SUICIDE RUN

ISBN-10: 1-940575-12-5
ISBN-13: 978-1-940575-12-4

First Printing: October, 2018

For more information or to leave a comment about this book, please visit us on the web at:

www.solarclipper.com

To Doreen.

For all her hard work
in helping me make this book
the best it can be.

The Golden Age of the Solar Clipper

Quarter Share
Half Share
Full Share
Double Share
Captains Share
Owners Share

In Ashes Born
To Fire Called
By Darkness Forged *

Milk Run
Home Run
Suicide Run

South Coast
Cape Grace*

Tanyth Fairport Adventures

Ravenwood
Zypherias Call
The Hermit Of Lammas Wood

* Forthcoming

SUICIDE RUN

NATHAN LOWELL

Durandus

CHAPTER ONE
DARK KNIGHT STATION: 2366, MARCH 15

THE CREDIT BALANCE blinked on the screen, mocking her. This was supposed to be so easy. Natalya Regyri looked up as the compartment door opened and Zoya strolled in, a carry-all trundling along behind.

"You still staring at that?" Zoya asked.

With a shrug, Natalya blanked the screen and eyed the carry-all. "Can't help it. If our unknown benefactor hadn't tossed a few credits into the account every month, we'd be living on the *Peregrine*. Probably starving."

"You still hell-bent on making a go as a courier?"

Natalya bit her lip and pondered the question for about the hundredth time. "What am I doing wrong?" she asked.

"Too much competition for a limited clientele." Zoya parked the carry-all beside the tiny table that served as combination desk, dining surface, and work bench in their apartment. "How many scheduled fast packets are making runs out of here alone?"

Natalya shook her head. "Seems like a new one every day."

"That's my point. You've got an antique ship. It's cramped as hell. There's not enough room to change your attitude in that galley. You and I have to hot bunk or there's no room for a passenger. How many times have you had to refuse a charter because they wanted two berths?"

Natalya sighed. "Too many."

"And we're not supposed to be carrying passengers anyway. So? When are you going to face it? The *Peregrine* is a great ship, but she's not a fast packet. She's barely a courier. She was built and designed for another place, another time. She's an antique."

Natalya glanced at the darkened screen. "You're right. She's a well-restored antique, but she's an antique."

Zoya started pulling groceries out of the carry-all. "Stop with the angst and help me stow these. I got some of that cheese you like and Morty had a flat of fresh vegetables in from the farms. There's still a bit of salami left. We can make a nice antipasto."

"But what are we going to do, Zee?" Natalya hated the whiny sound in her own voice.

Zoya thrust a package of tomatoes into her hand. "Stow the groceries. Make some tea. We'll think of something."

"We can't keep relying on getting paid for nothing. It's barely subsistence level as it is."

Zoya bit her lip and turned away, stashing a couple of cans in the pantry. "Well, it's not exactly for nothing," she said without turning back. "I might have been filing reports."

"Filing reports? With whom? About what?"

Zoya shrugged. "Ship traffic, mostly. Which one docked. Which one left. Scuttlebutt around the docks."

"You hang out on the docks?"

Zoya faced Natalya with a frown. "What else? Sit in this cubbyhole all day and wonder when we're going to do something?"

The words lashed Natalya, stinging deep. She felt the heat rising in the back of her neck. "If you don't like it, you don't have to stay." Natalya had to grit the words out between her teeth to keep from screaming them.

Zoya took a deep breath. Her jaw worked and her lips pressed into a line. She took another deep breath and blew it out, her whole visage relaxing. "Sorry," she said, her voice barely above a whisper. "That was low."

"I'm doing the best I can," Natalya said, feeling her own anger melting away.

"It's been almost three stanyers since we graduated. I can't leave you." Zoya gave a tiny shrug and looked at the half empty carry-all. "I wouldn't know what to do out here."

"What do you mean?"

Zoya leaned against the counter and crossed her arms, still not looking up. "This isn't what I thought it was. This Toe-Hold space station thing. I don't belong here."

Natalya took the few steps to the counter and leaned against it beside Zoya. "That's not true."

"Of course it's true. You fit out here. You've got the ship. You'll figure something out to make a go of it. Eventually." She offered Natalya a tentative smile. "I guess I'm just feeling like extra baggage."

"Well, at least you appear to be gainfully employed." Natalya bumped her shoulder against Zoya. "More than I can say for me."

"Gainfully employed?" Zoya asked.

"You're getting paid for filing your reports, aren't you?"

"Oh, yeah. Well. True."

"What are they paying me for?" Natalya asked. "Whoever they are."

"TIC," Zoya said.

"TIC?"

"That's where the credits are coming from. At least I assume." Zoya shrugged. "After the episode on Siren, I thought that would have been obvious."

"That's what I thought, but why are they still paying me? What if it's somebody else and we get a knock on the door from somebody wanting to collect that debt?"

Zoya shrugged and looked at the deck. "It's TIC. I don't know what they want any more than you do. All I know is that they want us out here and they're willing to pay us to do it."

"Both of us. Together."

"Yeah." Zoya glanced at the blank screen on the table. "Basic subsistence maybe, but yeah."

"But why, Zee?"

Zoya shrugged again. "No idea. Staged assets in advance of future need? Seems more likely than some master plan to establish a sleeper cell."

"Sleeper cell?" Natalya felt a giggle bubbling up in her chest. "Us?"

Zoya grinned at her. "Of course. Who'd suspect us of being spies?"

Natalya's giggle broke the tension in her gut. "But I guess we are, aren't we?"

"Yeah. I suppose I am, anyway. You're not filing reports on the sly, are you? Telling your controller what I'm doing?" Zoya bumped Natalya's shoulder in return.

"I couldn't," Natalya said. "I don't know what you're doing."

Zoya shrugged. "Well, we need to do something or we're both going to go stir crazy."

Natalya straightened up and started filling the tea kettle. "I guess we finish stowing the groceries and make some dinner."

Zoya nodded and bent down to pull their supplies from the carry-all. "Something will break, Nats. You'll see."

"I just hope it isn't us."

Zoya laughed. "Amen, sister. Amen."

3

CHAPTER TWO
DARK KNIGHT STATION: 2366, MARCH 16

NATALYA SIGHED AND surveyed the job board on KnightNet.
Her tea had gone cold and she wanted a cup of decent coffee. "I
wonder what I have to do to get some green coffee beans out here."

Zoya looked up from her breakfast and blinked. "Who sells
them?"

"Sarabanda over in Gugara," Natalya said. "I'm not sure where
to get any of the green arabasti varietals."

"Might be worth looking into."

Natalya shrugged a shoulder. "Maybe. Seems like somebody
would have done it by now."

"Somebody besides Kondur?"

Natalya laughed. "Yeah, but even he has problems."

"Does he?"

"Seems like he must or he'd be doing it on a commercial scale
instead of just personal consumption."

"What was that coffee we took over to Odin's?"

"Medium roast arabasti. Maybe we can track down the roaster
from the chandlery," Natalya said. "But we need the funds to buy
enough to make it worthwhile."

"I've got some funds," Zoya said. "We're living a little below
our means so we've got a positive cash flow."

"We could go harvest gases, come to that," Natalya said. "Maybe
getting out is what we should be doing."

"Is it worth going exploring?"

Natalya looked across the table at Zoya. "Exploring? Like
where?"

Zoya waved a hand. "Out there. It's a scout ship, after all.
You keep telling me how the early explorers found all these places

using ships like the *Peregrine*." She shrugged. "What's preventing us from picking up where they left off?"

"Survey probes, for one thing. Nobody makes them anymore. Exploration has been taken over by the big outfits, run by CPJCT."

"So, what if we got some probes? Maybe we won't find something big, but we might find something we can use. Or sell."

Natalya sat back in her chair and felt her mind spin into overdrive. "I wonder if that's what Dad was doing."

"What? Exploring?"

"Yeah. What if he found something?"

Zoya shrugged. "Didn't you say he had a place out here somewhere?"

"Yeah, but I never considered that he might have used the *Peregrine* to find it. I just thought it was some hole in the universe he bought or stumbled on."

"Is that where he is now?"

"I assume so. He never said much about it. What little he did say made me think it was an empty can with an airlock, a generator, and a chemical toilet."

Zoya laughed. "That's quite an image."

Natalya grinned. "You'd have to know my father to really appreciate it."

"Someday maybe I'll meet him."

"I wonder if we can find him," Natalya said, thinking out loud.

"Would the *Peregrine* have his location in the data?"

"Maybe. Maybe not. I don't know that he ever took the *Peregrine* out there. He always used a modified Unwin Eight when he came into the Toe-Holds by himself."

Zoya sipped her tea and gazed at Natalya. "That didn't strike you as odd? He takes a bigger ship when he's alone?"

"I guess. I never thought about it."

"But if he used the *Peregrine* to find a place, there are probably more places to find," Zoya said.

"There are always stories of lost colonies."

"Yeah, but we're not talking lost. We're talking undiscovered. Nothing big enough to register with the old Board of Exploration or the Confederated Planets, but big enough for a few people to make a living on," Zoya said. She shrugged. "Space is big and mostly empty but not completely empty."

"You think we'll strike it rich?"

"No, but we could strike it better-off-than-we-are." She smiled. "Besides, it'll get you back out where it's not so closed in."

"We'd need probes," Natalya said. "I don't think anybody makes them anymore."

"You think but you don't know. Have you looked?"

Natalya shook her head and dug into KnightNet again. "They'll be as antique as the ship if they're out here."

Zoya snorted. "I doubt it. Besides. How did the old timers do it? They must have used a lot of them and they didn't have places to buy fresh ones handy all the time."

Natalya looked up, the germ of an idea trying to take root in her mind. "No. They didn't, did they."

"There's not a ton of space in the *Peregrine* to stack them, unless they're really, really small. So how did they do it?"

"Like what was the process?" Natalya asked. "Or how did they actually accomplish anything?"

"Either. Both." Zoya shrugged.

"Prep a probe. Launch it. It jumps, runs some scans, and jumps back. It broadcasts its findings and does it again." Natalya felt her brow furrowing. "That doesn't seem like it should work."

"Clearly it did or we wouldn't have the Western Annex."

"The probes had to be jumping tiny distances," Natalya said. "Jump error would be huge in raw numbers. I don't even know what the power requirements must have been but just trying to broadcast radio across a couple of AUs would be time-consuming."

"So they have to come back near where they started?" Zoya asked.

"Within a fairly finite sphere, yeah."

"Any reason why they couldn't?"

"I don't know," Natalya said. "I wonder if we can find someone who does."

"It would also answer the question of where to keep them," Zoya said. "If they came back close enough to pick up and reuse? That wouldn't take many."

"That's true. I know the probe launchers are still mounted."

"I wonder if they picked them up. I can't see suiting up and going out to fetch it," Zoya said.

Natalya felt the sigh leave her like a last breath. "I can't believe I've had this ship this long and know so little about how to use it as a scout. There's good news, though."

"What's that?"

"We're in the Toe-Holds. If anybody knows—and is willing to tell—it'll be somebody out here."

CHAPTER THREE
DARK KNIGHT STATION: 2366, MARCH 17

THE JOBS LIST DIDN'T look any better in the morning than it did any other time of day. Natalya wasn't sure why she checked it when she got up. Just a habit. She'd make the tea, grab a snack, check the jobs. She was about to close her screen in disgust—another morning habit—when a window popped up with an incoming message.

Natalya read it twice, not quite believing what she read, before sitting back in her chair.

Zoya padded out of her room, blinking and yawning her way to the tea pot. "Mornin'," she said while slopping tea mostly into the cup. "I gotta stop staying up so late." She stopped halfway to the table. "You all right?"

Natalya looked up at her. "We just got a job offer."

"That's good, isn't it?" Zoya slipped into her chair across the table and blinked owlishly. "I'm not quite all the way awake but isn't a job good?"

"They're paying too much."

Zoya twisted her head sideways in each direction before taking a sip of tea. "Define too much."

"Fifty thousand a month."

"What for? Can't really call it too much if you don't know what it's for."

"Courier pilot. If interested, I'm supposed to meet them to go over the details."

Zoya took another slug of tea. "Sounds like it's what you always wanted. What's the problem?"

"Highest paid courier I've met out here is doing about ten thousand a month. Why do they want to pay me five times that?"

Zoya settled back in her chair and pulled the edges of her scruffy blue bathrobe together in front of her. "You'll have to ask them, won't you?" she said, peering across the table. "Maybe you just never met a high-paid courier pilot. Or if you did, they didn't tell you the truth. For that matter, you're getting ten grand from TIC every month, aren't you?"

Natalya shrugged. "Yeah? So?"

"So, maybe the pay scale isn't what you think it is."

"Or maybe they want me to do something unethical."

"Maybe you should go find out before you get your panties in a twist over what they might be, could be, should be asking you to do for the wage." Zoya reached for her teacup with both hands. "When do they want to meet?"

"Noon at Kondur's place."

Zoya shrugged. "Maybe it's Kondur and he needs a new courier."

"It's not Kondur." Natalya paused and looked at the message again. "At least I don't think so."

"Maybe Kondur's involved. It's not the only meeting place on the station but it's likely the most secure from what I've seen. What does it matter?"

"I don't know. Kinda weird having job offers come in over the virtual transom when I've been looking for jobs like this for weeks." Natalya stared at the screen.

Zoya snorted. "You've been looking for a job *exactly* like that for months. Who's it from?"

Natalya shrugged. "It doesn't say. Message headers dead-end with a High Tortuga routing."

Zoya sipped her tea again and looked across the table. "So, you go. You find out. You make a decision. You get the job or you don't."

Natalya worried her lower lip between her teeth and squinted at the screen as if to read between the lines. "What if it's TIC?"

"Seems unlikely. You're already on their payroll."

"You keep saying that like it's a fact. We don't really know," Natalya said.

Zoya shrugged. "Maybe not. Fits all the facts that we know. We might not know all the facts. That's possible. Call it a hunch. I'm relatively certain I'm being paid by them since they regularly ask me to do things they subsequently pay for. You're the pilot they sent me out here with. Makes sense you'd get paid, too."

"I don't want to be a member of the Trade Investigation Commission. I made that clear to them back at Port Newmar."

Zoya sighed. "Apparently they didn't take 'no' for an answer."

"But—"

"Just get some clothes on and go see, will you?" Zoya's voice crackled with irritation and she bit down on whatever she planned to say next. "You want me to go with you? You want me to stay here? What?"

"It doesn't say to come alone," Natalya said. "Not sure what the protocol is for taking a friend to a job interview."

"I can be ready to go. It's not like it's a job interview. The job is yours for the taking if they're talking credits already. Seems like more of a sniff test than a job interview. They clearly know more about you than you know about them."

"How do you figure?"

Zoya chuckled a little. "They know your KnightNet practices well enough to send you a private job offer that just happens to arrive as you're getting desperate for a job; they know you have your own ship or they'd have asked for you to be pilot instead of courier; and they've offered you enough of an incentive that you can't just blow them off. You know nothing about them, other than they want to meet you."

Natalya sighed and squinted even harder at the darkened display as if she could read something into the invitation simply by her force of will. After a few moments she relaxed into her chair and picked up her own mug of tea. "You're right."

"What's that? I didn't hear you," Zoya said, a smile twitching at the corners of her mouth. "I'm white? I don't think so."

In spite of herself, Natalya found herself chuckling along with Zoya. "I said you were right, all right? Happy now?" She threw up her hands in mock disgust. "On this 17th day of March, Zoya was actually right about something. I'll log it on the calendar. You are right."

"Thank you," Zoya said, putting her teacup back on the table. "Maybe the Toe-Holds *are* beginning to grow on me."

Natalya started to argue but had to admit, Zoya was right again. The woman across the table had grown a great deal since coming to Toe-Hold space. "I hope so," Natalya said. "You're still my wingman. I'm glad you're here."

Zoya smiled—a little wan, a bit sad, and completely honest. "Thanks, Nats. That means a lot."

Chapter Four
Dark Knight Station: 2366, March 17

KONDUR'S BAR AND RESTAURANT, The Roost, had become a familiar place for Natalya and Zoya. They knew the bouncers well enough to get a smile as they approached and ate there often enough that some of the service staff knew them as well. According to the scuttlebutt, Kondur played fair and paid well which kept the staff happy and loyal.

Natalya pushed through the door and smiled at the maÃ®tre d'. "Hi, Simon. I believe I'm expected?"

Simon smiled back. His balding head with white fringe and seamed face might have fooled some people but he moved with the smooth grace of a martial artist. His uniform fit him well enough that Natalya had no doubt that he served as more than maÃ®tre d' despite his apparent age. "You are indeed, Ms. Regyri." He glanced over her shoulder. "Will Ms. Usoko be joining you?"

Natalya looked back at Zoya before answering. "If that's satisfactory with my appointment?"

"Not unexpected. Right this way." He led the way past the bar and into one of the private dining rooms in the back. He gave a quick rap on the panel before holding it open for them to enter. "Enjoy your meal," he said, giving Natalya a wink and closing the door behind them.

Two men stood from the table as they entered. The taller of the two looked thin enough to fit through a thruster nozzle, while the shorter had the shoulders of a cargo hauler and the squat stature Natalya associated with heavy-worlders. Both wore shipsuits that might have blended in on the promenade outside in terms of cut and style, but fit too well to be off the rack from some chandlery.

The tall one reached across the table to offer a hand. "Ms. Regyri, I presume? And Ms. Usoko?" His voice carried no accent Natalya could place. Certainly not the clipped cadences common to the Toe-Holds. He sounded more polished, like Commandant Giggone. "I'm Brian Dorion."

Natalya shook his hand. "Nice to meet you," she said.

He offered his hand to Zoya with a nod. "Ms. Usoko."

Zoya returned the greeting.

The shorter one held out his hand. "Joe Allen, Ms. Regyri. I'm very pleased to see you." Natalya expected the deep, gravelly voice of a heavy-worlder, but she heard an airy tenor.

Natalya shook the offered hand, surprised by the man's careful, almost delicate grip. "Mr. Allen."

Dorion waved them into the waiting chairs. "Please. Make yourselves comfortable. Staff should be with us shortly and we can order."

Natalya took her seat across from Dorion and Zoya sat across from Allen at a table that was longer than it was wide and dressed with linens, rather than the more mundane hard-surfaced square four-top she was used to seeing at The Roost.

After the wait staff came and left, Allen leaned into the table. "You're probably wondering who we are and why we want you to come work for us. I assure you it's no trick. A legitimate offer."

"What is it, exactly, you want us to do?" Natalya asked.

Allen glanced at Dorion before answering. Natalya wondered who was the boss and who was the backup. She'd pegged Dorion for the boss job since he spoke first and Allen looked like the muscle.

"We want you to do some data pickup runs for us," Allen said. "We've a fixed route we need somebody to cover."

"Why us?" Natalya asked.

"The *Peregrine* has the legs to cover the route," Allen said.

"A lot of ships have those legs. Why us?" she asked again.

"The ships with that kind of range are all larger. We need something smaller," Allen said.

"Easier to hide," Natalya said.

"Harder to spot," he said with a conspiratorial wink. "We like to keep a low profile. It cuts down on complications."

"What happened to the last guy?" Zoya asked.

Allen tilted his head. "The last guy?"

"The guy who used to do this route for you," she said.

"He quit." Allen shrugged again. "We pay well. Some people don't like the work and leave us when they've earned enough. No hard feelings. You can quit any time. It's in the contract."

"But who are you?" Natalya asked. "Why should we trust you?"

"I can't answer that until you sign a non-disclosure agreement," Allen said.

"Non-disclosure for what? That we talked to you?" Natalya asked.

"Yes," Allen said.

Natalya expected something a little more elaborate. It took her a moment to recover. "What if we don't sign?"

"Well, in that case, you're free to leave here and tell anybody you want that you had a lovely lunch with Joe Allen and Brian Dorion," Allen said.

"So if we sign it, we can't tell anybody what we talked about over dinner?" Natalya asked.

"Correct," Allen said. "You're not allowed to disclose who we represent or what we talked about. You will, of course, be free to turn down our offer once we tell you what it is we want you do to. You just can't tell anybody else."

"Or what?" Zoya asked.

Allen smiled and it looked genuine to Natalya. "Or you pay us a very large sum. You really do not want to press that button." He looked at Natalya. "You can read the agreement before you make up your minds."

"That's a given," Natalya said.

Dorion chuckled and pulled a metal courier case up from beside his chair. He flipped some locks and the top lifted, blocking Natalya's view into the case. He pulled out two tablets and handed them across the table. "Non-disclosure agreements," he said. "Since you're both here, you'll both need to sign. We like it better when the whole crew signs."

Natalya opened the tablet and read the two paragraphs. She would never be able to reveal who she worked for to anyone for any reason for a period of twenty standard years following the end of her employment. The penalty clause invoked repayment of any earnings plus a million credits.

"Is this even legal?" Zoya asked.

"Why wouldn't it be?" Dorion asked.

"Who adjudicates a dispute?"

"High Tortuga provides the court of last resort," Allen said.

Zoya glanced at Natalya.

"He's right, Zee," Natalya said. "Contract disputes happen all the time. Even out here."

Zoya's brows inched toward each other. "What protection against liabilities do we have?"

"What do you mean?" Dorion asked.

"What if it turns out what you ask us to do violates some regulation? Makes us criminals with the CPJCT or persona non grata with a station so we can't dock there again?"

"It won't," Allen said. "But I appreciate your concern. You are free to turn down the offer. You'll have time to make up your minds when you know what we want to hire you for. You're just not free to tell anybody who we work for, that we made an offer, or what you're doing should you accept."

"It's for your protection as much as ours," Dorion said. "When you see the offer, I believe you'll understand better. Right now all we're asking is that you not tell anybody what we are prepared to reveal."

"Does Kondur know?" Natalya asked.

"Mr. Kondur has not been informed, no. We have no way to ascertain whether he knows. Asking him would be a violation of the agreement." Dorion smiled. "We're both bound by the same contract, as is the organization we represent."

Natalya nodded. "Understood." She pressed her thumb to the tablet and handed it back to Dorion, who added his own thumb before offering it to Allen.

Zoya stared at her. "Are you sure, Nats?"

Natalya nodded and leaned back in her chair. "I know who they are and what they want."

Allen's eyebrows rose. "Do you? I'm impressed."

"Thumb it, Zee. It'll be fine."

Zoya pressed her thumb against the tablet and handed it back. "I'm trusting you, Nats." Her tone made it clear how unhappy she was with doing it.

When Dorion had stowed the tablets, Allen asked, "Who do we work for?"

"High Tortuga," Natalya said. "You want us for data couriers to clear financial data around the Annex."

Dorion grinned and elbowed Allen in an I-told-you-so gesture, but didn't say anything.

A short knock on the door interrupted the discussion while the server brought in and distributed their meals. When he had gone, Allen raised his glass in a toast. "To profits."

Everyone joined him, but Zoya still frowned.

"You still seem unconvinced, Ms. Usoko," Dorion said as they addressed their food.

Zoya took a careful bite, chewed, and swallowed before answering. "If we've signed an agreement with High Tortuga, how can

High Tortuga adjudicate a dispute? They're hardly a neutral third party."

Dorion nodded. "Ah. Yes. Sorry. Ms. Regyri? Would you like to answer this?"

"High Tortuga is just shorthand," Natalya said. "It refers to a whole range of mostly independent entities that operate under the name. They all have separate names, separate management. The arbitration service handles disputes but has no fiscal ties to any of the others."

Zoya's frown deepened. "How do we know?"

Dorion looked at Natalya, but didn't speak.

"Profit," Natalya said. "Arbitration has to be above all others. Independently funded and managed, just like any station in the Toe-Holds. They get their income from the fees charged and rely on their reputation to keep those fees flowing."

Allen nodded. "Basically correct. While there's no absolute guarantee, the structure of the various entities operating in the Far Shores systems mandates that each operates independently. Finance, communications, arbitration, and several others operate as the High Tortuga Holding Company. They all get collectively referred to as High Tortuga, the same way all the stations and systems in CPJCT space are referred to as the High Line."

"Specifically, I represent Ravaine Communications," Dorion said. "As Ms. Regyri guessed, we want *Peregrine* to join the fleet that clears communications from the various outposts here in Toe-Hold space."

"Why us?" Natalya asked. "There must be more qualified people out here."

"The demand is always growing," Allen said. "Every time a new Toe-Hold gets established, we need to expand our network."

"We also have a fair amount of turnover," Dorion said with a shrug. "We're not going to lie to you. The job pays well but many find it tedious and far from exciting. Most of our pilots achieve some level of fiscal independence and leave us for greener pastures."

"They get rich and quit?" Zoya said.

"Basically," Dorion said. "The job is to fly a route we provide, sync up with the buoys in each system as discreetly as possible, and return to our station in Ravaine to clear it. We handle it after that."

Natalya finished her chicken sandwich and pushed the plate toward the center of the table, leaning in. "So? Terms? How long are the routes? How often would we have to fly?"

"The routes vary a bit," Dorion said. "We try not to have any courier always follow the same path. You'll see the same systems eventually, of course. There are only so many. Our routing algorithm shuffles systems and provides a route that generally takes no more than three days per leg. Each route may have six to ten legs. You'd be out for eighteen to twenty-four days with a week's downtime between."

Natalya nodded. "So we go out and clear the buoys for three days, then jump back to Ravaine to re-sync before going out for three more days and repeat."

"Basically. Some legs may be as short as jump out and back. Some might be a couple days before coming in again. You'd only dock when you're done with the whole route so you'd be out for something like two to three weeks, typically," Allen said.

"Time is of the essence in this business," Dorion said. "You'll be jumping into the outer edges of the systems, light-hours from the primaries so you only have to jump in, sync up, realign, jump out."

"Expenses?" Natalya asked.

Dorion grinned and pulled up his case again, extracting another tablet and handing it to Natalya. "I'm glad you asked. The details on food, fuel, and even routine maintenance allowances are all there. You can keep that and go over it in detail if you like."

"Can we have it vetted by a lawyer?" Zoya asked.

"We encourage you to do so," Allen said. "That contract has been sanitized to remove our name and affiliation. You're not violating our agreement so long as you don't tell the lawyer who 'The Company' references in the contract language."

"That wouldn't stand up in a CPJCT arbitration," Zoya said.

Allen's lips twitched in what Natalya suspected might have been a suppressed smile. "You might be surprised at that, Ms. Usoko. Let's just say, in the last two plus centuries, we've never had a problem."

"I have to take your word for that," Zoya said.

Allen shrugged. "Yes. Unfortunately. It's not something I can prove one way or another without showing we've had a problem. Since we haven't?" He shrugged again and raised an eyebrow at Natalya.

She nodded. "He's right, Zee. I suspect the contract would stand up in a CPJCT court."

"How can you say that? How can an anonymous contract be valid?"

"It's not anonymous," Natalya said. "It's sealed. If we were to challenge it in court, then somebody representing the company would defend against the challenge but the actual parties involved would never show in the record." She looked at Dorion. "Am I right?"

"Essentially," Dorion said.

"How do we contact you again?" Natalya asked. "Once we decide."

"At the bottom of the document you can thumb *accept* or *decline*," Allen said. "Whichever way you go will be communicated to us and we'll be in touch."

"If we don't accept?" Zoya asked, her brow still furrowed in a frown.

"If you decline, well, thank you for your time and consideration. If you accept, we'll send confirmation documents for your verification," Allen said. "We recommend you burn the contract to glass for your records."

Natalya began reading the contract.

"You're going to do that now?" Zoya asked.

"You got someplace you need to be?"

"Well, no, but that's going to take a while."

Natalya shrugged without looking up. "Order dessert. I want to see what kind of allowances we have for fuel and maintenance before I sign this and while I've got them here to get it adjusted."

"Told you," Dorion said with a glance at Allen.

"I'll have the berry pie," Natalya said. "With vanilla ice cream and a coffee."

Allen snorted and pressed the service button.

Chapter Five
Knight Station: 2366, March 17

ALL THE WAY BACK TO the apartment, Zoya said nothing. She stomped along, hands thrust into pockets, and chewed her mouth around like she had something nasty in it that she couldn't spit out and wouldn't swallow.

When the door closed behind them, she turned to Natalya. "You signed that contract. Without getting a lawyer to look at it."

Natalya filled the kettle with water and put it on the burner to heat. "Yes. You saw it. Straight boilerplate ship service contract. We've seen that language a hundred times. I think it came out of our Contracts IV course almost verbatim."

"What about the expenses clauses?"

"What about them? We got them changed upwards. They're even going to pay for the navigational upgrades. It's in their best interest for us to be as efficient as possible." She leaned against the counter and crossed her arms. "Real food in the galley? We'll eat as well out there as we do here. Probably better."

"You didn't even ask me if I wanted to do it."

A sick feeling filled Natalya's belly. "I'm not going to force you to fly with me. If you don't want to do this, I'm sure you can find something else to do."

Zoya threw herself into her chair at the table and scrubbed her face with the palms of her hands. "That's not what I mean," she said—not looking at Natalya, her voice uncharacteristically faint.

"What *do* you mean?"

"You just took the deal. We didn't discuss it. Nothing." Zoya took a deep breath and blew it out through her nose. She looked over at Natalya. "What's that going to do to our relationship with TIC?"

Natalya rolled the question over in her mind a couple of times before answering. "Well. First, I don't see how it has any bearing. Not like I signed up for it."

"Yeah, but I did and I can't tell them because I signed that damned non-disclosure."

Natalya shrugged and pulled the teapot and tea out of the cupboard. "We both did but there's no reason for you to tell them, is there? Do you even have a way to tell them?"

"I could include it in my reports, but I'm not going to be here any longer, am I?"

Natalya tossed some loose tea into the infuser as the kettle began to boil. "Is that what this is about? Keeping your TIC handlers happy? I thought I was your assignment."

Zoya didn't answer.

Natalya looked at her. "Zee?"

Zoya looked up and shrugged. "Honestly, I don't know."

"Well, would they complain if we hired onto another of Kondur's freight runs?"

"Probably not."

"You're my shadow. You report on what I'm doing, right?"

"You make me sound like a hall monitor."

"Sorry. Not my intention," Natalya poured the water over the tea and chose her words carefully. "I meant it when I said you're my wingman, Zee. I'm sorry I didn't ask you. I'm sorry I didn't *think* to ask you." She set the timer and faced Zoya. "Are you good with this? Can I make it up to you? Technically, they hired me and the ship. You're bound by the NDA but you're not bound to me or the ship. I can do this solo."

"I'm all right, I think," Zoya said after a few moments. "I hate not having that contract vetted. That's probably what scares me the most."

"What about TIC?" Natalya asked.

"They'll have to cope. You're right about the job. You're under no obligation to do anything specific and my only agreement—at least at the moment—is what it's always been. Go with you and keep track of what's happening."

"What will you tell them?"

She shrugged. "That we've got a courier job."

"Just think. You can tell them about the systems we're in."

"If we're only there long enough to sync a data buoy in the outskirts, there's not going to be much to tell."

"They'll live," Natalya said. "What are they going to do? Fire you?"

Zoya bit her bottom lip and looked down. "Maybe."

"Look at the bright side."

"There's a bright side?"

"Yeah. We'll get to see a lot of the Western Annex and we're getting a raise. Even if TIC stops paying us, we'll still be earning more per month. Until they do, we're going to be living fat."

Zoya gave her a tentative smile. "Did you see those annual raises?"

"Yes, as a matter of fact, I did." The timer dinged. She pulled the infuser and poured a couple of cups of tea. "I'm sure that's a function of just how tedious this job might be. They want to keep people from bailing on them so they keep sweetening the pot every stanyer."

Zoya laughed. "Probably right." She took the offered cup and sipped. "Are we doing the right thing?"

Natalya shrugged and took a seat. "We're on the hook for the next six months. That's going to set us up pretty well. Compared to what we've been doing?" Natalya looked around at their somewhat cramped quarters and shrugged. "We could probably afford a better place to live."

"Wouldn't be worth it if we're going to be in space three out of four weeks."

"Shall we keep this one?" Natalya asked.

"Won't we want one over in Ravaine?"

"Possibly. How much trouble would it be to move?"

Zoya looked around. "I'm not that attached to much here. I can be packed by this time tomorrow."

"We're paid through the end of the month."

"When do we have to be in Ravaine for the upgrades?"

"Contract stipulates thirty days. That would be April 16th."

"How soon can we get there?"

"Few days. I'd have to check, but no more than a week. We can cross the entire Annex in that amount of time." Natalya took a sip of tea and considered Zoya's expression. "So?"

Zoya grinned across the table. "So, I think we'd better get packing. I'd like some time to get settled before they start overhauling the ship."

Natalya grinned back. "You know what's another good point about this job?"

"What's that?" Zoya asked.

"No more hot bunking."

Chapter Six
CommSta Bowie: 2366, March 27

BRIAN DORION MET THEM at the dock with a big smile and a cargo hauler. "Welcome to Bowie," he said as soon as they cracked the lock open. "Hope Kondur didn't give you any trouble about leaving."

"I'm not sure he knows we're gone. We just signed out at station housing, paid the balance on our rental, and left," Natalya said.

Dorion chuckled. "He knows. Do you have much to move in? We've picked out a nice suite for you in the pilots' wing." He waved at the cargo hauler. "We can take a load over now if you'd like. Give you a chance to check it out. See if it meets your needs."

Natalya took a few moments to brace herself and to take a few deep breaths of station air. Even on the small-ship dock, it smelled fresh and clean—free of any mechanical odors except for the ubiquitous tang of cleaning solution and plastic. Even the scorched smell of maneuvering thrusters had been scrubbed. She looked at Zoya, who shrugged in return. "We can probably put all of it on one load, if you're game?"

"I'm at your disposal until 1800," he said.

Natalya checked the chronometer on the station's bulkhead—1400. "Let's do it, then."

Zoya led them back into the ship and aft to where a stack of cargo totes stood against an engine room bulkhead. With a few deft flips, she removed the tiedowns and grabbed the top box.

"Is that all?" Dorion asked.

"We've each got a few in our staterooms, but this is the bulk of it," Natalya said, grabbing the next box and following Zoya out. She grinned at the expression on Dorion's face. "We travel light. Most of it travels with us."

He added his crate to the growing pile on the hauler and grinned. "I've had pilots come in with metric tons of household effects."

"Yeah, but were they flying Scouts?" Zoya asked.

He shook his head and went back for another load. "No. This is a first for us, I think. We've never had a Scout flying for us as far as I know. Even in the early days."

"I'm surprised you don't have specialized ships for this work," Natalya said, grabbing the next box off the stack and starting back out.

"Funny you should mention that," Dorion said.

Natalya waited for Zoya to place her crate and then added her own on top of it. "You're developing them now?"

"You two might be the prototype. All our other crews are running fast packets in parallel with cargo."

"Lemme guess," Zoya said. "Unwin Eights."

Dorion froze and blinked for a few heartbeats. "Yes, as a matter of fact. Why do you say that?"

"Small, light, fast. Mass-produced and cheap. Beef the Burlesons and they can jump a long way with a pair of crew and still turn a good profit on a small, high-margin cargo," she said. "They're so common they're practically invisible."

Even Natalya stared at her.

"What?" Zoya asked.

"I had no idea you'd given it that much thought," Natalya said.

"Well, you've probably never thought of flying anything but the *Peregrine*, but some of us have." Zoya grinned and gave her a pat on the shoulder. "You should think about it. We could make a killing without risking a priceless historical artifact." She strode back through the lock leaving Dorion and Natalya blinking at each other.

"She's right, isn't she?" Natalya asked.

"Spot on, actually."

Zoya came back out with a cargo tote. "You guys gonna stand around or you gonna help?" She plunked her carrier on the stack with a cheeky grin and went back for another.

They laughed and followed her in.

By 1425, the hauler had all their goods aboard. Natalya locked up the ship and swung onto the back of the hauler. Dorion took the controls and Zoya tucked in beside him.

"I haven't gotten a statement from the station yet. What's our visa?" Natalya asked as he zipped them along the dock and down a wide passageway into the station proper.

"Permanent visa. All docking fees and charges are waived as long as you're under contract," he said, leaning his head back but not looking away from the path ahead.

Zoya met Natalya's stare with a look of surprised disbelief. "So if we get another ship we could dock it here, too?"

Dorion laughed. "Some of the pilots have private yachts docked. They use very little and the goodwill factor is high."

"As long as they're happy, they stay?" Zoya said.

"Spot on," he said. "We work hard to make you happy. Our business depends on it and we've had a couple of centuries' practice in not being penny wise and pound foolish." He glanced at Zoya. "Remember that going forward. If there's something you want, let the company know. You might be surprised what's possible." He tilted his head back toward Natalya. "That goes for you as well, back there."

Natalya didn't have much time to ponder his statements before the vehicle drew to a whining stop in front of a numbered door.

"Here we are," Dorion said. "Let me show you around. See if you like the place."

Dorion jumped down from the hauler and waited for them at the door before swiping a hand over the panel. The door opened and he waved them in. "First impressions," he said.

Zoya led the way with Natalya on her heels. The view over Zoya's shoulders made Natalya's brain zip. It didn't look like an apartment, at least no apartment she'd ever seen. Zoya stopped dead about three steps inside and Natalya had to step around her to see what caused the holdup. Once she saw, she stopped, too.

"This is big enough to park the *Peregrine* in," she said.

Behind her, Dorion chuckled. "Not quite. The overhead is a little low." He stepped around her and into the cavernous space. "This is your basic parlor. We'll get you some furniture from central stores. I didn't know what you were bringing or what you liked but we can fix that now you're here."

Natalya shared a look with Zoya and wondered if she looked as shocked as Zoya did.

"Through here is your kitchen. Galley. Whatever you want to call it. I call it kitchen. Food prep." He led the way around the corner to a galley area bigger than their whole apartment on Dark Knight. "Plenty of counter space. Full fridge. Freezer so you can store stuff while you're out and not have to worry about food when you get back. There's a concierge service that will keep it stocked for you if you just tell them what you want in it." He shrugged. "Basic stuff."

He led them back out and popped a door open. "Basic bath. All the necessities. Loo. Lav. Bathtub. Shower. Some linen storage." He went to the next door and popped that one open. "Spare room. Some pilots use it for an exercise room. Others a meditation space. We have a full gym at the end of the passage, but some people prefer to set up their own. Whatever you want to use it for."

On the far side of the parlor he pointed to two doors at either end of the long wall. "Matching bedrooms. Mirrored layouts with a shared bathroom in between." He walked into the nearer room, crossing it to open a walk-in closet. "They each have a closet. Bathroom through there."

"Two?"

He shrugged. "Yeah. This one has a steam room, a double shower, and paired sinks on the vanity." He popped the door and stepped back so they could look in.

Natalya took a deep breath and met Zoya's wide-eyed stare. "Um. Look, Mr. Dorion—"

"Brian," he said. "We don't stand much on ceremony here."

"Brian," Natalya said. "I know you're paying us well, but all this is ..." Her words failed her.

"Over the top," Zoya said. "You can't be serious."

Dorion frowned at her and then looked at Natalya. "What's the problem? I'm sure we can fix it."

"How much?" Natalya asked, her tongue suddenly sticking to the roof of her mouth. She waved a hand around at the space.

"How much?" he said. "What do you mean?"

"Rent?" Zoya asked. "Utilities, services."

His face relaxed and he looked back and forth between them. "How much do you think?"

"Five thousand?" Zoya asked.

He looked at Natalya.

"I was going to say ten," she said.

He shook his head, a devilish glint in his eye.

"More?" Zoya asked. "We're only going to be here one week a month."

He raised an eyebrow at Natalya.

"No," she said. "You can't be serious."

"Perfectly serious," he said. "It's yours, expense-free for as long as you fly for us."

"You can't mean that," Zoya said.

"The company wants you to stay. They need you to do the best job you can under trying circumstances. Being underway for three weeks out of four will be taxing. I think it's going to be particularly difficult in that matchbox you're sailing around in. It's bad enough for the Unwin crews and we want your home here to be as stress-free as we can make it. Believe me when I say we'll be getting our credits' worth out of you. If you find the lifestyle to your liking ..." His voice trailed off and he shrugged.

"We'll do it longer," Zoya finished, looking back into the bathroom again.

"Turnover is a problem," Dorion said. "Lots of people say they love to sail around the Deep Dark, but when you make it their job and keep them on a schedule, it gets tough to do week after week, month after month." He shrugged. "We know that. Over the last two centuries we've worked with shorter schedules, longer schedules, no schedules, rigid schedules. None of it made much difference in pilot satisfaction and turnover. Making more credits helps a bit, but a couple years of flying and most salt away a nice nest egg."

"So you make all this a noncash benefit of working," Zoya said.

"We still pay better than anybody else in the Annex for courier work. We pay regularly and reliably month after month."

"Gilded cage," Zoya said.

Dorion shrugged. "You're free to live anywhere you want. There are private rentals in-system here. Mostly short term contracts but there are longer term units available. With your ship and skills, you can live practically anywhere in the Western Annex. You could go back to Dark Knight if you wish." He paused for a moment before continuing. "Naturally, we'd prefer you to live on-station and we'll do almost anything to encourage you to do so. If you don't like this one, we have several units. Some have different floor plans but the same basic amenities. You can each have a single if you want it. I just picked this one because you were living together on Dark Knight. After a patrol, you might prefer to get away from each other. Would you like to see a single before you get moved in here?"

Natalya looked at Zoya with a raised eyebrow.

Zoya sighed and looked around the space.

"Oh, I almost forgot the best part," he said. He left the bedroom and went back to the central area. Crossing to a bulkhead, he tapped a key and the wall opened. "Armorglass. Twice as strong as your bridge," he said. "Opacity is controlled electronically. I don't understand the physics myself, but you can adjust this to be anything from this size and crystal to—well—pretty much anything you like. This is the default setting. All the suites have this feature but I think this one has the best view. The outside is silvered, so you can see out but nobody can see in." He offered a little chuckle. "Not like there are many people out there to look."

Zoya and Natalya stood transfixed by the view. Beyond the armorglass, the station structure extended only slightly and it framed the Deep Dark beyond. As they watched, an Unwin Eight packet drifted across the field, navigation lights blinking brightly against the soft colors and sharp points of light beyond. The view took Natalya's voice away and she felt a tightness in her chest. With an effort she dragged her gaze away and turned to Zoya.

Zoya looked back and said, "We'll take it."

Chapter Seven
CommSta Bowie: 2366, April 2

NATALYA WATCHED AS the tech put the finishing touches on the new navigational system. He glanced up at her and grinned. "Woulda been better if you'd let us upgrade the Mark Fourteens to Mark Eighteens."

"You'd still be upgrading. The fiber network won't support them," Natalya said. "I'm right on the edge as it is."

He nodded. "I wondered about that. The fiber looks new." He paused and shrugged. "Newer, anyway."

"Came with the Mark Fourteens. Got the package for scrap value and spent weeks rerunning the cables."

His eyes went wide. "You ran all that cable? By yourself?"

Natalya shrugged. "All eighteen kilometers of it."

"Eighteen kilometers? The ship isn't that big."

"Twenty meters length overall. Eight deep and seven at the beam," she said. "And yeah. It looks a lot smaller inside than out. Over half the ship is engineering or mechanical space."

"And you fly this out there?" His grin made her grin back instead of bridling at the insult.

"Ships like this made stations like that possible." She nodded at the dock outside the bridge.

He nodded. "No argument." He finished working under the console and snapped the cover back into place, then stood and wiped the surface down with a cloth from his pocket. "I heard about these Scouts. Everybody has, of course. Never thought I'd see one, let alone work on it."

"It's a labor of love, I guess," Natalya said, not sure how to respond.

"It's a priceless work of art," he said. "You have any idea how many of these are left?"

"At least one," she said. "We ready?"

He gave her a short laugh and nodded. "Fire it up. You should like the new interface, and you won't have any trouble with High Line regs either. The database automatically firewalls the 'unap-proved' destinations when you're in one of their systems."

She looked at him with a scowl.

He held up a hand. "You can still use them. They just hide from inspections." He looked around the tiny bridge. "A ship like this? I'd expect to get boarded a lot."

"Because they think we're violating some regulation?"

The tech laughed and shook his head. "Just to get a look at her from the inside."

Natalya dropped into the navigator's seat and brought up the new system. "It looks better, but I can't put my finger on why."

"A lot of it is cosmetic. The user interface tweaks are mostly font and contrast. Try plotting a course from here to Mel's."

She started laying out her path only to have the system fill in interim jumps for her. "That's slick. What parameters are driving this?"

He pointed to a clock icon at the top. "Least time based on the ship's drives and power curve. Click it."

She clicked and the icon changed to "CR" while the new plot mapped itself onto the chart display. "CR?"

"Credits," he said. "Least cost."

"More jumps is cheaper?"

"Shorter jumps use less power," he said.

"Of course," Natalya said.

"The system default is set so the capacitors aren't ever below fifty percent. Recharge cycles aren't as heavy or as long. It accounts for maintenance costs on both the fusactor and the drives as well as fuel for course adjustments based on ship averages. Right now, they're factory defaults but the system will track historical data going forward. You'll have a more accurate estimate within a few weeks."

"Slick," she said. "I suspect that adds up over the course of a month."

He nodded. "I'm not sure how much for this ship. The Unwins report at least a five percent improvement in expense costs over the older model consoles."

"Do they care?" she asked.

"Of course. Cutting down on expenses means they earn more. Five percent doesn't sound like a lot but in raw numbers that's a nice chunk of change."

"Don't they get reimbursed when they dock here?" Natalya asked, looking up from the display.

He shrugged. "They might if they docked here. Almost all of them have home ports outside of Ravaine."

"Why's that?"

"No idea. I'm not on a conversational basis with many ship captains. It's not something I've asked and they haven't volunteered. They'll dock here once in a while for system upgrades. They get refits done out at the yards sometimes. We've got a good repair dock on the other side of the station here so they can get routine maintenance done. Some of them don't even do that." He shrugged again. "No accounting for taste, I guess."

Natalya made a mental note to ask Dorion about it. "What about the new ships?"

"Not in rotation yet. We won't know for a while."

"When do you expect them?"

"Dock gossip says the first cohort will be coming out of the yards in August or September."

Natalya secured the console and stood up. "So we're ready to go?"

"The comms gang hasn't upgraded your array yet. They've been waiting on a module from home office to handle the encryption for you. That should be done by the time you're finished with training."

Natalya suppressed a sigh. "Speaking of which, I've got a hot date with a cold fish."

He grabbed his satchel and led the way down the passage and off the ship. "More training?"

Natalya sealed the lock and nodded. "Company-approved communications protocols in social engagements outside the company."

He snorted. "That's the name of it?"

"Afraid so."

"Sounds charming," he said.

"It's probably less charming than it sounds, but I don't want to break a rule because I didn't know about it."

"Good point," he said. He paused and looked at her a bit sideways. "If you ever need a social engagement within the company?"

Natalya looked at him trying to decide if he was asking her out or not.

"Buncha techs and dock monkeys hang out at Stay Frosty most evenings. You get bored, you'd be welcome."

"What do the dock monkeys call techs?" she asked.

"Techtards." He grinned. "We don't get many pilots or ship crews, but we don't discriminate."

"Thanks," she said. "I didn't catch your name."

"Doherty. Jeff. They call me JD."

She held out her hand. "Nice to meet you, JD. Natalya."

He gave her a lopsided grin and shook her hand. "Maybe we'll see you at Frosty?"

"Much stranger things have happened."

He nodded at that. "Well. I need to get going. Systems to break. Code to wreck."

She laughed and watched him scoot down the dock. "Much stranger things," she said to herself.

Chapter Eight
CommSta Bowie: 2366, April 7

NATALYA AND ZOYA TRUDGED the last few meters down the corridor toward Dorion's office. "Did he say what he wanted?" Zoya asked.

"Nope. Just be here at 1100."

"If it's another stupid training requirement, I'm going to scream."

Natalya grinned at her. "I'll scream in harmony."

"You'd think we'd never attended the academy. I swear we had that fraternization talk as second-year cadets."

"And third," Natalya said.

"Maybe he's going to finally put us to work."

Natalya stopped a couple of meters from the door. "Speaking of which. Does this station seem a little off to you?"

"Off? How?" Zoya shrugged. "The only station I've ever spent any time on is Dark Knight and that still seemed strange to me when we left."

Natalya looked up and down the passageway. It seemed to go on forever in a straight line. "How many people have you seen here?"

"Not counting the dozen or so at Frosty the other night?"

Natalya nodded.

Zoya frowned. "Four? Five? We've only had two different instructors doing the training. Dorion. The concierge, Ellis. What's his first name?"

"Tim," Natalya said.

"I guess it's not too surprising nobody's here," Zoya said. "Most of the crews must be out."

"Well, and according to JD, most of them don't live here anyway."

"True," Zoya said. "It explains one thing, though."

"What's that?"

"How that palace Dorion set us up with was available. I haven't even heard another person walking down the passage who wasn't coming to see us."

"That *is* odd," Natalya said. "I never noticed."

"You have to admit, that apartment is a long way from normal."

"I'll give you that," Natalya said. She nodded down the passage. "Best see what he wants. It's the least we can do to earn our daily crust."

Zoya chuckled and fell into step as they closed the distance to Dorion's office.

They found him seated behind his glass-topped desk. He looked up when they entered. "Good," he said. "I've got some plans I want to go over with you."

"Good morning to you, too," Natalya said.

He grinned. "Yeah. Sorry. Good morning. I'm excited and want your feedback." A large panel display on the bulkhead lit up with a ship model rendered in three dimensions. "Touch screen. Spin it. Look it over. Tell me what you think."

Natalya crossed to the screen and spun the ship. "What is it? It looks like a pillbug."

Zoya reached around Natalya and turned the ship so it was bow on. "What's the scale on this? Either those ports are huge, or this ship is really small."

"It's really small," Dorion said.

Dimension arrows appeared along the various axes of the display.

"That's smaller than the *Peregrine*," Natalya said. "What is it?"

"Latest iteration of our communications harvesting vessel."

"Got a deck plan?" Natalya asked.

A schematic of the inside of the ship replaced the model on the screen.

"Can you walk us through this, Brian? I'm not sure what I'm looking at," Zoya said.

"Everything aft of the airlock is engineering. Tankage is under the deck and in the overhead. She can fly for three weeks without refueling. Galley, which we largely engineered from old Scout blueprints. New materials and advances in Burleson drives and fusactors let us cut the mass by a third and boost her rating to twenty BUs with a six-stan recharge cycle on the capacitor."

Natalya whistled softly. "How many full jumps in the capacitor?"

"Just two," Dorion said. "That's still almost a third of the way across the Western Annex in less than a stan. Six stans later she can do it again, with short jumps possible within a few ticks."

Zoya stepped closer and peered at the diagram. "Cockpit instead of a bridge, but there's only one couch."

"Only one pilot needed," Dorion said.

Natalya looked at Zoya and read the look on her face. "You're going to send solo pilots out for three weeks at a time in this?" Natalya asked, turning to look at Dorion.

Dorion sat down behind his desk and pursed his lips. "Tell me what's wrong with it," he said after several long moments of silence.

"You a pilot, Brian?" Natalya asked.

He shook his head. "Communications analyst, originally."

"You called the *Peregrine* a matchbox, if I remember correctly," Zoya said.

His face flushed and he looked down at his desk. "Yes. I did. No offense."

"None taken," Natalya said.

"This is smaller," Zoya said.

"Not by much. It has about two-thirds of the volume of a Scout and only has a crew of one."

Natalya nodded and pulled at her lower lip with a thumb and forefinger. "Scouts are rated for solo operation. That extra space matters more when you're alone out there."

"Why?" Dorion asked.

"You need room to move around. Room to stretch out. Pace, maybe," Natalya said.

"You ever fly solo for three weeks at a time?" Dorion asked.

Natalya nodded. "Yeah. It's better when you have somebody to talk to."

Zoya's gaze raked the schematic again. "Where's the bunk?"

"Pilot's couch doubles as bunk," he said.

Natalya stared at Dorion who met her gaze with a bland expression.

Zoya turned away from the display and started to speak to speak but apparently thought better of it.

"You don't like it," Natalya said.

Dorion tilted his head to one side. "I beg your pardon?"

"This ship. This design. You don't like it," she said.

Dorion tapped the desk with his hands in a rapid pattering of fingertips. "Correct. I need your help to get this travesty pulled." He offered them a faint smile. "Tell me what's wrong in terms I can take to the board."

"It's too small," Zoya said.

"It's big enough for a single pilot," Dorion said. "From a cost perspective, one pilot is cheaper than a crew of two." He paused and gave a shrug. "No offense meant. That's the board's driver on this project. Keeping the costs down."

Natalya looked back at the screen but she wasn't really seeing the schematic. "Did anybody work up a two-seater model of this?"

"No," he said. "The design parameters specified a single pilot crew from the start."

"We haven't been out yet," Natalya said. She looked at Dorion. "We finished our training cycle two days ago."

Dorion nodded. "Yeah. I've been dragging my feet because I wanted you to see this. I got permission to show you last night."

Natalya nodded. "It's a good design."

"It is," Zoya said. "But it'll kill pilots."

"Literally?" Dorion asked.

"Probably," Natalya said. "You're already having turnover problems, right?"

His face blanked for a moment. "Why do you say that?"

"We talked about it before. I didn't realize the scope of the issue," Natalya said.

Zoya nodded. "Now it begins to make sense."

"What does?" Dorion asked.

"The palatial apartment. The docking fee waivers. The paychecks. All of it," Zoya said.

"How many systems do you serve?" Natalya asked.

"Twelve thousand and change."

Natalya felt her eyebrows rise at the number. "How many ships to cover that?"

"Something over five hundred. Depends on the day and who's quit lately."

"What's your turnover rate?" Zoya asked.

Dorion shook his head. "I'm not at liberty to say."

"It's a lot," Natalya said. "Most pilots won't dock here even with the free docking, will they?"

"I'm not at liberty to say," Dorion said.

"They have fewer than fifty docking rings that can take an Unwin Eight," Zoya said. She glanced at Natalya. "Yeah. I counted the other day while you were getting the new navigation system installed."

"Nobody but us lives in our wing. Right?" Natalya said.

"I'm not at liberty to say," Dorion said but after a moment he nodded his head.

Natalya turned back to the schematic. "This isn't an engineering problem."

"How so?" Dorion asked.

"It's a management problem," she said. "Why won't they dock here? The Unwins?"

"They claim it's too far away from their cargo points. They jump in, dump their data, and jump out."

"You don't believe them?" Zoya asked.

Dorion shrugged. "Oh, I'm sure that's part of it. They'll come in for routine maintenance. Sometimes one of them will dock with almost empty tanks and get a free refill."

"What about the yachts?" Zoya asked. "You said some of the pilots kept their yachts here."

"A handful. It's more like a cheap place to store them than anything they use regularly. Jump-capable yachts aren't that easy to park without incurring big fees. They get used infrequently and need station ties for maintenance."

"Yeah. Management problem," Natalya said again. "The freighters, you know how they keep crews happy?"

"Pay them?" Dorion asked.

"Well, that's part of it. You've got the pieces here. You've given us a great place to live. The food's great. I never worry about fuel or gases for the ship. All the extrinsic rewards are spectacularly high but nobody wants to live here. Do you know why?" Natalya asked.

"Do you?" His voice carried a bit of a snap.

"Hey, we're just the new kids on the block," Zoya said. "I'm betting we're almost the *only* kids on the block and that's the problem."

"Crews tend to stay together, sailing for weeks, even months at a time between docking. The ship docks for a few days. Everybody plays hard. Works hard. Then they do it all again," Natalya said.

"And?" Dorion asked.

"Everybody's different, but when you're part of a crew, you're in it together. You're part of something larger than yourself and your bunk and your paycheck. You're a crew." Natalya pointed at the model. "That's a good design. It will work well. But you're taking away the one thing that makes it all work."

"Making them single pilots?" Dorion asked.

Natalya glanced at Zoya before looking at Dorion again. "By not giving them a chance to be part of something bigger."

"How can we do that?" he asked. "There's only room for one on the ship."

"She's not talking about the ship," Zoya said.

"Your crews don't dock here because your crews don't dock here," Natalya said.

"What?"

"What a crew wants when they dock is companionship. Somebody to look at and talk to that's not the people they've been looking at for two months," Zoya said. "You know there's a decent pub here?"

"Sure. Everybody knows it," Dorion said.

"Do you know it's the only entertainment venue?" Natalya asked.

"Well, of course I know."

"That doesn't strike you as problematic?" Natalya crossed her arms to keep from slapping him.

"Why would it be?"

"What if I don't want to go to a pub?"

"Then don't go," Dorion said.

Natalya stared at him.

"What if she wants to go to a movie? Or go dancing? Or just have a quiet meal with friends in a place that doesn't serve pub food?" Zoya asked.

"Where do you eat, Brian?"

"At home."

"Always?" Natalya asked.

"Of course not. Sometimes we go to Frosty."

"We who?" Zoya asked.

"My wife and I. Who else?"

"What does she do? She works here on the station?"

"Yes. HR."

"How many people work in HR?"

"Ten, I think. They only handle the communication station staff. Not like there are a lot of them. The station is largely automated."

Natalya glanced at Zoya. "Tell me. Did that department handle our contracts?"

"Of course."

"Does that make us commsta staff?" Zoya asked.

"No, you're private contractors."

"Contractors you would like, ideally, to live on-station?" Zoya tilted her head to one side.

"The company would prefer it, yes."

"In theory you could have five hundred crews using this station as base. Do you have room for all of them?" Natalya asked.

"I don't see what this has to do with the ship." Dorion's face had taken on a ruddy glow about the cheeks.

"Your problem is not the ship. It's the station," Natalya said. "Crews won't dock here because there's nothing to attract a crew to stay here. They're going somewhere else. Anywhere else. Probably everywhere else. You were so proud of not being penny wise and pound foolish and you've overlooked the one thing that might—conceivably—cut your turnover in half."

Dorion's jaw tightened and his lips flattened into thin lines. "What might that be?"

"You're boring them to death."

Dorion's face went slack. "What?"

"How many permanent party here on this station?" Natalya asked.

"I don't know," he said. "I think it's around a hundred if you count all the techs, maintenance people, and support staff like the concierges."

"Where do you live?" Natalya asked.

"We have a wing on the other side of the station."

"What do you do for entertainment?" Zoya asked.

"The usual things. Dinner parties. I'm a member of a book club. My wife has her gaming friends. There's an active group of network gamers here. VR simulations. I play a little but I'm not very good. She's amazing. Top ten on the station. We'll take a vacation over to High Tortuga for the system finals in a few months." Dorion smiled. "I'm very proud of her."

"Right," Natalya said. "What will you do on High Tortuga?"

He shrugged. "Well, she'll have to play during her matches. In between we'll probably do a little shopping. Maybe see a show. It'll be nice to get a meal..." His voice petered out and his eyes grew wide.

"Some of your pilots dock over at High Tortuga?" Zoya asked.

"A few," he said. "It's not encouraged."

"So, here's the deal, Brian," Natalya said. "This place is a ghost town. That's a problem if you're going to try to cut a few pennies off by building these specialized ships and sending them out for weeks at a time only to have the pilots come back here and stare at the bulkheads until they go out again."

"So you're saying the ships are all right but we need to build what? A bowling alley?" His voice carried a hint of sarcasm that Natalya ignored.

"Bowling alley. Dance hall. Couple of different restaurants. A hotel." She shrugged. "Give the pilots who live here one week out of the month something to look forward to docking for."

"Free fuel isn't enough?"

Zoya sighed. "If it were enough, the passageways would be packed and the docks would be full."

"You want me to tell the board that they can save money by opening restaurants?"

"Just tell the board you need to diversify your revenues by leasing franchises to outside operators," Natalya said.

Zoya said, "Ideally, they'd be profit centers. The only expense the station would need to incur is getting enough spaces to accommodate the people who want to set up shop here."

"We can't just let anybody in here," he said. "This is a secure facility."

"So, vet them. Make it part of their contracts. Make them sign the nondisclosures," Zoya said. "You've got five hundred crews working for you now. They're flying all over the Western Annex. Docking who knows where. Talking to who knows whom. How secure do you think that is?"

Dorion's mouth opened and closed.

"How much less secure will it be to bring in fifty or a hundred service workers to make this place a station instead of a shell?" Zoya asked.

He took a deep breath and settled back in his chair. He looked at Zoya for several long moments before turning his gaze on Natalya. He glanced at the schematic on the display, then nodded as if to himself. "Of course. We'll need another wing for permanent party staff. I think we already have empty bays in the central station. We can isolate the actual secure communications gear in the tower easily enough." He looked up at Natalya and Zoya as if seeing them for the first time. "What about the ship?"

"If the couch is comfy enough, I think it's a winner," Natalya said.

"Unless you're going to give the ships to the pilots, I think you hire more pilots than ships and make the cycles shorter," Zoya said. "Pilots take the ship out for a two- or three-day run and come back, like they'd normally do. Instead of going right out, they dock and swap pilots."

"Put the pilots on a rotation schedule instead of the ships?" Dorion asked.

"I don't know how you schedule it now, but the only real difference would be that the ships dock every time they come back to unload data. That's more a function of time than capacity, am I right?" Natalya asked.

"Yeah. We want the financial data updates as rapidly as possible."

"An Unwin Eight would have to maneuver for what? A few days?" Zoya asked.

"To dock?" Dorion asked. "Maybe a week."

"The only problem with these is that jump error coming in on a twenty-BU hop could put them anywhere between here and the great beyond. They're going to need to end a run with a short jump so they can arrive somewhere near where they need to be," Zoya said.

"And start with a short one. *Peregrine* could jump a couple of stans after undocking." Natalya nodded at the display. "That ship could probably make a quick hop out within a stan."

Dorion stood and held out a hand. "Thank you. Both of you. You've given me a lot to think about."

Natalya shook his hand. "Sorry we didn't tell you what you wanted to hear."

He shook his head. "You told me what I needed to know." He held out his hand to Zoya. "Both of you."

Zoya shook it. "I wish you luck with the board."

He grinned. "They can be a bit stubborn when they get an idea."

Natalya crossed to the door and stopped. "So make it seem like it's their idea."

"Suggestions?" he asked.

"You have a chief of operations?" Natalya asked.

"We do."

"Catch him in the passageway and tell him you've thought about his idea of setting up some service franchises on the station to attract the pilots you'll need for the new ships," Zoya said. "Tell him you like the idea and that you're impressed with the creative way he's approaching the problem. Then walk away."

Natalya laughed.

"But that's your idea, not his."

"He doesn't need to know that. By the time he gets back to his office, he'll think it's his idea and will claim it when he presents it to the board," Zoya said.

"Naw. He's not that kind of guy."

"Bet?" Zoya asked.

"Bet what?" Dorion asked.

"Loser buys dinner at the first new restaurant," Zoya said.

"Bet," Dorion said and held out his hand again.

Zoya shook it and they both grinned. "I hope it's someplace expensive," she said.

"So do I," Dorion said. "By the way. Report to Dispatch. You're off on your first circuit tomorrow."

"Excellent," Natalya said. "It's time to test out the new toys your people installed."

"Haven't you tested them yet?" Dorion asked, frowning.

"Just in-system here. Not in field conditions," Natalya said.

"Well, it's all pretty easy. Jump in. Grab the data. Jump out to the next system on the route. Rinse. Repeat," he said.

"You forgot the 'don't get spotted' part," Natalya said. "You really think somebody would jump us? We're just a courier."

Dorion shrugged. "It's not common, but we've lost ships before."

"Enemy action or just bad luck?" Zoya asked.

"We believe bad luck. Law of averages. Our ships jump more times in a day than almost everybody else in the Western Annex does in a month. But we don't rule out somebody grabbing one of our ships to try to get the financial data."

"How can they?" Natalya asked. "We can't even access it."

Dorion shook his head. "They don't know that. We just don't take chances that we don't need to."

Natalya and Zoya traded glances and shrugs.

"We'll do our best to sneak in and out, then," Natalya said.

"Safe voyage," Dorion said.

Chapter Nine
CommSta Bowie: 2366, April 8

NATALYA STRAPPED DOWN while the coffee brewed. She grinned at Zoya. "You like the new nav?"

Zoya grinned back. "Did you check this itinerary they gave us?"

"Not in any detail but that's a lot of stations over three weeks. How many? Eighty something in almost twenty days?"

"Yeah. Eighty-four."

"How many can you plot at once?" Natalya asked. "Set for least time."

"I've plotted the first six. We have to come back here eight times, counting the last one. That's going to add a few stans to the run."

"How's it look?"

"Odd. I'd expect we need to hit them within a couple of days of the last data pickup or the whole scheme falls down."

"Yeah. That's what I'd expect."

"This list is in alphabetical order. That can't be right unless they always run in alphabetical order. We'd be jumping back and forth around the Western Annex rather than a least-time route between here and there."

Natalya paused. "Good point." She unbuckled and climbed out of her couch. "Come on. Bring the list."

"Where are we going?"

"Scheduling. I'd rather get it cleared up before we leave than try to iron it out after we've jumped away."

Zoya followed Natalya out of the ship and back onto the dock. It took them only a couple of ticks to get to the scheduling office. The clerk looked up from his terminal. "*Peregrine*, right?"

"Right," Natalya said. "We were prepping for departure and discovered that we didn't know what order this list is supposed to be in."

Zoya held up the drive.

He held out a hand and Zoya dropped the small device into it. He slotted it into his console and opened the file. Natalya could see the light reflected on his face as he scrolled down through it. "This is in alphabetical order," he said. "That can't be right. Where'd you get it?"

"Guy at Dispatch handed it to me this morning," Zoya said. "It needs to be in schedule order, doesn't it? So the data on the buoy isn't more than a day or two old?"

The clerk nodded. "Yeah, it should."

"Do you have the data for when the last pickup was on each of these?" Natalya asked.

"Of course."

"Can you generate the new query with that data appended to each station?" Natalya asked.

"Sure. One tick. Do you have the new Mark Twenties?" he asked.

"No. Sixteens," Natalya said. "Upgraded last week. Best we could do without ripping out the network and running new fiber."

He nodded again. "Your ship profile hasn't been updated. It's still showing Mark Tens."

"I don't think she's had Mark Tens since the '50s," Natalya said.

"It's a default template. That should have been updated. When you get back from this route, come see me and we'll reconcile the systems." He pulled the drive and handed it to Zoya. "You should be able to import that directly so the system will plot your course in order. You can choose best time or least cost and make adjustments for intermediate way points as you go."

"So all we need to do is fire it up and hold on?" Zoya asked.

He grinned. "Basically. The navigation system should be linked to your engineering systems so it knows how much leg you've got and when the capacitor should be charged. Most skippers just do a little manual fiddling to get the best approach."

"Thanks," Zoya said and nodded to Natalya.

"That was painless," Natalya said as they left.

"I'm glad you asked. This will save me a lot of time."

"I'm glad, too. That might have been embarrassing for the company if we'd failed to grab the data in time."

"Might have been embarrassing for us to botch our first route," Zoya said. "Makes me wonder if we've been initiated to the tribe."

"How do you mean?"

"What if they gave us the file in the wrong order on purpose?"

"To see if we knew the difference?" Natalya asked.

Zoya nodded and then jerked her chin toward the *Peregrine*'s lock. A group in station livery stood clustered around and grinned as they approached. Dorion stepped out of the group with a smile on his face and a package in his hands.

"Congratulations," he said. "You've passed with flying colors." He handed the package to Natalya. "I heard you like good coffee. Enjoy this on your first route."

"You were going let us get underway for the wrong place?" Zoya asked, her jaw clenched.

He shook his head. "Not at all. Traffic control wouldn't have approved your departure until we'd confirmed your itinerary and sent you the corrected one." He looked back and forth between them. "Whose idea was it to go to the source?"

Zoya looked at Natalya.

"I might have known," Dorion said.

"Well, she spotted the problem while we were trying to manually load the first jumps," Natalya said. "I just figured the best place to get what we needed was scheduling rather than dispatch."

"Good job. Both of you," he said. "Welcome to the team."

After everybody had shaken hands all around, Natalya and Zoya got back to work.

"That was nice of him," Zoya said.

"Giving us a bad routing list?" Natalya said.

Zoya shrugged. "I was talking about the coffee. He knows how much you like it. Not everybody has your fetish about it."

"Still feels like hazing," Natalya said.

"How many windows in Hutchins Gym?" Zoya asked with a sideways grin.

"Twenty-seven to the outside, six ticket, and twelve boxes for real people, not cadets." Natalya grinned back. "All right. Point made."

"Besides," Zoya said. "We apparently passed."

"Apparently." Natalya finished her pre-flight check and made sure her seat belt was latched. "I'm reserving judgment until I see what kind of coffee he gave us."

Zoya laughed and plugged the drive into her console.

Chapter Ten
Deep Dark: 2366, April 9

NATALYA RUBBED HER eyes. It didn't help the feeling that she had sand coating her eyeballs. "How long have we been at this?"

Zoya glanced at the chronometer on her screen. "We got underway from Bowie at 0930. It's almost 0120 now. I can't do the math. Twelve plus fourish stans. Call it sixteen in round numbers."

"How many buoys have we pilfered. Six?"

"Just five. We're coming up on number six now. Right on schedule according to the itinerary."

"How do the Unwin crews do it?" Natalya asked.

"Bigger crews, maybe. Maybe they don't just jump in, siphon off the buoy, and jump out again."

Natalya blinked and debated on whether another cup of coffee was a good idea. "That's what we're supposed to do, isn't it?"

"Yeah," Zoya said. "But remember what Dorion told us way back in the beginning?"

"What, two weeks ago?"

Zoya laughed. "Yeah. Unwin pilots also do some light trading while they're out here. They're probably docking up every other day and taking a break."

Natalya nodded. "Now that you mention it."

"I'm thinking we're doing the prototype run for the solo ships."

"Testing the theory before they build the ships?"

Zoya adjusted something on her console. "Yeah. I don't know if you noticed but that ship he showed us was a souped-up Scout. Lower mass, only slightly bigger drives."

"Way longer legs," Natalya said.

"Precisely. You were right about the cycle, too. We haven't been out a full day yet."

"This will get easier if we take watches," Natalya said.

"You'd trust me to jump into a system and out again?"

"Why not? You're doing the navigation now. I'm just pushing the button."

"These Mark Sixteens are doing most of the work," Zoya said. "I'm only approving the jumps as they come into line. I think we did most of the heavy lifting when we went through and added in the short jumps to get us into the system with a tiny error."

"Yeah. We're dropping in within a couple of light minutes of the buoys," Natalya said. "When we get this next buoy, we've got a big hole to jump into, right?"

"According to the database."

"Let's get there and get some downtime while the capacitors charge. We're running too close to empty for my comfort level."

Zoya pulled up the plot and stared at it for a few ticks. "That works out nicely. Do we need a bridge watch?"

Natalya sighed and stared out at the stars. "Maybe. Let's see how well we do jumping clear of this next station. Which one is it again?"

Zoya consulted her console. "Son Shine Station. Cosmological research station run by some Jesuits."

"Nearer my God to thee," Natalya said. She unclipped her belt and stood up to stretch. "You want another coffee?"

Zoya shuddered visibly. "I'm about coffeed out right now. I'll want one after a nap, assuming I can sleep after drinking so much of it."

"Food? We haven't eaten since 1800."

"Any of that ice cream left?" Zoya asked.

"We've got a couple gallons of it. You want some?"

"Thanks. Make it a double."

Natalya chuckled and headed for the galley. Ice cream didn't appeal to her, but a fresh cup of coffee and a couple of cookies would go down well. She glanced at the chrono. Two stans until they jumped into Son Shine and no more than one more to jump out. Just about right.

THE SMELL OF FRESH coffee pulled Natalya out of slumber. The chrono said she'd been out for six stans but it felt like two. She clambered out of her bunk, into a shipsuit, and grabbed a cup before joining Zoya in the cockpit.

"Did you sleep?" Zoya asked.

"Yeah. You?" She lowered herself into the pilot's couch and checked ship status.

"A bit. I think I was anxious knowing nobody was on the bridge. Woke up half a stan ago. Grabbed a fast shower and started coffee. What's for breakfast?"

"Looks like a couple of jumps and a side of buoy."

"That first jump is a long one. Margin of error is gonna suck," Zoya said.

"I see that. Let's jump and see how much correction we need to do on the other end. We can eat while we're getting ready to jump into—what is it? Macaroon."

"Yeah. No notes on it." Zoya shrugged. "Another unlisted station. Jump coordinates from our dispatch list and that's about it."

"Hiding out in the Dark," Natalya said.

"Can't blame them for that."

"I don't." Natalya took another sip of coffee before securing the cup and reaching for the console. "Let's get this over with and we'll get some breakfast going."

"Jump loaded," Zoya said. "Ready when you are."

Natalya punched it and the view outside the ship shifted only slightly. "Didn't look like that could have been seven BUs."

"It was only six and a half," Zoya said. "Lemme dial us in." She tapped keys while Natalya lounged back in her couch and sipped coffee.

"I'm in a bacon mood this morning," Natalya said.

"Throw some pancakes in and I'm with you," Zoya said. "Yeah. We're a bit off line, we'll need to shift our vector. Adjustment coming to helm now." She snapped a key and looked over at Natalya.

"Got it." Natalya stowed her coffee and accepted the course adjustment. "Perfect. We'll be here about a stan. Capacitor charging and programming the burn."

The star field looked like it was rotating around them as the ship spun on its various axes to align the heavy engine at the back of the ship. After a few moments, a low rumbling filled the ship as the kicker fired off.

"I'm keeping the power low and running the burn a little longer," Natalya said. "Give us time to eat, get cleaned up."

Zoya nodded and sat back in her couch. "You making breakfast or am I?"

Natalya released her seat belts. "You made the coffee. I'll make the food."

"In that case ..." Zoya pulled a coffee cup out of the holder and held it out to Natalya, who took it with a good-natured bow.

Chapter Eleven
CommSta Bowie: 2366, April 29

NATALYA SECURED THE thrusters and checked the station ties. "We still had half a tank of water."

Zoya released her seatbelts and stood up, stretching her back and rolling her shoulders. "We could probably both use a shower."

"I'm thinking of a nice hot soak in the tub myself." Natalya sat still, savoring the quiet for the first time in weeks. The lack of sound filled her with a kind of peace. The ship had held up well. "How many jumps?"

"Counting the one into here, I have no idea. A hundred and something. I stopped counting after the third day." Zoya looked around the cockpit. "We'll need to get the maid in."

Natalya snorted. "We did pretty well for practically living in these couches."

"I can't imagine doing this solo," Zoya said. "At least one of us could sleep while the other kept the ship moving."

Natalya clambered out of her couch and reached down to pull her coffee cup out of the holder. "Let's just leave it for now. Another day won't make much difference in here but a bath and a few stans of uninterrupted sleep will make a world of difference to me."

"Do we need to do anything for the ship immediately?"

Natalya looked around. "Nothing that can't wait until tomorrow. We'll need to take out the trash, change some filters. I'll want to run a full system check on the drives and a visual scan on the thruster nozzles. The old girl isn't used to this amount of use all at once."

"She did us proud," Zoya said. "Let's go see if they rented our room."

Natalya led the way aft, shutting off lights and securing equipment as she went. She cracked the lock and stepped out to a crowd. "What the—?"

Zoya stepped out behind her just in time for Dorion to emerge from the throng.

"Didn't we just do this?" Zoya asked.

He grinned. "Not exactly. Welcome back. You've just set a new station record for the most buoys serviced on a single route."

Natalya looked at Zoya. "You were right."

Zoya just shrugged.

"Right about what?" Dorion asked.

"Nobody else runs buoys back to back to back for three solid weeks, do they?"

He had the grace to look a little sheepish. "Actually, no. Three weeks per route? Yes. Two to three days per cycle, yes."

"But the Unwins dock somewhere every few days, don't they?" Zoya asked.

He nodded.

"Wonderful," Zoya said. Her tone made it clear she thought it was anything but wonderful.

"Anyway, thank you for a terrific effort and proving that the smaller, faster ships can make a significant difference to the processing time," Dorion said.

"You're welcome, I think," Natalya said. "Right now I need a bath and about twelve stans of sleep so if you'll excuse us?" She started forward but the crowd didn't separate for her.

He coughed. "Actually, we've laid on a bit of a celebration for you."

"What? Now? Are you mad?" Natalya felt the pressure rising at the back of her head. She looked at Zoya and took a deep breath. "Thank you. Thank you, all," she said turning to the crowd. "We both really appreciate the gesture. Don't we, Zoya?"

Zoya stepped up and nodded vigorously. "Yes. Yes, we do. Very much appreciated."

"But if I don't get into a hot bath followed by some cool sheets in the next thirty ticks, I'm going to break somebody's arm." She never raised her voice. She only stared at the people standing directly in front of her.

They melted to the sides, leaving a path down the middle.

"Thank you. Please enjoy the celebration and know we're with you in spirit if not in person," Natalya said. She and Zoya walked through the crowd.

They were halfway to the corner by the time Dorion caught up with them. Natalya eyed him but didn't stop and didn't speak.

"Yeah. Sorry about that. We, ah, that is, I wasn't thinking," he said.

"It was well beyond the tedium you promised," Natalya said, still striding along the dock. "We can do a lot with the *Peregrine*, but that death march is something we're going to need to talk about. We can't keep doing that to an antique. She weathered this storm. I think. We'll need to spend part of this week checking her out to make sure she's safe to take out again."

Dorion grunted like he'd been hit. "You didn't mention any problems."

"We haven't had a chance, have we?" Zoya asked.

"As far as we know, she came through with bells on," Natalya said. "I can't say the same for me. I'm exhausted, filthy, stressed, and would like a little bit of time without the floor vibrating and my chair rattling. I'd really like several stans where I could just sit and savor the quiet, maybe have a couple of drinks, and generally have a bit of down time after having practically zero for twenty-one days, two stans, and some odd ticks."

Dorion nodded. "We'd like to do a debrief."

They both stopped and stared at him.

He held up both hands, palms out. "Tomorrow. Tomorrow will be fine."

"Thank you, Brian," Natalya said. "I wasn't prepared for a reception committee. I get that we need to fill you in on what happened over the last few weeks, but right now? Not a good time."

He nodded. "You're breaking new ground for us. We appreciate it. Sleep well." He stepped back away from them and smiled. "I've got some news you might like but it can wait until tomorrow. Message me in the morning and we'll coordinate schedules."

Natalya nodded.

"Thanks. Again." Dorion turned and walked away.

Natalya sighed and they finished the walk to their apartment without saying another word to each other.

When the door closed behind them, Zoya looked at Natalya. "Think we were too hard on him?"

Natalya shrugged. "I don't know. We're not his prize puppies and the sooner he realizes it, the better off we'll all be." She paused. "You want dibs on the tub?"

"You take it," Zoya said. "I never was much for soaking. I'll grab the shower."

Natalya grinned. "Suppose we should have taken him up on the offer for separate apartments?"

Zoya stopped at the door to her bedroom. "Why? We got through four years at the academy in the same room. Three weeks in a can with you isn't that much harder." She paused and glanced at Natalya. "You want your own space?"

Natalya shook her head. "Not yet, anyway. I think we're a good team."

"I know we are," Zoya said and ducked through the door.

CHAPTER TWELVE
COMMSTA BOWIE: 2366, APRIL 30

A HOT BATH, A SOLID ten stans of sleep, and a hearty breakfast left Natalya feeling much more human. She slotted the dishes for cleaning as Zoya stumbled her way into the common room wearing one of the station's white terry robes.

"Mornin'," Zoya said. "I trust there's actual coffee to go with the aroma?"

"Of course. How are you doing?"

"Ask me after I've woken up." Zoya blinked her eyes several times. "Everything's still a little blurry."

"Felt good to sleep in a bunk that didn't vibrate, didn't it?"

"Oh, yeah." Zoya pulled a mug out of the cupboard and slopped coffee into it. She cradled the cup in her hands and held it up to her face. A couple of small sips later she sighed. "There. It's a start and my mouth is unstuck." She crossed to the nook and took a chair.

"We're going to have to see Dorion today," Natalya said.

Zoya nodded without speaking.

"Should I tell him we're awake?"

Zoya squinted at her with slitted eyes.

"Maybe I'll just go take a shower and freshen up," Natalya said.

Zoya put her elbows on the table and let her head hang over the mug. "Save some hot water for me. I'm going to need it."

Natalya laughed. "There are some breakfast packs in the fridge. Food will help."

Zoya raised an eyebrow and opened one eye to glare a warning.

Natalya laughed again and scooted into the other compartment on her way to the shower. Through long experience, she had learned that Zoya was not a cheerful morning person. After a cup of coffee and a bit of token grumpiness, she'd be ready to go. Natalya slid into the huge shower and let the water sluice over her skin. It felt so decadent as she played with the various nozzles and temperature settings until Zoya stuck her head into the bathroom.

"You're gonna get all pruney. Don't we have stuff to do this morning?"

Natalya shut off the water and pulled her towel down from the rack. "I was all pruney last night," she said. "And yeah. We do."

"What time shall I tell Dorion?"

"Tell him 1100. That'll give us time to make a first pass at cleaning up the ship. He'll want lunch at noon so he won't keep us too long."

"Good thinking."

Zoya disappeared, leaving her to get dried off and dressed in a fresh shipsuit.

"Amazing what a full belly, a good night's sleep, and being clean can do to your outlook," Natalya said when she joined Zoya in the common room.

"Ain't it the truth." Zoya lounged on the sofa in her robe with coffee and her tablet. "I need five ticks and I'll be ready to go."

"Did you message Dorion?"

She nodded and clambered up from the sofa. "No response yet. Think he's going to pull rank?"

"And tell us to come in earlier?" Natalya asked.

"Yeah. He didn't seem real happy with us yesterday."

"Wouldn't surprise me."

The doorbell rang followed by a rap on the door.

"Bets?" Zoya asked.

Natalya laughed and waved her hands. "Scoot. I'll hold him off until you've had a chance to get showered and dressed."

Zoya slipped into her bedroom while Natalya crossed to the door.

"What are you doing here, Brian?"

The pause lasted about three heartbeats. "How did you know it was me?" His voice sounded muffled through the door.

"Concierge has been here, maintenance isn't due for another stan, and you're the only other person we know."

The pause lasted a bit longer than before. "We need to talk. The board is after me for the debrief already."

Natalya opened the door to find Dorion in his usual impeccably tailored station uniform, leaning on the door frame. "Come in. We can have some coffee while we wait for Zoya."

He gave her a smile and slipped past her. "How was that coffee we sent along with you?"

"Very nice. Sarabanda varietal, wasn't it?"

He nodded.

"Would you prefer tea?" Natalya asked. "Zoya's going to be a few ticks."

The sound of a shower turning on came from the next room. Dorion's gaze flipped toward the sound. "I thought ... that is, she messaged me. I thought you were up."

"We are up. We're just not in the habit of accepting callers before we're ready."

Dorion sighed. Natalya thought his jaw clenched for just a moment. "Yes, actually. A cup of tea would be very nice. Thank you."

Natalya puttered in the kitchen and waved Dorion to one of the stools at the center island. "Ask," she said. "We've got a lot to do today. I'm sure you do as well."

"What's the issue? You two came off the ship yesterday like two wet cats climbing out of a bucket."

Natalya leaned back against the counter next to the cooktop and crossed her arms over her chest. "Apt simile."

"So?"

"So, you lied to us for starters."

Dorion blinked slowly a couple of times. "About what?"

"You told us everybody goes out on these three-week rotations. Three on, one off."

"They do."

"No, they don't. You also told us the Unwins—and I assume you have some fast packets in your fleet?" She paused and waited for him to answer.

"Yes. Mostly Unwins but a few Mercator couriers and a couple of Higbee one-tonners."

"You told us they do a little trading on the side, didn't you?"

He looked down at his hands as if surprised to find them knotted together in front of him on the island. He flattened them on the surface. "Yes. That's true. I told you that and they do."

"You implied they did that on their time off, but that's not true is it?"

"Well, I assume they do it then, yes."

The sound of the shower cut off as the kettle whistled. Natalya tossed some tea into an infuser and poured the boiling water over it before turning back to him.

"You didn't tell us that we're the only crew going nonstop for three weeks before we left, did you."

He looked at his hands again before looking back at Natalya. "No. I didn't."

"You strongly implied that we were just following the track of the last packet that made that loop, but that's not true either, is it?"

He shook his head.

"What's the truth? How many ships worth of buoys did we cover for you?"

"I'm not sure. Three. Maybe four."

She pulled the infuser with her fingers, ignoring the burn of hot metal against her fingertips, and slid the mug onto the island in front of Dorion. "Try five or six. Your fleet is on duty for three out of every four weeks on some kind of rotating basis but they only handle about one buoy a day, on average?"

"Something like that." He sipped his tea. "What tipped you off?"

"The route. A single packet—even a beefed-up Eight—couldn't cover it in that time frame. We only managed because we shifted to least time instead of least cost. We barely had the legs to cover it. Being able to jump fourteen BUs to a fast packet's seven to ten made a big difference on a couple of those legs."

He sipped his tea again and shrugged. "That's a big leap on thin data."

Natalya crossed her arms over her chest again. "When we went back to scheduling and got the correctly ordered list, we asked for last date of service."

"And?"

"And some of those legs were too damn long for one ship to have done them in that order in that time frame. That's a long jump into Son Shine and the jump from Son Shine to Macaroon took almost everything we had left. An Unwin Eight couldn't do it. It doesn't have the legs. Son Shine would have had to be the last buoy on a string before they jumped back here to dump data, and we were still on our first day out."

Zoya came out of her bedroom, shined and polished in fresh clothes and a smile. "And you confirmed it when we stepped off the ship."

Dorion's face went blank again.

"We pulled over eighty beacons in three weeks," Zoya said. "While I suspect your fleet could be more efficient if they paid attention to their routes instead of to their trading, I'm also pretty sure they wouldn't do it at all if they had to be out for the whole time." She crossed to the coffee maker and pulled a fresh cup from the cabinet. "So, maybe High Tortuga is an old company that's been around longer than the Western Annex, Brian, but something has changed and you're expecting the two of us to be the solution to a problem we don't even know about." She poured coffee into her mug and turned to face him again. "We've signed your NDA. We've signed your contract. We've proven that the *Peregrine* can make that route even if we would rather never have to make that run again. We have not proven that those one-pilot prototypes you're thinking about can do it."

"We'd have gone space happy without each other out there to lean on," Natalya said. "Just what we told you before we left. Maybe more than three days, but nobody is going to sign up for three weeks of solitary confinement with the added time pressure of trying to siphon off four buoys a day every day out there."

Dorion's lips pressed together in a tight line for a moment. He took a sip of tea and stared at the two of them. "We're growing too fast."

Zoya nodded. "That's why this shiny new station?"

He shrugged. "It's not all new. The communications core is a century old. The company migrated to it when High Tortuga broke from being a single entity. This wing? Yeah. New."

"Whose bright idea was it to put together a new fleet?" Zoya asked.

He shrugged. "What we have isn't working."

"So you pitched it to the board and now you're stuck trying to implement it," Zoya said.

He shrugged again.

"Spell it out for me, would you, Brian?" Natalya asked.

"Our systems all depend on fast promulgation of data across the entire Annex. High Line, Toe-Holds, everything. We get messages from one end of the Annex to the other in a matter of a few days. The longest any message takes to get from any High Line station to any other is four days. Toe-Holds is six. Most are within five. We prioritize High Line traffic because of our agreements with CPJCT. That's fixed. That's stable. CPJCT hasn't set up a new system out here in over half a century."

Natalya nodded. "Go on."

"Toe-Holds are different. Anybody who wants to can join our network. It's been a policy as long as High Tortuga has been in existence."

"Everybody wants to get paid," Zoya said.

"Yeah." Dorion took another sip. "For the longest time, it was pretty stable. The big stations like Mel's and Dark Knight have been around as long as High Tortuga. Ice Rock even longer. A new station would open up every few stanyers and request service. We'd send out a crew to set them up. For a century and a half we had two crews and they could handle it."

"Go on," Natalya said.

"Now we have ten and a backlog. A new station opens every few days. Most of them fail within a stanyer but everybody and his monkey seem to have it in their heads that heading out on your own is the way to fame and fortune. Or at least fortune." He shook his head. "One of our crews works full time just picking up the equipment and buoys from failed colonies."

"So the model you have has started to break down under the pressure?" Zoya asked.

"Exactly. We've relied on our fleet for a very long time. We've augmented it over the stanyers to just over fifteen hundred ships now. Not five hundred. Last stanyer, the projection for new Toe-Holds exceeded the production of fast packets within a decade. While a packet can service more than one station, we're not the only ones hiring packets to be couriers."

"That's why you hired us," Natalya said.

Dorion offered them a faint smile. "The Scouts have become mythical in their ability to go out, stay out, and jump long distances. It seemed a logical choice, but now you're saying you can't stay out that long." He paused. "Can you explain it?"

Zoya looked at Natalya.

"I can guess," she said. "Exploration—at least as I understand it—involves jumping into a known location and sending probes out to nearby locations to see what's there. While the explorer is waiting, the ship, if not stopped, is at least not moving very fast. The crew has days to hang out. Sleep. Waiting for the probes to come back. I don't know how long that is. I don't know what they're doing. Making baby explorers for all I know. The point is they're not pushing the ship to its limit every tick of every day over weeks. I'm a bit concerned for the ship and I wanted to spend this morning going over it to make sure we haven't damaged something. All we need is for another fuel coupling bearing to go on it." She sighed. "It's an antique. A well-restored antique, but still an antique."

"How many of the new ships do you have?" Zoya asked.

"None," Dorion said, looking down at his mug. "We have one that's almost spaceworthy and keels laid for four more."

"For what it's worth, we think it's a good design," Natalya said. "Based only on what we saw in your office. If you have twice as many pilots as ships, that could be the answer that you're looking for."

Dorion frowned at her. "You mentioned that before. I don't see how that helps?"

"Ships work while the alternating pilots rest," Zoya said.

"We were pretty played out by the end of the first day, but got a second wind by the end of the second," Natalya said.

"Of course, that was after we managed to get three hours of sleep in a row," Zoya said.

"There's that. Point is what you told us before. That ship can get from one end of the Western Annex to the other in something around a day. This station is almost in the middle. A ship only needs to travel half way across the Annex to get to almost any station or orbital out there," Natalya said. "Some careful routing and some good piloting, one of those ships could cover maybe ten buoys in a single day if they were clustered well. On average, probably five or six a day would be doable. We were doing four or five a day and one day we did eight."

Dorion sat and stared at his tea for several long moments. "So, if I'm hearing you correctly. The only problem with the new ships is the three-week cycle?"

Natalya and Zoya traded glances and shrugs.

"Why three weeks?" Zoya asked.

"It's what our contract boilerplate has always used."

Natalya sighed.

Dorion finished his tea and stood. "Thank you, both. I've got some work to do with the board and I need to contact the yard to find out how soon that ship will be ready for trials."

"You're thinking you have two pilots who can test it for you?" Zoya asked.

"We have a test pilot lined up for the trials but I still think I made the best deal of my life when I took a chance on a couple of junior pilots and an antique ship." His smile looked genuine to Natalya. "Would you be amenable to modifying our existing contract? You're both obviously qualified for this next phase of the project and it would be a waste to keep you out there for three weeks at a time when you could be doing much more for the company here."

"Does it come with a raise?" Zoya asked.

He grinned. "Possibly."

"What was the good news?" Natalya asked.

"Good news?" he asked.

"Yesterday. You said you had good news for us," Natalya said.

"Oh. The board approved developing two new restaurants and a movie theater for the station. Requests for proposals went out to operators while you were out."

Natalya had to pause for a moment to process the news. "That's more than I expected."

"Small push at the right time in the proper direction can move even a centuries-old monolith," he said, and winked. "I'll just show myself out. Thanks again. I'll be in touch."

Natalya and Zoya clinked their coffee cups together in a toast.

"Now what are they going to do about those ships?" Zoya asked.

"I don't know," Natalya said. "I think they'll be fine if they don't make the pilots run three weeks at a time."

"Would you take one out?" she asked.

"I don't think we're going to be getting much choice," Natalya said, then emptied her coffee mug in the sink and stacked her cup in the rack. "I better get down to the *Peregrine*. We left a bit of a mess and it's not going to clean itself."

Zoya finished the last of the coffee in her mug and stacked it in the rack beside Natalya's. "I helped make the mess. I'll help clean it up."

CHAPTER THIRTEEN
COMMSTA BOWIE: 2366, APRIL 30

NATALYA POPPED THE lock open and stepped into the ship. The air wasn't exactly stale, but carried the musky aroma of sweaty feet blended with fruit that had overstayed its welcome.

"Ugh," Zoya said. "What is that?"

Natalya chuckled. "That is what we smelled like when we left here yesterday." She headed aft to the engineering space. "We can afford a few new scrubber cartridges, I think."

"We probably should have changed them sooner."

"I'll make a note to check them if we're aboard more than a week," Natalya said. "Living in it, it's hard to notice."

"I'll get the recyclables and trash from the galley," Zoya said, heading up the passage to the bow.

Natalya pulled a couple of fresh cartridges from the stores locker and popped the lid on the scrubber. The funky stink assaulted her but she reached in to pull the nearly dead cartridges out, replacing them with fresh. She tossed the old ones in the nearest bin and looked into the scrubber, then pulled the remaining two and tossed them as well. A few more moments saw a full set of fresh cartridges in the cabinet. She slammed the door closed with her elbow so she wouldn't spread the noisome slime on her hands to the case.

"Scrubbers were that bad?" Zoya asked, stepping back as Natalya approached.

"I replaced all the cartridges. Soon as I get the slime off, I'll punch up the circulation fans."

"Good plan." Zoya hefted a trash bin and headed back down the passageway to the lock. "Back in a tick."

The slime came off her hands readily enough. Natalya slipped into her stateroom and got slapped with the sour smell of dirty laundry.

"What the—?"

She pulled the dirty shipsuits out of the 'fresher and checked the device over before kicking it.

"Something wrong?" Zoya asked, sticking her head in the door.

"This 'fresher. It took my shipsuits but didn't clean them. I can't see what's wrong with it."

"Lemme check the one in my compartment."

Zoya yelled from across the passageway. "Mine's working. You want to use it?"

Natalya tossed the dirty clothes onto the deck. "No. I'll take it all back to the apartment and do it there." She turned to her bunk, stripping the casings from her pillows and the sheets from the mattress. She folded the light blanket and left it on the foot of the bed as she gathered the rest of the laundry in one of the pillow cases.

"Do you do anything to clean the cockpit?" Zoya asked.

"I'll give you a hand. We should probably do a general sweep, swab, and polish. It's been a while."

They'd just cleared away their cleaning gear when somebody rang the lock-call.

Natalya checked the port and saw Dorion standing outside. She popped the latches and opened the hatch. "Didn't expect to see you here."

He shrugged. "You weren't at your apartment. I figured you'd be here. Zoya with you?"

"In the galley."

"Permission to come aboard?" he asked.

"Granted," Natalya said and led the way back into the ship. She pointed down the passage toward the bow. "Don't get lost."

He chuckled and slipped past Natalya, heading forward. Natalya closed the lock and latched it again before following him.

Dorion and Zoya stood in the galley, neither seeming to know what to do with their hands.

"So what do we owe this honor?" Natalya asked.

"The yard notified the board. They need a pilot," Dorion said.

"For the new ship?" Zoya asked.

"Yeah. It's about two weeks ahead of schedule."

"I thought they had a test pilot," Natalya said.

Dorion's face twisted like he had a toad in his mouth. "He backed out when he saw the ship."

Zoya and Natalya shared a glance.

Natalya asked, "Can he do that?"

"The company can't actually force him to fly it until it's certified spaceworthy."

"And because it's a new design under yard trials, it's not certified yet," Zoya said.

Dorion nodded.

"What was his problem? Do you know?" Natalya asked.

"Something about not wanting to sail a ship he had to put on instead of getting in."

"Is it that small?" Natalya asked. "I thought it looked almost as large as the *Peregrine*."

"It is," Dorion said. He stuck his hands in his pockets and looked around the galley.

Zoya shook her head and looked at Natalya who shrugged.

"What aren't you telling us?" Natalya asked.

Dorion took a deep breath and blew it out before looking at her. "The board thinks you two should do it."

"What? Take turns?" Zoya asked.

"Basically."

"I was joking."

"Yeah. I thought you might be. I'm not," Dorion said.

"Only one of us can fly it at a time," Zoya said.

"You can both fly *in* it. There's only one pilot's seat but there are a couple of jump seats on the aft bulkhead." He paused for a moment, chewing his lower lip. "It might actually be better if the two of you did do it together. A deck officer at the helm and an engineer backup. At least for the trials. If something goes wrong, having an engineer there to find—and maybe fix—the problem? Seems prudent."

"How soon?" Natalya asked.

"They're pulling it out of the construction dock tomorrow to make room for the first ship of the next flight."

"And the test pilot already backed out?" Zoya asked.

Dorion shrugged. "That's what I'm being told."

Natalya looked at Zoya. "I don't know about you, but now I'm curious."

Zoya smiled back. "New ship smell? I'm in."

"Have you ever smelled a new ship?" Dorion asked.

"Yes, actually," Zoya said. "I used to pick up the new ore haulers from Manchester for my grandparents."

"Ore haulers?" Dorion asked.

"The big Manchester mining support ships? We called them ore haulers," Zoya said.

"I thought they only made those in Margary," Dorion said.

"Well, they make them in other places, too. They're not jump-capable so you need a jump-tug to move them, but yeah. Those."

Dorion's eyes got round. "Usoko."

"Yeah. Zoya Usoko." She shrugged. "Don't think about it. It'll be easier that way."

"But you're—I mean—Usoko Mining." He all but swallowed his tongue.

Zoya sighed and glanced at Natalya.

"Brian. Over here," Natalya said, snapping her fingers in the air between them. "What do we need to do to get out to the yard?"

Dorion shook his head and looked Natalya in the eye. "Sorry. They'll have it out of the construction dock tomorrow around 1300. I can get clearance for you the day after. Take a company shuttle or the *Peregrine*. Whichever suits you."

"We'll take the *Peregrine*," Natalya said. "I need to get the 'fresher fixed in my stateroom but if we decide to hang around, it'll be easier to have a place to sleep."

Dorion nodded. "I'll make sure you're on the list."

"Who do I see about repairs?" Natalya asked.

"I'll send the dock master down. She'll line it up for you."

"Thanks," Natalya said.

Dorion nodded and beat what could only be described as a hasty exit.

Natalya followed him, making sure the lock was buttoned down after he left.

"Anything about that strike you as odd, Nats?" Zoya asked.

"Timing on the new ship seems like it was farther along than he said."

"He didn't know my connection with Usoko Mining."

Natalya felt her brain hiccup and she considered Zoya's observation. "For a guy who works in the network that keeps all that loose data piled up neatly, you'd think that wouldn't have come as a surprise, wouldn't you?"

"I certainly would," Zoya said. "Either he never looked or they never told him."

"Or he doesn't actually work for them," Natalya said.

"Given what we've seen and done over the last month, you think that's likely?"

Natalya shrugged. "Right hand, left hand. Central office might see it as beneath them to talk to the peons."

"Everything you've told me about Toe-Hold space implies that High Tortuga knows everything because they run the banks and communications," Zoya said.

"Yeah. That's my understanding, but Dorion as much as said the communications network is separated from the banking data. Arm's length and all that. Probably includes personal information."

"I'd like to see what Dorion's file on me says."

"Why?" Natalya asked.

"It wasn't too long ago we were chased off Port Newmar because we were murderers."

"Well, technically, I was the murderer and you were accessory after the fact, but we've suspected that was bogus for a long time now."

"That's my point. What else isn't on our records? Or what's there instead of what should be?" Zoya asked.

"Only one entity can do that, realistically," Natalya said.

"High Tortuga."

"Yeah. You think we can just sail over tomorrow and ask them?"

Zoya shook her head. "No, but I think we might be able to look up our own records to see what they say on the public side of the net."

Natalya took a few heartbeats to process that thought but nodded. "Yeah. There should be a record we can look at. Maybe we should just ask Dorion what he has?"

"You don't think he came to hire us just because of the *Peregrine*, do you?"

"Without even a background check? He's going to turn over all the company secrets to a couple of women who happen to fly an antique?"

Zoya frowned. "When you put it that way, sounds far-fetched. What company secrets do we have?"

"Well, for starters we know where at least some of their data buoys are hidden. We know the communications protocols for slurping the data off them."

"Actually, we don't," Zoya said. "The upgraded comms array they installed has a sealed encryption module in it. I have no idea how it communicates with the buoy. Only that it does."

"Has to be more to it than that. Otherwise we could just sail back to Port Newmar and sell the module to the highest bidder."

"That seems like a sloppy way to run a secure Annex-wide communications system. Every one of those other ships has the same array with the same encryption," Zoya said. "I don't know if we'd even need to dismount it. Just push the output into a spectrum analyzer and see what comes out."

"The whole operation seems a bit sloppy," Natalya said.

The lock-call buzzed. Natalya went to the lock to find a woman in a company jumpsuit waiting just outside.

Natalya popped the lock and stuck her head out. "Yes?"

"I'm Michelle Cecil. Brian said you had a problem with the ship?"

"The dock master?" Natalya asked.

"Yup. That's me."

Natalya stuck out her hand. "Natalya Regyri. Nice to meet you. Come aboard and I'll show you the problem."

Cecil shook her hand then followed Natalya onto the ship and into her stateroom. "The 'fresher stopped working. I can tear down and rebuild a Burleson drive, but I've never been trained on that." She nudged the unit with her toe.

Cecil grinned at her. "That's got to be original with the ship."

"Probably," Natalya said.

"I got a guy who might be able to fix it," Cecil said. "You'll be left with a working antique. Maybe."

"Choices?"

"We can pull that out and give you a new one. Probably use less power and be quieter." She looked at the unit. "We've learned a bit about this technology in the last two centuries. That the only one aboard?"

"Two. One in each stateroom."

Cecil nodded. "Makes sense. You want to replace them both. Same charge."

"How much is that?" Natalya asked.

"Free to you. Company dime."

"Generous," Zoya said, sticking her head in through the door.

"Michelle Cecile, Zoya Usoko. Zoya, Michelle is the dock master."

"Figured," Zoya said. "Why does the company care about keeping this antique flying?"

Cecil shrugged. "New kids always get the velvet glove treatment. This ship? I'm guessing you've done a lot of upgrades so it's not actually a stock issue Scout ship, right?"

Natalya nodded. "My parents had to do a lot of work on it just to make it spaceworthy. At least that's what they told me."

"So, upgrading this unit won't be a problem." She looked back and forth between Natalya and Zoya. "But even in refurbished condition, this baby is worth more credits than I'll ever see. Probably total in my life."

"What's that got to do with the company keeping it flying?"

"It's to keep you two happy, I suspect. They go out of their way for the new hires. Scuttlebutt says the turnover among courier crews is a monster. This is the first actual Scout I've seen come in, so that gives you a little extra cachet."

"Why do so many quit?" Zoya asked.

"Beats me. I'm never in the loop on that stuff. Ships come. Ships go. Few stay for more than a quick refit." She smiled at Natalya. "Or replacement, as the case may be."

"You heard the company has sent out RFPs for some new restaurants?" Natalya asked.

"About damn time," Cecil said. "I like Frosty's well enough but having a little competition for business around here could only help."

"You been here long?" Zoya asked.

"Coming up on my tenth anniversary. We've come a long way from the old comms tower in that time, let me tell you."

"Really?" Natalya said. "Let's get these replacements ordered and I'll buy you a beer."

"Coffee while I'm on duty, but I'd like that."

"I'll get it going," Zoya said, ducking out and heading for the galley.

Cecil pulled her tablet and flashed the ident tab on the 'fresher. "Lemme check the inventory and see what we got."

She flipped screens a couple of times, frowning.

"Problem?" Natalya asked.

"Not really. It may take us a while. I can't upgrade this after all. The replacements all call for more power than this unit uses."

"Which means we'd have to rewire the ship?"

Cecil nodded. "At least this piece."

"So?"

"So we need to fab one. I'm just checking to make sure we have all the models." She flipped a few more screens and her eyebrows rose. "Yeah. Looks like we've got all the models for the entire ship."

"You could make a new Scout?" Natalya asked.

"Apparently. Some of the stock is obsolete and I suspect we would want to upgrade some of these old units. The original consoles are Model 2s."

"You mean Mark 2s?"

"Nope," she said. "Model 2s. They didn't go to the Mark nomenclature until 2250. These are old, old models. I don't even know why we have them."

She poked the screen a couple of times and holstered her tablet. "Work orders filed. Now, coffee?"

Natalya grinned and led the way to the galley where Zoya had the coffee maker already gurgling away. The aroma of fresh coffee masked the scents of cleaning solutions and polish.

"This is a cool little ship," Cecil said. "But two of you in here for three weeks? You must be close."

"We were roommates at the academy," Zoya said. "After that, this isn't bad. We've each got a separate stateroom. The food's plentiful and the coffee's easy."

"I heard you weren't too happy after your first run," Cecil said.

"We don't like being lied to." Natalya pulled a covered mug from the cabinet and filled it. "It's one thing to live here for three weeks. It's another to do it while under time pressure and flying all over the ass ends of the Annex." She handed the mug to Cecil and started filling another.

"Lied to?"

"Let's just say, we were told we had a normal run. Something one of the Eights would normally cover," Zoya said.

"Technically, that was true." Natalya handed the mug to Zoya. "What they didn't tell us is that we covered the runs of five or six *different* Eights."

Zoya took a sip of her coffee. "We did it, but the stress of being in a new job, running a time-critical route, and trying to maintain that over three weeks made us a bit grumpy. It sorta boiled over when we got back and found out the truth."

Cecil took a sip of her coffee and smiled. "This is good. Private stock?"

"Last of our arabasti from Dark Knight Station. I still don't know where Kondur gets it," Natalya said.

"We need to find a new supply soon or we'll have to fly back to Dark Knight," Zoya said with a grin.

"You were going to tell us about the station," Natalya said.

Cecil propped her back in a corner and nodded. "When I got here, they'd just started construction on the expansion. This dock, the new permanent party wing, the pilots' wing. All new in the last ten stanyers."

"What did they have before?" Zoya asked.

"The main comms tower—that's the tall spire in the center of the station—that had a tiny facility around the middle. Basically room for the comms equipment and support staff."

"Ships didn't dock?" Natalya asked.

"It had three or four bays that could take a single ship each with a ten-meter docking ring and enough small craft dock for a half dozen shuttles. That was it."

Zoya frowned. "So all this is new?"

"New being a relative term, yeah," Cecil said taking another sip of the coffee. "I came on as dock maintenance crew just as they were finishing up the expansion."

"Why did they do it?" Natalya asked.

"The expansion?" Cecil shrugged. "Above my pay grade. They've been dubbing around trying to get the couriers to use the station as a base but I don't think we've ever had more than four ships here at a time."

Zoya snorted. "Chicken-egg problem."

"How's that?" Cecil asked.

"Nobody wants to dock here and be alone. So you need ships docking here regularly to have enough people to make it worthwhile."

Cecil nodded. "But without the people, it's not attractive enough."

Zoya shrugged. "Without the customers, there was no reason to expand the entertainment options. Without the entertainment options, that's one less reason to dock."

Cecil sipped her coffee. "Makes sense."

"My question is why didn't they realize this?" Natalya said. "It's not like it's a secret."

Cecil grinned. "The company rotated all the old staff out about the time they were building this up. The old guard wasn't happy with the upgrades. Rumor is they thought the building plan was unnecessary and expensive." She shrugged. "They may have been right. It's taken them almost all this time to finish."

"What? Ten stanyers?" Natalya asked.

"They only finished the pilots' wing about a stanyer ago. The dock didn't have bulkhead panels until about three stanyers ago. The apartment I got when I came aboard was basically a four-person dorm with a head and galley. Took them five stanyers to have enough space that we could all have our own rooms. Another two to get apartments."

"That seems excessive," Zoya said.

"Materials. The belts here in Ravaine got picked over early. Most of what's left isn't worth mining. They pulled miners in from all over and worked the other systems in the local group, but that meant delays while they ramped up production. They bought some finished materials to start the construction but relied on local production to finish it. It took a while, but I have to give them credit. They've created an amazing facility here."

"That nobody's using," Natalya said.

Cecil shrugged. "If they get some new restaurants and watering holes opening up, that will help. I think the reason they started the new shipbuilding program was so the company would own the ships and could dictate where they dock between routes."

"Might be cheaper, too," Zoya said. "Hiring one pilot is cheaper than hiring crews."

"They don't hire crews," Cecil said. "They charter the ships."

Zoya's eyebrows shot up. "They hired us."

Cecil blinked a couple of times. "They didn't charter the ship?"

"They didn't actually mention the ship," Natalya said. They just waved credits at each of us to come and fly for them."

Cecil's eyes narrowed. "Lemme guess. They're trying to get you to take over new ships?"

Natalya nodded. "We had some words about making us fly for three weeks before getting down time. They want us to check out the new couriers."

"We've been chewing on Dorion's ear over the doctrine. He thinks he can send a solo pilot out in one of those cans for three weeks at a time," Zoya said.

Cecil nodded. "That won't work, will it? When will they sleep?"

"The solitary confinement will drive most people over the edge within a week. I couldn't have lasted three weeks out there under those conditions without Zoya," Natalya said. "I think we pushed the limits on what the ship could do as well."

"Is he listening?" Cecil asked.

"We think so," Zoya said.

"My question would be whether or not he has enough standing with the board," Cecil said. "Some of the things they've passed down to me as dock master have been just dumb."

"Like what?" Natalya asked.

"Like turning off the lighting on the dock when there are no ships here."

"Why's that a problem?" Natalya asked.

"Because it's the main passageway between the various sections of the station and we have to do maintenance on the docks all the time. We can turn them off for a few stans during the night cycle but that's not going to add up to much in the way of cost savings. Even over a century."

"I can't imagine the lights use that much power," Natalya said.

"It's rounding-error level in the budget," Cecil said. "We spend more on deck cleaner than lighting."

"So who's Dorion's boss?" Zoya asked.

"Malachai Vagrant. He's the associate director for Communications Operations and reports to the board."

"Who's Joe Allen?" Zoya asked.

Cecil's eyes widened. "Allen is CEO of HTHC—the High Tortuga Holding Company. Why?"

"He and Brian interviewed us back on Dark Knight," Zoya said.

"Well, you must have made a good impression," Cecil said.

Natalya glanced at Zoya. "I'm not so sure. Maybe they just thought we'd be an easy pair to dupe into carrying the water on this new operation."

Zoya shrugged. "So which is better? Running that route for three weeks out of four or helping to shape the new protocols for High Tortuga?"

"Putting it that way ..." Natalya said.

"Exactly," Zoya said.

Cecil finished her coffee and put the cup on the counter. "Well, I need to get back to work. Thanks for the coffee and the gab."

Natalya led her back to the lock. "Any time. Thanks for filling us in on the station."

Cecil stepped off the ship. "Happy to do it. I'm looking forward to what's going to happen next. Getting this place converted from a ghost town to a real station would be amazing." She stopped at the dock and looked back at Natalya. "That new unit should be ready in a couple of days."

"We're going out to the shipyard day after tomorrow," Natalya said. "Any chance of getting it replaced by then?"

Cecil frowned. "Not sure. I'll see what I can do."

"Thanks, again."

"Glad to do it." Cecil waved and struck off down the dock, leaving Natalya staring after her and wondering what she'd gotten herself—and Zoya—into.

Chapter Fourteen
Pulaski Yard: 2366, May 2

TRAFFIC CONTROL DIRECTED the *Peregrine* to a shuttle bay along the dorsal ridge of the sprawl of girders, habitats, and construction docks. "What do you suppose they use this for?" Zoya asked, gazing out across the yard.

"What do you mean?" Natalya asked.

"Well, they hire most of their ships and crews. According to Cecil, they don't do a lot of repairs and upgrades." Zoya shrugged and waved a hand. "Why do they have all this?"

"Maybe it's an artifact of the old days," Natalya said, lining up on the docking bay. "They must have needed some significant construction when they set this up."

"Two centuries ago? It's still here?"

Natalya shrugged. "Maybe it's where they've been building the buoys and just expanded out as needed. Not like they needed to shut it down."

The docking light turned green and the doors slid open, allowing the *Peregrine* to slip in and settle to the deck beside a battered cargo frame and a sleek, shiny, bullet-shaped craft. Natalya secured the engines and triggered the shore ties. A soft thunk under their feet signaled the successful docking.

She took a moment to consider the lines of the ship next to them. "They can't be serious."

Zoya stood up from the couch and stretched. "It's pretty."

"Pretty small. The lines are wrong based on what Dorion showed us."

"Maybe they changed the design."

The lock-call buzzer sounded, interrupting Natalya's train of thought. She led the way down the passageway to see who'd come to meet them. She peeked out to see a stocky man with spacer-cropped hair peering back at her from the other side of the port. He raised a hand and waved—wiggling his fingers at her. He grinned and stepped back.

"This should be interesting," Natalya said and keyed the lock.

The hatch hadn't completed its cycle before the man was back, practically sticking his head through the crack as the lock opened. "A Scout. Holy guacamole. A real Scout. I never thought I'd see one of these in my life," he said, his eyes scanning everything in the cramped entry. "Do you think you could give me a tour before we get started?" He turned puppy-dog eyes on Natalya.

"You are?" she asked.

"Oh," he said and stuck out his hand. "Downs. Anthony Downs. Tony. Project lead. You must be Regyri?"

Natalya took his hand and gave it a firm shake. "I am. This is Zoya Usoko." She nodded at Zoya.

Downs extended his hand to her as well. "I'm very pleased to meet both of you. Thanks for coming out to look over our little project."

"We were in the neighborhood," Zoya said.

He paused for a moment as if trying to process what she'd said, but chuckled and grinned even wider—a feat Natalya couldn't have believed possible. "Indeed," he said. "Indeed." He looked at Natalya. "A tour? I've been working off the old design documents to build the new bird, but seeing one in the flesh as it were ..." He shook his head. "I'm speechless."

Natalya shared a look with Zoya who hid a smile behind her hand.

"Come aboard, Mr. Downs," Natalya said.

"Tony, please. We'll be working together and I don't do formal well." He stepped up into the lock as Zoya backed into the passageway to make room. "It's tighter than I imagined," Downs said.

"We don't usually get a crowd," Natalya said. "Or we didn't before we started working for Dorion. What would you like to see first?"

"Engineering?" he asked. "If it's not too much trouble."

Natalya took the three steps aft and opened the hatch. "Right this way, Tony. Nothing's very far away on this ship."

"Except a large room," Zoya said.

Downs barked a short laugh and shot her a rueful smile. "I bet that's true." He glanced up and down the passageway. "Still roomier than it looks."

The tour lasted only a few ticks. Downs barely took the time to look about a compartment as if measuring it with his eyes before nodding and moving on to the next thing. In the cockpit he paused and eyed the couches and consoles. "Those aren't originals," he asked, pointing at the displays.

"Upgrades. About as far as we can go without rerunning the data buses," Natalya said.

He nodded. "That's one thing I noticed on the original plans. These babies weren't overengineered in any aspect. Just enough to do the job. Nothing more."

Natalya nodded. "My father spent a lot of time getting her into shape. He and my mother replaced all the power runs fore and aft. They upgraded a lot of the data network, too, but that was some time ago."

Downs snorted. "And nothing changes faster than data requirements, eh?"

"Something like that," Natalya said. "There's room in the cable races to double up the cables, but just barely. What I need to do is pull it all out and upgrade to the forty-eight-channel fiber for the backbone."

Downs looked at the deck as if he could see through the surface to the cabling below. He nodded. "We put that in the new bird. Ran parallel systems for the ship services and comms."

"Forty-eights on each?" Natalya asked.

Downs nodded and shrugged. "Corp is bitching about the cost, but time is the expense they can't get more of. The less time the pilots spend syncing up the data, the more time they have to get to the next system."

"And the sooner they get back with it," Zoya said.

He smiled at her. "No flies on you, either, eh? You're not an engineer?"

"Deck officer," Zoya said.

"Nothing wrong with that. You the pilot, then?"

"It's her ship," Zoya said, nodding at Natalya. "I'm just along for the ride."

Downs looked back and forth between them for a few moments, then nodded as if making up his mind about something. "Well, you wanna see her?"

"That's what we came out here for," Natalya said with a smile.

He grinned and led the way aft and off the ship. Natalya and Zoya followed him out into the docking gallery and down the passageway toward the main station. "Not far. We routed you to the closest open bay," Downs said. He stopped at the next docking port and led them into the open bay. "There she is."

The ship crouched on three skids, looking much like a flattened egg. It looked to be almost the same size as the *Peregrine* in overall length, but not quite as tall. The black skin pulled at Natalya's eyes and made her blink. "Black body coating?" she asked, forcing herself to look away.

"Not as such, no," Downs said. "Just very good nonreflective skin. Almost invisible to radar across the spectrum and damned hard to see in space unless it's backlit."

Zoya pressed her fingers against her eyes and rubbed. "That's hard to look at."

Downs chuckled. "Takes some getting used to. You won't notice it from inside." He fished a small object from a pocket and tossed it to Natalya.

She caught it and examined it. "Remote door locks?"

"Yup. Open her up."

Natalya pressed the green button and a ramp clam-shelled open amidships, a soft yellow light glowing from inside. "Snazzy." She handed the fob back to Downs.

"We're trying to make it something you'll want to fly."

"Why'd the test pilot back out?" Zoya asked as they walked toward the ramp.

Downs ran a hand over his face, scrubbing it over his mouth before answering. "Let's take a look inside, shall we?" He walked up the ramp and stood waiting for them to follow.

Natalya glanced at Zoya, who shrugged before following Downs into the ship.

Natalya stopped at the top of the ramp and peered in. The entry lock was about the same size as the *Peregrine's* with some updated controls and fresh paint. "I'm not sure there's room for the three of us in there unless you open the inner hatch."

Downs shuffled back against the bulkhead and waved her in. "Plenty of room. Come on in."

Natalya saw something in his eyes and stepped into the airlock, crowding against Zoya. "Snug," she said.

Downs punched the lock control with a stubby finger and waited until the other doors closed with a whine and a *chunk*.

"They want me to say 'I don't know' but the truth is, I do." He scrubbed his mouth again. "He thought the ship was a flying coffin just waiting for a body."

"Is it?" Zoya asked.

Downs sighed. "We don't think so." He paused. "*I* don't think so." He paused again. "I'm not a pilot, I'm a structural engineer."

"Why did he think that?" Zoya asked.

"He didn't say. He took a quick tour, said, 'I'm not flying in that coffin,' and caught the next shuttle off the station."

"Why are we huddled in here talking about this?" Natalya asked.

Downs sighed again. "Black box recorders inside. Everything gets recorded. Safety feature."

"Bull," Zoya said. "Black boxes only work if you can recover them. Something goes wrong with this ship and you'll never find the pieces."

Downs nodded. "We all know that."

"But management has trust issues and wants to know everything that's happening in their ships?" Natalya said.

Downs's head bobbed once.

Natalya nodded. "Well, pop the top. Let's look inside this can. Thanks for the heads up."

Downs nodded again and punched the lock control again. The inner door slid open with a ping-ping sound. "We still need to fix the sensors so both doors can operate at the same time when the external pressures all match," he said. "That's something we plan on working on this week." He sidled out of the lock and into the passageway beyond.

"This looks familiar," Natalya said, following Zoya out of the lock and into the fore-and-aft passageway beyond.

"It should. The basic deck plan came from the old Scouts. We've modified it to bring it up to date in terms of engineering, life support, and navigation," Downs said, sounding more like a ship dealer than an engineer. He headed aft. "Power plant's back here." He opened the airtight hatch and swung it out, dogging it against the bulkhead. "Most of this should look familiar."

Zoya stepped aside so Natalya could go through first. "You'll know more about what you're looking at than I will."

Natalya grinned and stepped into the small space. She stopped and stared at the single drive hunkered down on the deck. "What's this?"

"That's your Burleson drive," Downs said, his mouth twitching as if not sure it should be smiling or not.

"Yeah, I get that it's a Burleson drive. Where's the other one?"

"What other one?" he asked.

Natalya looked at him. "I thought you said you used the Scouts as a basic deck plan."

"Well, of course," Downs said. "But we upgraded the power plant."

"And took away one drive?" Natalya asked, pointing to the massive machine. "You can't be serious."

"That drive is rated at three times the old ones," Downs said. "What's the problem?"

"This doesn't match the specs we saw in Dorion's office last month," Zoya said.

"Things change," Downs said, frowning. "A month is a long time when you're doing rapid prototyping."

"Have you ever designed a ship before, Mr. Downs?" Zoya asked.

Downs frowned and stepped back. "Well, I didn't design this one. We just took the Scout plans and upgraded them."

Zoya looked at Natalya and shrugged. "Looks like we're out of a job," she said.

Natalya nodded. "Maybe."

"Wait," Downs said. "You're walking away?"

Natalya stared at him. "You don't seem to understand," she said. She pointed at the drive again. "That's a single point of failure. You're a structural engineer. You know what that means."

"Well, of course," Downs said. "But—"

Natalya cut him off. "But nothing. That drive goes down and the ship never comes home. Period. The reason the Scouts survived is because they had two drives. One drive fails and the other drive takes them home again."

"That drive is rated at over twenty stanyers between failures," Downs said. "We don't intend to let it fall into disrepair so that a failure can happen."

"I'm not flying in this," Natalya said. "It's suicide."

"How can you say that?" Downs asked, looking back and forth between the two. "You're barely out of the Academy. What do you know about ship construction?"

Zoya's smile carried nothing like humor. "I've been sailing since I was tall enough to hit the lock button. I've logged thousands of hours in space. More than half of them in command. I'm not an engineering officer, but even I know that's not a viable design."

"And I *am* an engineering officer," Natalya said. "I've been up to my elbows in the *Peregrine's* guts for a decade and I'm telling you this design is going to cost you a ship, a pilot, *and* the data you need that pilot to bring back. It may not be the first run or the second or the hundredth but it *will* fail. How many of these are you going to build?"

Downs settled back on his heels. "First flight is ten."

Zoya frowned. "That's hardly cost effective."

He shook his head. "Shakedown prototypes," he said.

"How many?" Natalya asked, taking the three steps toward Downs. "A hundred?"

"Company wants a thousand by this time next stanyer."

Natalya stared at Downs. "What's the design criteria driver for this?"

"What? The single unit?" Downs asked.

"Yeah. Cost?"

Downs flinched. "Well, cost is a factor. They're expensive little birds."

"What's the incremental cost of two drives?" Zoya asked.

Downs looked at the deck and rubbed his palm over his lips again. "I'd have to look up the exact amount."

"Rough number," Zoya said. "Ten percent?"

Downs shot a glance at her. "These ships are expensive."

Zoya shook her head. "Not that expensive."

"How much would it cost to just build new Scouts?" Natalya asked.

Downs looked at her, eyes open wide. "You can't be serious."

"Why not?"

"They're old. We've learned a lot about ship building in two centuries."

Natalya gave a pointed look at the single drive. "Obviously not enough."

Downs looked back and forth between the two for more than a few heartbeats. "We can't change that," he said, nodding at the drive.

"Why not?"

"We'd have to upgrade all the power systems and reroute all the communications and power to add another drive."

"How much will it add to the cost?" Zoya asked. "Roughly."

Downs looked at the deck. "Another five percent."

"Five percent?" Natalya asked, her voice echoing down the passageway. "You've got to be kidding me. You're risking the viability of the ship for five percent?"

Down's shrugged without looking up. "Not my call."

"Whose call is it?" Zoya asked.

"Management."

"That's a department not a who," she said.

"Alison Pittman. She flies that yacht you're docked next to," Downs said.

"Fancy," Zoya said. "Why not use that design?"

"Doesn't have the power or the legs we wanted." Downs bit his lips and shrugged.

"And you can't get the license for it," Natalya said, guessing.

"And we can't get the license for it," Downs said with a sigh and looked at the deck.

Zoya snorted. "So management is too cheap to pony up for this project that's supposed to reimagine the backbone of what might be the richest operation in the Western Annex."

"You don't get rich by spending your credits," Downs said without looking up.

"You don't get rich by investing stupidly," Zoya said. The sharpness in her tone made Natalya shoot a glance in her direction. Zoya just shook her head and leaned back against the bulkhead, crossing her arms. "My grandparents didn't raise an idiot."

Downs sighed. "You're above my pay grade here. What do you want to do now?"

Zoya looked at Natalya and shrugged. "May as well see what else they've done."

Natalya nodded. "Let's finish the tour, Mr. Downs."

"Tony, please," he said, glancing up at each of them without lifting his head.

"Tony," Natalya said. "Where did you spend the money if it wasn't back here?"

Downs levered himself off the bulkhead and headed forward. "Cockpit is this way."

Zoya's lips twisted together in a rueful smile as she motioned for Natalya to go ahead. "Something tells me it wasn't on this ship," she said, her voice barely louder than the blowers.

Natalya snorted and Downs stopped at the lock. "You can leave now if you'd rather," he said, looking back down the passageway.

"One thing at a time, Tony. Show us your baby and we'll keep an open mind," Natalya said.

Downs nodded and moved along the passage. He tapped on a door. "Head."

Natalya opened the door and stuck her head in. "Interesting," she said.

"Same size and about the same place as the port-side head on a Scout," Downs said.

"Yeah, but it's laid out better," Natalya said and stepped back to let Zoya see. "You made the whole compartment watertight?"

Downs nodded. "The Scouts all use a modular head with separate sink, toilet, and shower. We just took out the booth and routed the plumbing so that the same valves feed the sink or shower, depending."

Zoya stepped in and looked around. She stretched out her arms to either side and smiled. "I couldn't do this on the *Peregrine*."

"That's pretty clever," Natalya said, nodding her approval to Tony. "What else you got?"

Downs shrugged. "Galley is next." He moved down the passage and took a turn to port.

Natalya followed him into the galley with Zoya right behind her.

"We used the space taken up by the stateroom on a Scout to expand the galley into something more than a closet with a coffeemaker," Downs said.

Natalya surveyed the expanded galley space, taking a moment to run a hand across the top of the new table and spin each of the four chairs on their gimbals. She pointed across the passageway. "What's over there?"

"Tankage. Potable water mostly," Downs said.

"So there really are no bunks?" Zoya asked.

"Only the pilot's couch," Downs said and led the way forward. "This is a one-person ship, so we got the best, most comfortable couch we could."

Natalya and Zoya stood at the back of the cockpit and stared at the couch.

"Try it out," Downs said. "I want one of these of my own."

Natalya waved a hand in an "after you" gesture to Zoya.

Zoya stepped over to the couch and slid onto it, almost gingerly, before lying back.

"Well?" Downs asked.

"How do I adjust it?"

"Adjust it?" Downs asked.

"Yeah. The lumbar support needs to move up and the head rest is too tall. It's only just catching the top of my head." Zoya put her hands up and stuck them between the back of her head and the headrest.

"Oh," Downs said. "We'll customize it for the pilot so it fits perfectly."

"You're going to trade out the couches for each new pilot?" Natalya asked.

Downs looked up at her blankly. "Each new pilot? How much turnover do you think we'll have?"

Zoya levered herself up off the couch. "Right hand, left hand," she said.

"How do you think they're planning to use these?" Natalya asked.

"The new pilots will each get a ship," Downs said with a shrug. "How else can they do their runs?"

"Dorion's planning on trading pilots every four days," Natalya said.

Downs blinked. "I think you misunderstood. The ships will be out longer than four days."

Natalya nodded at Zoya. "Right hand, left hand."

Zoya asked, "Why not just get an adjustable couch? What if I want to change it while I'm out there?"

Downs mouth moved like he might be working up a spit before he spoke. "That's why we custom fit them for each pilot. So you don't have to change it." He spoke slowly, as if to a somewhat dim administrator.

"Cost," Natalya said. "This was cheaper."

Downs glared at her.

"Am I wrong?"

His jaw tightened before he ground out, "No. You're not wrong."

Natalya and Zoya shared a glance and Zoya stepped up to Downs. "So, what's with the galley?"

"I told you. We had the space so we made it more livable."

"You took a perfectly viable galley for a one-person operation and added a dining room and four chairs," Natalya said. "Who's coming for dinner?"

Downs shook his head and his lips pressed together in a tight line. "Look. You don't wanna fly this ship. Fine. We'll find somebody who will. There's no need to get snippy with me, Missy."

Zoya stepped between Natalya and Downs before Natalya had a chance to process what Downs had said. "Tony. You're right. We don't want to fly this ship. We want to fly a safe and comfortable ship. This is neither. I get that it's your baby, but you'll have to pardon us for being critical of it. We're the ones who'd have to risk our lives to fly it."

"We don't need a couple of prima donnas coming in and tearing apart all our hard work—" A sharp ping-ping sound from the passageway cut into Downs's warming tirade.

Chapter Fifteen
Pulaski Yard: 2366, May 2

FOOTSTEPS ECHOED IN the silence and a slender woman in a pristine station jumpsuit smiled as she entered the galley. "Hope I'm not interrupting," she said.

"Ms. Pittman," Downs said. He gave the woman a short nod and backed up to the bulkhead. He looked like a kid just caught red-handed in the cookie jar.

"Hello, Tony," she said with a cold smile. Her brown eyes warmed considerably when she offered her hand to Natalya. "I'm Alison Pittman. You must be Natalya Regyri," she said.

Natalya shook the woman's soft hand and nodded. "Ms. Pittman." She nodded at Zoya. "My wingman, Zoya Usoko."

Pittman reached out to Zoya with another warm smile and an offered handshake. "Ms. Usoko."

Zoya took the offer firmly. "Ms. Pittman."

After a side-eyed glance at Downs, Pittman said, "We asked for you two because you've got more experience with small, jump-capable ships than anyone else in the system. Obviously, we've made some mistakes. How do we fix them?" She raised an eyebrow in Natalya's direction.

"First you have to accept that this ship isn't viable as it sits," Natalya said.

Downs opened his mouth but shut it with a click after another glance from Pittman. "Can you explain for me?" Pittman asked. "I'm not an engineer."

Zoya said, "Before I'd risk my life in this ship, I'd insist on a second Burleson drive, as a minimum. Before I'd sign a contract to fly it for any period of time, I'd insist on an adjustable couch.

The galley is the galley. It's dumb, and it doesn't make any sense to have a four-top table in a one-person ship."

Pittman looked at Natalya. "Ms. Regyri?"

"We're late to the game on this, Ms. Pittman," she said.

Pittman nodded. "I'd rather know the problems now—even as late as it is—than a stanyer from now when we've got a thousand of these things all built."

"I don't know enough to really talk about anything beyond what Zoya's said and which you've heard already." She glanced up at the overhead and shrugged.

"What do you need to know?" Pittman asked.

"Why one-person crews?" Natalya asked.

Pittman pursed her lips and nodded, folding her arms. "It seemed the most cost-effective approach. With a thousand of these ships, that's a thousand pilots. Every additional pilot multiplies the operating expense."

Zoya said, "How much do the ships cost?"

"I'm not at liberty to say," Pittman said. "A lot."

"Fair enough," Zoya said. "Losing one would be expensive, though?"

Pittman's lips flickered in a smile. "Yes."

"What's the breakeven?" Zoya asked. "A couple of stanyers?"

"More like ten," Pittman said, tilting her head to one side. "Depreciation, operational overhead, and variable costs."

Zoya nodded. "What's the cost of pilot turnover?"

Pittman blinked. "We don't have numbers for that."

"Because you've never had a fleet of your own ships?" Zoya asked.

"Right. All our data is run on a contractual basis with existing operators."

"So you're setting up a significant vertical integration of your operation. What's the estimated cost saving on that integration?" Zoya asked.

"We're actually a new division of the organization. What they pay in contracts now is privileged information."

Zoya smiled. "So, your mission is to bring the costs in below what they're paying. Preferably with higher reliability and better integrity of the process against a rapidly expanding demand. Right?"

Pittman tilted her head to the side. "Yes, although reliability and integrity have never been problems for them."

"What's the rate of growth on new demand?" Zoya asked. "Because reliability and integrity will suffer if it grows faster than you can expand service to cover it."

Pittman didn't answer for several long moments. Some kind of thought process was running behind her eyes, but Natalya wasn't sure whether it was "How much can I say?" or "Who the hell does she think she is?"

Before Pittman could respond, Zoya said, "We don't need to know. It's just—from an outsider's perspective—the organization appears to be incurring a massive expense to start up this in-house service. They're adding layers of management, new personnel, expansions to the space-based facilities, and additional support services for those pilots. That's a huge investment, and all of that investment depends on these ships and the people who'll crew them."

Pittman gave a slow nod. "Of course."

"Then—purely as an outsider—I think you're being short-sighted in sacrificing ship safety and pilot satisfaction on the basis of a few percentage points of cost," she said. "That twenty-stanyer failure rate gets multiplied across a thousand ships. With as many jumps as you're planning to make a day, in two decades you're going to lose a lot of ships, a lot of pilots, and a lot of data. You can replace the ships. You can hire new pilots. Losing data? That's reputation on the line. Once you lose that?" Zoya shrugged.

Pittman glanced at Downs and refolded her arms. "What do you suggest, Ms. Usoko?"

"Stop," Zoya said. "Whatever you've got on the ways now, stop construction until you can get a more reliable design." She looked at Downs. "Sorry, Tony, but this ship isn't safe."

Pittman looked at Natalya. "You?"

"I'm with Zoya. This ship isn't safe. I wouldn't fly in it."

"Would you fly in my yacht?" Pittman asked. "It has only one drive."

"Sure. Why not? Yachts don't fly that much. Twenty stanyers of reliability on a ship that needs a century to get twenty stanyers of use-hours? That's a long time. If you're willing to risk your life on it, I'll go with you."

"What if I wasn't going?" Pittman asked, her brow furrowed.

"No deal," Natalya said. "I'd want to see the maintenance records and check the parts lockers before I'd get underway on my own. Not just your ship. Any ship."

Zoya coughed into her hand and it sounded suspiciously like "Melbourne."

Natalya grinned at Pittman. "We've had some bad experiences lately and wouldn't want to repeat them."

Pittman gave another slow nod. "That's fair," she said. She paused and frowned. "What's with Dorion and four-day missions?"

Natalya looked at the overhead and sighed. "You two really should talk more."

Pittman's lips tightened. "We talked this morning. He didn't mention anything about four-day missions."

Zoya's head came up with a snap. She looked at Natalya. "He wouldn't, would he?"

"Yeah. He would," Natalya said. With a glance at Pittman, she bit her tongue against saying what she really thought.

"I still don't see what your problem is," Downs said.

Natalya looked at him. "What kind of structural work have you done, Tony?"

"Tony's the primary architect for the yard," Pittman said. "He designed the expansion that includes the new ways, the parts fabrication facilities, and housing for the workers."

"Before that?" Natalya asked.

"Look, I'm not the one in question here," Downs said, his back stiffening as he glared at Natalya. "My track record isn't the issue."

Pittman raised one perfect eyebrow in Downs's direction and he shut his mouth against anything else he might have been about to say. "Tony's been with the company for a long time," she said. "He's done a lot of good work for us. You two seem to take exception with his efforts here."

"We're not the first," Zoya said. "We're only here because your test pilot quit on you."

Pittman gave a dismissive toss of her head. "He'd been critical of the project since he came on board a month ago."

"Wasn't that about the time you changed the design?" Natalya asked.

Pittman looked at Downs. "Was it?"

Downs shook his head. "He came on when we laid the keel for this boat."

"And he didn't like what he saw then?" Natalya asked.

"He didn't like anything," Downs said, his mouth twisted like he tasted something rotten. "Coffee, food, ship, his quarters even. Nothing was ever good enough for him."

"But he stayed for a month," Zoya said.

"We paid him for it," Downs said.

"He drew the line at taking your money for flying this ship?" Natalya asked, looking at Pittman.

Pittman paused for a moment before answering. "Yes. Apparently."

"He liked our money well enough before then," Downs said, his voice a low grumble.

"You weren't asking him to risk his life before," Zoya said.

"Why'd you change the design?" Natalya asked.

Downs clamped his mouth shut and looked at Pittman.

"What change?" she asked. "We change the design almost daily."

"The drives. Why did you take out the second drive? Cost?" Natalya asked.

"Optimization," Pittman said. "Explain it, Tony."

Downs stood a little straighter. "Without the extra drive, we didn't need as much power generation capacity. The saving in mass gave the ship an extra two Burleson Units' worth of leg. We wanted the ship to be able to get as far as possible as fast as possible."

"And it cost less," Zoya said.

"Yes," Downs said, biting the word off. "Yes, it cost less. I still don't buy the safety argument."

"There's another factor to consider," Zoya said, looking at Pittman. "Accuracy."

Natalya's brain seemed to stutter as it adjusted to the realization. "Oh, of course."

Zoya smirked. "You'd have thought of it eventually."

Pittman frowned, the furrow between her eyebrows marring her serene visage for just a moment. "Accuracy?"

"Jump error," Zoya said. "Up to five percent plus or minus."

Pittman's head made a slow shake. "I still don't get it. What about jump error?"

"Navigators jump into the edges of a system," Zoya said. "Or try to. Sometimes they jump long, sometimes short."

Pittman's expression hardened. "Yes. I'm aware of that."

"When you jump two or three Burleson Units, the error is negligible. Just part of doing business. Six or seven, it's manageable," Zoya said. "When you're jumping fourteen? You need a big damn hole in space to shoot for or you run the risk of getting punched by a rock."

"Or punching into one," Natalya said. "You don't have to be too close to a gravity well to have a problem, even in a Scout."

"We had that problem with the *Peregrine* on this last run," Zoya said. "Finding spots big enough to jump into when the errors are larger than some systems."

"Having legs that long isn't really going to help that much if you can't plot courses that don't risk jumping long or short and into trouble," Natalya said.

Pittman's frown returned again. "So those extra two BUs aren't really useful?"

"Depends," Zoya said with a shrug. "There's a power consumption curve to calculate."

"When you push a drive closer to maximum, it uses more power per distance," Natalya said. "We can make a lot of shorter jumps for the same power consumption as one big one. Actually get farther but we lose time as we make the course adjustments between jumps. The *Peregrine* has more than enough power so we don't worry about it."

Downs's eyes grew wider. He looked back and forth between Zoya and Natalya. "What about the original Scouts? They looked seriously underpowered."

Natalya shrugged. "I don't know. My parents rebuilt the *Peregrine's* engine room from the drive mounts up."

Downs cast a glance at Pittman before leaning back against the bulkhead as if for strength.

"Tony?" Pittman asked.

Downs shook his head. "I need to run some numbers."

Pittman's frown deepened. "So what you're saying is that eighteen BUs would have been enough?"

"Probably overkill," Zoya said. "That's a big jump and the error on bending that much space is huge. From a practical standpoint, the pilot will be making short hops out of the system, a long hop to get close to the next one, then another short one to minimize error on the far end where it matters most."

"Those short hops will take time and the course corrections between jumps will take more," Natalya said. "The capacitors can recharge while those corrections happen."

"Any competent navigator should be able to balance the power drains against the draw," Zoya said. "We only ran into a couple of places where we needed the *Peregrine's* legs on our circuit. We had to pay for that in charging time."

Pitmann looked at Downs again.

He shook his head. "I need to run some numbers."

"Ballpark it, Tony," Pittman said.

Downs ran a hand over his mouth and shrugged. "Maybe. Yeah." He paused, gaze focused in the middle distance. "It makes sense." He focused on Pittman. "It wasn't one of our design drivers."

Pittman's frown didn't let up but she nodded. "Run your numbers." She looked at Natalya. "What do we need to fix, in priority order?"

"Add a drive, replace the couch," Natalya said. "I can't tell about anything else until we fly it."

"What about the galley?" she asked.

Natalya looked at Zoya who shrugged. "It's dumb and it's taking up volume that might be put to better use," Zoya said.

"Like what?" Downs asked, his chin thrust forward in challenge.

"Oh, I don't know. Stores? Maybe an extra freezer," Zoya said. "The chairs don't matter to the mission. It's not like the drive. Thinking ahead to what the ship will be used for? Stock it right and you'd be able to trade pilots in a matter of a few minutes. Only replenish the ship once every ten missions or so."

"That's an idea. Make it modular and you can have the replenishment waiting on the dock. Roll the empty out and roll the fresh one in. Give pilots a chance to load out their preferences," Natalya said.

Pittman's frown eased a bit. "Tony?"

"The drive is the problem," he said. "We can pull the couch and replace it with an adjustable one easily enough."

"Who's your supplier on these?" Zoya asked.

"Local construction," Tony said with a glance at Pittman.

Pittman's eyes narrowed. "Who's making bank, Tony?"

Downs shuffled his feet and found something interesting on the deck to look at. "Couple of the mechanics over in environmental got their hands on a Caldwell wide-bed printer. They're buying the stock from us and selling the finished goods back."

"Where'd they set it up?" Pittman asked, her expression more curious than furious. "Where are they getting power?"

"They set up shop in dock forty. I have no idea how they're doing it."

"Forty? That's not even pressurized."

Downs shrugged but continued his examination of the deck. "Is now."

Pittman shook her head. "All right. We'll deal with that later. Get an adjustable model. Something comfortable."

"A suggestion?" Zoya asked.

Pittman nodded.

"The company has the models for the original Scouts. If you've got access to a Caldwell, you'd only need a small parts printer and the stock to make the adjustable parts. Those couches would do for a couple of days." Zoya glanced at Natalya. "We've both slept on them. Not as good as a bunk, but they're good enough."

Pittman blinked. "Really?"

Natalya nodded. "Sure. I've slept on the couch quite often."

"Can you get your hands on those models?" Pittman asked.

Natalya looked at Downs. "You've got them already, don't you, Tony?"

Downs frowned and rubbed his lips with his hand. "Maybe. I didn't actually dig too far into the detail designs after we got the deck plan laid out. We just used current models."

"Find out," Pittman said. "And get the couch models to your brother-in-law."

Downs's face paled. "My brother-in-law?"

"What? You think I don't know who the mechanics are on this station?" Pittman asked. "If he's going to use our power and our facilities to feather his own nest, the least he can do is sell us something we can use."

Downs swallowed and nodded.

"And our deal is off. He can take back however many of these couches he's sent and recover the stock from them. I want to see the new orders and pricing by tomorrow's staff meeting."

"We've already paid for them," Downs said.

"No doubt," Pittman said, a storm rising on her face. "And they'll credit us for the returns or I'll have a station inspection team tearing through dock forty by tomorrow afternoon. Am I clear?" Her voice practically crackled.

"Yes, ma'am," Downs said.

"Good. Get this done. Now."

Downs looked back and forth between Pittman and Natalya.

"Now, Tony."

Downs looked like he might want to say something but bit back any comments, nodding to each of them before escaping down the passageway. After a few moments, the ping-ping sounded from the inner lock followed by a thunk as the outer lock door opened and closed.

Pittman steepled her fingers over mouth and nose. "Thank you," she said. "Your insights have been most illuminating."

"Glad to help," Natalya said. "How soon before we can take her out for a spin?"

Pittman's eyes widened. "I didn't think you'd fly this ship."

Natalya glanced at Zoya and shrugged. "I won't fly it on a live mission. Won't jump it out of the system. Doesn't mean I wouldn't take it out for a spin around local space."

"You'd do that?" Pittman asked.

"Sure. Zoya?" Natalya asked.

"You bet," Zoya said. "If you want to know what else is wrong with the ship, the only way to do it is to take it out and fly it around." She paused. "I do have one question, though."

"What's that?" Pittman asked.

"Does Downs have any other relatives working on this project?"

"I don't know." Pittman frowned. "I'll look into it."

"Might be a good idea. At least check the sourcing on the major machinery in case his uncle's younger sister built the Burleson drive from a construction kit." Zoya grinned.

Pittman chuckled but her eyes didn't reflect any humor. "I think I'll be getting my accountants to double check all of these orders. Just to be sure."

"I'd lean on Dorion," Natalya said. "He's got a stake in this, too, and I suspect he can get the forensics group from finance to come sift through the logs."

Pittman's gaze focused somewhere in mid-air and she nodded slowly. "That's not a bad idea. We're going to have to justify the project to them eventually. Bringing them in early could be an advantage."

After a moment of silence, Zoya asked, "So? When can we get the keys?"

Pittman's focus returned and she stared at Zoya.

"To the ship," Zoya said. "How ready is it?"

Pittman looked around, blinking as if waking from a nap. "It's supposed to be ready for shakedown now." She looked back at Zoya and then smiled at Natalya. "I'll get you both cleared for full access. You can look it over. Check the parts lockers. See for yourselves."

"That works for me," Natalya said.

Zoya nodded. "Me, too."

"Give me the rest of the day. That should give me enough time to get your credentials approved. You can start working tomorrow at 0800."

CHAPTER SIXTEEN
PULASKI YARD: 2366, MAY 3

NATALYA WOKE EARLY, oddly excited about the new ship. The aroma of brewing coffee drew her out of her stateroom and into the galley.

Zoya smiled over the top of her coffee mug. "Couldn't sleep," she said.

"It's barely 0600. What'll we do for two stans?"

"Make sure our wills are in order?" Zoya asked.

"That's probably something we should do tomorrow. I don't plan on taking the ship out today. Just want to rummage around in there and see if we can come up with a decent plan for a local shakedown."

Zoya sipped and nodded. "I wondered about that. Pop-pop always put the new barges through his own shakedown after taking delivery."

"Pop-pop?" Natalya asked.

"Oh, my grandfather. Was a joke growing up. Paternal grandfather is Pop's pop. So, Pop-pop."

Natalya sloshed some coffee into a mug. She leaned against the bulkhead and held the cup up to her face. "What'd he test?"

"About what you'd expect. Engine performance against fuel use. Max velocity. Navigational accuracy. He always recalibrated the instrumentation, just to be sure nobody'd missed it or messed it up."

"You ever run those shakedowns?" Natalya asked.

"Never in command, but I took a few runs with them."

"I was thinking we need to make sure the tankage is what the specs say."

Zoya grinned. "That's probably a good idea. I wonder if they'll let us pump them out just to refill them."

Natalya let a few sips of coffee warm her throat before answering. "Depends on whether or not there's anything in them yet. Downs might object but I got the feeling there's not a lot of love lost between him and Pittman."

"That whole business makes my skin itch," Zoya said.

"My father would call it 'hinky' but I'm not sure what the real story is. There's so much right-hand, left-hand stuff going on, it's hard to tell what's miscommunication and what's incompetence."

"True, but how did Downs get the job of designing that ship?"

"Nepotism?" Zoya asked with a shrug. "Second cousin's brother runs HR, maybe."

"Maybe, but why did Pittman agree? Modifying the Scout plans isn't exactly structural engineering."

Zoya shrugged. "Dunno. Maybe she doesn't know any better. Her yacht only has one Burleson drive."

"She's in charge of the project, though. Wouldn't you expect her to know better?"

"I'd expect that the big picture people over on High Tortuga assigned her to bring the yard up to snuff and to produce the next generation of communications couriers. Having actual ship design expertise might not have seemed as important as being a good administrator."

"Seems off to me."

"Does to me, too, but we're just spinning in space." Zoya sipped her coffee again, her gaze focused far away. "She did arrive on the scene awfully quickly when Downs started being an ass."

"He warned us that the place was bugged."

"True," Zoya nodded and looked into her mug. "I suppose it makes sense from a prototype perspective. Knowing what's happening in the ship and all." She looked up. "Doesn't it strike you as just a little odd that a one-person ship has audio bugs?"

Natalya snorted. "Who said they're only audio?"

Their tablets bipped, almost in unison.

Natalya pulled hers out and checked the message. "Looks like Pittman delivered."

Zoya looked up from her screen with a grin. "I think we should find breakfast before we go over there. Who knows when we'll think to eat again."

"Grab something here or try the yard cuisine?" Natalya asked, tipping the last of her coffee into her mouth.

"I'm up for yard cuisine. There's probably someplace handy to the docks."

"Sounds good. You look. I'll do the dishes." Natalya slotted her empty into the dish washer and held out her hand to Zoya.

Zoya drained her mug and handed it to Natalya. "Uniform of the day?" she asked.

Natalya gave a short laugh. "Shipsuit and tablets. What else?"

"Don't wanna break out the undress whites for inspection?" Zoya asked, flipping through her tablet screens.

"I could be convinced to go with khakis but this is still Toe-Hold space. Clothes won't impress them as much as doing something." She keyed the cleaning unit and headed down the passageway. "Doing something that doesn't blow the ship up on the first day would probably count in our favor."

Zoya laughed and followed along. "I've got a 'Rudy's' that should be just beyond where the ship's docked. Says it's open and serves breakfast all day."

"My kinda place," Natalya said and keyed the lock.

THEY ARRIVED AT THE new ship at 0745 and found a wiry, dark-haired yard worker leaning against the hull. "You the new test pilots?" he asked.

Natalya nodded. "That's us."

"It's a one-person ship," he said.

"We know," Zoya said. "We visited yesterday. Only one of us will fly it at a time."

The man's grin danced up his face and into his eyes. "Well, that's true of every ship, en't it? Only one skipper at a time?" He pulled a tablet out of his pocket and held it to Natalya. "I got your keys. One for each, and I'm supposed to work on this lock this morning, if that's not a problem."

Natalya took the tablet and held out a hand for the key fob.

He held it up between two fingers and nodded at the tablet. "Thumb first. Orders."

Natalya scanned the document on the screen and thumbed the pad.

The yard worker traded tablet for fob and handed the tablet to Zoya. He held up a second fob and raised his eyebrows. "One for you, too."

Zoya took the tablet, thumbed it, and swapped with him.

"Thanks," he said. "Name's Carroll, Charles Carroll. Call me Charlie. Everyone does. Even me mum." He stepped back and waved a hand at the ship. "It's all yours. Have at it."

Natalya nodded at Zoya who pressed her key to open the lock.

"I'll be opening and closing that all morning," Charlie said. "At least until I figure out why the override isn't working."

Natalya walked up the ramp and stood in the tiny lock. "I used to have the same problem on *Peregrine*. Check the couplings in the pressure sensors," she said. "It only takes one of the three to get a bit of a charge on it to keep it from signaling that there's equal pressure on each side of the lock."

"Thanks. That's already on my list to check, right after I make sure the sensors themselves are actually connected." He grinned ruefully. "You'd be surprised what I've found so far that was bolted in but not actually installed."

"That's my worry, too," Natalya said, stepping back to give Zoya room. "You need us for anything?"

He shook his head and tapped on the hull beside the door to pop open a cover. "Got the override here."

Zoya stepped into the lock, moving clear of the hatch.

"We'll get out of your way, then," Natalya said and pressed the lock cycle key. The external doors sighed closed and latched before the inner door opened.

"You think he believed you about the sensors?" Zoya asked as they took the few steps down the passageway and into the galley.

"Probably wasn't pleased that a kid was trying to give him advice on how to fix a lock," Natalya said. "He handled it well."

Zoya nodded and started to poke through the cabinets. "What do we check first?" she asked.

"You're doing it," Natalya said. "Let's see if the coffee maker works. While you're doing that, I'll fire up the systems and start poking around under the hood."

Zoya leaned back from the counter to look at Natalya. "I can check them while you're running through the engine room."

"I'd hoped you'd do that. Two of us checking means we're less likely to miss something."

Zoya nodded and opened the next cupboard in line while Natalya stepped into the cockpit and flopped onto the couch.

AT MID-MORNING, THEY took seats in the tiny galley and compared notes.

"Other than a poor taste in coffee and a really bad couch, I didn't find anything that would keep us from taking the ship out for a spin," Zoya said. "Did you?"

Natalya shook her head. She took a sip of coffee and sighed. "The coffee is pretty bad, but that's an easy fix. The couch is still horrible."

Zoya nodded. "What'd you think of the instrumentation?"

Natalya frowned. "I didn't notice anything terribly off. The couch was distraction enough."

Zoya stood and beckoned Natalya to follow. She stepped into the cockpit and waved Natalya into the couch. "What's the fuel status?"

Natalya pulled up the engineering display on the console. "Full," she said.

"How do you know?" Zoya asked.

"Green light on the monitor."

"Atmosphere? How's our gas mix?"

Natalya flipped to environmental and saw a similar interface. "Another green light." She frowned. "No data on the actual mix."

Zoya nodded. "Just the one green light."

"Presumably that means we can breathe but that's less than helpful."

"None of the instrumentation is actually calibrated," Zoya said. "They're all idiot lights."

Natalya frowned and pulled up potable water. Same problem. She flipped back to engineering and scanned through the various status indicators. "Capacitor charge level. Maneuvering fuel. They're all like this?"

Zoya lifted one shoulder in a half shrug. "Every single one that I checked. I think the only display I found with actual numbers on it was the clock."

"We'll need to get that reprogrammed," Natalya said. "I wouldn't have noticed until we got underway."

"I probably wouldn't have if I hadn't run into this same problem at home."

Natalya looked up at her. "Barge?"

"Manchester was working on a 'less taxing' pilot interface. It was so 'less taxing' that it was useless. Pop-pop wasn't happy with it but accepted it."

"I'll bet this story doesn't end well."

"No bet. The problem was the crossover point between green-for-go and red-for-stop."

"What about yellow-for-needs-attention?"

"They overlooked that part. We discovered it on potable water relatively early and close to station," Zoya said. "The indicator stayed green as long as there was water in the tank."

Natalya winced. "That's all well and good if you can run next door for a few thousand liters of potable water."

Zoya nodded. "Pop-pop made Manchester reprogram the system but they had to replace all the binary sensors before the programming would take."

Natalya sighed. "Lemme guess. The correct sensors were cheaper?"

Zoya tapped an index finger to the tip of her nose. "They tried to bill us for the repair."

"Pop-pop wasn't amused, I take it?"

"Gram runs the books. She accepted the invoice, paid it, and sent it back with a twenty-five percent service charge on all future metals deliveries to the yard."

Natalya pondered that for a few heartbeats. "Merciful Maude, that would have bankrupted them."

Zoya nodded. "They refunded the repair payment, tossed in a few crew amenities while they had it in the dock, and Gram dropped the service charge from their bills."

"I bet they weren't happy with that."

"They weren't but they thought they had us over a barrel because they're the only source for the barges we needed." Zoya sipped her coffee and grimaced. "They didn't like it when we just did it back to them. Without our metals, they couldn't make their ships."

Natalya looked at the display again. "You don't suppose our Mr. Downs knows anything about shorting the sensor suite on this boat, do you?"

"We're extrapolating based on a single data point," Zoya said. "The only fact we have is the couch."

Natalya looked up at Zoya. "You don't think he's skimming off the development budget?"

Zoya laughed. "Of course he is, but it's just my opinion. We don't have any proof except for his admission about the couch. Which is still dreadful and we shouldn't get underway until that, at least, is fixed."

Natalya bounced on the cushion and tried to find a comfortable position. She reached for the console and put her fingers on the keys. "Yeah. It's too far away for my short arms."

"It's too low for me," Zoya said. "I have to reach up to get there. The headrest is dumb and I can't imagine being strapped into it while the ship is maneuvering."

Natalya lay back and held out her hands. "I can't reach the console at all."

"I noticed that, too," Zoya said. "Maybe Tony will get his wish."

"His wish?"

"He said he wanted one of these for himself. Maybe Pittman will give him this one."

Chapter Seventeen
Pulaski Yard: : 2366, May 3

A PING-PING MADE NATALYA look down the passageway. Carroll stepped aboard and turned to look into the lock again. He fiddled with the control and smiled.

"Got it?" Natalya asked.

Carroll looked up the passageway and nodded. "Looks like it. Both hatches open if there's the same pressure on all sides."

"What was it? Bad sensor?"

He snorted. "Bad connection. The internal lock sensor was connected to its cable just fine, but somebody forgot to connect the cable in the junction box."

Zoya stepped into the passage and frowned. "How did it even work?"

"Normal cycle process doesn't check it. Just opens the hatch being keyed."

Zoya glanced at Natalya.

Natalya sighed. "That's got to change. What if there's no pressure in the lock and we open the inner hatch?"

Charlie shrugged. "I'm not sure the servos have enough oomph to open it against a vacuum."

"If there's pressure in it and we try to open the outer?" Natalya asked.

"It'll open as long as the inner hatch is closed. Blows whatever's in the lock out."

"That strike you as a good design?" Zoya asked.

He held up both hands, palm out. "I'm just the socket jockey. You need to take that up with the design team."

Natalya sighed. "Thanks, Charlie."

He nodded and gave her a jaunty wave before disappearing through the lock.

"That is how we throw out the trash," Natalya said, after the lock closed again.

"I know, but he didn't," Zoya said. "Are you thinking what I'm thinking?"

"That we have no idea if this ship is actually spaceworthy?" Natalya asked.

Zoya nodded. "That's the one."

"Verifying it is going to be a pain."

"We really need to make a checklist so we don't miss anything," Zoya said. "But I'm not sure we can think of everything when our basic assumptions about how things work aren't supported."

"Like the lock?"

"The lock. The couch. The instrumentation. What else would we assume was legit and not test before we needed it?"

Natalya sighed and rolled the question around in her brain for a moment. "Safety locks on the drives and rocket motors?"

"That crossed my mind," Zoya said. "I don't expect the coffee maker to check to see if there's coffee in the basket, but we've seen enough to make me question the fundamental design parameters."

A noise from the lock made them look down the passageway in time to see Pittman step aboard. "Knock, knock," she said. "The door was open ..."

"Welcome aboard," Zoya said. "We've got some questions."

Pittman offered a sideways smile. "I know. Tony said he'd have the new couch installed tomorrow. They're just doing the initial assembly this afternoon."

"That was fast," Natalya said.

"You were right about the models. We had them all along."

"You were monitoring our conversations this morning?" Natalya asked.

"I wasn't but my assistant kept a tally of the discrepancies." She held up a tablet. "I've got the list. The instrumentation suite is a problem?"

Natalya and Zoya both nodded.

"We really can't fly like that," Zoya said.

Pittman frowned but nodded. "Can I show you something?"

Natalya grinned. "That depends. What did you have in mind?"

Pittman nodded toward the lock. "Let's take a little walk."

They followed Pittman off the ship, pausing only to key the lock closed. "I don't suppose we can lock it," Zoya said.

"You can, but so many people have access, it's rather pointless. These prototypes have so many keys out that almost everybody on the production team has one."

"So anybody could fly away with it?" Natalya asked.

Pittman paused and frowned. "In theory," she said after a moment. "I'm not sure anybody would want to risk it in an untested ship."

Natalya and Zoya shared a glance.

"It would make a hell of a yacht," Natalya said.

Pittman's frown deepened. "You think so?"

Natalya shrugged. "Fast courier? Other people would like to have a ship with legs that long."

"Maybe," Pittman said, her frown smoothing out. "The prototypes are just that. Prototypes. Given what you've identified as problems, I'm not sure anybody would want them."

Zoya snorted. "That assumes that anybody agrees with us."

"Tony Downs didn't seem to have any problems with the design parameters," Natalya said.

"We'll see," Pittman said. "Come on. I want to give you a bit of background."

Pittman led the way down the passageway to the small craft dock next to the *Peregrine*. She keyed the dock open and let the way to her ship. "I reviewed some of your comments from this morning," she said, keying open the ship's lock. "I want to show you where some of those ideas came from."

She led the way into the tiny craft. The lock opened just behind what would be the bridge, but it looked more like somebody's living room. Armorglass wrapped around the forward half of the compartment, affording a good view of the *Peregrine*.

"It looks big from down here," Zoya said.

"Only by comparison," Pittman said. She dropped into the pilot's couch and touched a few keys, bringing the displays to life. She stood and waved at the couch. "One of you? Would you check my instrumentation?"

"I know where you're going with this," Natalya said, waving Zoya into the couch.

Zoya sat and started flipping screens. "All idiot lights," she said after a few moments.

"Well, the manufacturer calls them status indicators, but yes," Pittman said. "We took this idea and applied it to the new ship."

"How do you know when you're running low on—say—potable water?" Natalya asked.

"They're supposed to turn yellow at 20% but I've never run low," Pittman said. "It automatically fills whenever I dock. Gases, water, fuels. All of it."

"As long as you have the funds to cover the cost," Zoya said.

"That's a given," Pittman said with a faint smile.

"What about the lock's controller logic?" Zoya asked stepping away from the couch.

"I thought that was just a standard design," Pittman said. "You'll need to talk to Tony about that."

"Is he still speaking to us?" Natalya asked.

Pittman's eyes hardened. "If he wants to keep his job, he is."

Natalya pursed her lips and looked around the bridge, taking in the polished wood and chrome accents, the subdued lighting, and the small galley tucked away in an alcove. "How many people does she carry?"

"Room for four. Two couples or a cozy foursome," Pittman said. "I'm usually flying solo but once in a while I'll take a board member with me."

Zoya stuck her head into the galley. "This where Tony got the idea for the four-top?"

"I suppose he might have, but I don't think he's ever been aboard," Pittman said.

"Did you see the design before they rolled it out?" Natalya asked.

Pittman nodded. "I saw it but—honestly—seeing four seats in the galley didn't register as significant."

"What about the single Burleson drive?" Natalya asked.

"Like I said. There's only one on this ship." She sat on the pilot's couch and brought up the systems displays again. "This is what I brought you here for. This is what I have."

Natalya and Zoya leaned over her shoulders and watched as she flipped through screen after screen of green lights.

"It's not like I spent a lot of time going through the prototype's systems interface but even if I had, this is what I'd have expected to see." Pittman looked up at Natalya. "I've shown you mine. Show me yours?" She grinned.

Natalya nodded toward the lock. "Easily done, but can I see your engine room first?"

"Sure." Pittman stood and led the way aft. "The two ships are very similarly built."

"Only a few ways to stack up the pieces and have them work," Zoya said. "Old design principle."

"Form follows function?" Pittman asked.

"That's the one."

Pittman opened an airtight hatch at the end of the short passage. "More like engine closet than engine room," she said. "But here it is."

Natalya stuck her head through the hatch and surveyed the tiny compartment. "What do you use for maneuvering? I saw some kicker nozzles back there."

"There's a pair of auxiliaries under the deck. One on either side of the Burleson."

"Slick," Zoya said, peering around the combing.

"You actually have two Burlesons," Natalya said.

Pittman laughed. "Where is it? Hiding in the overhead?"

Natalya turned to look at her. "You really don't know what you've got here, do you?"

"That's ridiculous." Pittman frowned and looked at Zoya. "Do you see another drive in there?"

Zoya held up a hand. "She's the engineer. I'm just along for the ride."

"That's a Mellon-Merc Gemini," Natalya said. "I'd guess Alpha class but maybe Beta."

Pittman stood still for a moment, cocking her head as if listening for Natalya to say something else. "I got the upgrade to Gamma. Eight BUs but it drains the capacitors."

"Pravda fusactors?" Natalya asked.

"Yes."

"They cheated you by not upgrading the capacitor to Gamma class when they upgraded the drives," Natalya said.

"You keep saying drives. There's only one unit in there."

Natalya shrugged. "There's only one *casing* in there. It holds two drives. If one fails, the other will take you home."

"Now you're just teasing," Pittman said.

"Is it a Gemini?" Zoya asked.

Pittman paused, looking back and forth between them. "I think that's what the yard called it. Yes."

"Then that's two drives," Zoya said. "I may be a deck officer, but I know that much."

"I don't know of a single ship that has only one Burleson drive," Natalya said. "Not saying there aren't any. Just that I've never seen one designed that way." She paused and looked at Pittman. "Until yesterday when I saw your new courier."

"You really didn't know?" Zoya asked.

"I'm not an engineer," Pittman said, her words chipping off like ice. "I ordered a jump-capable yacht. I got a jump-capable yacht."

Natalya bit back a few sharp comments before speaking. "You still want to see what the *Peregrine* looks like?"

Pittman nodded. "More now than before." She paused and scratched her left ear. "Please."

"Let's go then," Natalya said and led the short parade to the next lock.

PITTMAN STOOD IN THE cockpit, her face a mask. "Two people lived in this ship?"

"We think so," Natalya said. "I don't know who originally owned it but these little babies mapped the Western Annex before it was the Western Annex. Generally two-person crews, sometimes three."

Pittman looked at Natalya. "This should be in a museum, not flying around Toe-Hold space."

Natalya shrugged. "It's not like she's in the original condition. Besides, she's my home."

Pittman stuck her head in the galley. "This is tiny. How do you eat in here?"

"We don't, as a rule, but mostly standing up," Zoya said. "We either eat in our staterooms or on the couches."

"So, two people flew these out for weeks at a time without contact with a station?" Pittman shook her head. "I mean I've heard the stories, but seeing it? It's unnerving."

"Two things make your courier different," Natalya said. "One person. Two people—assuming they get along—means you're not out there alone. There's somebody to talk to. With one person, you're putting the crew into solitary confinement. The question is, how long can they stand it?"

Pittman folded her arms and leaned against the bulkhead. "Seems like heaven to me."

"What's the longest you've been underway alone in your yacht?" Zoya asked.

Pittman frowned and looked at the deck. "I'm not sure. A couple of weeks. Maybe."

"What was the one thing you wanted most when you docked?"

"A bath," Pittman said, answering immediately. She seemed surprised by her own answer.

Natalya and Zoya both laughed.

"That's what we both went for after our first run," Zoya said.

"The showers are good, but a warm soak? That's different," Natalya said.

"What's the other thing?" Pittman asked.

"Schedule," Natalya said. "The people flying these made their own schedules. They didn't have any kind of responsibility to an outside authority."

"The financiers?" Pittman said.

Natalya nodded. "Having to make a payment is different from needing to perform on a schedule. They were free to make the decisions they wanted to earn enough to make the payments. Remember that few of them had bankers behind them. They were almost all financed by private money, one way or another."

"Loans aren't readily available to people who don't have collateral," Zoya said.

Pittman nodded. "I get that."

"So the early explorers were predisposed to autonomous operation," Natalya said. "People who knew they'd be out on their own in the Deep Dark for months at a time. They only needed to keep enough cash flow going to keep flying, keep probing. Gas scoops kept the consumables topped off as long as they found a gas giant or two to skim. Food was the most critical commodity, which is why the pantry space on this thing is almost a quarter of the volume."

"Three months of food for two people takes a lot of room," Zoya said. "Even prepackaged and frozen."

"You keep three months' worth aboard?" Pittman said.

"I think we're down to two months," Natalya said. "We'd top off before going anywhere but just hanging out around the station? That's enough."

Pittman looked around the cockpit. "This isn't that much bigger than the new ship."

"About half again, I think," Natalya said. "We get more out of the volume because the ship's much blockier."

"Can I see the engine room?" Pittman asked.

"Sure." Natalya headed aft with Pittman and Zoya in tow. She undogged the hatch and stepped in. "This space is pretty cramped but—again—the shape of the hull gives us more space inside."

"That rounded ovoid is pretty," Zoya said. "It's not terribly practical."

"If the plans we saw back at Bowie haven't been changed that much, our length overall is only a couple of meters more than your courier," Natalya said. "We're about the same in beam, but we've got a lot more headroom."

Pittman eyed the pair of Burleson drives and then measured the compartment with her eyes.

"Kickers are behind the bulkheads on either side," Natalya said. "Tankage below us."

"Where are these gas scoops I keep hearing about?" Pittman asked.

"They're amidships under the decking along with a refining plant," Natalya said.

"Probe launcher?" Pittman asked.

"Amidships over the passageway. There's a hatch for loading the launcher in the overhead," Natalya said.

"I didn't know that," Zoya said.

"Not exactly something we use," Natalya said, grinning. "No probes to launch and no reason to launch them."

Pittman nodded. "I can see why you're not exactly enamored of the new ship."

"I'll admit I'm spoiled," Natalya said. "This ship has been my home for a long time. Even our apartment isn't really home. Just a place to go when we're off the ship."

"Having seen this, I'm wondering why we didn't just update the model for this and roll it out instead of starting from scratch." Pittman sighed. "I suppose it's not too late to do that."

"There are a lot of aspects of the new ship I think will work well," Zoya said.

"Like what?" Pittman asked.

"Long legs. Specialized for data collection and dissemination. The solo pilot will work well on shorter missions." Zoya shrugged. "The galley is kind of silly, but that's not a show stopper. The couch is a cheap fix. The drive will be the problem."

Pittman looked at Natalya. "What do you think?"

"I think she's right," Natalya said. "Adding the second drive won't actually change the power system that much. You'd never run them both at the same time. Generally, the navigation systems alternate between the two to spread the load. Having enough capacitor to actually drive it matters."

"So I've learned," Pittman said with a grimace.

"Punching a slot in the decking and rearranging the drive compartment will take some fiddling. If Downs really did use a scaled-down Scout model for the basic layout, there'll be room to put a clone of the existing drive right beside it. They'll be cramped but they'll fit," Natalya said.

"Shorter mission means less fuel, food, gas," Zoya said. "I suspect that if you re-spec it for two weeks instead of two months, you'll find a lot of space you can recover."

Pittman cast her gaze around the compartment again. "That's probably true. What is Dorion thinking in terms of actual mission run?"

"We recommended no more than three days," Natalya said. "Jump out, pass traffic, jump back and dock instead of downloading and jumping out immediately."

"Won't that docking delay be significant?" Pittman asked.

"We can jump pretty close in the *Peregrine*," Natalya said. "Very close if we can find a hole nearby to jump into."

"Zero out the jump error?" Pittman asked.

"Yeah," Zoya said. "We'll have to check the charts to see if we can find some locations that are within a Burleson Unit of the station. Setting those up as doctrine for the pilots will mean they can probably jump close enough to dock within a standard day."

"So, three days in space. Dock. Change pilots?" Pittman said, counting the days on her fingers.

"Something like that," Natalya said. "One ship, two pilots. You can keep the birds in space almost nonstop without burning out the pilots."

"Probably find that certain runs need an extra day, or maybe one day less," Zoya said. "Depending on navigation and accrued jump error."

"Modularize the replenishment," Natalya said. "Swap out the consumables. Top the tanks. Trade pilots. The ships should be able to turn around within a couple of stans."

Pittman nodded. "A couple of totes for freezers. Another for fresh food. The galley could handle that."

"Give the totes to the pilots so they can pick their own food and drink," Zoya said. "Cut down on the bitching."

Pittman grinned. "Give them something to do on their days off."

"That and it means you can keep turning pilots out even if their designated ride is a day later than schedule. Just drop them into the next available ship," Zoya said.

"I'd keep a couple in reserve," Natalya said. "Alice got a bad bounce coming in so rather than keep Bob waiting at the dock, you toss Bob into a reserve ship while Alice motors in from outside. You can keep a tighter schedule if you're willing to keep a ship or two idle to take up the slack."

Pittman looked back and forth between Natalya and Zoya. "You two seem to have given this a lot of thought."

Natalya shrugged. "We had some time on our hands."

"Besides, we were hired to make these runs," Zoya said. "That run we made together was a nightmare. I don't really feel like repeating it—even in the *Peregrine*. To say nothing of running solo in a new, untried ship."

"You've given me a lot to think about," Pittman said. "Thank you."

"You're welcome. It's our hides on the line and we'd like to keep them," Natalya said.

"You'll let me know when you're ready to take the new ship out for a spin, right?" Pittman said.

"Maybe tomorrow. Certainly by the next day," Natalya said, looking to Zoya.

"We got a good look at her today," Zoya said. "I'd like to take part of tomorrow and see how bad the instrumentation really is."

Pittman frowned and tilted her head. "The status indicators?"

"Yeah," Zoya said. "They may just be an overlay on top of the actual sensor suite. If that's the case, I should be able to strip them down and get the underlying data displayed."

"Sounds feasible," Pittman said. "The indicators must have actual readings under them somewhere."

"That's what I think," Zoya said. "If not—if they're just binary switches—we don't want to be flying around out there when the green light switches to red to tell us we're out of fuel."

Pittman's eyes grew wide. "Is that likely?"

Natalya shrugged. "It's not likely, but it's possible."

"I've seen it happen on new ship construction," Zoya said. "Not something I'd like to see again."

Pittman grimaced. "I'll leave that to your investigation. Do you want to meet with the design team? Talk to any of the personnel?"

"Maybe later," Zoya said. "The original team is gone so I'd kinda like to look under the hood without knowing what the current crew thinks should be there."

"I'd like to see the plans as built for the prototype," Natalya said.

"I can arrange that." Pittman pulled out a tablet and tapped a few keys. "I'll route them to you here and you can look them over."

"Thanks. That should do us for now," Natalya said.

"Let me get back to the office. I've got a lot of work to do, thanks to you two." She smiled. "And I really mean that. Thanks."

"You're welcome." Natalya nodded toward the passageway. "Lemme show you out."

"Not like I could get lost," Pittman said.

"There aren't that many places to hide, either," Zoya said, following them back to the lock.

As the hatch closed behind Pittman, Zoya looked at Natalya. "Are you wondering what I'm wondering?"

"How did she get a job she's so obviously unqualified for?" Natalya asked.

Zoya pursed her lips and pondered a moment. "That too, but I was wondering who wants this project to fail and set her up to take the fall."

Natalya blinked. "That escalated quickly. What makes you think it's not just basic incompetence? She could be an excellent administrator and whoever set this show up thinks a manager doesn't need to understand the job."

"Has High Tortuga ever demonstrated that level of incompetence?" Zoya asked. "On the surface, this project is probably going to save the company from taking a beating when they grow beyond their ability to scale their network."

"You think that's likely?" Natalya asked.

Zoya shrugged. "You're the expert in Toe-Hold space. You tell me. The CPJCT space is static. All their new growth is coming from Toe-Holds, if what they've said is true."

Natalya chewed her lip for a moment. "Good points. Now I want to know why the Toe-Hold stations are growing so fast."

Zoya snorted. "That one's easy. I just said it."

Natalya frowned for a moment, then stared at Zoya. "CPJCT space is static."

Zoya nodded. "That's one of the problems Pop-pop has with Margary and Manchester. Red tape, regulation, and a smattering of corruption."

"Makes sense," Natalya said.

"When the business environment gets too restrictive, business finds a less restrictive environment," Zoya said.

"You didn't learn that at the academy," Natalya said.

"At my grandmother's knee," Zoya said. "With what I've seen out here over the last couple of stanyers, it wouldn't surprise me to find a Usoko Mining fleet tucked away in a belt somewhere."

Natalya grinned at her. "You've come a long way, Fleet."

Zoya shrugged. "Nothing like the deep end of the pool to motivate you to learn to swim."

Natalya laughed. "Another of your grandmother's sayings?"

Zoya paused in thought for a moment. "First mate on my first barge used to tell me that all the time. Crusty ole fart named Furtner. He flew the first Usoko barge with Pop-pop when Gram was running the smelters. Older than rocks and tougher than a titanium deck plate."

"And you were his skipper?" Natalya asked.

Zoya shrugged. "Yeah."

"How old were you?"

"It was a present for my twelfth birthday."

"What? The barge?"

Zoya nodded. "I've been sailing since I was old enough to put on a suit by myself. Pop-pop had them made special for me. Nobody else was that small."

"How did Furtner take it?" Natalya asked.

"He was terrific. Wouldn't make any of the decisions for me. Made me do it. Even the bad ones. Most of the time the routine was deadly dull. I always felt like an imposter sitting in the captain's chair. Furtner had them weld a bar onto the captain's chair so my feet had something to rest on. Everybody knew what to do and how to do it. I just had to sit there and agree."

"Most of the time?"

"Sometimes the crew got a little feisty. We had a fight aboard. A deck hand insulted an engineer. Words led to fists. Fists led to a wrench in the ribs."

"Ouch."

Zoya nodded and she looked down at the deck. "Furtner made me handle it."

"You were twelve?"

"Almost thirteen by then. Deep end of the pool. I pulled them up to the cabin. Held a formal captain's mast. The works."

"What'd you do?"

"Well, the deck hand was in the auto-doc for three days while his ribs mended up. I made the engineer stand the deck watches in addition to his own."

"How'd that go down?"

"He got about four stans of sleep a night for three days. He might have had some extra punishment from his section chief that the captain didn't know about."

"Was that the end of it?" Natalya asked.

"Mostly. Last I heard the two of them had gotten married and were running a small smelting operation in one of the Margary Lagrange points."

"So Furtner threw you into the deep end of the pool."

"It was his stock answer to everything. Got to be a joke between us." Zoya shook her head. Her eyes glistened. "It was the last thing he said to me before he died. Heart attack on final approach to the Manchester yards to drop a load of refined metals. Keeled right over on the bridge. He lasted long enough to smile at me. I was sixteen."

"You're kidding."

"Wish that I were. I still miss the old fart." Zoya shook her head. "Come on. We got work to do, don't we?"

Natalya blew a breath out and shifted her mental gears. "Checklist. We need one."

"That could get messy," Zoya said. "How far down in the weeds do you think we need to go?"

"Root level," Natalya said. "It could take a while."

"Design team should have one, shouldn't they?"

"Probably, but I'm not sure I'd trust them to be complete enough for me to risk my life on."

Zoya sighed. "It's place to start."

Natalya nodded. "Not a bad idea."

"It's your turn to make the coffee," Zoya said. "I'll contact Pittman to see if there's a design checklist to go with the models."

Natalya nodded and headed toward the bow while Zoya started clicking keys.

CHAPTER EIGHTEEN
PULASKI YARD: 2366, MAY 10

NATALYA TOSSED HER tablet onto the table. It clattered across the smooth surface, fetching up against an empty coffee mug. "What were they doing?"

Zoya didn't look up from her screen. "It's a prototype. You have to expect problems."

"We've been at it a week and I'm less confident about this bird than I was when I started."

"Well, a week ago we didn't know how bad it was," Zoya said, looking up and reaching for her mug. "At least the galley has been useful. Can you imagine standing around for a week while we ran the checklists?"

Natalya's short laugh took her by surprise. "All right. Good point."

"What's the latest screwup in engineering?" Zoya asked, tilting her head to look at the discarded tablet.

"Only half the maneuvering thrusters seem to be working."

Zoya's eyebrows shot up at that. "Are they not connected?"

Natalya shook her head. "They show up on the control diagnostics scans, but they're not getting fuel." She paused. "At least I think they're not getting fuel. They use so little, I'm not sure the amount would show up even if we had the actual gauges."

"Sorry about that," Zoya said. "I'm still waiting on Bates and his crew. They promised me a software update but it hasn't shown up yet." She sipped her coffee and frowned. "I can't do a damn thing without the source and they won't give me access to it."

"Think they're stalling?"

"I don't know. It's the loosest shop I've ever seen and I've seen a lot of loose operations." Zoya gave a shrug and slid her cup back

117

onto the table. "Generally you get good results when people have a little leeway. This group? I don't know."

"Maybe they've got too much leeway," Natalya said.

Zoya shrugged and addressed her tablet again. "Any idea why the pilot's console is overheating while the long-range scan is running?"

"Overheating?"

"The display subsystem redlines on temp whenever the long-range kicks on."

"It's not the display itself?"

"Nope," Zoya said. "I stress-tested the whole display system with everything running at once. No issues. Shut it down and started long-range, it redlined within ten seconds and I never opened the display. I left it blanked."

"Does it need the display on for some reason?"

"I tried that, too. Still hot. I can't test it long enough for decent diagnostics without burning out a board."

"Did you pull the cover?"

Zoya looked up, her eyebrows drawn together. "I pulled the cover on both systems. Smelled hot, but there was nothing obvious."

"Where's the long-range controller?" Natalya asked, mentally tracing the system components.

"Main system bus rack," Zoya said.

"You know which slot?"

Zoya flipped through a few screens and paused. "Says slot alpha-sixteen. Last slot on the first card."

"How about the display system controller?"

Zoya consulted the readout again. "Hotel-one."

"That's it," Natalya said. "There's probably a short in the power supply where those two controller cards intersect. Only shows up when they're both active."

"How's that possible?"

"Four slot buses per side. Alpha on the top is hotel on the bottom. Last slot in alpha butts against first slot in hotel." Natalya stood and nodded toward the cockpit. "Let's look."

Zoya crossed to the pilot's console and clicked through a few prompts. "Power's secured to that segment," she said.

Natalya popped the cover off and the tangy stink of hot electronics wafted out. They started into the rats' nest inside. "This would be much easier if they actually ran the cables instead of just stuffing them in wherever they'd fit."

"No argument from me," Zoya said, consulting her tablet. She pointed at the racks. "That's the controller bus rack."

Natalya nodded and crouched down to look at the underside. "There's hotel. They run left-to-right on the top and right-to-left on the bottom."

Zoya craned her neck a little sideways to read the labels on the cards. "Yeah. That's the display controller and the long-range is above it, but I still don't get the connection. Why is this causing the display system over there to overheat?" She pointed at the pilot's console.

"That's just a repeater," Natalya said. "I suspect that these controllers are overheating in the rack, which makes it look like the problem is in the console."

Zoya frowned and pursed her lips. "I think I can buy that. Shall we test it?"

"Swapping the cards?"

Zoya nodded.

"What do you want to swap?" Natalya asked, peering at the racks.

"Short- and long-range," Zoya said. "I know short-range works now. If it overheats in the slot?" she shrugged.

"Which one is short-range?"

Zoya looked at her tablet. "Delta-four."

Natalya nodded. "Same side of the plane. Just a different slot. Should be plug-and-run."

"That's my thinking," Zoya said.

As she pulled back from the cabinet, Natalya saw something glint where there shouldn't be anything. She leaned back into the rack and stared into the slot between the top and bottom halves of the bus plane.

"What are you looking at?" Zoya asked.

"There's something in there," Natalya said, pointing to the gap.

"How can there be?" Zoya asked.

Natalya shrugged and pulled a small screwdriver from a sleeve pocket. "Let's get this off so we can take a look."

Zoya holstered her tablet and leaned in to help. "Hope this doesn't void our warranty," she said.

Natalya snickered and started pulling the hold-down screws. It took only a few moments to pull the top half of the rack off. "What the—?" Natalya said and pointed with the tip of her screwdriver.

"What is that?" Zoya asked, leaning in.

"Just a piece of litter," Natalya said, looking at Zoya then nodding toward the overhead.

Zoya eyed the rack, her eyes narrowed and brow furrowed.

Natalya nudged her. "I need to stretch my legs. Fancy a stroll down the dock?"

"Yeah. We've been at this for three solid stans. I'm ready for a break," Zoya said. "Rudy's?"

"Sounds good," Natalya said. She grabbed her tablet and took a digital of the rack, leaning in close to get a good image. "I could use a piece of Rudy's pie."

RUDY'S ALWAYS SMELLED of fresh pastry and hot coffee. Even during the breakfast rush, the aroma of fresh breads, muffins, and Rudy's signature cinnamon rolls overpowered the scent of bacon, eggs, and fried potatoes. Natalya slid into a booth where she could watch the entrance.

Zoya grimaced. "You always make me sit with my back to the door."

"I watch the front so you can watch the back," Natalya said with a small nod to where the kitchen doors swung on their hinges. "You wanna swap?"

Zoya shook her head. "I want pie."

A server sidled up to the table with a smile on her face and her tablet poised. "I heard that. What kind? Darberry? Got a granapple just out of the oven. It's more cobbler than pie, but it's still hot."

"I'll have that and a coffee?"

"Black?"

"Yes, please."

"And you?" The server looked at Natalya.

"Sounds good. I'll have the same."

The server tapped her screen a couple of times and nodded. "Be right up."

After the server disappeared through the kitchen doors, Zoya asked, "Did you get a good look at it?"

Natalya pulled out her tablet and displayed the digital image, zooming it in. "Looks like just a piece of scrap," she said, spinning the tablet on the table so Zoya could look.

Zoya leaned in and squinted. "Conveniently placed," she said. "And conductive."

"Rather a long-shot coincidence for random garbage."

"And linking two systems that wouldn't be getting a lot of use until the ship was underway," Zoya said.

"As it would have been if we hadn't disrupted the schedule," Natalya said.

The server bustled up to the table and slid two warm plates of granapple cobbler topped with a small scoop of ice cream onto the surface. Mugs and a carafe appeared as if by magical conjuration; the combined aroma made Natalya's mouth water.

"How's that look?" the server asked. "Can I get you anything else?"

Zoya picked up a fork. "I'm good."

"Thanks," Natalya said. "Looks wonderful."

The server nodded and gave them another smile. "You're the two working on the new bird, aren't ya?"

Natalya nodded. "That's us."

She smiled. "That project has been a godsend. Got busy enough I had to hire more help."

Zoya's eyebrows rose. "You're Rudy?"

She laughed. "No. I'm Sandra. Rudy's my father. I took over the joint when he retired. Kept the name because, why not?" She laughed again. "I see you come in here for breakfast. Good to see new faces."

"Well, it's convenient and the food's good," Zoya said. "You have a lot of regulars."

She nodded and looked around the almost empty dining room. "Mid-afternoons are slow, but it'll start picking up for dinner in a bit."

"What did you do before the new project started?" Natalya asked.

"The best we could," Sandra said. "We had our regulars. The docks have always had a bit of business and the company kept a permanent party here. It was pretty cushy work for them." She smiled. "The company gave us a good rental and we made do."

"Much changed?" Zoya asked.

Sandra snorted. "What hasn't? The engineers came in what? Two stanyers ago? Something like that. The new construction crews started arriving about six months ago. Seems like there's more people here every day now."

"How'd that go over with the existing crew?" Natalya asked.

"Most of them took it with good grace. A couple of the hotheads thought they'd been overlooked for promotions or some such. Whining about lost overtime." Sandra shrugged. "Change is hard for some people."

"Most people, actually," Zoya said.

"True," Sandra said. "If there's nothing else? I'll let you get on with your day. Thanks for stopping in." With a little wave, she went back through the doors to the kitchen.

"Two stanyers?" Natalya asked.

"That's not a long time for a new ship design." Zoya took a bit of the cobbler and smiled. "This is really good."

"I wonder where they spent the credits," Natalya said, savoring the nutty, sweet flavor of her dessert.

"The ones they were supposed to spend on a new design?" Zoya asked.

"Yeah. Other than the fancy shell and slightly smaller footprint, that's a Scout."

"That's also not the design Dorion showed us," Zoya said. "The galley. The engine room. All that changed in a month when they've been working on this for two stanyers?"

"Where does our old friend Tony fit in this picture?" Natalya asked.

"How does a structural engineer get put in charge of a ship design?" Zoya asked back.

"Back to basics," Natalya said. "Who's setting this up to fail? And why?"

"Can we trust Pittman?" Zoya asked, scraping the last of the cobbler off her plate with the side of her fork.

Natalya sighed. "I don't know."

Sandra strolled in from the kitchen. "Can I get you anything else?"

Zoya placed her cutlery and napkin on the used plate and pushed it back from the edge of the table.

"I don't think so," Natalya said.

Sandra held out the tab. Natalya thumbed it.

"You know any of the engineers?" Zoya asked.

Sandra looked up. "What? Personally?"

"Yeah. Any of the designers who started in the beginning?"

Sandra pursed her lips and shook her head slowly. "Not offhand. Most of them left when production started ramping up."

"Where'd they go?" Natalya asked.

Sandra shrugged. "It's how it's always been. Arrive without notice. Leave the same way."

"So? Like us?" Zoya asked with a grin.

Sandra smiled. "Well, I hope you're not going to disappear any time soon. About time that project got some brains." Her eyes opened wide for a moment as if she'd just realized what she'd said. "Anyway. Thanks for coming in." She turned and scurried back into the kitchen.

Zoya raised both eyebrows. "We're the brains?"

"I'm good," Natalya said. "I don't think I'm *that* good."

"How do we unravel this one?" Zoya asked, sliding out of the booth.

"Maybe we need to visit Ms. Pittman."

Zoya frowned and shrugged. "You think she knows she's being set up?"

"To take the fall?" Natalya asked. "Might be a good thing to ask her."

"Are we?" Zoya asked, pushing through the door and out into the passageway beyond. "Being set up?"

"Most assuredly." Natalya shrugged. "I just don't know what we're being set up for."

"First principles," Zoya said.

"Feed the crew?"

"Follow the money," Zoya said. "Who benefits if this project fails?"

"All those ships with courier contracts now," Natalya said. "They get to keep them. Dorion didn't say as much, but I'd bet my mattress that they're planning on phasing all those contracts out once the new couriers come online."

"That's my thought, too, but how does that help us?"

"Somebody in the company who could orchestrate this but doesn't have the pull to quash it outright," Natalya said. "They're making a big investment in infrastructure over at Bowie. That's going to be next to useless without these ships and pilots."

They sauntered back along the docks toward the small-ship locks without seeing another person.

"It's almost spooky," Natalya said. "Nobody moving on the docks."

Zoya shrugged. "Not a lot of ship traffic so no people. My question is about the engineers."

"The ones who left?" Natalya asked. "That's decidedly odd."

"Since when do you release the designers while the ship is still in development?"

Natalya shrugged. "I wonder if we can get a meeting with Pittman."

"Should be easy enough," Zoya said, stopping beside their dock.

"You think?"

"The last few times, we only needed to make some noise inside the new ship and she came to us." Zoya shrugged. "Seems like it might work again."

Natalya grinned. "We should probably get her in the loop on this piece of sabotage to her ship sooner rather than later."

"That's my thinking, too," Zoya said. She keyed the lock on the new ship and strode up the ramp.

CHAPTER NINETEEN
PULASKY YARD: 2366, MAY 10

ALISON PITTMAN MIGHT have made a good poker player. Her face gave nothing away as she peered into the data cabinet. "What am I looking at?" she asked.

Natalya reached in with her small screwdriver and pointed to the piece of scrap lying on top of the card socket. "That's shorting out and making the long-range scanner overheat."

Pittman's hand moved toward it, but stopped. "It's still in there for a reason?" she asked, turning to look at Natalya.

Natalya nodded. "We haven't decided the best way to deal with it yet."

Only a single raised eyebrow disturbed Pittman's bland expression.

"Take a walk with us?" Natalya asked, nodding toward the lock.

Pittman looked back and forth between them for a moment and nodded. "Of course."

Zoya led the way off the ship and out into the docking gallery. "Fancy a cup of coffee, Ms. Pittman?"

Pittman stopped and folded her arms. "I'd fancy an explanation."

"Sabotage," Natalya said.

"A piece of crap in the data closet and you're leaping to sabotage?" Pittman asked.

"Here's the thing," Natalya said. "That piece of crap isn't just any loose piece of crap. It didn't fall in there by mistake."

"How can you be sure?" Pittman asked.

"It's conductive," Zoya said. "Most loose litter isn't even metallic, let alone conductive. It's placed precisely so that the short causes the devices to overheat until they get so hot they melt. All without actually impairing their functionality until they fail. That's stupidly difficult to do on purpose. I've a hard time believing it's an accident."

"But it's possible," Pittman said.

Zoya shrugged. "I'd say it was possible except for one thing."

"What's that?"

"We had to take the rack apart to get to it. The piece of crap is too big to have fallen in between the rack units on its own. It had to have fallen in there when the rack was assembled originally." Zoya shrugged again. "Or been placed there after the rack was installed on the ship."

"Why?" Pittman asked. "Why there? Long-range scanners? Displays? Doesn't seem like it would be a fatal problem."

"Without the display subsystems, you can't navigate. You can't run the engines. You can't even communicate," Natalya said. "Long-range doesn't usually get used while docked. Whoever did it probably didn't think we'd test it before getting underway."

"Or didn't think we'd notice the problem until we needed both those systems at once," Zoya said.

"What was your test pilot planning to do before he quit?" Natalya asked.

"Labark had a checklist," Pittman said. "First Flight Protocol. I gave it to you."

"So he'd have just taken the ship out and run that list?" Natalya asked.

Pittman nodded. "I presume so. You'd have to take it up with engineering. They're the ones who drive that process."

"So, Downs?" Natalya asked.

"Of course," Pittman said.

"Who hates you enough to want this project to fail?" Natalya asked.

Pittman's facade barely quivered. "Pardon me?"

"Why are you here, Ms. Pittman?" Natalya asked.

"It's my project," Pittman said, her voice like cracked ice. "Where would I be?"

Zoya held up a hand. "Yes, sorry. Wrong question, Ms. Pittman." She shot a quelling look at Natalya. "We've just noticed some ... irregularities."

Pittman refolded her arms. "Irregularities, Ms. Usoko?"

"The project has been here in design for a couple of stanyers?" Zoya asked.

Pittman nodded. "About that. I think the first teams convened in August or September of 2364. I fail to see the bearing."

"You weren't part of that group?" Natalya asked.

"No, I was brought in about five months ago. The early construction phase was a mess and they needed a strong administrator to sort it out. They tapped me," she said, lifting her chin just a fraction.

"Why did the engineers leave?" Zoya asked.

"Leave?" Pittman asked. "Why would they leave?"

"Where are they?" Zoya asked. "Those members of the first teams?"

Pittman blinked, opened her mouth as if to speak, then closed it again.

"They were already gone when you arrived, weren't they, Ms. Pittman?" Zoya asked.

Pittman shook her head slowly. "No engineers have left the project since I've been here. The only person who left was the test pilot, Labark."

"Do you know who they were?" Natalya asked.

"I'm sure I have a roster in the files," Pittman said. Her professional mask reasserted itself and her expression went blank. "What has that got to do with my involvement and this project failing?"

Natalya glanced up and down the dock. "We could take this someplace more private, if you prefer."

"I'm happy right here," Pittman said. She closed her mouth around whatever else she might have been going to say but her jaw worked as if she were chewing the words back.

"What do you know about ship design and manufacture?" Zoya asked.

"I have people for that," she said. "My job is to keep to the plan. Make sure the production goals get met."

Zoya nodded. "I'm sure you're very good at it, but how do you know when they're lying to you?"

"Who?" Pittman asked.

"Those people you have who understand ship design and manufacture," Zoya said.

Pittman paused, her brows wriggling together for a moment before her forehead cleared. "Numbers don't lie."

"How many of those couches have you bought?" Natalya asked.

"Only twelve," Pittman said. "I just reviewed the records. They've all been returned and we've been reimbursed."

"Why twelve?" Natalya asked.

"Enough for the first flight and a couple spares," Pittman said. "What's your point?"

"Who runs your inventory?" Natalya asked.

"We have a whole logistics team," Pittman said. "They're responsible for purchase and inventory of all the materials used on station."

"Yes, but who runs the inventory for the couches?" Natalya asked. "How do you know the numbers match the parts?"

"There are checks," Pittman said, biting off each word. "We're not so cavalier about this as you may think, Ms. Regyri. I still fail to see where you're going with this and I don't take kindly to being accused of incompetence."

Natalya held up her hands palm out. "I'm not accusing you of incompetence, Ms. Pittman. I'm suggesting that somebody— maybe some group of people—is purposefully setting up this project to fail and for you to take the fall."

Pittman's face flushed and she pressed her lips together in a line so tightly they turned white around the edges. "And you've come to this conclusion on the basis of a piece of litter stuck in an electronics rack on a ship that's only just come out of assembly?" The words ground out of her through her clenched jaw. "I think it's time for you both to get into your antique and get off my station."

Zoya shrugged and nodded to Natalya. "Sounds like a good idea to me."

"Good luck, Ms. Pittman," Natalya said and walked away down the docks toward the *Peregrine's* lock with Zoya beside her.

Chapter Twenty
Pulaski Yards: 2366, May 10

NATALYA SEALED *Peregrine's* lock behind them and made her way to the galley. "I need coffee."

"Shall we leave immediately?" Zoya asked.

"I'm about done with this project. Is there any reason to stay? She *did* order us off."

"What'll we tell Dorion?"

Natalya finished loading up the brewing station and punched the button. "The truth. Those boats aren't safe to fly, let alone secure enough for their needs. Somebody's setting her up to fail."

"Why the sabotage?" Zoya asked, pulling mugs out of the rack.

Natalya slumped against the bulkhead, letting the soothing aroma of fresh coffee waft over her. "Good question. If I wanted the project to fail, I'd sabotage the production run, not the prototypes."

Zoya frowned. "Maybe. Maybe not. I supposed it would depend on your goal."

"Like what?"

"What if you only wanted to discredit Pittman?" Zoya spoke slowly as if refining the idea with each new word. "What if you wanted to take over the project yourself?"

Natalya weighed the idea in her head. "Maybe. Would that explain why she was given the program just a few months ago?"

"Could," Zoya said, grabbing the pot and filling their mugs. "The timing might be significant."

"How so?"

"Well," Zoya said, pausing to sip before speaking. "The design engineers worked for what? About a stanyer?"

Natalya nodded. "That's what Sandra said."

"So they worked up a design, got it ready for early prototyping and left."

"That part is dumb."

"Agreed," Zoya said. "But it might support the notion that somebody behind the scenes is operating to either control it or scotch it completely."

"Why ship the engineers out?"

"Maybe to replace them with people you control?" Zoya said, her eyes focused someplace in the distance. "Maybe to change the design without opposition." She looked at Natalya. "Kinda makes me want to see the history of the design revisions."

"We're not exactly in the pool on that one anymore," Natalya said, letting the aromatic steam wreathe her nose.

"Might be something to take up with Dorion."

Natalya nodded. "Still. This whole project reeks."

"It sounded good," Zoya said. "It still might be the only way to solve their data collection and dissemination problem."

Natalya stiffened. "That's the problem."

"What? That it's the only solution?"

Natalya shook her head. "No. That it's not."

Zoya cocked her head to one side. "You lost me."

"What if it's not the only solution? What if it's not even the best solution?"

"Why would they adopt it if there was a better one?" Zoya asked.

"That's the question. If we find the answer to that, we'll find out why this project is a mess and why Pittman got set up to hold the bag."

"I'll grant you that, but do you have a better solution?"

Natalya sipped her coffee for a moment. "I've got some pieces. I don't really know enough about what goes on behind the curtain."

"Sharing is caring," Zoya said with a lopsided grin.

"What's wrong with the design as it stands? Sabotage aside."

"Single Burleson," Zoya said.

"Why is that a problem?"

"Single point of failure loses the ship and the crew. Even with a good mean time between failures, the number of ships in space will almost guarantee regular losses."

"Exactly."

"I'm still not following," Zoya said.

"Single point of failure. They're trying to solve a growth problem with engineering and they're overlooking the larger problem because it's been there all along."

"Single point of failure?"

Natalya nodded. "Where do they collect all the data?"

Zoya shrugged. "Bowie, isn't it?"

"That's what we've been led to believe."

"I still don't get it," Zoya said.

"The problem is getting all the data in and out of Bowie in a timely manner, right?"

Zoya nodded. "Nearly exponential growth putting more demand on their distribution network than they can accommodate."

"What if that's not the problem? What if the real problem is a single point of failure?"

Zoya's eyes widened. "If the hub fails, the wheel breaks."

"So why aren't they addressing that?" Natalya asked.

"Maybe they are and we're not aware of it," Zoya said. "It's not like these are amateurs cobbling together a network out of bits and pieces they found in a closet."

Natalya paused and let that sink in a moment. "Possible. We weren't given any options when we made our run, though."

"And Dorion keeps talking about getting the data back to Bowie," Zoya said. "If we could do anything, what would we do?"

"The new boats are a good idea," Natalya said. "Fast, specialized, long legs, and hard to see."

"Relatively low cost," Zoya said. "Exchanging pilots to keep the ships flying even when the pilots are tapped out makes them cost effective."

"So, what if there were regional hubs?" Natalya said.

"How does that help the single point of failure?"

"If every hub has the same data, no single hub failure could kill the network."

"How do you reconcile them? Don't you still have the same problem you have now?" Zoya asked.

Natalya let the question play in her brain while she took another slurp of coffee. "No," she said. "Now Dorion needs to have every ship dump their data here. If the collectors had a hub closer to their operating region, they wouldn't need such long legs. The ships assigned to that hub could service each node without the long jumps between nodes."

"We didn't have that many long jumps," Zoya said.

"We also don't know how indicative that route was."

"True." Zoya nodded. "We're back to reconciliation."

"That could be done easily with a few ships dedicated to humping the data once a day."

"Is a day frequent enough?" Zoya asked.

"What's the gap now? It's got to be at least three days based on the schedule we flew."

"It solves another problem," Zoya said after a few moments.

"Which one's that?"

"Places where there's more growth can get more ships. As the demand density builds in a region, the mechanisms would be in place to allow the infrastructure to scale up. First with more ships and eventually with a dedicated hub."

Natalya nodded. "I like this. It's a better solution than what they're doing now."

"If that's all they're doing," Zoya said, a cautionary note in her voice.

"It doesn't answer the question about Pittman and who's trying to kill the project."

"Follow the money," Zoya said. "Who gains if the project fails?"

"Or who lost out because they didn't get the project for themselves?" Natalya asked.

"Like who's trying to hurt it just enough to replace Pittman?"

Natalya nodded. "Downs has a pretty fat cushion of credits to skim and it sounds like he's already grabbing his slice. What if he had the whole project to skim from and nobody looking over his shoulder?"

"Could be a lot of golden eggs out of a goose like that," Zoya said. After a moment, she said, "We need to talk to Dorion."

Natalya raised an eyebrow. "What if it's Dorion?"

Zoya shrugged. "Have to start somewhere. Pittman would be my first choice but she slammed that door in our faces."

"Let's go talk to Dorion, then. What's the worst that can happen?"

"I don't even want to think about that," Zoya said with a mock shudder. "We're kind of exposed."

Natalya paused. "I was thinking the worst thing might be he'd fire us."

Zoya snorted. "I guess I'm a pessimist. My thought was more fatal."

Natalya nodded. "Well, he could space us, I suppose, but he doesn't strike me as the type."

"We know an awful lot. Can they let us go?"

"We signed the nondisclosures and we're bound by them. We break that contract and High Tortuga can get retribution pretty easily," Natalya said.

"What's to stop them from getting it anyway?"

"Nothing, I guess." Natalya paused on her way to the cockpit. "So we better make sure we're more valuable alive than dead."

Chapter Twenty-one
CommSta Bowie: 2366, May 11

DORION MET THEM AT the lock. His face could have broken asteroids. "What the hell, Regyri?"

Natalya stood in the hatch and stared him down. "Which part? The part where that ship is a death trap? The part where it's been sabotaged? Or the part where Alison Pittman is being set up to take the fall for the failed project?"

His hard-rock face dissolved into disbelief. "What? What are you talking about? Pittman had me on the blower for half a stan complaining about you two insulting her and how she had to kick you off the station."

"Some people just can't deal with reality," Zoya said.

"You wanna come have a cup of coffee or would you prefer to broadcast this up and down the docks?" Natalya asked, stepping back out of the way.

Dorion shot them both a poisonous glare as he mounted the ramp and entered the ship.

Zoya keyed the lock closed while Natalya led the way to the galley.

"All right," he said, leaning against the bulkhead. "Spill."

Natalya started prepping the coffee maker, looking over her shoulder at him. "First, the plans you showed us don't match the ship."

"What do you mean?" he asked.

"I mean that the plans you have are for a different ship than the prototype they wanted us to test."

"You've been there a week and this is the first I've heard about it."

"Pittman heard about it within a stan of our arrival," Zoya said. "We're just the hired help. Don't you two talk?"

"What's different?" Dorion asked.

"The most important change is that there's only one Burleson drive," Natalya said, punching the button to start brewing.

"Is that a problem?"

Natalya leaned against the opposite bulkhead and crossed her arms. "It's a showstopper in terms of viability, but the larger point is that you don't know the prototype for the ship you're betting the station on doesn't match the one they've told you they're building. Doesn't that bother you?"

"I'm sure they have valid reasons," he said. "Why is it a show-stopper?"

"Burlesons fail. Not often but when they do, it could cost the ship. That's why every jump-capable ship has two. Even the *Peregrine*," Natalya said. "You're investing in a network to make it more reliable, not less. Sidestepping the issue of lost ships and pilots, you'd also lose the data and your business depends on that data. How much of it can you lose and still maintain your reputation?"

Dorion paused at that. "Did they say why?"

"Cost," Zoya said. "They spun some floss about the second drive adding a few percentage points to the cost. I doubt that it would stand up to a stiff breeze, let alone a forensic audit."

"Wait? Forensic audit? Who said anything about a forensic audit?"

"If I were your boss, I'd insist on it," Zoya said. "That whole project is rotten."

"Back up. Start at the beginning."

Natalya sighed. "The prototype is actually pretty sweet. The chief engineer on the project may be criminally inept, but the ship itself could be the answer to part of the problem you're trying to solve."

"Who's the chief engineer?"

"A structural engineer named Anthony Downs," Natalya said.

"I know Downs," Dorion said, his brow furrowing in a frown. "Structural engineer, right. Helped us set up this place."

"Pittman is working through her books to find out how much he's skimming," Natalya said. "But he's way over his head in terms of ship design."

"I'd bet he didn't design it," Zoya said. "I suspect he just took the base design the original team gave him, fired them all, and started skimming off the top while his cousins and in-laws provided the parts at the low, low price of twice retail."

His eyes all but bugged out of his head on stalks. "You're making some pretty serious accusations. Can you prove any of this?"

Zoya held her hands up, palms out. "I'm not accusing anybody of anything. I'm just saying somebody with skin in this game needs to take a real hard look at what's going on over on Pulaski."

He looked at Natalya. "What's this about Pittman taking the fall?"

"She's flailing. She's been there five months and still didn't know that Downs was buying parts from his family," Natalya said. "She's probably an excellent administrator who's used to dealing with well-structured problems of information flow. She has no idea who's blowing smoke up her pants or who's dealing from the bottom of the deck."

"It's worse than that. She doesn't seem to believe that it's even possible," Zoya said. "She kicked us off the station when we suggested that she needed to check into her inventory processes to see how badly she's being robbed."

Dorion frowned and bit his lower lip. "Maybe she's in on it."

Natalya felt her eyebrows trying to crawl into her hair at that. "I thought you were on her side."

"I'm not on anybody's side," he said, biting off his words. "I need those ships because I need to get this network service issue solved. I need them now but I'm not going to get them for weeks yet. I was counting on you two to get that shakedown done and here you are. Banned from the yard. On Pittman's shit-list. Spouting tales of incompetence and sabotage? Who do you think you are?"

Natalya pulled three cups from the rack and let him stew. She poured his coffee and handed him the mug before filling the other two. She paused to take a sip of hers before turning back to him. "I think we're the small-ship experts you hired to help you figure out how to use those new boats. If you don't want our expertise, we'll be happy to butt out and leave you to it."

Dorion's brows met over his nose with a tectonic furrow. He took a sip of coffee without taking his eyes off Natalya. "Uh-uh," he said. "You signed a contract. You don't get to walk away just yet."

Natalya shrugged. "You're the boss. You tell me. How do you want it?"

He swallowed his coffee and glowered into the mug. After several long moments he asked, "Why do you think Pittman's being set up?"

"They started development on this ship, what? Two stanyers ago?" Zoya asked.

"Something like that," he said, dipping into his coffee again.

"It took them a stanyer to come up with a design and then all the original engineers left," Natalya said.

"That would have been about the time they started building the prototypes," he said. "What of it?"

"Who ordered them off? Where did they go?" Natalya asked.

"Their work was done. They moved on. What does it matter?" Dorion asked.

"Their work was just starting," Zoya said. "They had a theoretical design and just as it's about to be tested, they're removed."

"That's not normal," Natalya said. "Who changed the design? How did they change it?"

His eyes narrowed. "I'm not sure I'm following."

Zoya sighed, the exasperation clear on her face. "You can't just slop a design on the page and expect it to work. No designer I know would do that. No competent engineer would walk away just as the building starts. What if they miscalculated? What if they measured wrong? What if—any number of things that might need a correction in order to make the ship work?"

"Why all of them?" Natalya asked. "Fine, reduce the overhead, but removing *all* the designers? That smacks of coverup."

He leaned his head back against the bulkhead and seemed to stare at the overhead for a few moments. "Sabotage?"

"The ship was sabotaged," Natalya said. "Somebody jimmied the computer rack to short out the long-range against the display subsystems."

Dorion straightened and looked at her. "That's a pretty strong accusation. Can you prove it?"

"Not at the moment," Natalya said. "We don't even know when it might have been done, but it had to have been done on purpose."

"It's a new ship. Maybe a tolerance was off?" he said.

"It was a piece of conductive scrap lodged between the card racks in such a way that it shorted out two cards," Zoya said. "The system would only fail if both display and long-range get used at the same time. Long-range doesn't usually get started until you're away from the station. Everything needs display."

"Why couldn't it be an accident?"

"Some things are just too improbable to be credited," Zoya said. "Stick a piece of conductive material between two powered cards, they generally sizzle for a split second and die. This particular piece of conductive material managed to connect just enough of the two cards to make them both overheat without failing immediately. I only caught it because we were running pre-launch diagnostics on the ship and I spotted the temperatures spiking."

He stared at her. "So you pull it out and keep going, right?"

"The original test pilot's checklist didn't include systems testing," Natalya said. "He wouldn't have found the problem until his ship died around him someplace between stations."

Dorion stared at her for several long moments. "What the hell were you two doing out there?"

"Pittman gave us carte blanche to test the ship any way we wanted as long as we agreed to give it a shakedown run," she said. "We found a lot of things out of whack. Connections not solid. Components missing. Normal stuff that you'd think would have been caught but wasn't."

"I was running a full systems diagnostic suite because I wanted to find the underlying sensors for the various ship functions," Zoya said. "The whole ship was rigged with idiot lights instead of actual data displays."

Dorion's head twitched once. "Let me get this straight. You were trying to revise the pilot's systems access before you'd take it out?"

"Yes," Zoya said. "It's not safe to operate as it sits. It still wouldn't have been safe but with decent instrumentation, we could have evened the odds a bit."

He shook his head. "So you two decided you know better than the team of engineers who put the ship together?"

"We don't *know* the team of engineers who put the ship together," Natalya said, exasperation spitting onto the deck. "That's the whole point. The ship we saw has fatal flaws. Flaws any ship designer would have spotted. Do you, by any chance, have the first draft design?"

He paused at that. "Maybe," he said. "I'd have to check my archives."

"Somebody must have it, and I'd like to see it," Zoya said.

"I'm still not seeing the point of sabotage and trying to kill this project," he said. "What makes you think that's happening?"

"Who gains if this project fails?" Natalya asked. "If the new ships don't take over the network, who wins?"

His head shook back and forth slowly. "Nobody wins."

"What about the chartered ships? Won't they lose their contracts when the new ships come online?"

"No," Dorion said. "We'll still need them. We're only rolling out a few of the new ships until we see how well they work."

"Pittman is planning for a thousand," Zoya said. "That's a lot of ships."

"She also thinks they're going out for weeks at a time," Natalya said. "You two really need to talk more."

"Well, we may have to revisit that," Dorion said, sipping from his coffee.

Zoya and Natalya shared a glance.

Zoya sighed.

"All right, boss. What's our next assignment?" Natalya said. "We may as well make as much as we can before this blows up."

He stared at them for a full tick. "We need those ships," he said.

"You need a solution to the correct problem," Zoya said. "The ships are a piece of it, but they're not the answer."

His lips flattened over his teeth. "Can you just trust us to know our own business?"

Zoya shrugged. "I'm not convinced. How are you going to scale this solution when you've got another thousand stations to service?"

"That'll take decades," Dorion said.

"High Tortuga has been running this network for over two centuries," Natalya said. "They've always kept it all in-house. Banking, communications, data. All under one roof. Everybody in the company is happy to spin off this subsidiary?"

He shook his head. "I'm not that naive."

"Who gains if it fails?" Natalya asked again. "You keep saying nobody, but somebody has a vested interested in seeing it doesn't come to fruition."

"Or wants to be in control of it when it does," Zoya said. "That would explain Pittman being set up."

"Who was supposed to be in charge?" Natalya asked. "Who led the design team originally?"

"And what happened to them?" Zoya asked. "Do they want the job back?"

Dorion paused, chewing on his tongue for a moment before answering. "He died."

"That's not suspicious," Natalya said, feeling her eyeballs rolling.

"It was an accident," he said.

"I'm sure," Zoya said. "Project leads die from accidents every day. Radiation poisoning from poring over a hot console all day? Infected paper cut?"

"Airlock malfunction. He got sucked into a dock that was supposed to be pressurized but wasn't."

"You've *got* to be kidding," Zoya said. "Who certified the lock?" Natalya asked.

"A team from home office did the inquiry. They ruled it an accident." Dorion shook his head. "You can't seriously believe somebody would have the opportunity to fake that, can you?"

"I don't know," Zoya said. "We trust the machinery to what it's supposed to do, but how much of it depends on somebody else doing their job correctly and thoroughly?"

"She's got a point," Natalya said. "The lock on the new boat had a malfunction in the pressure overrides so you couldn't open both doors at the same time. How easy would it be to rig it so they both opened at the same time?"

"They can't," Dorion said. "The inner door can't open against a vacuum. They don't have the muscle to break the seal."

"Obviously, that's a flawed assumption," Zoya said. "I'm not an engineer but I can think of at least two ways it could happen."

He opened his mouth but closed it again without saying anything.

"So, back to the new ship. What do you want us to do about it?" Natalya asked. "Pittman's kicked us off the station. We had a week but couldn't do more than get a start on checking all the systems. A crew of engineers could do it faster, but you can't use the engineers who designed it to test the build."

"Some software help from High Tortuga would help," Zoya said with a shrug. "Even a couple of deck officers who know what a ship is supposed to do would help."

"We'd need to be reinstated in Pittman's good graces," Natalya said. "We called her baby ugly and that's going to be a hard pill for her to swallow."

Dorion frowned and sipped his coffee. "You said part of the problem." He looked at Natalya.

Natalya had to backtrack in her mind to find the reference. "Yeah. The ships aren't going to solve your problem."

"Why not?" he asked.

"The network doesn't scale. I'm surprised your technical boffins at High Tortuga didn't point it out," Natalya said.

"We're not planning on getting that big," he said.

"They weren't planning on being in business for two centuries when they started either, were they?" Natalya asked.

He drained his cup, placed the empty on the sideboard, and crossed his arms. "Give."

"Pittman's building a thousand ships over the next stanyer. I don't think she'll make it, but how many new stations will come online in that time?"

Dorion shrugged. "No idea. Seems like they run in batches. Nothing for stanyers and then a spike."

"I know you won't tell us peons, but you know the numbers. How many new stations have come to you in the last five stanyers?"

The last three? If that rate continues, how many ships will you need?" Natalya said.

"It's worse than that," Zoya said. "What if this station has a catastrophic failure?"

"We've got backups," he said. "Three new comms spikes that we can bring online in a matter of a few stans."

"They're all here?" Zoya asked.

"One is. The other two are in other Viceroy systems. No, I won't tell you which ones."

"You know they're there?" Zoya asked. "You've visited them? Seen them?"

He shook his head and looked at the overhead. "Yes, I know they're there. I've toured one of them in person."

"How do you know the other two are there?" Natalya asked.

"We test one of them each stanyer. A crew powers it up. We run data through it in parallel for a few days, then put it to sleep again."

Zoya nodded. "Triple redundancy and actual live testing. More than I expected."

Dorion shot her a foul glance. "We've been doing this for a very, very long time without your help and I don't appreciate your attitude. I'll trust you know your job if you can trust me to know mine."

Zoya held up a hand, palm out. "Fair enough. Sorry. I'll keep a lid on it."

He looked at Natalya again. "So what's the problem? In small, plain words that even an administrator can understand."

"Central processing works as long as the hub is secure and none of the spokes are too long," Natalya said. "Two centuries ago, there weren't many spokes so having them stretch halfway across the Annex wasn't a problem."

"Go on," Dorion said.

"Now you've got too many spokes and you're getting more all the time. The more ships you put out and the longer they have to stay out, the greater the chance that something will happen."

"You're barely keeping up with the data load now," Zoya said.

"Why do you say that?" he asked, his gaze focused on her.

"Because you're desperate for the ships," Zoya said. "The project has been live for at least two stanyers. Probably more than five. Corporate inertia keeps large companies from moving very fast, so it was probably a serious problem before the project even started. Nothing you've said makes me think it's getting any better."

Dorion started to speak but bit back whatever it might have been, chewing the side of his mouth for a moment. "What about the hubs?"

"The ships are the slowest form of communication *except* across interstellar distances," Natalya said. "What happens when the number of spokes exceeds the capacity of the hub?"

"We just add more processing power and keep grinding," he said. "That's easy."

"It is, but I'm talking about too many ships, too many pilots, too many long jumps out into the dark with all the accumulated errors," Zoya said.

"It's what we do," he said, refolding his arms.

"It's what you've *done*," Natalya said. "Nothing says you have to keep doing it that way."

"What's your solution to this problem we don't have?" Dorion asked.

"Regional hubs," Zoya said.

"Regional hubs? That's your idea?" he asked. "How does multiplying the problem help me solve it?"

"It's the scalar factor. Put the hubs where the demand is. Balance the demand across the hubs and use the new ships to provide the fastest service."

"You're suggesting we recreate this hub? How many times?" Dorion asked.

"Not this hub," Zoya said. "That would be overkill. Keep this as the main hub, it's where the central data storage is and you'll need to keep feeding that data in here, but for transient data? Nothing says you have to pull it all in here in one step."

"Won't that delay it?" he asked. "Dropping it off at an intermediary and having to ferry it out here again?"

"Might reduce the average time per packet," Zoya said.

His frown relaxed just a fraction. "How?"

"Put the hubs one jump out from here," Zoya said. "Well, three jumps but a short one on each end with a big jump in between. Minimize jump error. You can retrieve from all the hubs in a single day with just a few ships."

"What about the delay at the hubs?" he asked.

"What delay?" Natalya asked. "If you're pulling the data from the hub every day, that's faster than waiting two or three days for a ship to make a loop and come back. It shortens the cycle times for the ships because they're only working the local area and you're not having to cover the whole Western Annex from here."

"Those ships are small, fast, and have long legs," Zoya said. "With some careful plotting for the new hubs, you can keep them in the Deep Dark. No need to put them in a system at all. Locate them where a single ship can cover several data buoys in a day. Provision the stations with fuel, gases, and some bunk space. Rotate the crews in and out from here where you've got the long-term facilities to handle a few hundred at a time."

Dorion shifted his weight from one leg to the other and stared at Zoya for several long moments. "How many hubs?" he asked.

"I don't know," Zoya said. "You're the man with the numbers. It would depend on where the load is and how many stations you need to cover. At least three, I should imagine. Six would give you a lot of coverage. Perhaps as many as eight."

He shifted his weight back and refolded his arms, still staring at Zoya with an occasional frown in Natalya's direction. After a long, awkward pause, he said, "We need those boats."

Zoya nodded. "That's going to be true whatever plan you decide on."

"Those ships are almost what you need," Natalya said. "They're this close to being right." She held up her index finger and thumb in a near-pinch. "But somebody's messing with the project."

Dorion pursed his lips and focused his stare at Natalya. "Malice or ignorance?"

Natalya looked at the deck and shifted her own weight back and forth. "Could be ignorance," she said, hating that she had to admit it. She finally looked up at him. "We're the new kids on this block. You're in a better position to tell. Why Pittman? She's probably an ace admin, but what she knows about ships wouldn't fill a coffee cup. If she's going to run that show, she needs an engineer who can be her bullshit detector."

"What about Downs?" Dorion asked.

"Downs is one of the problems," Zoya said.

"Why?" he asked. "He's been with the company longer than I have. From all reports he's a solid engineer."

"He's a *structural* engineer," Zoya said. "Maybe he's a good one. Even a great one."

"But you don't think so," he said.

Zoya shook her head and sighed. "No."

"Why?"

"If he were a *good* engineer, he'd know he's outside of his area of expertise. I'm sure he can design and oversee building dry docks and habitation units. Probably even dealing with the logistics of power and air. He might know enough about closed environmental systems to deal with the plumbing." She paused and shook her head. "He's not a ship designer. While a lot of his skills go into designing and building ships, he's got nothing on propulsion, navigation, and communications."

"He has no idea how a ship actually works," Natalya said. "It's not a station that just happens to fly around."

"He has people to advise him on that," Dorion said.

"Who?" Natalya asked. "The ship designers all left."

His frown deepened at that. "You keep saying that. How do you know?"

"You ever visit the yard?" Natalya asked.

He shook his head. "I've been rather busy here."

"All right," Zoya said. "If you wanted to know the skinny on what's happening here—and you weren't the administrator? Who would you talk to?"

His frown relaxed for a moment and his head tilted to one side. "Why wouldn't I talk to the admin?"

"Maybe you would," Zoya said with a nod. "But how could you verify it?"

Dorion's entire face relaxed. He looked bemused by the question. "Where are you going with this?"

"Where do you go for the gossip?" Natalya asked.

"Frosty's," he said.

"Can you trust it?" Zoya asked.

"Not as such, no."

"Right," Zoya said. "But you can use that as a place to start. Maybe the grumbles are just crew bitching. It's their right to bitch. It shouldn't take long to figure out."

"You want to know what's happening on the station, talk to the *staff* at Frosty's. Not the regulars," Natalya said. "They've got their paws on the pulse."

"And you talked to the staff at Pulaski?" Dorion asked.

"A place called Rudy's. It's central to the yard and the docks. They're quite happy with the new personnel but disappointed that the original team has left the station," Zoya said.

"Pittman's looking into it now. She didn't realize her team wasn't the actual team that designed the new ships," Natalya said.

"How could she not know that?" Dorion asked.

Natalya and Zoya shared a quick glance. "Now you know why we think there's something rotting in the ductwork," Zoya said.

He frowned. "First things first. We need the ships."

Natalya nodded. "You'll also need a deployment doctrine, and it would be good if you and Pittman coordinated a bit so she doesn't sandbag you with something because she's not in the loop."

He shot her a sour look. "You made your point."

Natalya shrugged. "How can we help? We're not allowed on Pulaski."

"I'll talk to Alison," Dorion said.

Natalya's tablet bipped and Zoya's echoed a heartbeat later. Natalya pulled up her screen. "Maybe you won't have to. It's Pittman. She wants to talk."

"Apparently, she did a little poking around after we left," Zoya said, reading her tablet. "She didn't like what she found."

"Did she say what it was?" Dorion asked.

Natalya shook her head. "Only that the numbers don't tally."

Zoya pocketed her tablet and nodded. "She must have taken it to heart and spot-checked the inventory data against the warehouse."

CHAPTER TWENTY-TWO
PULASKI YARDS: 2366, MAY 13

THE COMMS STATION PINGED as the *Peregrine* settled into her berth. "Bet that's Pittman," Natalya said, checking the station ties.

Zoya opened the window and snorted. "No bet. Invitation to dinner." She glanced at the chrono on the console. "Just over a stan from now. Her quarters."

Natalya nodded. "Time enough to grab a coffee at Rudy's."

"Rudy's?"

"I wanna check in with Sandra."

Zoya frowned. "You expect much has changed in the last four days?"

"Not really, but if anything has? Sandra will know about it."

"You don't trust Pittman?"

Natalya secured her console and shrugged. "Let's just say I'd prefer to have a foundation under me before Pittman starts spinning her vision of reality. I don't completely trust the sudden turnaround."

Zoya snickered and led the way to the lock.

When they stepped into Rudy's, the dual scents of cinnamon and coffee washed over Natalya making her sigh. She felt her entire body relax. Sandra looked up from filling salt shakers at the counter. Her eyes widened and she smiled. "Well, look what the cat dragged in. I didn't expect to see you two back here." She waved them into a booth off to the side.

Natalya glanced around the empty restaurant and raised an eyebrow as they slipped into the seats. "I guess we didn't need a reservation, huh?"

Sandra gave a low chuckle. "You just missed the last group and the shift change happens in about half a stan. It'll pick up after that for a bit."

Zoya frowned. "Long hours for short pay."

Sandra shrugged. "Nothing better to do and I can just as easily do it here, but what's with you? Last I heard you'd been booted."

"Heard from Tony Downs lately?" Natalya asked.

"Downs?" Sandra asked with a short shake of her head. "Not likely. Why?"

"Just wondering," Natalya said.

"Uh huh," Sandra said, rolling her tongue around in her mouth a bit. "What can I get ya?"

"I need some coffee that I didn't make," Natalya said.

"I might have a fresh cinnamon roll to go with it," Sandra said. "I'm not above trading pastry for good goss."

"Not much to tell," Natalya said. "We thought if anybody knew what was happening on-station, it would be you."

"Why Downs?" Sandra asked.

"We had a bit of a run in with him last time," Natalya said. "Ms. Pittman didn't like our take on it."

"That why she booted you?" Sandra's eyebrows rose.

"We might have suggested she didn't know what she was doing," Natalya said, studying the table top.

"And you're back already?" Sandra asked. "How'd that happen? She's not known for backing off."

Natalya looked up and shrugged. "Not sure. We figured something must have happened here to change her mind."

Sandra looked at Zoya with a raised eyebrow.

Zoya grinned. "None for me, thanks. Just coffee. We've got a dinner date coming up."

Sandra snorted. "I'm guessing it's not with Tony Downs."

"You've not heard anything from the yardbirds?" Natalya asked.

Sandra chewed the corner of her mouth a moment and frowned. "Couple of the guys were in this morning. Jawing about some airlock problem. I didn't hear what. They weren't happy, but that's normal." She shrugged.

Natalya glanced across the table at Zoya. "You know who they were? Where they work?"

Sandra laughed. "Honey, this is a big station and with the guys coming and the guys going, I'm lucky I know myself in the mirror in the morning." She looked back and forth between them and sighed. "Guess I can't blame a woman for askin'. Lemme get you some coffee."

"Thanks," Natalya said and offered an apologetic smile. "We don't know anything or we'd share."

"Maybe we'll know more after dinner," Zoya said.

Sandra shrugged and disappeared into the kitchen only to return in a few moments with cups and a carafe. "Enjoy," she said, winking at Natalya before returning to her salt shakers behind the counter.

Natalya hunkered down over her mug, letting the warm steam float across her face as she stared into the dark depths. "Coincidence?" she asked, her voice barely audible.

"Not likely," Zoya said, her voice not any louder. "Hard to shrug something like that off as an accident a second time."

Natalya took a sip and placed the mug back on the surface with a quiet click. "Depends on who sees it and where it happens, I suppose," Natalya said.

"And who knew about the first one," Zoya said.

Natalya nodded. "That, too."

"I'd have expected there to be more gossip," Zoya said.

"Depends on who knows what and how fast things are moving here, I suppose."

"What? You think she hasn't confronted Downs?"

Natalya lifted one shoulder and let it drop. "Maybe it's not Downs. We're assuming based on a cryptic message."

Zoya lifted her coffee and blew across the top of the mug, her eyes narrowing. "Possible," she said after a few heartbeats. "It's more likely she hasn't taken any action yet."

"What's she waiting for?" Natalya said, more to herself than Zoya.

"Maybe for us to get back." Zoya shrugged and sipped her coffee. "Maybe she'll tell us over dinner."

"What's with the airlock?"

"Maybe it's a simple production problem. The first prototype had an airlock issue."

Natalya shot an incredulous look across the table.

Zoya chuckled. "It could happen." She paused and looked into her mug. "I'm pondering the different ways something unfortunate could happen in an airlock."

"Probably the easiest would be to jimmy the cycle control. You get in and punch the cycle button to open the outer door, but instead of cycling—poof," Natalya said. "Out like the trash."

"Ouch." Zoya winced.

"Wouldn't take that much," Natalya said. "Somebody on the inside punching the eject buttons with a person in the lock." She shrugged. "It's almost impossible to protect against authorized execution of routine actions taken with bad intent."

Zoya tilted her mug up and drained it. "Shall we?"

Natalya nodded and followed suit. She held up her thumb toward Sandra.

"It's on the house," Sandra said with a smile and a wave. "See you at breakfast." She paused for a beat before saying, "I'll expect gossip then."

Natalya grinned and nodded. "If we have any by then, we'll share."

"I'll hold you to that."

Natalya followed Zoya through the door and back down the passageway toward the ship. They stopped at the dock. Natalya eyed the lock's control keys.

Zoya glanced at her. "You worried?"

"Notice anything odd?"

Zoya frowned and examine the controls. "No override?"

Natalya nodded. "If I were designing a station, I'd only have the overrides on a couple of carefully controlled locks."

"What if you didn't need an override?" Zoya asked.

"How would that work?"

Zoya shrugged. "You get in, find the outer door closed and press the cycle button. Somebody comes along and keys the inner door while the cycle is running. Wouldn't take much of a software change to read that as 'eject' and open the outer door."

Natalya felt her breath leave her in a rush. "Even simpler to change it back."

Zoya scratched her nose with an index finger. "Maybe not easier, but certainly no more difficult. Hiding your tracks after might be a little harder, but it would depend on your systems access. Maintenance activity is normally logged somewhere." She nodded at the lock controls. "Feeling brave?"

Natalya contemplated that notion for several long moments before keying the lock open. Both doors opened onto the hangar. She shrugged and stepped through into the docking bay. "This lock's too exposed. Too much chance of error. It'll need to be one that can't space the wrong target."

"You think whoever's doing this is that careful?"

Natalya shrugged as she keyed the lock on the *Peregrine*. "I think they'll want to keep the number of incidents down. Too many 'accidents' would give the game away. They've already had one. Two is coincidence. Three would be highly suspicious." She shook her head. "No. If there's another one, it won't be on an obvious lock. It'll be obscure."

"Like the prototype?"

Natalya considered that as she stepped aboard her ship. "That would be my guess. Most likely while underway where it would happen quickly and without witnesses."

"How would that happen?" Zoya asked. "It's not something you're likely to test on a shakedown."

Natalya stopped in the passageway. "No, but it wouldn't be too hard to jimmy the lock so that both doors open at once on some kind of timer or computer trigger."

"I didn't think the inner door could open against a vacuum," Zoya said.

"It can't," Natalya said stopping at the door to her stateroom. "But if the lock is pressurized before the key sequence triggers, there's no vacuum inside so both doors can open and depressurize the whole ship."

Zoya's eyes widened. "And no airtight hatch between the bridge and the lock on the new ship."

Natalya nodded at the cockpit just ahead of them at the end of the passageway. "None here, either."

"Design flaw?"

Natalya pondered that for a moment. "I don't know. It never occurred to me that it might be a problem until just this tick. Getting into the *Peregrine's* systems to set that kind of booby-trap would be exceptionally difficult without the command override codes." She paused, chewing on her bottom lip.

"But not on the prototype," Zoya finished the thought.

"Probably not on Pittman's yacht either," Natalya said. "Wonder how much 'routine maintenance' she gets done here."

Zoya's eyebrows shot up. "Maybe something we should ask her about?" She paused. "Are we being paranoid?"

"It's not paranoia if they're really out to get you," Natalya said, a tiny smile flickering across her mouth. "The problem is that we still don't know who—if anybody—is trying to set the project up for failure."

"True," Zoya said. "All the evidence seems to be circumstantial at best."

"Yeah, but if it looks, quacks, and swims ..." she shrugged.

Zoya nodded. "We better get a move on. It's almost time."

"Still makes me nervous not knowing what Downs's status is," Natalya said. "You'd think there'd be more scuttlebutt if he'd been sacked."

"Maybe he hasn't been."

"Yet," Natalya said. "Which makes me think Pittman has a surprise in store for him."

Zoya snorted. "Or us."

"That's what I'm worried about," Natalya said.

"We won't know until we get there. Better get changed." Zoya stepped into her stateroom and latched the door behind her with a click.

Natalya sighed and considered what she'd wear. She closed her own door and pondered her wardrobe. She popped open her gravtrunk and pulled down a tab in the top, revealing a collection of weapons. "Accessories," she said. "This calls for the proper accessories."

Chapter Twenty-three
Pulaski Yards: 2366, May 13

ALISON PITTMAN ANSWERED her own door with a sheepish grin. "Come in." She stepped back to let them enter, then bolted the door behind them. Natalya noted the physical bolt and raised an eyebrow. Pittman shrugged. "I never really trust electronic locks," she said.

"Bitter experience?" Zoya asked.

"Something like that," she said and led them down a short corridor into a modestly sized living-dining room. Delicious smells wafted out of the kitchen. The space seemed spartan, as if she'd never moved in. "Dinner will be ready in a few ticks. I hope you like pasta."

"I'll eat anything," Natalya said. "Pasta sounds lovely and that sauce smells divine."

Zoya nodded. "It really does."

Pittman stood awkwardly in the middle of the room as if unsure about what to do with guests. "Make yourselves comfortable." She gestured at the living room. "Wine?" The question was almost an afterthought.

"I'll have some with dinner," Zoya said.

"Yeah, that's fine with me, too," Natalya said, lowering herself onto the nearest couch.

Pittman nodded. "Let me just check the kitchen." She scuttled through the door, disappearing into the next room.

"She seems a bit rattled," Zoya said, taking a seat beside Natalya.

"Something's not quite right here."

Pittman came out of the kitchen and settled across from them. "Well." She examined her hands for a long moment. "I'm sorry," she said, looking up. "You were right. I was wrong."

"You took a physical inventory?" Natalya asked.

She nodded. "I tapped one of the dockworkers to help me." She looked to where her fingers writhed in her lap and then forcibly flattened her hands on the tops of her thighs. "He knew what he was looking at and we ran a fresh inventory on the fixtures storage." She shrugged. "There were a lot more units there than should have been. Worse, some of the crates were empty."

"You opened them?" Zoya asked.

Pittman looked at her lap again. "He did. I didn't know enough to look."

After a too-long pause Natalya spoke. "So, Ms. Pittman? Pardon my asking, but what did you do before you got tapped for this job?"

"Alison, please," she said. "I was in charge of HR for High Tortuga Holding Company." Her spine straightened and she stared straight ahead, looking somewhere between Natalya and Zoya but not looking at either. "I was very good at my job."

"I'm sure you were," Zoya said. "Lots of work. Many people reporting to you. A critical role in the organization."

Pittman's gaze jerked to Zoya. "That's ... not the usual reaction."

Zoya chuckled. "My grandmother always said the company isn't a company without the right people. I can't imagine how difficult it must be in Toe-Hold space."

"It was a challenge. Finding the right people. People with the right skills and attitudes," Pittman sighed. "Keeping all the balls in the air made me a pretty good juggler."

"Sounds like you enjoyed it," Natalya said. "So why'd you take this position?"

Pittman sighed and offered a shrug, looking around the room—anywhere but at Natalya. "I thought I was bored. It was a dead-end position. Head of the department and no more rungs to climb."

"You didn't want to move up to one of the management slots?" Zoya asked.

"That *was* a management slot. No place to go except into one of the chief slots—CEO, CFO—and those people weren't going anywhere. My boss was the chief operating officer. I had about as much chance of replacing him as walking outside without a suit."

"Not even with the new divisions opening up?" Natalya asked.

"All those slots are filled already. Have been for over a stanyer. I helped fill most of them." Pittman looked down, seeming to notice her hands had started grappling with each other again. She pressed them palm down. "I was passed over."

A *ting-ting-ting* sounded from the kitchen and Pittman stood as if shot from a gun. "Dinner's ready. Shall we dine?"

"I think we better before I drool down my shirt," Natalya said. "That smells wonderful."

Pittman gave a small smile and nodded at the table. "Just give me a moment to get it on the table."

"We can help," Zoya said. They followed Pittman into the tidy kitchen and soon had a baked pasta dish, fresh bread, and a large bowl of salad positioned on the table. The requisite dishing out took only a few moments. Natalya and Zoya addressed the meal and left the obviously uncomfortable discussion for later.

Natalya pushed back from the table slightly, a bit surprised that her plate and glass lay empty before her. She looked up with a grin. "That was wonderful, Alison. If you decide to give up this management thing, you have a real future as a chef."

Pittman grinned back. "I love cooking, but seldom have a good excuse. I think you're the first people I've had to dinner since I got here."

"Why's that?" Zoya asked.

Pittman shrugged. "You know how it is. Bosses and help. When you're the boss, you can't get too friendly with your staff."

Natalya felt her eyebrows rise at that.

Zoya nodded. "Never know when you might have to fire them."

Pittman's head twitched just slightly to one side. "Well, no. It's not that. It's just difficult to maintain proper discipline with your friends." She shrugged again. "I'm the director. Everybody here reports to me and I wouldn't want to put them—or me—in a difficult position."

"Doesn't that apply to us?" Natalya asked.

Pittman pursed her lips. "You're contractors. Not on my org chart." She sighed. "And I owed you an apology."

Zoya finished scraping the last of the pasta off her plate and pushed it toward the middle of the table. "Well, Alison, anytime you want to cook for us, feel free. That was unbelievable."

"You two don't eat well on that ship?"

Natalya glanced at Zoya. "We eat fine, but it's mostly ready-to-eat freezer food. Zoya's a pretty good cook when we're not underway and can take the time."

Zoya grinned. "Natalya's not so bad either. It's just when we're underway, there's always something more important than fixing a meal."

Pittman nodded and offered a smile. "I don't cook like this for just myself, either." She paused, casting her gaze across the table. "If we're done here, would anybody care for dessert? I've a bit of cheesecake and fresh strawberries."

Natalya felt her eyes widening. "Where'd you get fresh strawberries?"

"Grew them. The hydroponics team on station here does wonders. They're not the same as grown in dirt under direct radiation, but they're not bad."

"I haven't had strawberries since we left Port Newmar," Zoya said.

Pittman tilted her head to one side. "You were on Port Newmar?"

Zoya seemed to freeze for a moment. "You didn't know?" she asked.

"Why would I?" Pittman asked.

Natalya nudged Zoya's arm. "Looks like we're rubbing the fleet off you."

"I figured you'd have run a background check on us," Zoya said with a grimace at Natalya.

Pittman sat back in her seat. "I thought Dorion had." She pursed her lips. "I probably should have. It would have been the first thing I'd have done in my old job." She looked at Zoya. "What would I have found?"

"Nothing too incriminating, I hope," Zoya said. "You mentioned strawberries?"

Pittman laughed. "I did. Come help me dish up." She stood and gathered surplus plates and cutlery with their help.

Once settled again over tea and cheesecake, Pittman looked at Zoya. "So, you never answered. You were at the academy?"

Zoya nodded at Natalya. "We were roommates."

"You stayed together after?" Pittman's eyes widened. "That's rather unusual, isn't it?"

"She had a ship. I didn't." Zoya grinned at Natalya.

"You could have had a ship anytime you wanted," Natalya said. "Your grandfather would have had one built for you."

Zoya's lips twitched like she was hiding a smile behind the movement. "Probably. It's worked out all right."

"You two aren't a couple?" Pittman asked.

Natalya shook her head. "Roommates at the academy. We left Port Newmar in a hurry and never looked back."

Pittman sat back in her chair, lounging with one forearm on the table. She looked back and forth between them for a few heartbeats. "There's a story there."

"Yes." Natalya met her gaze. "There's a story there."

Pittman gave a small nod. "Maybe someday you'll be able to share it. I love a good story."

"We'll have lots of stories to share by the time this project is done, I think," Natalya said.

Pittman looked at Zoya. "So, you come from money but you're bumming around in an antique?"

"Money?" Zoya asked.

"Your grandfather would have built a ship for you? I know how much ships cost. That's a pretty generous grandfather."

Zoya took a moment to slide a slice of strawberry into her mouth before replying. "Well, he probably wouldn't have had it built just for me. It would've been something the company needed and he'd've let me captain."

"The company?" Pittman asked.

"Usoko Mining. They supply Manchester over in Margary, among others," Zoya said.

Pittman's eyes widened. "You're *that* Usoko?"

"Well, no. I'm not but that's my grandfather, yes." Zoya placed another strawberry on her tongue and sighed.

Pittman looked at Natalya with her eyebrows raised.

Natalya nodded. "Yes. That's her."

"Are you a secret heiress, too?" Pittman asked.

Natalya scoffed. "Hardly. I'm not sure where my father is at the moment. Somewhere out here in the Toe-Holds." She paused. "Now that I think of it, I haven't heard from him since before—well, for a very long time. I hope he's all right."

"Is that normal? Having him disappear for long periods?" Pittman asked.

"Perfectly. When I was growing up, he'd sometimes take off for months at a time. Generally, he'd stay in touch with my mother. She's an engineering officer somewhere up in the High Line. Toe-Holds don't really appeal to her."

"It's been stanyers, hasn't it?" Zoya said. "Have you heard from him since Port Newmar?"

Natalya shrugged. "No, but—honestly—that's just like him. He's probably up to his armpits in some engineering job. Either for himself or somebody else. I'm pretty sure I could reach out to him if I needed to."

"Inky?" Zoya asked.

Natalya nodded.

"You two are something else," Pittman said. "Now I want to run you both through a background check just to see what you're not telling me." She grinned.

"Speaking of not telling," Natalya said. "How'd you get this job?"

"That's rude," Zoya said.

Natalya bit her lips together. "Sorry. It was, rather. Don't answer unless you want to."

Pittman pressed her lips together and leaned forward, resting both forearms on the table. "Oddly enough, I was asked to take it."

"Your boss?" Natalya asked.

Pittman frowned. "No. He knew I was feeling a bit dead-ended but the request came from a member of the board of directors. I didn't think he even knew who I was."

"But your boss approved it?" Zoya asked.

"Yes. This project has been plagued with problems—mostly related to personnel—ever since it began two stanyers ago. It was a perennial topic on the board's agenda."

Natalya glanced at Zoya before looking at Pittman again. "Didn't it strike you as ... well ... odd?"

"At the time? Not really. I guess they turned my head with compliments. How they needed my strong hand for personnel to get the project back on track and under control."

"At the time, you didn't know they'd released all the original engineers?" Zoya asked.

"No. I didn't even think to ask that until you brought it up." Pittman shrugged. "Now? I'll confess. I'm feeling completely off the beam on it. Nothing makes sense."

"In what way?" Natalya asked. "If you don't mind telling a pair of contractors."

Pittman smiled. "You've given me good advice, even when I wasn't smart enough to take it." She paused and looked down at the table for a moment. "I'm a lot of things, but I'm not stupid. At the moment, I'm coming to understand that I really don't know how to do this job. I'm the best human resources administrator in the Western Annex, but I'm in charge of a shipyard engaged in R&D for a new ship design. What I know about ship design is less than what I know about running a shipyard. As an HR guru I should have twigged sooner. We don't have the right people doing the right jobs. Including mine. My whole career I've depended on the management team to tell me what they need. Now I'm in the hot seat and I have no idea what I need." She looked across the table at Natalya, staring hard before giving Zoya the same treatment. "Call me crazy, but I think you two wild cards might be what I need to turn this into a winning hand."

Natalya shared a glance with Zoya before answering. "We think you've been set up to fail."

"I knew that. Who would do it?" Pittman asked.

"Whoever would benefit from having you fail here," Zoya said.

"When you were working HR, did you ever run across somebody sabotaging their boss, or maybe the team lead on another group?" Natalya asked.

Pittman snickered. "That's a way of life out here. Especially in this company."

"It's universal in any organization above a certain size, I think," Zoya said. "Drove my grandfather crazy."

"Who benefits if you fail?" Natalya asked.

"Tony would have, until this whole episode happened."

"But Tony was in place already?" Natalya asked.

"Yes," Pittman said, her head nodding slowly. "He might have thought I took his job away. It won't matter now. By this time tomorrow he'll be off the station."

"He's still here?" Zoya asked.

"I can't toss him off the way I could you," Pittman said with a shrug. "He's got too many friends in high places. He's being transferred back to the main office for rehabilitation."

"Meaning he knows where too many bodies are buried?" Natalya said.

Pittman shrugged again but didn't answer.

"How can we help?" Natalya asked.

Pittman scooted her chair forward and leaned over the table. "I was hoping you'd ask. Normally, I'd just toss this upstairs but I'm just stubborn enough—and pissed enough—to make this work. What's the highest priority?"

Natalya started to speak but Zoya placed a hand on her forearm and gave her a subtle shake of the head.

Pittman looked at Zoya, her eyes wide.

"What do *you* think it is?" Zoya asked.

"Clearly, I don't know what goes into new ship construction," Pittman said. "I didn't even know my own ship had two Burleson drives. If I put on my HR hat, I'd say I was out of my area of expertise and too reliant on my staff to be effective."

"So? Putting on your HR hat?" Zoya said. "What would you advise the manager to do?"

Pittman pursed her lips, staring into the middle distance. "Well, given that I wouldn't tell a manager to step down, I'd recommend finding somebody with the expertise he needed to be effective."

"How would you pick that person?" Zoya asked.

Pittman grimaced. "I can't very well advertise for one. Not after trashing Tony Downs."

"You didn't trash Downs," Natalya said. "You removed a problem employee. One who stole from the company and lined his own pockets. I think he's a lot deeper in the mess than we know."

Zoya nodded. "I agree. So what would you tell this hypothetical manager to do?"

Pittman smiled at that. "Well, I've already taken the first step." She looked back and forth between Zoya and Natalya. "I've brought in outside troubleshooters."

Zoya laughed. "All right. What's next? What would you advise?"

Pittman's smile faded as she pondered. "Consult with a trusted colleague," she said after nearly a whole tick.

"Do you have any?" Zoya asked.

"Dorion," Pittman said. "He's about my only colleague at the same level. Everybody else is either lower on the food chain or a higher level director."

"You and Dorion have independent operations under a board?" Zoya asked.

"Under the same board, yes," Pittman said. "Members of the main office board, some industry leaders. The usual suspects."

"What expertise do you need?" Zoya asked.

"You tell me," Pittman said. "I need an engineer, but there are too many engineering specialties." She sighed. "Downs shouldn't ever have been lead on this project. I'm not sure he should have ever been on it at all. I need a ship designer and a shipwright."

"This is a shipyard, right?" Natalya asked.

"Yes," Pittman said, her eyes narrowing.

"Who's the most senior team lead?" Natalya asked. "Somebody who was here before the program started. Is there anybody like that?"

Pittman tilted her head to one side and squinted her eyes. "I don't know, but I can find out." She smiled. "We've got a great HR department."

Zoya nodded. "She's right. Find the people who know ship-building. They'll tell you what's wrong with the ship you're building."

"Can I believe them?" Pittman asked.

Zoya shrugged. "You know you can't trust Downs or his buddies. I'd bet they trampled a bunch of people getting into positions of power. I suspect any of those people will be happy to tell you how to fix the problems. They'll be the ones whose names will be on the ship—even if only figuratively."

Pittman smiled and raised her teacup. "To new beginnings," she said.

Natalya and Zoya joined in her toast, clinking the cups together.

CHAPTER TWENTY-FOUR
PULASKI YARDS: 2366, MAY 13

ZOYA LOOKED AT NATALYA as the door closed behind them. "Anything strike you as odd?"

Natalya took a few steps down the passageway, Zoya at her side. Natalya glanced back at the closed door. "She's lonely."

"Yeah. Obviously. Anything else?" Zoya asked.

Natalya frowned at the deck as she strode along. "I don't know where you're going with this."

"She may be a great administrator but she's no leader. She needs external direction for even the simplest tasks. I suspect that if you gave her a chart and a destination she'd get there in the least cost, fastest time."

Natalya nodded as the idea slotted home in her brain. "But she can't navigate without the chart."

Zoya nodded. "Any idea how this will shake out?"

"Nope. And she never did say who it was that put her in for the job."

"One of the directors," Zoya said.

"But which one? We don't even know how many there are."

"Or whether the person who stuck her in this hole was named to the board overseeing this project."

Natalya glanced at Zoya. "That's a scary thought."

"There's a big pile of what-if here."

"Like what if the last project director was murdered?" Natalya asked.

Zoya grunted. "That's the one that has me most concerned."

"If they're willing to do it once, why not twice?"

"Or three or four times," Zoya said.

They walked in silence until they got to the docking gallery. "You think she can turn this around?" Zoya asked.

Natalya sighed as she thought about it. "Maybe Dorion can take her under his wing. Help her sort out her leadership."

"I don't understand how she could have been a great administrator without picking up leadership skills. HR isn't exactly free of the kinds of challenges she's facing here," Zoya said.

Natalya glanced at Zoya and smiled. "There's a big difference between being a department head and the captain. It's one thing to have to call the shots. It's another to have to figure out which shots to call."

Zoya nodded. "True."

"I still think somebody set her up. I bet she's a great HR director but she's floundering because she's never worked outside that box."

Ahead of them, a man in a shipyard coverall stepped out of a docking bay and started toward them. His head came up and he stared at them before turning on his heel and walking away.

"That was odd," Zoya said.

"Wasn't that the tech who repaired the lock on the new ship? What's his name?"

"Carlyle?" Zoya asked. "No, Carroll."

"Yeah, Charles—call-me-Charlie—Carroll," Natalya said.

They stopped at the docking bay and looked inside.

"Ship's still there," Zoya said. "What do you suppose he was doing?"

"Maybe just his shift," Natalya said.

Zoya snorted. "You don't believe that any more than I do. Why'd he turn away? Forgot his watch?"

Natalya rummaged in a pocket and pulled out her fob. "Wanna take a look inside?"

"Think it still works?" Zoya asked. "They shoulda changed the codes after they kicked us off."

"Shoulda and did are miles apart on this job," Natalya said. "Easy enough to find out."

They crossed the dock. The lock opened with a single press of Natalya's key. "For a big-time operation, these people are pretty sloppy."

"When you're the biggest dog, you tend to forget about the puppies," Zoya said.

Natalya raised an eyebrow in her direction. "More wisdom from your granny?"

Zoya shrugged.

"What the hell does that mean?" Natalya asked.

"Big dogs all start out as pups. When you've been the only dog that matters long enough, you tend to think the little dogs can't hurt you. High Tortuga has been the biggest dog for centuries." Zoya nodded at the open lock. "They've forgotten that they're not the only dog."

Natalya felt a chill down her back. "This isn't about the ship."

Zoya shrugged. "That's a possibility. Somebody wants this project to fail. If they're on the inside, they probably know more about High Tortuga's weaknesses than we do."

Natalya nodded and led the way into the ship.

Zoya headed for the cockpit while Natalya cracked the hatch on the tiny engineering space. A quick survey showed nothing changed since the last time she saw it. She dogged the hatch and followed Zoya to the bow.

"Nothing's changed in the engine room. Still has just the one Burleson drive."

"Not much has changed here," Zoya said, her mouth twisted in sour expression. "Just one little thing." She pointed at the exposed card rack.

"They didn't put it back together?" Natalya asked, peering into the tangle of cards and wiring.

"On the surface it doesn't look like anybody's been aboard since we left it," Zoya said.

"On the surface?" Natalya asked and then stopped, staring at the cards. "It's gone."

"Yeah," Zoya said. "Somebody knew enough to take away the evidence."

Natalya pulled out her tablet and put the image she'd taken on the screen, looking back and forth between the image and the rack. "Not only that. They swapped the cards around."

Zoya's eyebrows shot up and she leaned in to look. "I'll be damned." She spent a few minutes looking back and forth between Natalya's screen and the card rack. "They swapped the long-range with—what is that?"

"Looks like the electrical systems status board," Natalya said. "ELSS-32."

Zoya pulled out her tablet and accessed the schematics for the rack. "That should be on delta-six."

Natalya scanned across the delta segment of the bus cabinet and pointed to the sixth—empty—slot. "Somebody doesn't want that card found," she said. She crossed to the couch and fired up the terminal.

"Will that work with the bus system screwed up?" Zoya asked.

"Not as a rule," Natalya said, staring at the screen for a moment and then holding down two keys at the upper corners of the keyboard. "But sometimes you have to have the computer running even if all the peripherals aren't working correctly." After a few seconds, the display flipped on. "It isn't pretty," Natalya said. "But we can look at the logs."

Zoya grinned. "Like the lock access logs?"

"Just like that." Natalya typed a few commands and keyed the lock activity log open. She stared at the screen for several long heartbeats.

A single entry, time stamped 2145, blinked on the screen.

"Well, crap," Zoya said, looking over Natalya's shoulder. "What is it now? 2148?"

Natalya nodded. "Pittman needs to see this."

Zoya placed a hand over her own mouth and nodded at the overhead.

Natalya nodded. She aimed her tablet at the console, grabbed a digital image, shut the terminal off, then holstered her tablet. Without another word, they left the ship, closing the lock behind them as they left.

In the docking gallery, Zoya asked, "Where to now? Back to Pittman's?"

Natalya stopped walking and frowned. "That was my first inclination, but I'm not sure that's the right one."

"We can't stand around here all night," Zoya said with a grin.

"Back to the *Peregrine*, then. Spend a little time sorting this out," Natalya said, turning down the gallery toward their docking bay. She fished her tablet out and started typing on it while they walked. She stabbed the send key and put the tablet away.

"What was that?" Zoya asked.

"Note to Pittman. Copy of the digital and a warning."

Zoya's eyebrows shot up. "Warning?"

"Don't trust any airlocks."

Zoya paused, then nodded. "Good advice."

"Advice we should take, too," Natalya said, stopping at their docking bay.

The access lock stood open, proving the bay had pressure.

"What would we have done if it were closed?" Zoya asked.

Natalya grimaced. "Good question. One we should probably find an answer for before we run into the situation again."

Chapter Twenty-five
Pulaski Yards: 2366, May 14

RUDY'S WAS PACKED AT 0600. Sandra and two assistants kept the coffee flowing and the food coming while Zoya and Natalya held down a small table in the corner. The smell of fried potatoes and onion mingled with the sharp scent of coffee and the yeasty aroma of fresh bread.

Sandra stopped by to fill up their coffee cups. "Anything else I can get you?"

Natalya swallowed a bite of toast. "I'm good."

"Nothing for me," Zoya said.

"Lucky you got here early. This is our busiest shift." Sandra surveyed the dining room.

A trio of men in shipyard coveralls came through the door and stopped just inside, heads turning as they scanned the room.

"We're almost done," Natalya said. "Got the check?"

Sandra fished a tablet out of the pocket of her apron and placed it on the table for Natalya to thumb. "Thanks," she said, retrieving the device. "I'll just tell them it'll be a moment. You two finish up and have a terrific day." She slipped between the tables on her way toward the door.

Natalya popped the last of the toast into her mouth and washed it down with a healthy slug of coffee. "We need to see Pittman."

"I want to know what she's done about Downs," Zoya said.

"Not enough if they're still messing with the ship."

"What if he's not the mastermind behind this whole thing?"

Natalya winced at that idea. "You done?"

Zoya took a final drag from her coffee mug and slid the cup back onto the table. "Let's get some air."

After the hubbub inside, the passageway seemed practically silent. Individuals and small clusters of workers wearing Pulaski Yard coveralls streamed toward the docks at the far end.

"What time's shift change?" Zoya asked.

"Probably 0700," Natalya said. "They'd have to punch in at half past. There'll be a half-stan to change over the crews." Her tablet bipped. She pulled it out, checked the message, and nodded to herself. "We're not the only ones up early. Pittman wants to see us." She headed down the passage toward the administrative offices.

"It makes me nervous that Downs is still here," Zoya said, falling into step.

"Makes me wonder why they're still messing around with the new ship."

Zoya nodded. "Maybe Downs isn't the ringleader."

"And maybe he's not really leaving," Natalya said.

Zoya glanced at her with a raised eyebrow.

Natalya shrugged but kept walking.

Only a few people occupied the front office at admin. One sleepy-looking man in a fresh coverall propped himself behind the counter, holding a mug of coffee as if it were the only thing keeping him upright. A couple of workers near the back of the small entry tapped keyboards at their consoles. Half a dozen workstations sat unattended.

The man at the counter blinked at them a couple of times, stretching his face out as if he'd just crawled out of his rack moments before. "Lost?" he asked.

"Ms. Pittman wants to see us," Natalya said.

He blinked again and jerked his head toward a door at the back. "Through there."

"Thanks," Zoya said, giving him a bright smile.

The smile seemed to register with him. At least he smiled back. The door buzzed as they approached. Natalya grabbed the handle and pulled it open, allowing Zoya to enter first.

A short corridor ran past a half dozen closed doors and opened into a large conference room at the end. Pittman looked up from her place at the head of the table as they entered.

"Morning." A small smile flickered across her lips before disappearing in a frown. "Help yourself to coffee." She nodded to a coffee service on the sideboard. "Airlocks?"

"Your predecessor died in an unfortunate airlock accident," Natalya said. "Twice would only be a coincidence."

Pittman stiffened at that. "What was that image of?"

"The lock entry log on the new ship," Natalya said. "Ours was the only one listed."

"You went to the ship last night?" Pittman sat back in her chair and cradled her mug between her palms.

"We saw Charlie Carroll come out of the docking bay on our way back to the *Peregrine*," Zoya said, topping off a mug. "When he saw us, he turned and left in the opposite direction."

"Carroll? Wiry guy? Dark hair? Mid-forties? Call me Charlie?" Pittman asked.

"Everyone does," Zoya said. "Even his mum."

Pittman snorted. "I know who you mean. Not like he could hide in the passageway. Did he think you didn't see him?"

Natalya grabbed a mug for herself and shrugged. "I don't know. Maybe he didn't think we got enough of a look to recognize him."

"So you went aboard?"

Natalya settled on Pittman's right. "Yeah. It seemed an odd time for a day worker to be messing around with the ship."

"Find anything?"

"The scrap is gone," Zoya said.

"The little piece that was shorting out the system?" Pittman asked.

Natalya nodded. "We left it there. It's gone now."

Pittman reached into a pocket on the sleeve of her shipsuit and pulled a small bag out, sliding it across the table. "Is that it?"

The clear plastic bag held a small piece of scrap.

Natalya looked at it for a moment and pulled out her tablet. She compared the image she'd taken with the scrap on the table. "No," she said, looking at Zoya.

Zoya leaned in and examined the object. "Nope. Wrong material. Wrong shape. That's a piece of plastic strapping."

Pittman frowned. "I was afraid of that. May I see?" She pointed to Natalya's tablet.

Natalya spun the screen so Pittman could see. "I took that when we found it."

Pittman looked at the image and at the scrap in the bag. "Yeah. Same size and rough shape but not close."

"Where'd you get this?" Natalya asked, pointing at the bag.

"After I found the inventory discrepancies, I went aboard and found that laying on the disassembled card rack. Called security to come bag it and document the scene."

"Nothing on this, was there?" Zoya asked, picking up the bag and holding it up to the light.

"Nope. It's not conductive either," Pittman said.

"It wouldn't be," Zoya said. "It was put there as a distraction."

"It was put there to discredit you two," Pittman said. "I may be new here but I know crap when I smell it."

Zoya sat back in her chair and lifted her mug to sip. "So, how do you monitor the ship?"

"From here?" Pittman asked. "I have a clerk in shipyard engineering who keeps an ear open and notifies me when there's something I should know."

"You record it?" Natalya asked.

"Of course. Round the clock."

"How long do you keep the recordings?" Zoya asked.

"Permanent. Burned direct to glass." Pittman shrugged. "Seemed prudent to keep track of everything we could in case something else untoward happens."

"Whose idea was that?" Natalya asked.

"Monitoring? That was part of the design team's plan for the first few prototypes. Black boxes only take you so far. The monitoring system is part of the ship's intercom."

"It is on most ships," Natalya said.

Zoya lifted an eyebrow at that.

"What? You didn't know?" Natalya asked.

"We'll talk later," Zoya said.

"What about the glass?" Natalya asked.

"That was the lawyer," Pittman said. "If it ever comes to court? Glass can't be tampered with."

"Well, it can," Zoya said. "But it's difficult."

"It can?" Natalya asked.

"I'd be interested in that tidbit, myself," Pittman said, leaning forward in her chair.

"Just need a blank with the same sequence number. Record the contents onto a nonpermanent medium. Edit it to be what you want it to be. Use a burner to lay the corrected tracks back down. Since the glass has the correct sequence number, the tracks all lay down and pass validation."

"That seems like it would be too easy," Natalya said.

"Getting the blank with the right number on it is the problem," Zoya said. "You need special gear to label it and a good source of blanks. That's not easy to come by."

"We get our blanks from the main office," Pittman said. "Formatted with our custom disk architecture."

Natalya paused and stared into space for a few heartbeats. "So Downs knows the ship is being monitored. I assume you back up the logs?"

"We image the system every day at midnight," Pittman said. "There's a crew of data people who scan it for discrepancies."

"They ever find any?" Zoya asked.

"None reported."

"So today, they're looking at yesterday's logs. The one where the only entry was us entering the ship?" Natalya asked.

"Presumably," Pittman said.

"And you should have a recording of the evening on glass?" Natalya asked.

Pittman nodded. "Yeah."

"Whoever swapped the cards should be on one of the recordings," Zoya said.

"Swapped the cards?" Pittman asked.

"Whoever tampered with the ship changed the layout of the cards in the rack," Natalya said. She pointed to the image on her tablet. "This card is the long-range sensor control bus. It's not in that slot anymore."

Pittman's eyebrows went up and she tapped some keys on her tablet. "Let's see when that might have happened." She keyed some more and slid her tablet to the side. "Security took images of the cockpit in general and that rack in particular. I've just asked for copies."

"How soon before Downs is off the station?" Zoya asked.

"This afternoon," Pittman said. "I still need to find a replacement."

"What's HR say?" Zoya asked.

"Nobody who's ranked above yard worker has been here longer than Downs." She shrugged. "There are a couple hundred yard workers who've been here for decades."

"Who's the most senior?" Zoya asked.

Pittman consulted her tablet. "A Marti Lawrence." Her eyebrows rose as she read. "That's odd. She's well past retirement age but still working as a clerk in procurement."

"Maybe she just likes to keep busy," Natalya said.

"What shift?" Zoya asked.

"Days," Pittman said, scrolling down. "She should have just come on."

"Maybe talk with her?" Zoya asked. "Seems like a good first step."

Pittman looked across the table with a smile. "I've a better idea."

ZOYA CHUCKLED ALL THE way down to the procurement office. "How'd we get roped into this?"

Natalya nudged her with an elbow. "Pittman has a point. We're more likely to know what to ask and understand what she answers. Lawrence has worked at almost every job in the yard over the last four decades."

"Why's she tucked away in procurement, though?"

Natalya stopped in front of a door. "Maybe we should ask her." She opened the door and stepped into the humming office.

A clerk behind the counter looked up as they entered, his gaze flipping back and forth between them for a moment and then scanned their chests. "No badges," he said. "You're not allowed in here."

"Pittman sent us." Natalya leaned her elbows on the counter. "We'd like to see Marti Lawrence."

"No badges," he said again, a little bit louder. "This area is restricted to yard employees only."

"Fine," Natalya said. She flipped out her tablet and snapped a digital of the man's badge.

"What are you doing?" Belatedly he clapped a hand over his badge. "I'm calling security." He started banging furiously on the keyboard in front of him with his one free hand.

"Excellent," Natalya said. "That'll save me some time."

He looked up at her, his eyes wild. "What's going on?"

"Well, now I have your badge here." Natalya held up her tablet. "So when Ms. Pittman asks why we didn't talk to Marti Lawrence, we'll be able to point out the dumb-ass keyboard jockey who called security on us and had us removed." Natalya smiled at him. "You didn't like this job that much, did you?"

A diminutive woman with more wrinkles than a walnut and iron gray hair gathered back in a short ponytail stepped up to the counter, nudging the clerk out of the way. "Relax, dear," she said to the clerk. "They're not here to steal secrets." She smiled at Natalya and Zoya, the creases beside her mouth and around her eyes giving her a jovial appearance that belied the steel in her voice. "I suspect they already know more than we do. They're the test pilots for the new bird. I'm Marti," she said. "Can I help you?"

"Gotta minute?" Natalya asked. "Can I buy you a cup of coffee?"

"I'm not due for break for another couple of stans but why don't you two come back to my office and we'll have a little chat?"

She led them through the warren of desks, half walls, and free-standing offices to a quiet corner where she pointed to a pair of chairs nested in front of a pristine desk. She settled into the large chair behind it and folded her hands on the top, leaning forward slightly, and offered a smile. "Now, what brings Alison Pittman's bird dogs into my corner of the station?"

Natalya smiled. "You, Ms. Lawrence."

"It's Marti. Always has been. Will be until they launch me into the cold." She paused for a heartbeat. "Could you be a little more specific?"

"You may have heard rumors about a change in personnel?" Natalya asked.

"I hear many rumors every day, my dear."

"Tony Downs will be leaving the station today," Natalya said.

"You think so?" Lawrence asked. It was less a question than a challenge.

Zoya glanced at Natalya. "It's what we've been told."

Lawrence nodded. "Words are words. We can weigh them but they don't have much mass. What makes you think he'll go?"

"Ms. Pittman seems to think so," Natalya said.

Lawrence pursed her lips and nodded once. "Be that as it may, you still haven't answered my question, young lady."

"Ms. Pittman needs some advice about ship building," Natalya said.

Lawrence gave a small snort that sounded half a laugh and half exasperation. "Ms. Pittman needs to find somebody who knows which end of a ship spits out the fire."

Natalya smiled at her. "Then we're all in agreement."

Lawrence blinked slowly a few times. "Who's 'all' in this equation?"

"Me, Zoya here, you ... and Alison Pittman."

Lawrence sat back in her chair, tenting her fingers in front of her mouth while staring across the wide desk at Natalya. "She sent you down here to recruit me."

"Yes," Natalya said.

"Little late for that, isn't it?"

"Can you be a little more specific?" Zoya asked, a faint smile playing across her lips.

Lawrence snickered. "I asked for that," she said. "Yes, I can. She's been letting those jackboots run roughshod over this whole facility for months. Downs may know how to feather his nest and cover his ass, but what he knows about shipbuilding wouldn't fill a G-string. Somehow you two got through to her when nobody else could. How?"

"We called her baby ugly to her face and got kicked off the station," Zoya said.

Lawrence nodded a couple of times. "I'd heard that, but now you're back."

"Ms. Pittman decided to stop believing everything she saw on a report and decided to look into a few things on her own," Natalya said.

"That's why she had Davie off the line for two days," Lawrence said, more to herself than anybody else. "He said they were checking inventories and your Ms. Pittman didn't seem too happy about it."

"That's when she called us back. We just got back on station yesterday," Zoya said.

"Typical. Woman gives us all a bad name. Can't make up her mind and even when she does, she doubles back." Lawrence sighed. "Why me?"

"You're the most senior employee still left at the shipyard after Downs got done stripping out the middle management and replacing it with his own crew," Natalya said.

"His own toads, more like." Lawrence practically spat the words onto her desk. "They're the reason you're not going to be shut of Downs for a very long time."

"You think they'll just close ranks?" Zoya asked.

Lawrence nodded her head slowly. "Yes. Everybody will be smiling and pleasant and taking orders from Downs behind her back until Pittman finally screws the pooch and gets replaced."

Natalya grinned and traded glances with Zoya. "So, Marti. You want a new job?"

"I like my current one, thanks." Lawrence patted the arms of her chair. "No stress. No drama. Quiet corner. Close to the tea cart and the bathroom and a long way from the door, if you catch my drift. I'm too old to be looking for another job."

"What's wrong with the current design?" Zoya asked.

"What? That new bird?" Lawrence asked.

Zoya nodded.

"What isn't?" Lawrence snorted. "Stupid shape. Damn foolish power plant setup. Underpowered. Overly long legs. Suicide basket on the way to an early grave for the first generation of pilots who'll get stuck with them."

"Don't sugarcoat it for us, Marti," Natalya said. She felt like her grin might split her face in half.

"How would you fix it?" Zoya asked.

Marti grimaced. "Scrap it. Some things can't be fixed."

"What's wrong with the shape?" Zoya asked.

"You don't need aerodynamic in deep space. It's moderately efficient in terms of skin-to-volume ratio but ridiculously inefficient for doing things where people might want to stand up and walk around. Stupidly expensive to fabricate. Too many curved pieces that need extra supports. I'm not telling you anything you don't already know. You've been aboard," she said. "I may be old but my ears get around."

"Underpowered?" Natalya asked.

"Dumbasses only put one Burleson drive in there and half a power plant. They didn't realize paired Burlesons don't both draw power so they shaved half the power off the top. The drive is rated for something like eighteen or twenty BUs but I'd be surprised to see that crippled bird fly more than six. Empty and with a tail wind." She paused and squinted at Natalya. "Your Scout would be a better design. The original concept design wasn't bad but the project manager took a short swim in vacuum. Still don't know what brain-dead bureaucrat thought they could improve on the design with the design team gone. Downs, probably."

"So why don't you want to help Ms. Pittman fix the design?" Natalya asked.

Lawrence squirmed a bit in her seat and worked her jaw a little. "I'm not a designer. I can look at a design and tell you if it'll work or not, but making them up?" She shook her head. "I'm a mechanic. Give me a blueprint and the tools. Some material. I can build it."

"Your personnel jacket says you were once a line chief," Zoya said.

Lawrence's white eyebrows tried to join the gray hair on her scalp. "You did some homework."

Zoya shrugged. "We're the out-of-town consultants. It's what we do."

Lawrence sighed. "Long time ago. Things changed. I changed. I know a lot about ship construction. Mostly, I know I can't do that job."

Natalya nodded. "I see."

Zoya asked, "Who does?"

Lawrence sighed and her eyes focused somewhere in the distance. "If I wanted a ship built, I'd get Ernst Panko on it," she said after a very long pause.

"You know how to reach him?" Zoya asked.

"Pittman can find him," Lawrence said. "He's somewhere on station. Keeping his head down and his nose clean, I hope."

"What makes him special?" Zoya asked.

"He's been building ships since he was old enough to spin a spanner."

"How old is he now?" Natalya asked, the question slipping out before she knew she was going to ask it.

Lawrence smiled. "A spry old man of thirty-something, I think. I don't know for sure."

"That seems kind of young for a genius shipbuilder," Natalya said. "That's not much older than we are."

"It would have taken anybody else a couple of decades longer to get the reputation," Lawrence said with a grin. "Unless I miss my guess, you two aren't exactly lacking in aptitude or talent."

Natalya sat back in her chair, wondering what Lawrence had seen—or heard—that she'd draw such a conclusion.

"Don't look so surprised," Lawrence said. "I told you. My ears get around and they hear all kinds of noises." She paused and nodded. "Alison Pittman is a lot of things—including a damn poor judge of character for somebody with two decades in HR—but she's big enough to admit when she's wrong and smart enough to try to make it right. From what I hear, you two kids have spanked her with a wake-up call and now here you are bracing me about getting her off the hook. Nope. You're the pair that could take down a full house. I'm surprised you didn't get tapped for project development already."

"We're just the test pilots," Natalya said.

Lawrence laughed. "Keep telling yourself that while you make your way back to the executive suite, dear. Find Panko—or get Pittman's HR team to find him. See what he says. See if you agree with him."

"What if we don't?" Natalya asked.

"Come back and see me again. I'll put out some feelers. See who else may be in-system." She stood. "Let me show you out so you can report back. I have to get on with my day and fight with a supplier over a titanium stock shipment. They always think they can put one over on the little old lady." She tsk-tsked. "Dumbasses."

Chapter Twenty-seven
Pulaski Yards: 2366, May 14

MID-AFTERNOON FOUND them pushing open the door to Rudy's. The place was all but deserted. Sandra emerged from the kitchen carrying a tray full of napkin holders and gave them a nod. "My two favorite test pilots," she said. "Come for your afternoon coffee?" She slipped the tray onto the counter and reached for the coffee pot.

"Actually, we've come for your dishwasher," Natalya said, pulling herself onto one of the stools and resting her arms on the counter top.

"Which one?" Sandra asked. "I've got three."

"Guy named Panko?" Zoya asked.

"Ernst?" Sandra asked. "What do you want with him?"

"We just want to talk to him," Zoya said. "His name came up as a top-shelf ship designer."

Sandra looked back and forth between Natalya and Zoya. "You're kidding, right?"

"Nope," Natalya said. "Is he here?"

Sandra frowned and kept shaking her head. "No," she said. "He's off-shift until the dinner rush. He'll be back around 1800."

"You know anything about him?" Zoya asked.

Sandra snorted. "Not enough, apparently."

"He been with you long?" Natalya asked.

"About a stanyer, I think. He's been on station—well—I don't know. A long time. Always trying to get into the yard and never quite making it." She leaned on the counter. "A ship designer?"

"That's the word," Natalya said. "Why couldn't he get into the yard, if he's that good?"

Sandra shrugged. "Something doesn't add up. I didn't know he had more than basic mechanical skills. He's sure helped me around here more than once. But a ship designer? Don't you have to be an engineer for that?"

"Usually," Zoya said. "And I'll take that coffee."

Sandra pulled a pair of mugs off the rack and filled them from the carafe behind the counter. "There has to be some mistake. I don't think he ever graduated from anything, let alone engineering school."

Natalya looked at Zoya. "Could she have been pulling our legs?"

"She who?" Sandra asked.

"Marti Lawrence," Natalya said. "You know her?"

"Mama Marti? Of course. Everybody on station knows her," Sandra said. "She told you Ernst's a designer?"

"Yeah. Just this morning," Natalya said.

Zoya sipped her coffee and shook her head. "Not exactly."

Natalya looked over at her. "Not exactly?"

Zoya nodded. "What she said was something like 'If I wanted a ship built, I'd get Ernst Panko on it.'"

"That's a subtle distinction," Natalya said. "Was she a lawyer, too?"

"Pittman said he didn't have the qualifications," Zoya said.

"Well, not on the record, but your record doesn't show your qualifications either," Natalya said.

"That's kinda my point. There's qualifications and there's credentials," Zoya said. "You're a lot more qualified than your credentials would indicate. There aren't many people could keep that antique flying."

"Don't be bad-mouthing my ship," Natalya said. A mock scowl furrowed her brow.

Zoya laughed. "You know what I mean."

Natalya nodded. She had to admit that Zoya had a point. "That would explain why he couldn't get into the yard through the front door."

"You know where he lives?" Zoya asked.

Sandra shrugged. "He's got an apartment somewhere in the permanent party area. At least I assume he does. We don't exactly have a lot of places you can live on-station."

"His record in HR lists an address," Zoya said. "Gold Section. Unit fifty-seven."

Sandra frowned. "That can't be right."

Zoya nodded. "That's why we're here. It's not right. There's no Gold Section."

"Not anymore," Sandra said. "That's where the new construction lines are. The company gutted that section and put in the new equipment when they started this project."

"So he might have lived there once?" Natalya asked.

Sandra shrugged. "It wasn't exactly the high-rent district, but yeah. It's entirely possible he moved without notifying the administration."

"When's his shift over?" Zoya asked.

"He's usually done around 2100."

"That his only shift?" Zoya asked.

"No. He does a morning shift that runs into the lunch rush," Sandra said. "He has a couple days off a week. He's off tomorrow, actually."

Zoya took a long drink from her mug and slid the cup back onto the counter. "Thanks."

Natalya looked at Zoya, startled at her abrupt action.

Zoya looked back, her face a flat mask.

"Yeah, thanks, Sandra," Natalya said, taking a last sip of her own coffee, relinquishing the mug, and making a flexing motion with her thumb.

Sandra waved her off. "On the house." She grinned. "I'll gouge you at breakfast tomorrow."

Natalya laughed. "Fair enough." She followed Zoya's retreating form out the door and down the passageway. "Something?" she asked.

"He's not living on-station," Zoya said.

Natalya's brain gave a little hiccup. "Say that again?"

Zoya stopped and looked at Natalya. "I said, 'He's not living on-station.' He can't be or they'd have his corrected address in the database. As soon as he signed into his new place, the system would have reconciled his records."

"Where else would he be living?"

Zoya laughed. "We don't live on-station either."

Natalya put the pieces together and felt her eyes widen. "That's a pretty big leap on scant information."

"Not really. He was probably displaced by the new construction. Maybe he couldn't afford any of the offerings so he found a way to live really, really near the station without being on it."

"In a docking bay?"

"Can you think of any other place?" Zoya asked.

Natalya paused and squinted at Zoya while she thought about it. "If he lived in the shadows between the buildings top-side, that would probably work."

"That assumes he has a ship," Zoya said.

"So does living in a docking bay."

Zoya nodded. "That's my point."

"Too poor to rent a room but he has a ship?"

"Maybe he inherited it."

"Or built it," Natalya said, unable to stop the grin forming on her lips.

"One way to find out," Zoya said.

Chapter Twenty-eight
Pulaski Yards: 2366, May 14

THE SIGN ON RUDY'S said "Closed" but the door wasn't locked when Natalya and Zoya went back at 2030. The door gave its customary bell-tinkle sound as they entered. The dining room overheads were off, but spot lighting around the edges gave enough light to navigate by.

Sandra burst from the kitchen, flapping the door hard against its stop. "We're closed. Oh." She smiled at them. "Wondered if you'd forgotten. Come on back. I'll introduce you." She held the kitchen door open for them and nodded.

"Ernst? Those women are here to talk to you."

They stepped into a steamy galley. The scents of grease and detergent fought for dominance. Heat rolled off the big dishwashing machine rumbling in the corner and a wiry man wearing blue jeans, a black tee, and a soggy apron wrestled with a large pot in the deep sink. He looked up at Sandra's hail and turned to face them. He pulled a towel off his shoulder and dried his hands. He nodded and held out a hand. "Ernst Panko. You are?"

Natalya shook his hand, noting the callouses, the redness. "Natalya Regyri." His handshake felt solid. The strength in his fingers, unmistakable but controlled.

"You're the engineer?" he asked.

"Yeah." Natalya hadn't really known what to expect, but this young-looking ginger with chapped hands didn't match any of the possibilities she'd imagined.

"Zoya Usoko," Zoya said, shaking his hand in turn. "I'm the deckie." She grinned. "We don't want to interrupt but wanted to make sure we caught you."

Panko nodded to each in turn. "Fair enough. You caught me. I've still got half a stan's worth of work to do here." He waved a hand at the pots still in the sink.

"Buy you a beer when you're done?" Natalya asked.

"Prefer coffee, but this place is closed." Panko shrugged and his smile crinkled the corners of his eyes.

"We may know where you can find a good cup," Natalya said.

"You two fly that Scout, right?"

"That's us," Zoya said. "Her ship. I'm just along for the ride."

"I haven't seen a Scout in a very long time. Toss in a tour along with the coffee?"

"Not much to see, but sure," Natalya said.

He grinned. "Gimme half a stan and I'll meet you there."

Natalya glanced at Zoya.

"I'm not going to dodge ya, if that's what you're thinking," he said. "The coffee is enough of a draw but the tour sealed that deal." He glanced at Sandra. "And if what Sandra said is true, I definitely want to hear what you have to say."

PANKO ARRIVED JUST as the coffee maker finished brewing. He grinned as he came through the lock, his head on a swivel as he tried to look everywhere at once. "Man, I wish I could have gotten my hands on one of these."

"You've seen one before?" Natalya asked, leading the way to the galley.

Panko nodded. "Oh, yeah. Back at Mel's. I'd been knocking rocks on the B-97 belt. Good money in those days, but we only got back to civilization about once a month. Just long enough to resupply the ship and back out."

Zoya poured the coffee and handed a mug to Panko.

"Thanks," he said. "There used to be this guy with a Scout. It was in pretty rough shape but he was putting it back together."

Natalya felt her eyebrows climbing her head. "You remember his name?"

Panko sipped the coffee and his gaze focused somewhere else, his eyes squinting. "Reggie, I think. Older guy. Older than me at the time, which probably wasn't that old. Twenty-five stans ago and I've never forgotten it. That got me into shipbuilding."

Zoya raised an eyebrow in Natalya's direction.

"You sure it wasn't Demetri?" Natalya asked.

He frowned and took another sip. He shook his head. "Nope. Not sure. Good coffee, by the way. Thanks."

"So, pardon us for being nosy," Zoya said. "Where do you live?"

He looked back and forth between them. "You must have seen my address."

"Yeah, we did. We're new on-station, but we're not that new. Your address of record doesn't exist anymore," Zoya said.

"Well, technically, it still exists, but it's part of Fabricator Assembly Dock Two now." He offered a sideways smile and shrugged a shoulder.

"But you don't live there," Zoya said.

"I live in a box just off the visitor's dock."

"As in a box box?" Natalya asked. "What, cardboard? Old packing crate?"

He chuckled. "You're not going to narc me out to Pittman, are you?"

"We're going to try to get you a job with Pittman, but your living arrangements are really none of our business," Natalya said. "Except you've got no credentials. We're hoping you have some qualifications."

He took a big slug of coffee and stared at them over his mug for a few heartbeats. "I built my first ship—such as it was—when I was ten. We lived on a mining station over in the Monarch system. Not a lot for a kid to do but fiddle around with parts. I built a little station-hopper. Used it to shuttle myself and loose scrap to the recycle hub there. It wasn't much. A repurposed thruster as main engine. A saddle on the fuel tank. Some CO_2 jets for steerage."

"How'd you navigate?" Zoya asked.

"Mark 1 eyeball and the seat of my pants. Thruster was on a push button. Press it for fire. Let go and it stopped pushing." His gaze unfocused as if he watched the memories in his head. "Learned a lot about thrust, mass, and acceleration." He shrugged. "Stopping was always an adventure. Banged into a lot of hard things before I got the hang of it."

"Your parents let you do this?" Natalya asked. "Mess with rocket parts?"

His smile faded a bit. "Yeah. Well. They worked long hours." He buried his face in his coffee mug and didn't look up for a long time. "By the time I was fifteen, I was working along with them so ..." He shrugged. "Kids grow up fast in the belts."

"Indeed they do." Natalya looked at Zoya. "We promised you a tour. This is the galley."

He laughed. "Just as roomy as I remember."

Natalya led him on a tour of the tiny ship from cockpit to engineering and back to the galley without bringing up his past again. "You want a warm-up on that coffee?" she asked, reaching for the pot.

He shook his head. "Thanks. I'm good." He leaned against the bulkhead and raised his eyebrows. "So? Now you want to tell me why we're here?"

"Marti Lawrence said we should talk to you," Zoya said.

"She did? About what?"

"Ship design and construction. She seemed to think you knew a thing or two."

"They don't want me at the yard."

"Maybe they didn't, but things have changed a bit in the last couple of days," Natalya said.

"Long as Downs is in charge, he won't let anybody else near that new ship."

"Downs isn't in charge anymore." Natalya pulled the key fob from her pocket and held it up. "Wanna see it?"

His eyes widened. "Has anybody told Downs?"

"He's on his way to the main office," Natalya said.

He frowned. "I saw him this afternoon. He didn't look like a man who was moving."

A chill slipped down Natalya's back. "We'll look into it, but in the meantime?" She jiggled the fob in the air. "I'll show you mine if you'll show me yours."

Zoya snickered.

Panko grinned and emptied his mug before putting it in the sink. "Let's go."

Chapter Twenty-nine
Pulaski Yards: 2366, May 14

PANKO'S EYES NARROWED as he surveyed the black hull. "Seriously? Who's getting the kickback on this?"

Zoya hid a smile behind her hand and Natalya snickered. "Don't sugarcoat it for us," she said.

"What's wrong with it?" Zoya asked. "Specifically."

Panko paused before answering. "It's useless. An insignificant detail that adds nothing in terms of real stealth in deep space." He leaned in close to sight along the curved lines. "The curvature might—and I emphasize might—help to reduce the radar return, but radar isn't one of the main sensors in the suite."

Natalya nodded. "Heat signatures."

Panko nodded at her. "Yeah. You can't help but show a heat bloom anytime you maneuver. The hull itself will be considerably warmer than the space around it simply because there's nowhere else for the heat to go than to the hull." He stepped back and scanned the hull with his gaze. "It's pretty, I'll give them that."

"Just not particularly practical?" Zoya asked.

"Curves are hard," Panko said. "Getting everything to line up. To bolt down solid. Sure, surface-to-volume ratios are best in a sphere, and pressure vessels hate square corners, but spheres don't work well with regular solids. Even irregular ones. Like people."

"What would you do differently?" Natalya asked.

"Your Scout is pretty much perfect for the task. More or less rectangular solid. Tanks where you need them. Headroom all the way across the hull, so you're not ducking down to keep from bashing your forehead against the overhead when trying to get to a storage locker against the outer bulkheads. Enough curves to maintain pressure without undue bracing." Panko waved a hand at the black ship perched on its landing struts. "This? It's a romanticized version of what a spaceship should look like when envisioned by somebody who doesn't know what they're doing."

"That's pretty harsh," Natalya said. "I agree with you. Would it make a difference if I told you it was based on a yacht design?"

He pursed his lips and considered. "No. Yachts—small yachts in particular—are designed more for show than performance to begin with. They're not very efficient in terms of useful volume or power-mass ratios."

"Have you seen Ms. Pittman's yacht?" Natalya asked.

He snorted.

"I'll take that as a yes, then." Natalya pulled out her key fob. "Shall we look inside?" She pressed the button and the lock clam-shelled open.

Panko shook his head. "I'd give it three cheddars and a slab of gouda."

"That cheesy?" Zoya asked.

"All it needs is a robot doorman," he said.

"Probably true, but what's wrong with it?" Natalya asked.

"Extra point of failure. How do you get in if you don't have the fob?"

"There's an override panel beside the lock," Zoya said.

"Do you know how to open the lock using it?" Panko asked.

Natalya felt the stab in her gut. "No."

"Can you imagine not knowing the code on your ship?" he asked.

"Point taken," Natalya said. "We need to know that."

"Yeah, and if you do, you don't need the fob," Panko said. "And don't give me the security of logging individuals through the lock. That's just bull. Give everybody their own code and two emergency overrides—one for duress situations to warn people aboard and one for a bogus lock malfunction so it won't open." He shook his head again. "This is just expensive theater."

"And we haven't even gotten inside yet," Natalya said.

"You've not seen this ship before, Ernst?" Zoya asked.

"No. I saw the plans for what it was supposed to be. This doesn't look like I remember."

"They built this in a month," Natalya said.

Ernst frowned at her and looked back at the ship. "I don't think so."

"We saw very different plans for the ship a month ago," Zoya said. "Those were supposed to be the ship in process."

Ernst rubbed a hand across the back of his neck and stared at the deck. "I was here. They laid this keel in February."

Natalya and Zoya shared a glance.

"Fair enough. That's a problem for somebody else to solve," Zoya said. She waved a hand at the open lock. "Shall we?"

Ernst stepped up the ramp, moving slowly like he expected the thing to collapse around him. His head moved in a robotic pattern as he looked up and down, left and right, working systematically over every surface as he went. He turned aft toward engineering and didn't stop at the airtight door. He grunted a couple of times as he made a circuit around the compartment. He stopped at an inspection panel and pulled the cover, peering in at a breaker box. "Missing half its power supply." He glanced over his shoulder at the Burleson. "And half its capacitor." When he got back to the entry, he stopped and glared at the Burleson unit. "If that were a Gemini, it *might* make sense," he said, almost to himself.

"Yeah. That's a nonstarter for me," Natalya said.

"It's dead weight for an in-system transport and completely useless for interstellar," Ernst said. "Downs's work, no doubt."

"You don't like Downs?" Natalya asked.

"Not even a little," Panko said. He pressed his lips together as if to hold back further commentary.

"Wait'll you see the cockpit," Zoya muttered and turned toward the bow.

They only got as far as the galley before Panko stopped. "What was he thinking?" he asked.

"It's been handy for us while we run our checklists," Natalya said.

Panko paused and tilted his head to the side. "It might make sense on the prototypes. I hadn't thought of that." He looked from Natalya to Zoya. "What's going to go in that space for the production runs?"

The women both shrugged and Panko hissed. "Sloppy, sloppy and stupid."

"Who, us?" Natalya asked, grinning at his distress.

He laughed. "No. Downs and his bully boys." He waved a hand at the galley as if to dismiss it. "Somebody's been getting a cut of that action."

"Seems like the way the project went," Natalya said. "It wouldn't be the only nest-feathering activity going on."

Natalya entered the cockpit and stepped to one side to make room for Zoya and Panko. "You'll have to pardon the mess. Maid's day off."

Panko smiled and his eyes crinkled at the corners as his gaze swept the area. He stared at the open bus cabinet for a moment. "Redecorating?"

"There was a short between the display routing bus and the long-range scanner system," Zoya said.

"Burned them out?" Panko asked.

"Nope. Shut them down in time," Zoya said.

Panko raised an eyebrow in her direction. "Somebody had fast reflexes."

Zoya shrugged.

"What would you change in here?" Natalya asked.

Panko braced his shoulders back against a bulkhead and his gaze swept the cockpit in the same kind of near-robot precision he'd started the tour with. "Couch is a monstrosity."

"That was the first kickback we discovered," Natalya said. "Pittman's trying to put a stop to it and get a replacement."

"Good luck with that," Panko said. He continued his examination. After a full tick he shook his head. "Couch is the only thing that stands out. It's supposed to double as bunk?"

"Yeah," Zoya said. "Makes a certain amount of sense for a solo flight. If you're the only one aboard, you don't need much to camp out for a couple of days."

"Agreed," Panko said. "If it's comfortable. That one looks terrible. My back hurts just looking at it."

"It is just as uncomfortable as you imagine," Zoya said. "Maybe worse."

Panko winced. "I didn't see a head."

"We walked by it," Natalya said. "That actually looks like the best-designed compartment on the ship." She led them back down the passageway and swung the door open. "Sanitation facilities."

Panko stepped in and looked it over. "Not bad," he said, his gaze taking in the fixtures and arrangement. "I'll bet this one's a kickback, too."

"Why do you say that?" Zoya asked.

"That shower-sink combo? Stock fitting. Cheap as chips. Buy a container load for next to nothing and sell them in ones and twos to the company for a big markup that still looks reasonable." He shrugged. "That would have been an easy pocket to pick."

"Would you change anything?" Natalya asked.

Panko shrugged. "Don't see anything crazy enough to warrant fixing. Under the deck might be a different story depending on what they used for clean, gray, and waste water connections."

"You willing to tell all this to Ms. Pittman?" Natalya asked.

"The larger question is whether or not she's willing to listen to me."

Natalya met his gaze. "You might be surprised at who she'd listen to these days."

CHAPTER THIRTY
PULASKI YARDS: 2366, MAY 14

ALISON PITTMAN DID not looked pleased. A scowl twisted her face while her fists pressed the top of her desk. Her glare raked Panko from top to bottom with enough heat left over to warm Natalya and Zoya. "You want me to what?"

"Start over," Panko said, seemingly unaffected by the hostile gaze.

"Why?" she asked.

"Because the design as built is not viable," Panko said.

"I got that part," Pittman said. "Why isn't it viable?"

Panko paused for a couple of heartbeats before answering. "It's too expensive to build, contains too many single points of failure, and operational costs will be monstrous once it's in the field."

"You've divined this from a single walk-through in the middle of the night?" She spared a glare for Natalya.

"Yes," Panko said. "The problems are obvious."

"Not to me," Pittman said, her scowl deepening.

"You're too close to it," Panko said. "It's hard to see the problems with a ship you're invested in."

Pittman's face, already red, took on a darker hue. "You're saying I don't know what I'm doing?"

"Not at all." Panko relaxed in his chair, recrossing his legs and smiling. "I have the same problem myself. It takes a lot of practice to step back and be objective on a project with so much invested in it. I'm not invested." He shrugged.

"Why should I believe an over-aged dishwasher?" Pittman asked.

"Alison?" Zoya said, her voice lowered and sounding soft against the hard wall of Pittman's ire. "HR hat?"

Pittman's eyes glittered as she stared at Zoya. "What?" She spit the word as if it burned her tongue.

"You asked us to find somebody who understands design and ship building. Somebody outside of Downs's influence," Zoya said. She nodded at Panko. "Mr. Panko comes highly recommended by at least one person who should know and has proven his knowledge to Natalya and me."

"You're biased because he's just saying what you've already told me." Pittman said. "I'm wearing my HR hat, as you put it, because I've reviewed his record and there's nothing in it to indicate he has any skill or knowledge of basic engineering, let alone ship design and construction."

"I understand," Zoya said. "But name calling?" She raised an eyebrow.

"She's right, you know," Panko said, looking at Zoya. "I'm an over-aged dishwasher with no credentials to speak of." He looked back at Pittman. "What I have is an example of my work, if you'd care to examine it."

Pittman drew back in her chair a bit. "You've never worked in a yard. How can you have an example?"

"I have worked in a yard, actually," Panko said. "Just not a yard that's on my record."

"How convenient."

"Not really," Panko said. "It's been difficult to get people to take me seriously."

"You have a ship that you designed and built," Pittman said.

"Yes. Down in Bay Twenty-Five."

"How do we know it's your work?" Pittman asked.

Panko shrugged. "You'll have to take my word for it."

Pittman snorted. "That's not exactly a great way to prove your credibility."

"It's not, no," Panko said. He paused, then stood, offering his hand across Pittman's desk. "Thank you for your time, Director. I'll show myself out."

Pittman reached across her desk and shook his hand. The heat in her glare dropped a few degrees as he turned on his heel and left.

Pittman stood there staring at the closed door.

"Great job, Alison," Natalya said, slumping in her chair.

Pittman frowned at her. "What was that about? Why did you bring him in here?"

"Is that how you became a good HR director?" Natalya snapped back. "Insulting candidates. Refusing to listen to what they brought to the interview."

Pittman settled into her chair, taking a deep breath. She placed her hands flat on the desk in front of her, staring at them for a few heartbeats. "Yes," she said, biting the word off. "Yes, it is. People lie. They exaggerate. They tell you what they think you want to hear. Their records lie. They get on the job and can't do the first thing." She closed her eyes and took another deep breath. She opened her eyes and looked at Natalya. "I learned early that I could never trust what an applicant said. Only what they do."

"Yet you wouldn't look at what he's done," Zoya said.

Pittman's lips pursed. "I couldn't believe that the ship represents his work experience just because he said so."

"What were Downs's credentials?" Zoya asked.

Pittman blinked as if just waking up. "Impeccable. Advanced degrees in structural engineering. Years of experience with the company designing and building habitats, factories, and even communications stations."

"And a streak of larceny so wide, it borders on breathtaking," Natalya said.

"One instance," Pittman said, stiffening her spine.

"That you know about," Natalya said. "All those projects? Wanna bet he wasn't skimming from them?"

"You forgot murder," Zoya said.

Pittman's eyes widened. "That's a pretty hefty allegation to be tossing around without proof."

Zoya shrugged. "Maybe. Somebody murdered your predecessor. So far Downs is the only one we've discovered who has the motive and opportunity."

"It was ruled an accident," Pittman said.

"Of course. Expert shipbuilder just manages to be in the only lock that accidentally malfunctions and tosses him into vacuum without a suit. Perfectly understandable. Happens every day," Natalya said.

Pittman's head twitched to the side. "Motive?"

Zoya shrugged again. "You think he started skimming when you came on?"

Pittman frowned. "What are you saying? He wasn't the project lead until ..." She paused.

"Until?" Zoya asked, when Pittman didn't continue for too many ticks.

Pittman refocused on Zoya. "Until after Jeffrey's death."

"What was he before?" Zoya asked.

"Head of yard engineering."

"So, he managed the maintenance and expansion of the yard itself?" Natalya asked.

"Precisely. He built the new ways and expanded the habitation section. Upgraded all the life support." Pittman paused and stared at her hands for a moment. "At least that's what's on his record."

"Who took over that job?" Zoya asked

"His second-in-command moved up."

"Why did Downs take over the project?" Natalya asked.

Pittman frowned. "I don't know. He was already project lead when I came over from the main office. I never asked."

"But you checked his credentials," Zoya said.

"Of course."

"You checked ours?" Natalya asked.

"Yes," Pittman said. "Finally."

"But it didn't show Zoya is connected to Usoko Mining."

Pittman started, her brown furrowing in a frown. "It's not in the records."

"Why do you suppose that is?" Natalya asked.

Pittman paused. "Clearly your records are incomplete."

"Possibly. I don't know what records you have access to or what they say about us," Natalya said.

"Or it could just be that my record doesn't reflect the work I did for my grandfather as part of the family business," Zoya said. "I trust it showed that I went to the academy at Port Newmar."

"Yes," Pittman said. "Four stanyers. Graduated with honors and took a job as third mate on a tanker in the High Line. You're still receiving income from a blind trust."

"That's in my record?" Zoya asked. "Nothing about working here in the Toe-Holds?"

"Well, yes. Toe-Holders are notoriously closed-mouthed about what they do and what they've done."

"Yet you question Panko's credentials? A man who's been living in the Toe-Holds his entire life?" Natalya asked.

"His record shows pretty clearly. He's been here on this station for a decade. Drifting from one low-skill, low-paid job to another the whole time."

"Does it show he applied to work in the yard?" Natalya asked.

"Why would it?" Pittman asked.

"Probably wouldn't," Natalya said. "Doesn't mean he didn't or that he hasn't spent the last decade trying to get through the door."

"What about her record?" Zoya glanced at Natalya with a raised eyebrow.

"Port Newmar. Graduated with honors. Took a job as engineering third on a Saltzmann freighter out of Venitz. Citation of merit from TIC a couple of stanyers ago before dropping off the grid. Financials show she worked for Dark Knight Enterprises with no indication of job duties."

"I didn't know they gave me a citation," Natalya said.

"What did you do?" Pittman asked.

"I'm not at liberty to say." Natalya paused, then asked, "So no mention of the murder?"

Zoya coughed into her fist.

Pittman's eyebrows flashed upwards. "Murder?"

Natalya grinned. "And nobody mentioned the rebellion either? How about the mutiny in Dunsany Roads?"

"You want to mention the hijacking while you're at it?" Zoya asked, looking at Natalya.

Natalya nodded. "Best not."

"True." Zoya sat back in her chair and folded her hands on her lap. "Less said, the better."

Pittman edged back from her desk, her frown focused on each of them in turn. "When you're done, you might explain what just happened."

"What?" Natalya said. "You have the records. Clearly none of that appears in our records so none of it happened."

"And since you know we attended the academy—graduating with honors—we couldn't have been involved with anything nefarious, could we?" Zoya asked.

"Because fleet officer is a sign of credibility and trust. Right?" Natalya said.

Pittman scowled. "What's your point?"

"Most of that record is false," Zoya said. "Either missing experience that's occurred outside of official channels or flat-out fabricated."

"I've never worked for Saltzmann," Natalya said.

"I haven't worked on a tanker since I graduated," Zoya said.

"How can that be?" Pittman asked, her frown returning. "It's the official record from High Tortuga. Nobody can change that."

"Nobody had to if they gave it incorrect data to begin with," Zoya said. "Stuff that happened in the family company would be opaque since I was never on the official payroll, never an employee." She paused. "Who set up the trust fund?"

Pittman shrugged. "Blind trust. Somebody in the Toe-Holds set up the trust with a wad of credits. High Tortuga administers it and pays out the interest earnings monthly."

"We should look into that," Natalya said.

Zoya nodded, but focused on Pittman. "Why do you trust us?"

"Who says I do?"

"We're here."

"You're here because I have nobody else with your expertise."

"What expertise?" Zoya asked. "The record only shows we graduated from the academy. That part is true, by the way."

"Well, Dorion hired you because of your small-ship experience."

"Yes, but what *credentials* do we have?" Zoya asked. "There's nothing in our record to indicate we ever saw a small ship."

Pittman gave a short laugh. "You're flying around in one of the smallest commercial vessels there is."

"How do you know that?" Zoya asked. "It's not on file."

Pittman sank back, her eyes wide. "It's *not* on file."

"So? How did Dorion know? How do you know to trust Dorion?" Zoya asked.

"I've known Brian Dorion for decades," Pittman said. "He didn't get to be the head of that division by being stupid." She paused, frowning. "How *did* he know?"

"Maybe Joe told him," Natalya said.

"Joe?" Pittman asked.

"Joe Allen," Natalya said. "I believe he's somewhere up there in the Tortuga hierarchy."

"You met Joe Allen?"

"He and Brian interviewed us back at Dark Knight," Zoya said.

"Well, to be fair, Brian did most of the interviewing. Joe didn't say much," Natalya said.

"So how did he know?" Zoya asked again. "Whoever knew. It wasn't because they searched the records for people with credentials. I suspect the company has a database full of courier and fast-packet crew they could call on."

"Certainly," Pittman said.

"But they hunted us down all the way over on Dark Knight to check us out," Natalya said.

"How did they even know we existed?" Zoya asked.

Pittman sighed and gave them a wry grin. "All right. That horse is dead now." She leaned back in her chair and stared at the overhead. "I could have handled that better," she said.

Natalya bit back her initial response. "It's not too late," she said instead.

"Will he talk to me after that?" Pittman asked, sitting up and looking at Natalya.

"Why do you suppose he's washing dishes at a shipyard?" Natalya asked.

Pittman shrugged. "It's the only job he could get?"

"A man with his skills and talents? Maybe it's the only job he could get *at your shipyard*," Zoya said.

"Alleged skills and talents," Pittman said. "We only have his word for it."

Natalya sighed. "Somebody else in this yard knows. Somebody who's been here longer than Panko. Even CPJCT accepts performance to certify credentials. Why don't you?"

"I haven't seen him perform," Pittman said. She held up a hand as Natalya started to speak. "But I'll remedy that if he'll let me."

"Well, we know where his ship is," Zoya said.

Chapter Thirty-one
Pulaski Yards: 2366, May 14

THEY HAD TO WALK THE entire length of the visitor's docking gallery to get to Bay Twenty-Five.

"He doesn't like neighbors?" Pittman asked when they finally made it to the lock.

"This bay isn't set up for shore ties," Natalya said. "It's the cheapest bay in the yards."

"Low overhead," Zoya said. "As you've pointed out, washing dishes doesn't exactly lend itself to a high-roller lifestyle."

Pittman paused and looked down for a moment, chewing on the corner of her mouth. "Point taken," she said after a few moments.

They pushed on into the bay and found it littered with a collection of small craft: everything from one-person open sleds to battered cargo jacks to a two-seater jitney missing half its forward armorglass. A small ship rested on landing skids off to one side, out of the direct view of the lock. Roughly oblong with wrap-around armorglass at the bow, on its squarish side the ship boasted a mural showing a sunrise from orbit over a ringed planet.

"That's gotta be it," Natalya said.

Zoya nodded.

"How can you be so sure?" Pittman asked.

"First, that looks like the only operational ship in the bay," Natalya said. "Second, it's clearly been inspired by a Scout. Panko all but drooled on the *Peregrine* last night."

"Wonder who his artist is," Zoya said.

"I am."

They turned to find Panko entering the lock behind them, a couple of bags of groceries in each hand.

"You painted that mural?" Pittman asked.

"Yeah. Paint's cheap. Even for an over-aged dishwasher," he said.

Pittman sighed. "I deserved that." She looked Panko in the eye. "I'm sorry, Mr. Panko. That was ... not my best interview ever."

Panko gave her a half smile. "It was far from my worst interview at Pulaski."

She held out a hand. "Can we start again? I'm Alison Pittman and I think you can help me."

Panko looked at the hand, then glanced at Zoya and Natalya. He shook her hand. "Nice to meet you, Ms. Pittman. I think so, too. Can I show you my ship?"

"Yes, please."

PANKO SHOOK HANDS ALL around. "Sorry to have to rush off, but I'm due at Rudy's."

Pittman covered his handshake with her other hand. "Thank you, Mr. Panko. That was most enlightening." She paused. "I really am sorry about before."

"Air out the lock, Ms. Pittman. I hope you'll consider my work here in lieu of more traditional credentials?"

She released his hand and stepped back to admire the mural. "I certainly will."

Panko nodded. "Thanks, Natalya. Zoya. I really need to scoot." He gave a jaunty wave and jogged out of the bay.

Pittman glanced back at Panko's ship for a moment. "Talk to me, ladies."

"What do you want to know?" Natalya asked.

Pittman smiled at her. "You've seen his ship. Is he as legit as he seems?"

Natalya chuckled. "He's way more legit than that."

Zoya nodded. "No question. I have no doubt that he built that ship. It's a one-off, custom job from the deck up and the skin in. He either built it or bought it from a genius and I don't think he has that kind of credit. Nats is right. He took a lot of inspiration from the Scout, but what he did with it is just short of a miracle."

"I noticed he included a gas skimmer. He can probably make his own fuel and water. And it's about a third bigger than a Scout," Natalya said. "That extra size and using only one stateroom gave him the space for his galley and mess deck."

"Why is his mess deck brilliant but the one in the new ship is stupid?" Pittman asked.

"The new ship is a specialist. One pilot. Always underway. Long legs. Short cycles," Natalya said. She pointed at Panko's ship. "That? That's a home. One might presume that Mr. Panko might entertain periodically. He really only seems interested in ship design."

"Did you see that drafting setup in his office?" Zoya asked.

"Dual one-meter screens? How could I miss it?" Natalya asked.

"That wasn't being run off the ship's systems either."

"I saw the unit racked into the bulkhead but didn't recognize the model."

"That was one of Manchester's design computers. I've seen them in the yard at Margary. Supercomputer. Sex on a stick. I'd bet he's got their design suite installed on it too."

"Why do you say that?" Pittman asked.

"The models he had on display. One of them is a standard printer test model Manchester uses to calibrate their designs for printing."

"So? What is that telling you?" Pittman asked.

"He learned to design at a Manchester yard somewhere," Zoya said. "I don't know if it was in the High Line somewhere or if Manchester has a Toe-Hold yard, but you don't just pick up one of those boxes at the flea market."

"They do," Pittman said. "Have a Toe-Hold yard. Two, actually."

"So, you're willing to believe he's a legit designer?" Natalya asked.

Pittman stared at the mural for several moments. "I'm beginning to believe I've been a little hasty." She looked at Natalya. "Why are you so sure he's what he appears to be? You believed it before today's little performance."

"You have to admit, it was a good one," Natalya said, trying not to gloat.

Pittman nodded. "Yes. It was, but you didn't answer the question."

"Honestly, I don't really know. I think it was his enthusiasm."

"No," Zoya said. "It was his anger."

"Anger?" Pittman asked.

"When we showed him the new ship. He was angry that somebody would build a ship like that. Like it was an affront to his sensibilities. If he'd been a faker, I don't know that he'd have been quite so mad."

"Good point," Natalya said. "I mean, when I first saw it I was dismayed. I could see the potential, but it didn't make me angry."

"You seemed mad enough to me," Pittman said.

"I was ready to rip Downs down the middle," Natalya said. "Just because he was such an ass."

"He would have needed a ladder to look any farther down his nose at us than he did," Zoya said. "You could practically hear the 'don't worry your pretty little heads about it' coming off him."

Pittman sighed. "He's out of the picture now. We need to pick up the pieces. Retooling is going to kill our timeline."

"Maybe not," Natalya said.

"Panko wants us to start over," Pittman said. "That what he said in the office this morning."

"Yeah, he did," Zoya said. "But that might not mean what you think it means."

"Explain it slowly with small words an administrator can understand," Pittman said.

Natalya snorted. "That's what Dorion said."

"I've known him a long time," Pittman said.

They started the long walk back up the gallery.

"One of the things that takes time is the ship's shell," Zoya said.

"Yes," Pittman said. "I didn't think the shell was a problem."

"We didn't think of it either," Natalya said. "He pointed out that the curved pieces take a long time to print."

"Do they ever," Pittman said. "The big printers take forever and they're not always accurate."

"If we used a boxier design, that wouldn't be the case," Natalya said.

"The internals could be more stock parts and fewer specialty parts that have to fit in the curved bulkheads," Zoya said. "It would add extra headroom and make the interior of the ship feel roomier."

"How much room does one pilot need?" Pittman asked.

"Enough that they can get up and move around a little bit. Even on a short-cycle mission, periodically getting off the couch matters," Natalya said. "It might be mostly psychological, but there's a physiological value, too. You want the pilots to be alert, and alert means active."

Pittman frowned at the deck as they walked. "So, even if we lose time retooling, we'll make it up by being able to produce the ships faster?"

"That's the theory. We'd have to get Panko to check it. He'd need access to the current production data," Zoya said.

"If I hire him, he'd have all that," Pittman said. "What about the drive?"

"You actually gave us the answer to that one," Natalya said. "Panko confirmed it yesterday."

"I did?" Pittman asked.

"The volume problem of adding a second drive," Zoya said.

"Yeah. It already feels cramped back there," Pittman said. "How do we solve that?"

"Use Geminis like you have on your yacht," Natalya said. "The footprint would be just a bit larger, but the deck template wouldn't change very much, if at all. The larger problem is upgrading the power supply to be able to push the Burleson to its rated capacity."

"What's wrong with the power?"

"It's only half of what the ship needs," Zoya said. "Whoever cut out the second drive halved the power generation and capacitors."

"Well, sure. It's not trying to power two drives," Pittman said.

"That's not how Burleson drives work," Zoya said. "Only one of them fires at a time, drawing down the capacitor charge based on the drive rating, the distance, and the mass of the ship. Without a big enough capacitor, you can only jump as far as the capacitor will let you. Doesn't matter what the drive is rated for if you don't give it enough power to get there."

"And without a big enough fusactor to refill the capacitor, it takes forever to refill it between jumps," Natalya said.

"Well, if we need more generation and storage, aren't we going to need a bigger ship?" Pittman asked.

"Yes," Natalya said, feeling the smile stretch her face. "But you're getting a bigger ship—at least in terms of interior volume— by getting rid of those curved pieces and squaring up the hull."

Pittman's eyes widened. "Will that be enough?"

Natalya shrugged. "We'd need a designer to tell us that."

Pittman smiled. "All right. All right. That horse really is dead. I'll get back to my office and see what I can do about expediting the red tape. You two." She paused. "Security says they're done with the ship. Continue with your pre-flight testing."

"You sure?" Natalya asked.

Pittman nodded. "Yeah. We may not use that ship design, but I want to know if that thing has any more surprises."

"Fair enough," Natalya said.

Pittman headed for the docking gallery. She paused before leaving the bay. "Try to stay out of trouble."

Zoya laughed as Pittman strode down the gallery toward her office.

"Think she's on board?" Natalya asked when Pittman disappeared down a side corridor.

"Hard to tell," Zoya said. "She's at least attracted to him."

Natalya felt her mind go zip. "Are we talking about the same thing? Panko?"

"Yeah. Panko," Zoya said. "She's attracted to him. I think she'll hire him in spite of it."

"She's old enough to be his mother."

"I'm not so sure of that. Ernst's older than thirty-something. He's just well preserved." Zoya grinned at her. "Even if he's not, don't be so judgmental. He's old enough and she's allowed."

Natalya stared at Zoya. "What makes you so sure he's older?"

Zoya held up her right hand and wiggled her fingers. "Academy ring."

Natalya paused, trying to recall his hand. "How'd you notice that?"

"The inlay caught my eye. When we ordered ours, I looked back through the catalog. Class of '49 was the last one to get the gold inlay on the brushed zirconium. Class of '50 onward has silver."

"And you remembered?"

Zoya shrugged. "I wanted gold and they wouldn't let me have it. Tradition. I argued that the gold was more traditional. I took it all the way to the provost."

"What'd she say?"

"They changed to silver because the company didn't make the gold ones anymore."

"Silly you had to go all the way to the provost for that."

"Personally, I think she was blowing smoke up my pants, but I let her get away with it."

"I don't think I've even worn mine since graduation," Natalya said.

"I know I haven't, but it's interesting that he wears his here." Zoya shrugged. "More interesting that his records don't show he was fleet."

Natalya nodded and pondered what else his records didn't show as she keyed open the lock and climbed the ramp into the *Peregrine*.

Chapter Thirty-two
Pulaski Yards: 2366, May 14

ZOYA LOOKED AT THE disassembled bus rack. "Are you sure about this, Nats?"

Natalya stuck her head out of the galley and nodded. "Most of the systems will be the same once Ernst gets done with the redesign. It's pretty likely that anything we discover here would still be useful in that process. Even if it's only 'this part works,' it could inform the next generation."

"I was hoping you'd say something else." Zoya sighed, pulled a screwdriver out of her sleeve pocket, and started the reassembly process.

Natalya went back into the galley and started a fresh pot of coffee before settling in to review her notes on the engineering section. She highlighted the power generation system and capacitor linkages on her schematic and sketched a rough expansion based on Panko's idea of squaring off the hull design.

"Whatcha doin'?" Zoya asked, peering over Natalya's shoulder.

"Just trying to see how much space is taken up and what we might recover with a squarer hull." She glanced up at the coffee maker. "There's fresh coffee."

"Good. I put the main bus cabinet back together and reset the boards to their original positions as best I could. We'll need a new long-range board."

"I hope we're not disturbing evidence," Natalya said.

"Fine time to think of that."

Natalya shrugged. "Pittman's the boss."

Zoya poured two cups of coffee and settled across from Natalya. "And security doesn't think there's anything to investigate, so they won't find any evidence of wrong-doing here."

Natalya picked up her mug and toasted Zoya. "To pretty little heads and the men who have them."

Zoya snorted and held up her mug in return.

Natalya settled back in and continued tracing out where the additional power and capacitor might go based on the larger hull.

"Do we have enough power to get underway?" Zoya asked, looking up from her tablet.

"What? Maneuvering power?"

"Yeah," Zoya said.

"We don't have any fuel to test it, but the specs on maneuvering power are fine. Everything's buried behind the bulkheads and under the decks. Why?"

"These fuel lines seem kinda skimpy to me." She held up her tablet and highlighted an area under the deck in engineering.

Natalya looked up the same view on her ship schematic and zoomed in. She scowled. "That can't be right."

Zoya shrugged. "Wanna dig around under the deck?"

"Not if we have to cut it open," Natalya said, staring at her schematic. "Not yet anyway."

"Well, if they're as small as I think they are, we can probably spit out the lock and get better response," Zoya said.

"I agree and I'm ashamed to admit I didn't catch it," Natalya said. "But there's an inspection hatch in the passageway by the lock." She highlighted another area and showed the display to Zoya. We should be able to get in there. The fuel lines run under the decking, past the ventral maneuvering thrusters, and up to the bow harness. My schematic says they're the same size."

Zoya consulted her screen and nodded. "Mine, too."

"We'll need a hatch puller and I think the nearest one is on the *Peregrine*," Natalya said.

"There isn't one in the engineering locker?" Zoya asked.

"That locker is empty at the moment. Just like practically every other locker, drawer, and cabinet on the ship. We wouldn't have coffee—or mugs to drink it with—if we hadn't brought it with us." Natalya paused. "How are you coming on the idiot lights?"

Zoya shook her head. "I got distracted by the system bus problem. I need to finish that test suite and get back into it. I still think there are more than binary sensors at the end of the cables."

"Can we go to the source, rather than trying to find our way back to it through the system?"

Zoya frowned and stared into the distance for a few moments. "Maybe. I don't know where the sensors got mounted in the various systems. Even if we found one, we have no way of knowing if all the sensors are the same. Some could be legit and others only binary.

And we'd still need to drill into the software application layer to change the displays."

Natalya nodded. "Good points."

Zoya heaved herself out of her chair. "I better get back to it. I'll be glad when they get that couch replaced."

Natalya stood and started down the passageway. "I'll go get the hatch puller and we can check the fuel lines."

Natalya keyed the lock open and walked off the ship, triggering it closed with her fob as she left. She paused as the ramp retracted. She ran a hand over the hull where the lock override must be hidden. Most ships had the override plainly marked but this one's black hull coating masked the location. On one hand, it made some sense to hide it from casual view. On the other, the lack of visible cues scratched Natalya's engineering itch. It just didn't seem right. She couldn't feel any difference as she ran her fingertips back and forth across the hull. The coating had just enough texture to keep her from feeling it. She tried to picture where Carroll had it open, closing her eyes and replaying in her mind how he'd accessed it. He'd just tapped on the hull. She opened her eyes again and reached for the hull just forward of the lock and right at the mid-line of the curve. A firm tap popped the cover open, revealing the keypad inside. She smiled and reached up to close the cover just as a tiny green light pulsed near the top of the compartment.

"What the—?"

She leaned in, standing on tiptoe to get a good look. A tiny module, not much bigger than her little finger, rested across the top edge of the opening. Made from the same material as the key-pad assembly, it blended in almost perfectly. The little green light pulsed again.

She settled back on her heels and examined the keypad. A detail tickled the back of her brain. She pulled out her key fob again and pressed the button to open the lock. A tiny red light pulsed and the lock started to cycle. She felt her eyebrows climbing her forehead.

Zoya stuck her head out and looked at her. "Forget something?"

"Come look at this, would you?"

Zoya hopped down and looked at the keypad just as the green light pulsed. "What am I looking at?"

Natalya pointed. "That seems to be the module that senses the key fob signal. Watch."

She pressed the button again, the red light pulsed twice, and the lock started to cycle closed.

Zoya nodded. "Good hypothesis. What else?"

"What's missing in there?"

"Missing?"

"I'm looking at this and I can't help think there's something that's supposed to be there that isn't."

Zoya hmm'd and took a step back, squinting her eyes a little before looking around at the hull. "Override jack?"

"That's it," Natalya said. "Even the *Peregrine* has an override jack."

Zoya reached into the compartment and plucked the small component out with two fingers, revealing the data jack behind it. She rolled the component over in her hand to show the plug on the back. "Voila."

Natalya pressed the button on her key fob. The lock didn't move. "That answers one question. Odd solution but makes getting rid of the fobs easier."

"Maybe the fobs are only for the yard," Zoya said. "Giving everybody a fob would be easier than trying to add a code for everybody who needed access."

"I suppose," Natalya said. "They'd still have to tell the ship which new codes to allow, unless they gave everybody the same code."

"Unless the codes aren't just strings of digits but solution sets. Pass a value to the lock. If it evaluates to a valid solution, the lock opens," Zoya said. "Heck, even a quick close-field comms blip from the station system would be enough."

Natalya nodded. "That would work, too."

A red light pulsed twice on the unit.

"There must be an off switch somewhere," Natalya said.

Zoya rolled the unit around until she found a tiny slider on the top. She got a fingernail on it and slid it with a soft click. They watched the unit for a tick. "That's probably it," Zoya said, flipping the switch back. The unit pulsed blue a few times before repeating the double-red. She pressed it back into the socket and it pulsed blue once before flashing a double green pulse.

"Looks like key fobs are optional, after all," Natalya said. "All we need is the keypad code."

Zoya pulled out her fob and keyed the lock open. "You were going for the hatch puller?"

Natalya nodded as Zoya slipped back into the ship. The lock closed behind her. Natalya slapped the cover closed over the keypad and headed for the gallery. Something still niggled at the back of her brain. "I'm missing something," she said. "I know it."

A few ticks later she had the inspection hatch pulled up from the deck. She got down on her belly and shined a light into the cramped space below the decking. Zoya stood over her, hands on knees.

"That's a first," Natalya said, reaching in and putting a couple of fingers on one of the tubes running fore and aft. "This looks like the size it should be. Not the size on the blueprint." She rolled to one side. "What do you think?"

Zoya got down on her stomach and reached in. "Blueprint indicated they'd put in twenty-five millimeter tubing, but you're right. That's more like fifty." Zoya looked up at Natalya. "You're the engineer. You tell me."

"I'm pretty sure fifty's what I'm running on the *Peregrine*. At least to the maneuvering thrusters. Kickers are running paired hundreds."

"What are the odds?" Zoya asked.

"That they did it right back there?"

"Yeah," Zoya said, leaning farther into the inspection port. "What all's down here?"

Natalya leaned in beside her. "Well, you know the thruster fuel line. That conduit with the green tape should be the data run going back to engineering. Red is electrical power. Blue is potable water. Sewer and gray water should be off to port." She craned her neck to look under the decking. "Yup."

Zoya followed suit and nodded. "Makes sense. Head and galley are on that side of the ship."

"Exactly," Natalya said, pulling herself back up onto the deck. "We can check the kickers tomorrow. How soon before we can take this baby out for a spin, d'ya think?"

"Well, if we go with the idiot lights, probably as soon as we can get the sensor bus rack rebuilt and fuel aboard," Zoya said. "I didn't see anything else out of whack."

"We'll need that couch replaced," Natalya said.

Zoya nodded. "That's a given. You have a test protocol?"

"I was just going off the original," Natalya said. "We know it would have been enough to catch most of the problems we've found."

Zoya snorted. "I'm not sure we've found them all."

"Me either, but I'm also pretty sure we've done about as much as we can do in terms of checking the ship out before we try to take it out for a test run."

Chapter Thirty-three
Pulaski Yards: 2366, May 28

PANKO STOOD OUTSIDE the lock and glared at Natalya. "Look, you two got me in the door, now you're not going to let me do my job?"

"Ernst, I don't know how to say this any plainer," Natalya said. "You're right. This ship is a catastrophe in the making. I don't trust it enough to jump anywhere in it for fear it wouldn't go where I asked or that it wouldn't get me back. But—" She held up a hand to forestall whatever it was he was about to say. "But local? Sure. If we get it out there and lose power, somebody can come get us. Tow us back and you'll have one more data point to design for in the next iteration."

Panko ran a hand over his forehead and across his cropped hair. "We'll have a new prototype off the ways in a month."

"Great," Natalya said. "It's looking good. I visited this morning. Love the new hull. Your new design is going to be off the ways before they finish the first prototypes for this design."

"Well, yeah," Panko said. "I made them stop construction. We're recycling as much of the material as we can."

"Why don't you want us to take this out?" Zoya asked, sticking her head out of the lock.

"Because you're getting underway in a stupid design, engineered by a plumber, constructed by some great workers being overseen by monkeys. Even the people who built it don't trust it," Panko said.

"We're just going to run it around the system," Natalya said. "Can you give me one concrete reason why we shouldn't test it?"

"It's not safe."

"That's an opinion. Are there any systems that are so badly flawed that they might cause a catastrophic failure?"

"I don't know," Panko said. "That's why I'm against this."

"Noted," Natalya said. "In the absence of any logical reason to scrap the only working model of the ship, I see no reason not to take it out."

Panko took a step forward, his lips pressed together and his fists clenched at his sides. "Look," he said, his voice so low Natalya could barely hear it over the machinery noise in the bay. "Look, the problem is that the only way we can verify that nothing is bugged or booby trapped on that ship is to tear it down and build it over."

"Do you think that's really likely?" Natalya asked.

"Yes," Panko said. "I do. I've watched this project from the sidelines since before it was the gleam in some pirate's eye. I've seen what Downs and his cronies are willing to do to keep their gravy train on the tracks." He paused and looked to Zoya and back again. "They've killed already. More than once. You two have helped me. More than I can ever repay. I can't just stand by and let you take this coffin out for a test run."

"Downs is over at the main office now. He's out of the equation," Natalya said.

"Theoretically, but you know as well as I do that his crew is still here, keeping a low profile, and just biding their time," Panko said.

"He's right about that," Zoya said, stepping out of the ship to stand beside Natalya.

"And this ship was built before he got deported," Panko said. "It's been clear for a long time that Alison Pittman was put here to fail. I have to admit that she's doing a lot better lately, but think of it this way. If the ship blows up, that's going to be a slap in the face for the project."

"If it doesn't, it will be a small success in the face of a sea of disaster," Natalya said.

Panko sighed and looked around the bay as if seeking the answer he needed to convince them. Or perhaps the question he needed to ask. "What's the harm in waiting another month? We'll have the new bird off the ways by then."

"What do we do in the meantime?" Natalya asked. "We've spent the better part of two weeks tearing this ship apart, examining everything to make sure it works as designed. Now what? We cool our jets in the docking bay until the next ship comes off the ways and we have to do it all again?"

"I'm fine with that. Take up a hobby. Learn to play the piano," Panko said. "Sandra still needs a dishwasher. Pay sucks but the job is exhausting. You won't have much time to worry about the new ship there." He grinned. "I'll put in a good word for you."

Natalya looked at Zoya. "Jump in here any time."

"He has a point, Nats."

"I know that. I still think we can learn a lot by actually firing up the kickers and tottering around the system for a few stans, just to see if it works. If it does, then we know the base design is sound and we can work to improve it in the new hulls. If it doesn't, we'll know what to look for in the new flights. Other than the ship blowing up and tossing us into the cold, there's not that much risk."

"You have to admit, that's a pretty big risk," Zoya said.

"It's not going to blow up," Natalya said.

"Can you think of a better way to hamstring Alison, though?" Zoya asked.

"Than blowing up the ship?" Natalya sighed and stared at the deck. "Not really. No."

Panko stepped forward. "So, meet me halfway. Sleep on it. If you still feel like you want to go out for a limited test run, I'll support it."

"How limited?" Natalya said.

"No jumps. Stay within a quarter million kilometers of the yard. We take a chase ship out so we can get you off there in a moment's notice."

"You think we need baby-sitting?" Natalya asked. "You think we're going to run off with the ship you don't even like?"

He sighed and shook his head. "Did I say that?"

"No," Natalya said with a sigh of her own. "No, you just said you're going to send out a herd-dog to keep track of us."

Panko clenched his teeth and took several deep breaths. "Take it or I'll recycle that ship this afternoon."

Natalya rolled her jaw around a bit, glanced at Zoya who returned the glance with raised eyebrows, and finally said, "I'll take it. We get underway day after tomorrow."

"Submit a test plan," Panko said.

Natalya sighed. "All right. If I'd known what a pain in the ass you were going to be about this, I'd never have brought it up."

Panko grinned. "There's more where that came from. If you'll excuse me, I need to see a man about some loose ends before you take this thing out and crash it into a planet or something."

"As if," Natalya said.

Panko left the bay and Zoya sidled up to Natalya. "What was that all about?"

"What?"

"The chase ship. There was always going to be a chase ship."

"I know," Natalya said. "Standard operating procedure."

"Then why fight him on it?"

"Because he's cute when he's frustrated?"

Both of Zoya's eyebrows rose well up her forehead before she frowned. "You're kidding."

"Yeah," Natalya said. "I wanted him to focus on that and forget all the other obstacles he could have thrown in our faces."

"That's pretty sneaky. What did you think he'd try?"

"I thought he might try to play the 'I'm the new boss' card—or maybe just drag it to the scrap heap and slag it while we weren't looking."

Zoya pursed her lips and nodded slowly. "I could see him doing either of those."

"He's agreed to the test now, so I don't think he'll pull anything underhanded," Natalya said. "I also wanted to see how far he'd go to get his way. What kind of logical arguments he'd try."

"And?"

"He and Pittman are going to get this program back on track and shock the living hell out of whoever thinks it should fail."

Zoya laughed. "I hope you're right."

CHAPTER THIRTY-FOUR
PULASKI YARDS: 2366, MAY 29

NATALYA STOOD UP FROM the table and arched her back, stretching out all the muscles that felt like they'd been permanently crippled. "All right," she said. "Are we set on this?"

Zoya nodded. "You're the engineer, but I agree that these are the systems that make the most sense to test."

Panko sat back in his seat and tossed a stylus onto the table. "I hate to admit it, but this looks good. The handling profile isn't going to be that much different so testing out the kickers and maneuvering thrusters makes sense. The data backbone will be virtually identical on the next gen but with the upgraded fusactors and capacitors, the power grid will have a lot more pushing it. Knowing how much these crippled systems can do will be handy." He nodded. "Chase ship will be ready at 0800."

"What are you using to chase?" Zoya asked.

Panko gave her a small grin. "I happen to know of a ship I can use."

"You can't tow us with that," Zoya said.

"Wanna bet?" Panko asked.

"No bet," Natalya said. "I didn't see the specs on your ship, but if you say it'll tow this bird, I believe you."

"It's got about twice as much muscle as the *Peregrine*," Panko said. "And nearly double the mass of this bird. It may not be a tug now, but it used to be. It'll be enough to get you back to the dock."

Zoya looked at Natalya.

Natalya nodded. "I'm good."

"If she's good, I'm good," Zoya said.

"Then we're go for tomorrow," Panko said. "When do you want to start pre-flight?"

"We can start at 0700," Natalya said. "Time enough to get some breakfast at Rudy's. We'll be back in time for lunch."

MORNING FOUND NATALYA prowling around the *Peregrine* much earlier than she'd intended. Having given up on sleep, she'd crawled out of her bunk at 0430 and made coffee. She settled into the pilot's couch in the cockpit and stared mindlessly out at the docking bay beyond the armorglass. Pittman's yacht gleamed in the bay's stark lighting, a bright toy ship surrounded by drab working vessels. A lone pilot wandered across the bay and clambered into a dinged-up shuttle sitting on the far side of the bay. Warning lights strobed red moments before the small ship rose off its pad, lifting out of the bay and into the departure lock above. Its maneuvering thrusters made a quiet roar, which quickly cut off as the lock closed behind it.

"I thought I smelled coffee," Zoya said, sticking her head into the cockpit. "Did you leave any for me?"

Natalya held up her mug. "Only the first cup from the pot. Should be plenty."

Zoya rummaged about in the tiny galley for a few moments before settling into the navigator's couch beside Natalya. "You couldn't sleep either?"

Natalya shook her head. "Not sure why. Nerved up."

"Scared?"

"No. I don't think so. Mostly excited to be the first pilot to fly the new ship."

"Um," Zoya said, drawing the syllable out and looking sideways at Natalya.

Natalya returned the side-eyed stare. "First crew. You'll be the first pilot," she said. "You know what I mean. We'll be the first to fly the new couriers."

Zoya sipped her coffee before replying. "Well, technically, the first courier prototype."

Natalya looked at her and found Zoya staring straight ahead, her coffee mug propped in front of her face with both hands, elbows on the couch's arms. "I suppose that's true. That ship is never going to be a courier, is it."

"No, it's not. I think you're right about the test, for whatever that's worth," Zoya said. There are more systems that won't change than will. If we find something wrong, I'm sure Ernst can fix it in the next generation."

"I can't believe he's come so far so fast."

Zoya smiled. "Say what you will about Alison. Once she buys in, she's all the way in."

"Think they'll hook up?"

"Naw. Ernst would, probably, but Alison's too hung up on appearances." Zoya took another sip. "Probably wise given their relative positions on the org chart."

Natalya sighed. "True." She sipped her coffee for a few ticks, savoring the quiet, enjoying the easy companionship. "You ever get lonely?"

Zoya turned her head to stare at Natalya. "Lonely? We're joined at the hip."

A short laugh escaped Natalya's lips. "You know. A relationship? With somebody?"

"You propositioning?" Zoya's brows drew together. "You're more sister than lover material."

Zoya's serious expression made Natalya giggle. "Not with me. Sister. With somebody special?"

Zoya grinned and looked back out over the docking bay. She sipped again. "Sometimes," she said. "We've been a bit isolated of late. Scrambling for work. So much happening. Haven't really had time to think about it much." She glanced at Natalya. "You?"

Natalya shrugged a shoulder. "Just seeing Panko and Pittman maneuvering."

"They're cute together," Zoya said. "I still think it could happen."

"How soon before Rudy's opens?"

Zoya lifted her elbow out of the way to look at the console in front of her. "Another stan, maybe. You thinking of getting an early bite?"

"I could eat."

Zoya settled back again. "What you really want to do is go run the pre-flight checklist."

Natalya grinned over at her. "You know me too well."

"We're not going to jump that ship," Zoya frowned across the narrow space. "Right?"

Natalya chuckled. "Not in this lifetime. We could probably do a short jump. One BU. Maybe two. With our luck? The drive will toast on the very first try and we'll be stuck there."

"It's not like it would be a meaningful test," Zoya said. "Ernst's going to replace that whole drive chain."

Natalya nodded. "Shall we go over?"

Zoya grinned. "Thought you'd never ask." She tossed her mug back and drained the last of the coffee. "Let's take our softsuits and see how far we can get before breakfast."

"I like the way you think. We can stash them aboard, run the first half of the checklist, then go eat."

"That's what I was thinking," Zoya said. "Suit up after breakfast and run the rest of the pre-flight while we wait for Ernst and his magic bus."

Natalya chuckled. "Let's do it."

CHAPTER THIRTY-FIVE
PULASKI YARDS: 2366, MAY 30

NATALYA FELT A LOT calmer once she started pulling her gear together. "You got the first aid kit?"

Zoya held up the oblong box. "Suit sealer and all the basics. Should I take the forensics kit?"

"The one Blanchard gave you after Siren?"

"Yeah. Not sure what we'd use it for but with the number of fingers that have been in that pie, it might be useful," Zoya said.

"Throw it in a carry-all. We can tie it all down in engineering."

She pulled her softsuit off its rack and spread it on her bunk, rolling it up into a bulky package she could tuck under her arm. It wouldn't give her much protection from sharp edges but could make a difference if the ship lost pressure. She flexed her fingers, thinking about trying to use the console with the gloves on. It was doable, but she wouldn't win any speed challenges with it. She went aft to engineering and grabbed her small tool kit and a deck puller from the storage locker.

"You think you'll need that?" Zoya asked, eyeing the heavy clamp.

"I hope not," Natalya said. "But if we get out there and need it, we're really going to need it."

"Good point." Zoya looked around at all the gear they'd amassed. "Can we carry all this?"

Natalya grimaced. "We can but it would take three trips, probably."

"We should have done this yesterday."

"We should have had the yard do this last month," Natalya said. "With their own supplies."

"Would you trust it?" Zoya asked.

Natalya chuckled. "Probably not." She looked around at all the gear. "We could wear the suits over. The rest of it isn't that much."

Zoya pursed her lips and did another quick visual scan. "You're right."

Within a couple of ticks they'd pulled the suits on, strapped in the extra air canisters, and grabbed their loose gear. The walk to Bay Two had Natalya sweating from the exertion of moving in a suit designed for zero-gee and carrying almost half her body weight in tools.

"We shoulda gotten a grav-pallet," Zoya said, puffing along beside her.

"We're almost there."

They staggered into the bay before Natalya realized her mistake. "The fob is in my pocket."

Zoya looked at her, bemusement coloring her expression. "Your shipsuit pocket?"

Natalya nodded.

They both started giggling and dropped their gear beside the ship.

"We got it this far," Zoya said and started stripping out of her softsuit.

Natalya wasn't far behind, stepping clear of her own softsuit before patting her pockets to find the fob.

It only took a few more ticks to get their gear stowed in the lockers in the tiny engineering space, locking the tool kit and deck puller into the tool bay and stowing the rest of their kit in a cupboard in the galley.

"Where shall we start?" Zoya asked settling on the couch.

"Start at the beginning," Natalya said. "We can bring everything up until we get to the engines."

"We can put them on ready standby, can't we?"

Natalya shrugged. "We could but I'd feel better if they were cold if we're not going to be here to watch them." She looked at Zoya. "We are still going to Rudy's for breakfast, aren't we?"

"I hope so," Zoya said. "I've worked up an appetite."

"They open in a stan. Let's see how far we get."

Natalya pulled the pre-flight checklist up on her tablet and started reading down through the long and detailed protocol for bringing up all the systems in the tiny ship. She plopped down in the jumpseat right behind Zoya's couch—reading the instruction while Zoya worked the console, bringing up displays, checking status, adjusting settings, and lighting up all the on-board systems together for the first time.

"Ships status markers green for power, gravity, and atmosphere," Natalya said, after what seemed like a week-long checklist.

"Three greens. Power, gravity, and atmo," Zoya said.

Natalya nodded. "That's it for now. Next steps bring up the kickers and Rudy's should be open."

"Did we really make that list?"

"Yeah. We've got another half a stan or so to go after we eat."

"Should we make a pot of coffee for when we get back?" Zoya asked.

"Let's hold off for now," Natalya said. Her stomach rumbled loud enough that Zoya looked at her. "I'm hungry." Natalya shrugged and stood, stashing her tablet and rolling her shoulders to stretch her back. "I think the pre-flight will take longer than the actual first flight."

"What are we scheduled for?" Zoya asked. "Two stans?"

"Yeah and we're already at almost that on the checklist."

Natalya keyed the lock closed behind them as they left the ship. "What are we missing?"

Zoya fell into step as they strolled up the gallery toward Rudy's. "There's so much that could go wrong. We've checked everything we could think of but what haven't we thought of?"

Natalya sighed. "Short of tearing the ship down and reassembling it?"

"I thought of that," Zoya said. "The problem is that it could be anywhere."

"Ernst would probably just as soon we scrapped this ship like he did the others," Natalya said.

"He may have a point."

"Yeah. That's the part that bothers me."

"That he's right?" Zoya asked, looking at Natalya with wide eyes.

"No," Natalya said. "Somebody's trying to get this project killed—or at least removed from Pittman's management."

Zoya bit her lip and nodded. "You're wondering what they'll do now that Downs is out and Panko is in?"

"Yeah." Natalya pulled the door open and waved Zoya in ahead of her. "That's why I want to take this ship out."

Natalya stepped into the busy morning rush and let the door close behind her. Sandra waved from behind the counter and pointed at a table near the kitchen doors. Natalya waved back and started to thread her way through the throng.

"You want to make it a target?" Zoya asked.

"It might flush out some of the unknown actors."

"Why would they waste time on this ship now that the whole wing has been scrubbed?"

"You ever hear the expression 'pecked to death by ducks'?" Natalya asked.

They settled into their seats and Sandra plunked the coffee down. "The usual?" she asked.

"Yes, please," Natalya said.

Zoya nodded, coffee already halfway to her mouth.

Sandra sped off, dispensing coffee, grabbing dirty dishes, and joking with the regulars.

"Sounds unpleasant," Zoya said.

"I think they'll chip away at the current management team with dozens of small, awkward failures. Just like they have so far by throwing away the valid design that everybody outside of the yard is expecting and replacing it with this monstrosity. Now that we've scotched that, they'll need to do something else. Nothing big enough to attract attention but a small failing."

"You ever been pecked by a duck?" Zoya asked.

"No. Have you?"

"Yeah. Pop-pop took us on holiday to Dunsany Roads when I was little. He wanted to show us a planet up close."

Natalya took a sip of her coffee. "Oh, Margary. Not much by way of planets there."

"Yeah. Bunch of us. Aunts, uncles, cousins. Made quite a parade of it."

"Fun?"

"It was pretty shocking for kids raised in cans. That's a lot of open sky and walking outside without a suit." Zoya grinned, her gaze focused on the past. "One of the cousins wouldn't leave the shuttle for the longest time. Once he got coaxed out, he didn't want to go back."

Natalya chuckled. "Figures, right?"

Zoya nodded. "They have this big park in the middle of Dunsany City. Lots of grass, trees. A big pond. I thought it was a lake. It looked huge."

Sandra slipped dishes onto the table and refilled coffee. "Good?" she asked.

"Thanks," Zoya said.

"Good," Natalya said.

She saluted them with the coffee carafe and continued on her way.

"Anyway. Pop-pop doled out food. Little pellet things for us to feed the ducks at this pond. It was apparently the thing to do."

"Uh, oh."

"Yeah. I didn't throw the food far enough away and the next thing I know, I've got these big-ass birds all around me. I held out one of the kibbles instead of throwing it and three ducks came at me. I dropped everything and ran. Damn ducks chased me halfway across the park."

"How old were you?"

"Seven." Zoya dug into her breakfast. "Anyway, I tripped and the ducks ran right up over me and started rooting around in my hair, my clothes. I kept trying to swat them away. One of them started pecking at my hands and arms before Pop-pop caught up with me and shooed them away."

"That must have been terrifying," Natalya said.

"It was." Zoya took a swig of coffee. "I've never heard that saying, but I can tell you from firsthand experience. Being pecked by ducks hurts like hell."

Natalya nodded. "I figured it must."

"Then why do you want to get pecked?" Zoya asked.

"I'm willing to be the peckee if we can catch some of those little peckers who are screwing with this project." Natalya gave breakfast her full attention as Zoya tried to stifle a giggle.

Chapter Thirty-six
Pulaski Yards: 2366, May 30

SANDRA CAME BY TO CLEAR away the dirty dishes and offered the tab. "You two really taking that ship out today?"

Natalya nodded. "That's the plan. Why?"

Sandra loaded up her tray. "Just everybody's talking about it. Half of them think it's a waste of time what with the new ships coming off the ways next month."

"What do the other half think?" Zoya asked.

"It's going to blow up and you're both going to die in a fire." Sandra smirked. "I may just be a glorified waitress, but I don't think there's that much oxygen where you're going."

"The explosion would probably kill us before the fire could," Zoya said.

Natalya nodded. "Yeah. Any kind of explosive would probably ruin our day long before a little fire."

Sandra looked back and forth between them, her mouth slightly open and her brow furrowed. "You're not joking," she said after a few moments.

"We hope we are," Natalya said. "But there's a chance that things could go horribly wrong out there."

"Not like we're going very far on this first run," Zoya said. "But there's always the chance."

Sandra rested the loaded tray on the edge of the table and stared at them. "You're crazy. Both of you."

Natalya shrugged. "Probably, but I plan on being back in time for dinner."

"Any scuttlebutt on Downs?" Zoya asked.

"Tony?" Sandra asked. "I wouldn't hear it anyway. His crews stopped coming in here a few weeks ago. Right after he got kicked off the station."

"Who's running his gang now?" Natalya asked.

"My ex-dishwasher, I thought," Sandra said with a little shake of her head. "At least I assume that's what Ernst's doing. If not directly, then he's appointed a yard boss for the project. That's what Tony's official title was as far as I know."

"Yeah," Natalya said. "He had the new prototype all laid out on his computer before we ever met him."

"He's had a lot of time to think about it," Sandra said. "He wasn't known to hang out on-station and get into trouble."

"It'll still be a full-time job refining the design to take advantage of as much of the current design as he can," Natalya said. "Which is why we need to take this poor doomed prototype out for a spin around the system. At least we can verify what works and what doesn't."

Sandra hefted the tray and started toward the kitchen. "You two be careful out there. I'll expect to see you for dinner. The special's gonna be fried chicken."

"Thanks," Natalya said to Sandra's retreating back.

They slipped out of the booth and threaded their way through the boisterous breakfast crowd. The hubbub of clinking cutlery and conversations shouted across small tables diminished as soon as the door closed behind them.

"Think it'll blow up?" Zoya asked, casting a sideways glance at Natalya.

"Nope. At least not right away, and it won't be something that screams of sabotage. If it's sabotaged, whoever has done it really can't afford to do something too blatant."

Chapter Thirty-seven
Pulaski Yards: 2366, May 30

AS SOON AS SHE ENTERED the ship, Natalya keyed the coffeemaker on. "We're going to need this, I think."

Zoya grinned. "Probably, but it'll be hard to drink in our softsuits."

"We've still got at least a stan of pre-flight to get through and
Ernst won't be ready to escort us for at least two."

"Well, sooner started, sooner done," Zoya said, settling into the
couch and pulling up the window with the checklist on it. "You
ready?"

Natalya pulled out her tablet and accessed her copy of the list.
"We left off at the start of engine initialization."

"Roger that. Requesting clearance from station control for engine initialization," Zoya said.

They ticked items off the list for a stan before getting to releasing
the station ties and starting the maneuvering engines.

Zoya looked up. "That was too smooth."

"We did a lot of homework to make it smooth," Natalya said.
"How many times have we run through these systems? Ten? Twenty?"

"At least," Zoya said. She clambered out of the couch and lifted
her arms above her head, arching her back in a stretch. "Time for
suits."

Natalya nodded and walked aft to the engine room where they'd
left the softsuits. She sent off a quick message to Ernst before
stashing her tablet in the outside pocket of her suit and starting
the process of getting the suit on over her clothes.

"This is gonna suck if we have to pee," Zoya said.

"That's the only problem with having coffee now." Natalya shrugged. "This flight's only scheduled for half a stan. I can hold it that long."

Zoya finished pulling the flexible material up her torso, stuffed her arms into the sleeves, and sealed the front. "It's the 'scheduled' bit that gives me pause."

"How so?"

"Everything we've done on this ship since we got here has taken longer than we expected. What makes you think it's going to change now?"

Natalya snorted. "A good point, but history is a poor predictor of the future."

"Murphy was an optimist," Zoya said, settling her gloves into place and fussing with the connections. "I hate flying in these things."

"Safety first," Natalya said.

"I know. I know," Zoya said. "They're supposed to be easy to type in and they work with the touch screens, but I still feel fat-fingered with them on."

"You could leave them off until we're ready to leave the dock," Natalya said.

Zoya grimaced. "May as well get used to it."

Natalya's tablet bipped, the sound coming through her helmet speakers as well as her pocket. "At least that still works." She read the message. "It's Ernst. He's undocking now and will meet us outside as soon as we're ready."

Zoya's face folded into a deep frown as she started pulling her gloves off and fumbling with her helmet.

"What?" Natalya asked.

"Why is it I never have to go until I'm locked into one of these suits?"

Natalya started to laugh but thought better of it and started getting out of her own suit.

"You, too?" Zoya asked.

"I'm pretty sure that I'll have to as soon as you're done," Natalya said. "Just figured I'd save some time."

Zoya finished peeling her suit off again and stepped into the head. "The glamorous life of test pilots."

"We could have asked for hardsuits," Natalya said. "At least those have plumbing."

Zoya shuddered and closed the door. "I hate that more," she said, her voice muffled by panel.

Natalya nodded, even though Zoya couldn't see. "I'm with you there."

It didn't take them long to get back into their softsuits and settle once more into the pre-flight checklist.

"I show 'Request clearance for embarkation' as our next task," Natalya said, buckling into the jump seat.

Zoya settled into the couch and strapped down. She checked her console. "Concur. Requesting clearance." She typed a few lines and settled into her seat.

"Secure shore ties," Natalya said.

Zoya nodded, her helmet bobbing with the motion. "Securing shore ties." She pulled a new window up and clicked some icons on the screen. "Shore ties secured." The console flashed an incoming message. "Station local grants clearance for departure."

"Establish voice comms with local traffic," Natalya said.

Zoya synced her suit's comm relay with the ship. "Pulaski Local, *Echo One*, ready for departure. Over."

"*Echo One*, Pulaski Local. You're cleared to the inner markers. Your escort is waiting just outside the lock. Over."

"Thank you, Pulaski Local. *Echo One*, out." Zoya grabbed the navigational control sticks and picked the ship up from the deck. She lifted until the ship was even with the departure lock and spun the ship on its vertical axis until the ship lined up with the open door. A few deft shots from the thrusters moved them into the lock. She signaled the lock controls to cycle and shook out her hands while they waited for the air to be pumped out.

"How's she handle?" Natalya asked.

"Can't really tell," Zoya said. "She came up smoothly enough. She's really responsive, but not skittish. She seems to go where I want her to go."

The red light above the exit turned green and the outer door opened.

"Here we go," Zoya said, pulsing the throttles to push the tiny ship into space for the first time under her own power.

Panko's ship rested on-station just inside the inner markers.

Zoya brought up a secondary receiver and keyed the channel open. "*Serendipity*, *Echo One*. Over."

"*Echo One*, *Serendipity*. Looking good. Over."

"*Serendipity*, we're cleared for inner markers. Over."

"Roger that, *Echo One*. *Serendipity* standing by."

Zoya steered toward the inner markers and the outbound lane markers flipped up on the pilot's HUD. "I really like this heads-up display," Zoya said. "Reminds me of the shuttles back at Port Newmar."

"It does. I wonder if it's the same software," Natalya said.

"It might be an updated version," Zoya said. "The shuttles only had the path indicators. This has velocity, heading, and delta-vee right where I can see it."

"But the ship's status indicators are idiot lights," Natalya said. "You'd think anybody who could do that would know enough to use actual instrumentation on the critical sensors."

"I'd bet we can thank our friend Tony Downs for this one. It seems like something he'd do to put his stamp on this project."

Natalya snickered. "Like peeing in the corners to mark his territory?"

Zoya snorted. "That's a visual I could have done without." She eased the throttles up to build a little momentum and then zeroed them to kill their acceleration, relying on the maneuvering thrusters to get them through the inner rank of ship traffic around the station. "Whoever put this package together got it right as far as I can tell," she said. "Other than the idiot lights, maneuvering feels terrific."

"I wonder why Alison didn't come to see us off," Natalya said.

"Maybe she didn't think it was significant. With Ernst out here with us, somebody has to be riding herd on the new ships in the yard. She's probably up to her armpits in administrivia right about now."

The scent inside the softsuits cloyed at the back of Natalya's throat. She swallowed hard and wished for a cup of coffee to wash it away. "I hate these suits."

Zoya glanced back at her. "Something wrong?"

"No, but the plastic smell mixed with the antiseptic wash they use on them always sticks in my throat."

"Yeah, you'd think they'd find something better. I got used to them on the barges. The smell inside the ships wasn't anything to write home about either, so getting stuffed into a softsuit for a few stans didn't seem like such a big deal."

"Coming up on outer markers," Natalya said.

"I got it." Zoya tossed a grin over her shoulder before turning to the console again. "Just because you're sitting behind me doesn't mean you can be a backseat driver."

"Just reading the next item on our test protocol."

"Uh huh." Zoya said. She keyed her mic. "Pulaski Local, *Echo One* on the outer markers. Over."

"*Echo One*, Local. You are cleared for open space. Please shift to Pulaski Traffic on channel foxtrot four. Over."

"Local, *Echo One*. Roger cleared for open space. Shifting to channel foxtrot four. Out." Zoya reset the comms array to the correct channel and keyed her mic again. "Pulaski Traffic, *Echo

One outbound at outer markers and shifting from Pulaski Local. Over."

"*Echo One*, Pulaski Traffic. Welcome to the party. We've got two heavy mixed freight inbound and a tanker outbound. Over."

"Pulaski Traffic, *Echo One*. Roger that. We'll keep a scanner on them. Out." Zoya flipped through the short- and long-range scanners. "Doesn't look like anybody's going to be in our way this trip."

"Let's get through our checklist and get this bird back to the nest, shall we?"

"What's next? Fifty percent throttle for ten seconds?"

"Yeah. How's our vector?" Natalya asked.

"Clear for a few million kilometers. I'll notify Ernst." She tapped the mic on. "*Serendipity, Echo One*. Go for fifty percent throttle for ten seconds. Over."

"*Echo One, Serendipity*. We'll try to keep up."

Zoya snorted and tapped the throttles forward. A low rumble came from the back of the ship as the rocket nozzles thrummed with the passage of superheated gas. In just a few seconds, she tapped the throttles back to zero. "Velocity just over a kilometer a second." She checked a couple of screens. "I can't tell how much fuel we used."

"In spaceship terms, we're barely moving," Natalya said.

"We haven't actually tried moving very fast."

"True. We have a series of sensor and system tests next."

Zoya opened her mic again. "Serendipity, *Echo One*. Still with us?"

"*Echo One*, did you move yet?"

A movement outside the cockpit drew Natalya's attention and she saw the bow of Ernst Panko's ship sliding into view. The ship flipped vertically and she could see Ernst Panko in the cockpit of the other ship. *Serendipity* flew backward and upside down relative to *Echo One*. He waved and grinned.

"*Echo One, Serendipity*. You need any help with the calibration tests?"

"*Serendipity, Echo One*. Just watch your vector, showoff," Zoya said and flipped him a rude one-fingered gesture.

The low rumble started up from aft again and Zoya's gaze jerked back to her console as the ship scooted ahead.

Panko's ship slipped out of the way just enough for them to slide by.

"*Echo One, Serendipity*. Everything all right?"

"*Serendipity, Echo One*. Stand by."

"What's happening, Zee?" Natalya asked.

"The engines have come back online but my throttles still say zero. I can't shut them down because my controls all say they're already off."

Natalya slapped the release on her seat belts. "Tell Ernst. I'm going aft to see if I can kill the pumps."

Zoya keyed the mic but Natalya didn't wait to hear what she said.

She arrowed down the passageway and tried to remember which of the circuits controlled the fuel pumps. She pulled the dogging lever on the airtight door and almost stumbled over the threshold in her hurry to get into the engine compartment. The noise from the rocket motors just under the flooring vibrated through the soles of her boots. She pulled the breaker panel door open and peered at the panel. She found the label for the main fuel pumps and pulled the tab to interrupt the power.

The rumbling under her feet grew louder and the vibrations from the deck got stronger.

"Zee, that didn't work."

"Try something else, Nats. We're burning through fuel fast. If we don't get them off soon, we won't have enough thrust to turn around."

"I'm thinking." Natalya pulled her tablet out of its holster and scrolled to the engineering schematic. She'd looked at it a hundred times in the past weeks but a runaway auxiliary wasn't one of the scenarios she'd thought of. "It's always the things you don't expect," she said.

"What?" Zoya asked.

"Nothing. Talking to myself." She ran a finger along the circuitry diagrams and tried to think of some other way to shut off the engines.

"You sure you hit the right breaker?" Zoya asked, the stress in her voice obvious in her tone and compressed speech.

Natalya looked at the breaker panel again. "No," she said. "I only tried the one labeled as fuel pumps."

"We're running up to the point of no return. If you got a rabbit in that hat, now would be a good time to pull it out."

Natalya reached in and pulled the main breaker which disconnected the ship's power generation system from the ship. The engines cut out almost immediately—along with the lights, life support, and the ship's computers.

"Well, they're off," Zoya said. "So is everything else."

"One thing at a time," Natalya said. "We're still going too fast and without power we have no maneuvering thrusters, do we?"

"Ship systems are on batteries for a bit," Zoya said. "Not sure that'll give us enough push to flip the ship."

"I can try turning power back on," Natalya said.

"Comms are out," Zoya said.

"Is Ernst still with us?"

"Can't see him. Last time I checked the short-range he was keeping up. I can't tell now."

"Let me see if I can isolate this," Natalya said. She ran a gloved finger down the rows of breakers, flipping every one of them off before putting the main breaker back on. "I'm going to turn on breakers one at a time, until and unless the kickers fire up."

"Roger that."

Natalya started at the top and worked down and across, feeding power to the ship's systems one at a time. She got to the end of the first column. "How're we doing?"

"The short-range sensors came back online. Ernst's about a hundred kilometers aft. Still no maneuvering power."

"As soon as we get some, flip the ship."

"Way ahead of you. Keep hitting them."

Halfway down the middle column, the engines coughed under the deck. Natalya flipped the breaker out. "That's the one," she said.

"I'm guessing it's not labeled as main engine," Zoya said.

"Nope. It's labeled galley outlets."

"We won't be needing coffee until we get back anyway. Keep clicking. I don't have comms or navigation back but the main computer system seems to be trying to come back."

Natalya skipped the faulty breaker and kept clicking down the line until everything was on. "Computer back?" she asked. "I'm done."

"Come look. Something's not right."

Natalya made her way forward again and leaned over the back of the couch. The console showed a blinking prompt. Natalya reached over Zoya and held down the two upper-corner keys at once. "It worked before," she said. The screen blanked and then a boot screen popped up. "Here she comes."

"I hope we have comms at least," Zoya said.

"I hope we have nav," Natalya said. "If we can flip the ship, we can start decelerating."

The system finished booting but instead of the normal console interface, a single line of text appeared in the middle of the screen.

"How long can you hold your breath?"

"What the hell does that mean?" Zoya asked.

A sharp ping-ping sound from the passageway and Natalya's entire body went cold inside her suit. She dove for her jump seat as the inner lock door opened on its own. "Hold on," she said, reaching for the seat belts. She got the first one buckled before the outer lock door opened and the air in the ship ripped past her, nearly dragging her out of her seat. She managed to lock the second belt, pulled them both tight and got a good grip on them.

The buffeting stopped almost as quickly as it began. Natalya heard her heart beating in her ears and the rasps of her breath as she struggled to get herself under control. The quiet sounds of Zoya's breathing came over the suit speakers. It sounded loud and just a bit ragged in the silence of vacuum.

"Now we know how the lock can open direct to space," Zoya said.

"The inner door doesn't have to open against the pressure if it's already open," Natalya said. "You all right?"

"Yeah," Zoya said, her hands moving across the console. "The engine room still has pressure but the rest of the ship, such as it is, seems to be without atmosphere."

"Do you have navigation?" Natalya asked.

Zoya flipped through a few screens before grabbing the handles. She twisted the stick and the star field outside the armorglass started to pan sideways as the ship twisted on its vertical axis. "Looks like we have some. Not sure how valuable that is, given we can't get to the breaker panel now." She stopped the rotation when the ship had turned completely around.

Panko's ship was little more than a tiny collection of winking lights.

"There's Ernst," Natalya said. "You have scanners?"

"Short-range is up. Long-range is still out." Zoya flipped a couple of screens and keyed the radio on. "*Serendipity, Echo One.* Over."

"*Echo One, Serendipity.* You have no idea how happy I am to hear your voice. How can I help?"

"Main thruster runaway boosted us out. We've got it shut off and restored basic navigation but we can't slow down or change this vector very much. Short-range scanners are up, but long-range is down. Over."

"*Echo One, Serendipity.* Roger that. It looked like you lost hull integrity. The telemetry data has shut off. Are you both all right? Over."

"*Serendipity, Echo One.* The lock decided to open on its own. Vented all our atmosphere. We're both in softsuits and strapped down. I think the only thing we broke is the coffee maker. I don't know if it's rated for vacuum. Over."

"Roger, *Echo One*. I suspect the plumbing might be a bit damaged as well. How long can you stay in the suits? Over."

"Longer than we want to, *Serendipity*. Five stans at least." Zoya looked at Natalya with a raised eyebrow.

Natalya checked her suit's gauges and nodded.

"*Serendipity*, *Echo One*. At least five, possibly more depending on how energetic we need to be. Over."

"Roger, *Echo One*. This is your show. How do you want to handle this? Over."

"Stand by, *Serendipity*." Zoya tapped a few keys and looked at Natalya. "Well?"

"Somebody needs to pay for this," Natalya said. "I don't think whoever it was expected us to be wearing suits or be strapped in."

"Probably not."

"We really need to get this ship back to the yard if we can," Natalya said. "I don't want to die doing it."

Zoya nodded. "I can get behind that. The question is how to get the ship under control."

"The lock has a manual override. If we can manually latch one or both of the doors, we might be able to pressurize the ship again," Natalya said. "Once we can get into the engine room, I can reset that breaker so the engine will fire to slow us down. If we can slow down enough, Ernst can probably tow us—or have the yard send out a tug—but we're really moving fast at this point."

"Agreed," Zoya said. "Bring Ernst in on it?"

Natalya nodded. "See what he suggests."

Zoya keyed the communications system back on. "*Serendipity*, *Echo One*. Over."

"Go ahead, *Echo One*."

"We want to get the ship back to dock but at this point securing the ship and towing it back seems the wisest course. Over"

"Roger that, *Echo One*. If we can match vectors, I can tow you but I can get a yard tug on its way out as backup. Any idea how to cut that velocity? The tug could probably brake you, but you'll be halfway to Mel's place by the time he could get here at this rate. Over."

"*Serendipity*, *Echo One*. We're working on it. We're going to use the manual override on the lock and try to repressurize. If we can get into the engine room, we can restart the main engines. Unfortunately, the door opens the wrong way. Over."

They stared at each other for a long moment before Panko replied. "Roger that, *Echo One*. Can you get to the manual override? Over."

"Nats is heading that way now. We'll know in a tick or so, *Serendipity*. *Echo One*, out."

Natalya pulled the releases on her belts and stood. The grav plates kept her on the deck but she still felt exposed. "Zee, make a note to add a safety line to our kit."

"Just take it slow and easy."

"I'm going for the inner door. If we can get some pressure behind it, that trick won't work again."

Natalya eased down the passageway as far as the head. She gave the open lock a wide berth as she went by it and felt marginally safer with the open door between her and eternity. She knelt on the deck and popped the hatch cover off the manual override. It took her more than a few heartbeats before she got her gloved fingers around the control and gave it a tentative tug.

The airlock door moved almost imperceptibly.

"I'm at the control. It seems to be connected."

"That's the good news," Zoya said. "Is there bad news?"

Natalya gave the lever a solid pull and the door closed a small fraction. She pushed the lever back to the starting position and pulled again. The door moved another small fraction. "Yeah. This is going to take a while."

"Take your time. Done right is always faster than done twice."

"Your grandmother?" Natalya asked.

"Yup."

Natalya chuckled and worked the small handle back and forth, each pull inching the door closer to the latch.

After a few long ticks, Zoya said, "We may have a problem."

"Another problem?" Natalya asked. "Or just a complication in the current one?"

"I think this would classify as a new one. The Burleson drive just came online. The capacitor has a full charge and the navigation system is set for a programmed jump."

"Let Ernst know and send him the coordinates," Natalya said, leaning back on her haunches to give her knees a break. "I take it you can't stop the drive?"

"Nope. I'm locked out of that routine."

Natalya cursed under her breath. "Do we abandon ship and let it go?"

Zoya sighed. "I don't know. *Serendipity*, *Echo One*. If we jump, can you catch us? Over."

"*Echo One, Serendipity.* I'm trying to match your velocity now but I'm still a thousand kilometers behind you. Why?"

"*Serendipity, Echo One.* The Burleson drive just lit up. The capacitor is full and there's a destination programmed into the navigation system that we didn't put there. Over."

"*Echo One, Serendipity.* I can track the ship. I don't know that I can track two softsuits on their own at this range. How are you coming on the lock door?"

"Natalya's working the latch but it's slow. Over."

"Roger, *Echo One.* I'm trying to catch up with you but it's going to be a few ticks yet. Over."

"Zee?" Natalya said.

"Go ahead, Nats."

"If we jump we'll still be going as fast as the ship. If the Burleson punches a hole before Ernst catches up, we'll just follow the ship through and we won't be able to get back aboard without a lifeline or a thruster."

Zoya sighed. "You're right."

Natalya got back to work, pumping the handle as fast as she could, watching the door close one tiny fraction at a time.

"*Serendipity, Echo One.* We can't jump until you're alongside and can take us aboard. Over."

"*Echo One, Serendipity.* Yeah. I was just considering that. If I don't get there in time, you'll drift through with the ship and I'd never find you. Hang on. I'm trying to match vectors with you. Over."

"Zoya, how far is that jump targeting?" Natalya asked.

"Four BUs."

"What's there?"

"It's not showing up in the database," Zoya said. "Could be nothing. Could be the middle of a star."

Natalya sat back on her heels again and wished she could scratch her nose. "Four BUs will have enough error in it to keep us from jumping directly into a star. At least on purpose."

"I'm more worried about jumping into a dust cloud at this speed," Zoya said.

"That would be bad."

"How you coming on the door?" Zoya asked.

"It's closing but slow—" Natalya bit down on the word as the lock door swung shut. "It just closed on its own," she said.

Zoya whooped. "We have hull integrity back. I'm pumping atmosphere as fast as I can."

Natalya pushed up off the deck and grabbed the handle for the airtight door into engineering. "I'm at the door." From that vantage point she could look down the short passageway amidships and see the back of Zoya's head.

"Fifty percent and climbing," Zoya said.

Natalya could feel the difference in the way her suit moved and could make out some sounds from outside her suit.

"Seventy percent."

Natalya pulled the dogging lever but couldn't get enough shoulder behind the door to move it. "I only need a crack here."

"Eighty percent," Zoya said. "It's going to be close. There's not that much left in the air reserves."

Natalya tried not to do the math in her head. A kilogram per square centimeter times too many square centimeters. She wedged herself against the door and pressed. The only thing that gave was her shoulder. She backed off before she ripped her suit.

"Ninety percent," Zoya said. "More than enough to breathe."

"Still too much pressure on the inside of that door. Whose idea was this door anyway?" Natalya felt inordinately angry. "I just need a wedge. Something I can get a seam open with."

"Butter knife in the galley?" Zoya asked.

"Don't think it's got the tensile strength to hold up to the pounding I'd need to give it to drive it into the door jamb."

"Ninety-five."

"This door is about a meter and a half by two. That's what? Three thousand square centimeters?" Natalya slumped against the door. "We'll need better than ninety-eight to break the seal."

"That's all we got," Zoya said. "Ninety-eight percent. The tanks are dry now. We can generate a bit more over time but I don't know how much time we have."

Natalya saw Zoya pull her seat belts off and climb out of the couch. "What are you doing?"

"Maybe both of us can put enough muscle behind it to get it started," Zoya said.

Natalya shifted herself to give Zoya as much room on the edge of the door as possible. They both got a firm grip on the dogging handle and braced themselves as best they could on the decking.

Zoya nodded and began a count. "One. Two. Three."

They threw their combined weight against the door, straining against the pressure inside, pushing with their legs. And promptly fell forward into the engine room as they broke the airtight seal, letting the pressure equalize almost instantly.

"Must not have been full pressure in here," Zoya said. "Can't say I'm surprised."

Natalya scrambled to untangle herself from Zoya and dove for the breaker box. She yanked the door open and reached for the main breaker.

"Wait!" Zoya said, scrambling to her feet. "We just jumped."

CHAPTER THIRTY-EIGHT
DEEP DARK: 2366, MAY 30

ZOYA DISAPPEARED DOWN the passage while Natalya examined the drive. Nothing seemed out of place. The indicators showed the capacitor was three-quarters depleted with at least five stans before it would be fully charged. She checked the gauge on her suit. Barely four stans left.

"We're somewhere," Zoya said. "Astrogation scan shows us four-ish BUs from Ravaine. The database doesn't indicate this place was ever surveyed."

"We need to start heading back as fast as possible," Natalya said. "What's your suit status?"

"Just about four stans," Zoya said. "We're almost five before the capacitor is fully charged."

"We've got to unbutton," Natalya said. "The ship's life support can handle us, which should buy us some time."

"Pressure's coming up slowly. The environmental system seems to be replenishing the atmosphere, but I don't know what it's using as a source."

Natalya unlatched her helmet and let it fall back on its hinge. "It's probably scavenging from the potable water," she said. "Shall I fire up the thrusters?"

"Better. We need to get moving in the other direction if we're going to try to jump home." Zoya's voice sounded a bit tinny after listening to it in the speakers in her helmet.

Natalya pulled the breaker panel open and flipped the breaker on. Nothing happened. "Breaker's on. Do you have control of the thrusters?"

In a couple of heartbeats the ship rumbled with the vibrations from the rocket nozzles. "Yeah. For the moment, they're working."

Natalya made her way back to the jump seat. She gave the air a sniff. "Smells like something burned. You seeing any systems alerts?"

Zoya flipped through console screens. "Nothing showing up. No alerts. No warnings." She flipped through a couple of windows. "We have long-range scan back. Nothing showing."

"I was hoping we'd see Ernst jump in," Natalya said.

"He may already be here but out of range. I don't know what our jump error was but if one of us was short and the other long, we could both be here but too far away to see each other. It could take a few stans for a radio message or long-range scanner pulse to make the round trip. We're only reliable out to a million kilometers."

"*Serendipity* wouldn't make much of a return blip at that range," Natalya said.

Zoya nodded, but clicked on her mic. "*Serendipity, Echo One,* over." She turned off the mic and made sure the speakers were patched into the cockpit. "Maybe he'll hear us and reply before we jump out."

Natalya buckled in, her mind racing through the various problems. "We need to make sure that lock door doesn't pop open again," she said.

"You have any ideas?" Zoya said, her fingers dancing over the console's keyboard. "I think I can plot a jump back but the question is whether or not we'll have any main thruster fuel left when we get there."

"Do we have enough air for a full day?" Natalya asked.

Zoya sighed and pulled up a window. "Scrubbers are new so we're good there. You're right about the potable water being broken down for oxygen. The hydrogen's going to the maneuvering thrusters. We should have enough for a day. Maybe a little more."

"So a day plus about four stans with the suits. We really need to make sure that lock doesn't play any more games."

"Too bad we can't weld it shut," Zoya said.

"What if we cycle the lock?" Natalya asked. "Suck all the air back into the ship so it's vacuum in the lock itself. The door can't open against atmosphere with the vacuum on the outside."

"That might work, but what stops the system from just pumping the air back in again?" Zoya asked.

Natalya nodded. "Yeah. That's a flaw. Is there pressure in the lock now?"

Zoya consulted a window. "Looks like it."

Natalya grinned. "Hold that thought." She jogged back down the passageway and retrieved her tool kit from the locker in the engine room. She opened the inner lock door and popped an inspection hatch off the bulkhead inside the lock itself. In a matter of a couple of ticks she dropped a component into her kit and snapped the hatch back on. As she left the lock, she pushed the door closed and dogged it down, resting her weight on the dogging handle. She took her tool kit back to the cockpit and settled into the jump seat. "That'll do it."

Zoya glanced back. "What'd you do?"

Natalya opened the tool box and pulled out a fist-sized hunk of metal and wires, holding it up for Zoya to see. "Actuator solenoid."

Zoya grinned. "Shall I bring up the thrusters a bit more?"

"Are we carving down the vector?"

Zoya nodded, consulting a readout on her screen. "It's slow but it's steady."

"We're still almost five stans before the capacitor is full," Natalya said. "How much do we need to jump back?"

"We only used three-quarters of it on the jump out, so if we can get at least half of it back, it should be enough for a return jump—assuming it doesn't decide to jump us somewhere else."

"So, in theory we could jump in just over two and half stans?"

Zoya nodded. "That's what the system says."

"Can you program a burn that will get us moving in that direction in two stans?"

Zoya frowned. "It should be possible. We were only pushing hard for a few ticks before you got the thrusters shut off."

"Fuel?"

Zoya's hands tumbled across the keyboard for a few moments. "We used a lot but there's still almost half a tank. Lemme run some numbers." After a tick she nodded. "If we can keep control of the thrusters, we should be able to goose them up to reverse our current vector. That's assuming the thrust is properly calibrated for this ship. It was one of the things we were supposed to do before we left Ravaine."

"So we're guessing based on uncalibrated readings?"

Zoya gave a little shrug. "They're not too far off. Our velocity vector seemed pretty near the estimated value for the low-speed test."

"Can we do some calibration out here in the Dark?"

"Probably not," Zoya said. "We don't have anything close enough to bounce a ranging signal against and we don't have enough velocity to read direct from the stars."

Natalya sighed. "I was afraid of that. I was hoping I overlooked something."

"The only thing we haven't considered is that this spot in the Deep Dark doesn't appear to have been charted. We could get punched by a high-velocity rock at any moment," Zoya said.

Natalya's heart sank into her stomach. "We better burn, then."

Zoya's only reply was to goose the throttle up a notch. The rumbling from aft picked up as the large thrusters pushed harder to stop their momentum and begin to nudge them in the other direction.

Natalya went into the galley to survey the damage. The coffee maker had apparently survived its immersion in vacuum. "Shall I try to make some coffee?" she asked.

"Check to see if the head survived, first," Zoya said. "We went before we left, but I don't really feel like pissing down my own leg if I can help it."

Natalya chuckled, grabbed her tool kit and headed aft. "If it's broken, I don't have any spare parts to speak of."

"You'll figure it out," Zoya said. "I got faith in ya."

Natalya snorted and headed down the passageway.

NATALYA STRAPPED INTO the jump seat, taking care to hold her mug level while maneuvering the straps. "We got lucky with the head."

Zoya held her own cup up to her face and nodded. "Somebody knows this ship isn't spec'd out correctly."

"How do you figure?" Natalya asked.

"You saw the specs. How far do you think the ship had enough power for?"

Natalya took a sip and thought about it. "Five with a tailwind," she said.

"I agree. The official line is that she can jump twenty."

Natalya nodded, granting the point. "The drive is rated high enough for that but the capacitor doesn't have the power to deliver it."

"Exactly," Zoya said. "And what happens if the capacitor doesn't have enough power to make the programmed jump?"

"It shuts down," Natalya said. She stared at Zoya, realizing the implication. "Somebody wanted the ship to jump and be lost after the decompression pulled the pilot out."

"I don't think so," Zoya said.

"What then?"

Zoya looked over her shoulder at Natalya. "If they weren't wearing a suit, they'd have died. The ship jumped out to avoid having the evidence found."

"Why close the lock?" Natalya asked. "It's not like the ship couldn't jump with the door open."

Zoya shrugged. "Locked room mystery if the ship ever got found?"

"So whoever programmed this horror show planned on killing the test pilot, then throwing the ship out into the Deep Dark to hide the evidence?" Natalya asked.

"Who was supposed to be the target? Us or somebody else?"

"It's us," Natalya said. "We've been on this for weeks now. This goes way beyond embarrassing the management to take over the project."

Zoya sat and stared at the console for several long moments. "What if it's not that simple?"

"How so?"

"What if somebody wanted to steal the ship?"

"Whatever for? It's a mess," Natalya said. "Any half-assed designer with a shred of knowledge could do better than this in a weekend."

"I don't know, but if the goal was to make the ship disappear— along with the crew—it seems odd that they'd jump us into a rel- atively clear spot in the Deep Dark."

"Not like they could jump us into a star," Natalya said.

"That's true but there are a lot of dirty places out here. Many of them marked on the charts. Why not jump there where the probability that the ship would be destroyed is greater?"

Natalya let that idea play around between her ears for a bit. "What if it's not the ship? What if it's something on it?"

"Like what?"

"The comms array?" Natalya asked.

"Not installed," Zoya said. "What good would it do anybody if it were? Not like they can't bribe somebody to give them one. There are thousands of them flying around out here."

"Nothing makes sense," Natalya said.

"I can't argue that," Zoya said. She consulted her console. "We're just coming up on the reverse vector. Capacitor will be at two-thirds power in a bit over a stan."

"We'll have enough velocity to go through the hole?"

"Yeah. We won't be going very fast, but fast enough to slip through a hole."

"You jumping direct to Ravaine?" Natalya asked.

"That's what we agreed, wasn't it?"

Natalya nodded.

The long-range scan bipped.

Zoya pulled up the display and swore. "Somebody's closing on us."

"Some*body* or some*thing*?" Natalya asked.

"Judging from the deceleration profile, it's manned. They're coming fast and braking hard. They'll close on us in under a stan."

"We need to be somewhere else by then," Natalya said.

"Much as I'd like to know who's out there, I agree. Now if there's only someplace we can jump to." Zoya flipped through the astrogation data and pulled in a sector barely one BU away from the shipyard. "Yeah. We actually jumped to it on our way back from that last messenger run. Right distance. Fairly large region. Clean."

"Will we have enough capacitor to jump before they catch us?" Natalya asked.

Zoya worried her lower lip between her front teeth as she tapped keys and stared at the console. "Yes. Should have. Probably."

"You're not filling me with confidence, Zee."

Zoya tapped keys and ran a finger over the screen. "Yeah. Programmed. Jumping in half a stan."

They sat, waiting. Watching the capacitor fill, even as the fuel for the thruster fuel level fell.

"We going to make it in time?" Natalya asked.

Zoya shrugged. "Can't tell. They've changed their deceleration profile. They're not slowing as fast so they'll be here sooner."

"Won't do them much good if they're going too fast when they go by."

"Good point," Zoya said after staring into space for a couple of ticks. "We've got the juice now. Course is locked in. When do you want to go?"

"Now is as good a time as any to find out if the drive still works."

Zoya grinned and punched the button.

Chapter Thirty-nine
Deep Dark: 2366, May 30

NATALYA PEERED THROUGH the armorglass at the sprinkling of stars. "Did we jump?"

Zoya nodded, her hands busy on the console. "Yeah. At least here we have the advantage of knowing we're not likely to get hit by a stray rock."

"Or picked up by somebody who wants the ship more than us. Anything on long-range?"

"Not yet," Zoya said. "Short-range shows a Barbell pulling away from us. Vector's consistent with a jump out of Ravaine."

"How close are we to jumping home?" Natalya asked.

Zoya keyed an engine burn on the navigation panel. "We'll be ready to go by the time we're lined up." She consulted a meter on the panel. "No more than a stan."

Natalya settle back in her jumpseat and pondered. "Something doesn't feel right."

"Oh?" Zoya asked, glancing back over her shoulder. "What's giving you that feeling? The runaway thrusters? The airlock opening us to vacuum? Or maybe the preprogrammed jump to nowhere?"

"Where's Ernst? He knew where we were jumping. Why didn't he follow?"

Zoya frowned. "Good question. He was on track. Only had to charge his capacitor."

"*Echo One, Serendipity.* Over."

Natalya felt her eyes widen and Zoya snapped back to her console. "*Serendipity, Echo One.* Over."

"*Echo One,* I'm so glad to hear your voice. I have you on the edge of my long-range. I'm maneuvering to match vectors now. Over."

Zoya shifted windows and nodded. "Roger, *Serendipity*. I see you. We're lining up for a jump home. Over."

"*Echo One*, *Serendipity*. I should be alongside in a few stans. Do you have enough atmosphere to wait for me? We should talk before you jump back. Over."

Zoya glanced back at Natalya. "As long as the water holds out, we're good with oxygen. Probably as much as another whole day."

"Scrubbers will be fine for that amount of time. We're a little short on food, but I can live on coffee that long," Natalya said. "I'd really like to know what happened after we jumped and how he happens to be here now."

"You can't suspect him of sabotaging the ship. He tried to talk us out of testing it." Zoya frowned. "You're the only one who thought this was a good idea."

"I still think it is," Natalya said, rubbing at her nose. "Or can be if we can use this to smoke out the rats at the yard. Ernst might be able to help with that."

"What are you thinking?" Zoya asked.

"If we jump back in with Ernst, his arrival can mask our jump. He can probably get us into a docking bay without anybody being the wiser."

"And once we're there?" Zoya asked.

"I think there's an advantage in having people think we're lost in the Deep Dark." Natalya said. "I want to know how Downs did this—and who's behind him."

"What good will that do?" Zoya asked. "Does Alison strike you as the kind of administrator who'd space somebody?"

Natalya slumped back into her jump seat. "Not really." She paused. "But sabotage of a critical project, attempted murder? That's going to be harder to sweep under the rug than a little skimming off the construction budget."

"*Echo One*, *Serendipity*. I should be alongside in four stans. Over."

Natalya nodded. "My gut says wait."

"My gut says it's been a long time since breakfast, but all right." Zoya keyed her mic. "Roger, *Serendipity*. We'll wait. You got any sandwiches? We left without lunch. Over."

"Roger, *Echo One*." Panko's voice sounded like he was trying not to laugh. "Lunch is on me. *Serendipity*, out."

"Now what?" Zoya asked.

"You want me to spell you so you can stretch your legs?" Natalya asked.

"It seems like a lot longer but we've only been out here a few stans," Zoya said. "I'm good for the moment."

Natalya settled back in her seat and rested her head against the bulkhead behind her. "Fair enough," she said. "Wake me if something else happens."

"If something else happens, I'm guessing you'll know as soon as I do," Zoya said with a chuckle.

Natalya closed her eyes but she didn't sleep. Her mind kept working on the problem. Somebody wanted them dead and she wanted to know why.

THE *SERENDIPITY* CLOSED to within a kilometer of the ship, only its marker lights visible against the starry background. At that distance, it appeared no larger than a child's toy. "*Echo One, Serendipity*, over."

"Go ahead, *Serendipity*," Zoya said.

"One moment, *Echo One*."

Natalya sat and watched for several long moments. "What's he doing?" she asked.

Zoya frowned at her console and flipped a couple of toggles. "He's painting us with microwave. I'm bringing up the tight beam receiver."

"At this range he may fry it before we link it up," Natalya said.

"As long as he doesn't fry us ..." Zoya said.

The speakers crackled a couple of times before Panko's voice became clear as the tight beam system synced up. "*Serendipity*, over."

Zoya patched the mic into the tight beam array. "*Serendipity, Echo One*."

"*Echo One, Serendipity*. What's your status? Over."

"*Serendipity, Echo One*. We've got atmosphere for about twelve stans. It's going to be tight docking unless we get very lucky with the jump. The system is peeling oxygen out of the potable water and that tank is almost full, so we could—theoretically—last a lot longer. The mains have a bit of fuel. We had enough to reverse course and we're saving some for docking. The ship itself is mostly intact. Over."

"Roger, *Echo One*. I can tow you if it comes to that. You need food? Over."

"*Serendipity, Echo One*. We're fine for the moment, but it's been a long time since breakfast. Over."

"Roger, *Echo One*. How do you want to handle this? Over."

Zoya looked at Natalya. "You want to talk to him?"

Natalya nodded and Zoya transferred the mic to Natalya's suit. She pointed.

"*Serendipity, Echo One.* Over."

"Go ahead, Echo One."

"*Serendipity, Echo One.* Are your towing grapples good enough to jump us into Ravaine? Over."

Zoya's eyebrows rose as the pause lengthened.

"Roger, *Echo One.* I believe so. As long as the ship doesn't pull any new maneuvers. Over."

"*Serendipity, Echo One.* Perfect. Get us snugged in and we'll pull the breakers and come aboard. Over."

"Roger, that, *Echo One.* You can tell me about it when you get here. *Serendipity*, out."

"*Echo One*, out."

"We're not going to jump ourselves?" Zoya asked.

"We have no idea if the ship will even make another jump," Natalya said with a shrug. "This way we'll be aboard his ship with food and water. We can get out of these suits and try to keep the ship from doing anything else strange."

Zoya snorted and turned to her console as Panko's ship closed on them.

"*Echo One, Serendipity.* Ready to latch on. Over."

"*Serendipity, Echo One.* Ready when you are. Over."

Natalya watched over Zoya's shoulder as the other ship linked up the towing harness. The engineering schematic showed *Serendipity* as slightly larger while the towing fields snugged the prototype to the ship's ventral side.

"*Echo One, Serendipity.* I show full latch on my end. Over."

"Roger, *Serendipity.* Same here. We're ready to come aboard. Do you have a line you can toss us? Over."

"I can do better than that, *Echo One.* Secure the ship and stand by at the lock. Over"

"Will do, *Serendipity. Echo One*, out."

Zoya pulled her seat belts off and stood, flipping her helmet into place while Natalya worked her way aft. She stopped with her hand on the breaker.

"Zoya? We can't actually pull the main breaker."

"Why?"

"Airlock needs power to cycle."

Zoya stuck her helmeted head into engineering. "Of course. Shoulda thought of that."

Natalya started flipping switches on the main components on the small room. Rather than pull the breakers, she disabled each device in turn starting with the kickers and moving methodically through engineering until she got to the Burleson drive. "That should keep us mostly out of trouble," she said.

Zoya nodded and went back to the lock.

Natalya joined her in the small cubby, squeezing in beside her and closing the inner door.

Movement outside the port made her flinch before she saw Ernst Panko's helmeted face peering in from outside. He gave a thumbs-up signal and held up a D-ring with a lifeline.

Their suit speakers crackled for a moment before Ernst's voice came through. "Ready out here. Open her up."

Zoya keyed the lock and the air pressure dropped, deadening the sound around them until the only thing Natalya heard was the sound of her own breathing and the blood rushing through her ears. When the pressure dropped to vacuum level, Zoya opened the outer door and joined Ernst hanging on the life line like laundry hung out to dry.

Ernst handed her a short chunk of line connecting two D-links and then passed another to Natalya.

They each clipped a link to their suits and the other around the lifeline.

Natalya stepped out of the lock and closed the door behind her.

Ernst led them up the line, hand over hand into the slightly larger lock on the *Serendipity*. There was room—barely—for the three of them and Ernst keyed the outer door closed, starting the lock's cycle.

Zoya popped her helmet as soon as they stepped aboard the ship proper. "Thanks," she said.

Ernst nodded. "That's why we have a chase ship for these runs. Just in case."

"How'd you happen to be here?" Natalya asked, pulling her arms out of the suit and beginning to feel a little more human and a lot less like a sausage in a stuffed casing.

Ernst finished shucking off his suit, hanging it in a locker just across from the airlock. "I'm embarrassed to say your jump caught me flatfooted without a charged capacitor. By the time I told Alison what had happened, I only had enough charge for a short jump. That location you gave me isn't in my database. This one is on a direct line and I figured if you had to hop back in short jumps, you'd most likely hit it." He ran a hand over his scalp and looked at the deck with a little laugh. "I was actually surprised when you showed up. I figured I'd jump out to you once I had enough capacitor."

Zoya raised an eyebrow in Natalya's direction. "What did Alison say?"

Panko looked up at her. "Find them." He turned and headed toward the galley at the bow. "Food, fluid. Let's get moving toward the jump vector while you eat."

Natalya's stomach rumbled so loudly Panko looked back at her. "Sorry," she said. "Been a long time since breakfast."

Panko smiled and nodded at the seats around his small table. "Have a seat. Sandwiches all right? Fresh bread. Cheese. Some ham."

"Where do you get fresh bread?" Zoya asked.

"I make it."

"Here?" she asked.

"Don't get too excited. It's just a civilian-grade bread machine. Throw in some flour, water, yeast, sugar, and salt—push the button and come back in four stans. The ingredients stay fresher longer than the bread would, and it gives the ship a great homey smell while I'm working." While he talked, he pulled sandwich fixings out of the cupboards and coolers. "Beverage?"

"Coffee?" Natalya asked.

"Uh." Panko shrugged. "Water. Juice. Tea. I've got the coffeemaker but good beans are hard to find."

Natalya nodded. "We've found the same thing, but I've got some back on the *Peregrine*. Water, please."

"I remember," he said. "That's a lot better coffee than I'm used to at the yard. Zoya?"

"Water's good for me, too," she said.

Panko pulled a couple of covered cups from a rack and filled them with ice water from the cooler, placing one in front of each woman. "Help yourself. I'll get us moving and then we can talk while we cruise into the yards."

"Can you sneak us into the dock?" Natalya asked.

"If I just fly into my normal berth, nobody will think twice. It would never fly, though. Alison is going to be on the blower as soon as we jump in. We can't keep the ship secret, but we may be able to do the next best thing."

Panko plopped into the pilot's couch and started punching keys. A low rumble worked through the ship while Zoya and Natalya helped themselves to the sandwiches. "You were almost on the vector," Ernst said after a few ticks. "We'll be ready to jump in half a stan." He turned the couch to look at them. "So? What happened?"

Zoya swallowed a bite of sandwich before answering. "After the thrusters started firing by themselves?"

"Yeah. You managed to stop that."

"I pulled the main breaker," Natalya said. "The thrusters were cross-wired to a different switch and I didn't have time to try them all. I pulled the main and then shut off all the individual circuits until we found the one that went to the thrusters."

"Fast thinking."

Natalya shrugged and took another bite of her sandwich.

"What happened then?"

"When we got the ship restarted, the computer didn't come back up so we refreshed the console," Zoya said. "It didn't reboot immediately. Just a message about how long we could hold our breath."

"From where I was sitting, it looked like you lost a lot of air. I saw a plume of crystallized water even from way back there."

"The inner lock opened first," Natalya said. "A second later, the outer door opened and sucked all the atmosphere out of the ship except for the engine room. I'm not sure about that door opening in like that."

"It's always a fifty-fifty thing whether to design the door opening in or out. I suspect the design team went with opening in to guard against an engine room explosion," Panko said. "If the engine room malfunctions and punctures the hull, the rest of the ship still has atmosphere."

"And no way to get into the engine room to repair it," Natalya said.

"You obviously got around that."

"Just before the Burleson fired, the lock closed. I was able to get some atmosphere reloaded and we almost had full pressure again," Zoya said, wiping her mouth with a napkin. "It was enough to get the engine room door open but by then we'd jumped."

"It took about three-quarters of the capacitor to jump just four BUs," Natalya said. "I don't know if we could have jumped more than six."

"So somebody knew the ship couldn't jump as far as the yard claimed," Panko said.

"That's what we figured too," Natalya said.

"Why there?" Panko asked.

"Somebody wanted the ship," Natalya said.

"We got turned around just in time to see somebody coming in hot trying to intercept us before we could jump out," Zoya said. "Good bread, by the way."

Panko grinned. "Thanks."

"I can't figure out why somebody might want to steal that ship. It's a hot mess," Natalya said.

"It's not that bad," Panko said. "It's a pretty ship. A few upgrades and it would make an interesting yacht."

"But who'd want it? It's such a novel design that it would stand out like a sore thumb," Zoya asked. "Steal a Barbell and rename it. It looks like every other Barbell. That ship is unique as far as I know."

"That's a good point," Natalya said. "It would be pretty easy for High Tortuga to track it down anywhere in the Western Annex."

Panko pursed his lips and frowned. "How deep into the ship did you dig while you were doing your pre-flight?"

"Not deep enough," Zoya said. "I found a few of the sensors so I could reprogram the levels of atmosphere, water, and main thrusters. I never did find maneuvering fuel levels, gray water levels, or anything approaching heat sensors for hull or thrusters."

Panko's frown deepened. "We need to get that ship back on-station and tear it apart."

"I can get behind that," Zoya said. "I've wanted to take a laser cutter to it for the last week."

Panko snorted a short laugh. "I can only imagine."

"Why do you say that?" Natalya asked.

"What? Tear it apart?" Panko asked.

Natalya nodded.

"I think you're right. Stealing the ship doesn't make much sense. What if it's not the ship?" Panko asked.

Natalya cocked her head to the side. "I don't get it."

"I do," Zoya said. "We even thought of it but we didn't go far enough."

"We did?" Natalya's brain wouldn't latch on but she could almost feel the itch inside her head as if she should know and would kick herself once somebody enlightened her.

"What if it's not the ship, but something in the ship?" Zoya asked.

"What could be in the ship?" Natalya asked. "We went through all the systems. There's nothing there worth stealing. Especially not so elaborately."

"Chips," Zoya said.

Natalya felt her eyes widen. "Somebody's smuggling credit chips?"

Panko shrugged. "There are a lot of ways to get chips off the station. If you spent a lot of time amassing credits that you didn't want anybody to know about, I can see where it might be tough to get them all out without raising questions."

Natalya frowned. "A few large-denomination chips? You could carry millions away in a small pocket."

Panko nodded. "True, but what if they're not legitimate chips."

"What? Forgeries?" Zoya asked.

"I think the word you're looking for is counterfeit," Panko said.

"I didn't know you could do that," Natalya said.

"You're not supposed to be able to," Panko said. "But what if somebody has figured out a way?"

Zoya put the remains of her second sandwich down on her napkin and stared at Panko. "Chaos."

Panko nodded. "If word got out that chips couldn't be trusted, the entire banking system would take a massive hit. Nobody would trust the chips and since they're used extensively on transactions between the High Line and Toe-Hold space, that's a major problem."

"Can they?" Natalya asked. "Be counterfeited, I mean?"

Panko shrugged as a long beep sounded from his console. He glanced at the display. "We're ready to jump."

"You think the chips might be hidden in that ship?" Zoya asked.

Panko shrugged without looking back. "If it's not the ship—and whoever did this clearly did not want the ship lost—then it's something on or in the ship. I don't know what else it could be." He held one hand poised over the keyboard and glanced back. "Ready to jump?"

They both nodded.

Panko pushed the button.

CHAPTER FORTY
RAVAINE: 2366, MAY 30

PANKO SAT BACK FROM the console and nodded as if to himself. "All right then. We jumped a bit short but we'll be docked by this time tomorrow."

"The extra mass?" Zoya asked.

He shook his head. "I don't think so. I adjusted the base mass to account for it. We're only a percentage point off."

"Time enough for everybody to get the news that we're missing," Natalya said. "Before we're close enough for the station to get a good look."

"Yeah," Panko said. "My thinking as well." He spun around in the couch. "So, what do we do in the meantime?"

"Run through the telemetry data?" Zoya asked. "I assume you were recording it."

He grinned. "Come see." He stood from the couch and led them back to his office. "I've modeled the old design—your design. I wanted to see how much space I had to work with based on squaring up the hull a bit but keeping much of the floor plan." He slipped into the chair in front of the drafting station and brought up a screen. It showed the egg-shaped design from each axis. "This is the original," he said, then tapped a few keys.

A gray, boxy shape surrounded the original. The new shape was almost exactly the same width, length, and height as the original. "The new hull gives us about twelve percent more interior, cuts the estimated production time by a week, and has lower material costs because there are fewer custom parts that need to be fabricated."

"Nice," Natalya said. "What's that do for the engineering space?"

Panko tapped a few more keys, replacing the external hulls with the layout of components inside. "There's more than enough room for another drive and the capacitors to drive it to full capacity. The new space gives us extra room to upgrade the fusactor. That should cut recharge time between jumps by about twenty percent."

Zoya nodded. "That'll make up for any loss of leg. Taking smaller jumps faster will get the route done in less time."

He glanced back at her. "Even with the Gemini, she's got so little mass that I think the reduction in jump range isn't going to be much. My numbers say she'll jump eighteen BUs instead of the twenty Downs claimed."

"Which was only about four or five as built," Natalya said.

"Yeah. There's that small point," Panko said. "Still—there was plenty of room for the extra capacitor and drive. It's hard to believe they shorted that when the volume was already reserved for it."

"Focus on the cost per unit. Once they decided to make it as cheaply as possible," Zoya said with a shrug.

Something tugged at a corner of Natalya's brain. "Can you show that space on the original design?"

He frowned at her but nodded. A few keystrokes later, the original hull design displayed showing an oblong volume highlighted in green under the deck plates in engineering. "That's the space that the larger capacitor would have taken up, along with the connections needed for a Gemini. The difference in volume for a full Gemini is too small to show at this scale."

Natalya leaned in to peer at the screen. "How much volume is that?"

"Something over a cubic meter," Panko said.

"And it's empty?" Natalya asked.

"There's nothing on the plans I have."

Natalya pulled up her tablet and looked at the plans she got from the yard. She flipped through the layers and zoomed in on the same area. "My copy shows that as being filled with capacitor." She held the tablet over to show Panko.

"Mine will show the same thing," Zoya said. "We just copied the one we got from the yard."

"What's the date on yours?" he asked.

"Last update, December last year," Natalya said checking the file's metadata.

He nodded and pulled open a small tab on his screen. "That's probably the design. I got mine from the actual fabrication and construction unit from the yard. It's dated last month." He looked up at Natalya. "Something?"

"They designed a larger capacitor but shorted it in construction to leave a cubic meter under the deck empty," Natalya said.

Panko's eyes widened.

"We wouldn't have found it doing the pre-flight," Zoya said. "Our plans show it as being filled with the capacitor. There wouldn't have been anything to see if we pulled the deck plate. We already knew the capacitor was underpowered."

He nodded. "Wanna bet it's not empty now?"

"No bet," Natalya said.

"We've got a few stans," Panko said. "Shall we go look?"

The thought of suiting up and going back into the ship sent a chill down Natalya's back. She glanced at Zoya, who gave her head the tiniest of shakes. "Let's wait until we have it in the station," Natalya said. "I've seen enough of that ship for the moment."

"I'd feel better about it if we were safely docked someplace myself," Zoya said.

He nodded. "I don't blame you." He pulled up another window. "Here's the model animated by your telemetry." He played several ticks of animation—pausing it when the thrusters started firing. "The acceleration was very good," he said, pointing out the vectors painted on the screen. "I know the ship doesn't have that much mass, but the kickers are more than up to the task."

Natalya nodded. "Maybe too much?"

"How so?" Panko asked.

"Well," Natalya said. "If you're looking to jump in and out again quickly, you don't want too much way on the ship. Just enough to ride through the jump but not so much that you have to spend a day adjusting the vector to point to your next jump."

"Once you've made it out to jump range, going fast isn't that much of an advantage," Zoya said. "You have to burn more fuel to adjust your heading."

He frowned and looked back at the frozen monitor. "Good point. I hadn't thought of that." He grimaced. "I should have." He started the animation again and they watched the small ship pull away. He paused it when the lock opened as a plume of atmosphere jetted from the open port. "That's just an animation. There aren't any sensors to show that. You were smart to wear your softsuits and stay harnessed in."

"We had everything locked down for the test run," Zoya said. "With all the accidents around airlocks here, that was an easy one to guess."

"Even the head survived with just a few frozen pipes," Natalya said.

"We were able to have coffee, even. I was surprised the coffee maker survived the decompression without being knocked around," Zoya said.

Panko restarted the animation. After what seemed like a long time, the outer door closed and he stopped the replay again. "How'd you get the door closed? I've seen that manual override. It's damn near impossible."

Natalya shrugged. "I didn't. It closed on its own. Somebody with a lot of time on his hands had a field day programming that ship."

"We were lucky he's not a spacer," Zoya said.

Panko and Natalya looked at her. "What makes you say that?" he asked.

Zoya shrugged. "He wouldn't have wasted time on evacuating the ship. Not for the shakedown. Any pilot worth his water is going in with a softsuit. Closing the door? Really? The ship didn't need that door closed. It actually worked in our favor because we got enough atmosphere to get back into the engineering compartment. As a phase two plan, closing the door worked against him."

"Well, if the depressurization had worked as planned, you'd have been dead," Panko said.

Natalya's brain twitched at that. "What if it wasn't the plan? To kill the test pilot. To kill us."

Panko looked at her, his eyes squinted and his mouth screwed into a grimace. "It certainly looks like attempted murder. Complete with the cheesy warning message."

"What then?" Zoya asked.

"What if it was just to scare us into abandoning the ship?" Natalya asked. "Somebody's known for weeks that we'd be taking the ship out and that Ernst here was going to chase us."

"So we were supposed to dive out and Ernst would pick us up?"

Natalya nodded. "Yeah. We considered it. Remember?"

"Yeah, I do," Zoya said.

"Why didn't you?" Ernst asked.

"We worried that the drive would fire before you could get to us and we'd follow the ship through the hole," Zoya said.

Panko scrubbed a hand across his mouth and nodded. "Valid point."

"You weren't close enough to follow us through the same hole, depending on when the drive kicked us. We tried to shut down the drive but we got the engineering door open just as we jumped. By then it was too late anyway," Zoya said.

"*Serendipity*, Pulaski Local. Over."

Panko stood and bolted for the cockpit. "Pulaski Local, *Serendipity*. Go ahead."

"*Serendipity*, Pulaski Local. Switch to channel alpha four for secure communications with the director please? Over."

"Pulaski Local, *Serendipity.* Roger, alpha four, secure comms. Out." He fiddled with the communications gear for a moment until the signal locked. "Pulaski, *Serendipity.* Over."

"*Serendipity,* Pulaski. Stand by."

Panko looked over his shoulder at Natalya and Zoya. "I knew we wouldn't be able to hide the ship."

"What will you tell her?" Natalya asked.

"Depends on what she asks," Panko said.

"*Serendipity,* Pulaski. Over." Alison Pittman's voice sounded like she was in the next room.

"Pulaski, *Serendipity.* Go ahead, Director. Over."

"*Serendipity,* Pulaski. Spill it, Ernst. What did you find? Over."

"Pulaski, *Serendipity.* I have the ship in tow. Nobody is aboard. Over."

His communication was met with a pause much longer than the time it took radio waves to travel all the way to the yard and back.

"*Serendipity,* Pulaski. Roger that, Ernst. Bring it home and I'll talk to you after you've secured the ship. Over."

"Pulaski, *Serendipity.* Roger. I'll be back at the yard in a few stans. *Serendipity,* out."

"Pulaski, out."

Panko secured the communications equipment and turned to the women. "Think she bought it?"

"More to the point, do you think the people overhearing us bought it?" Natalya asked.

He blinked a couple of times. "That was a secure channel."

"Yes, but we overheard your conversation easily enough," Natalya said.

"Aren't you being a bit paranoid?" he asked.

Natalya shrugged. "Maybe, but somebody in Pittman's crew is dirty. I don't know who or how, but there are just too many weird things happening."

"You don't think it's Pittman herself, then?" Panko asked.

Natalya looked at Zoya. They both shook their heads at the same time.

"No," Natalya said. "She's the patsy. She's going to take the fall for the failed program."

He frowned at each of them in turn. "You still think it's going to be a failed program?"

"Yeah, but no fault of your design. There are enough people working against this project that I'm pretty sure somebody will make a move on Pittman and take over."

"You suspect Downs," Panko said.

Natalya saw Zoya chewing on her lower lip. "Zee?"

Zoya looked at him and shrugged. "I think he's the distraction. I think we're supposed to pay attention to him instead of the real mover behind the scenes."

"We already know he's skimming," Panko said. "That's why he's been tossed off the station."

"Yes, but we don't know how many people worked either for or with him. He was at the yard a long time," Zoya said.

He rubbed his mouth with the fingers of one hand and frowned. "Longer than I have, actually."

"So, what?" Natalya asked. "How many different factions do you think there are?"

"Occam's Razor," Panko said.

Zee pursed her lips and squinted. "If—and it's a big if—somebody's trying to get control of the project, we don't know who they are or why they want to."

"Agreed," Natalya said. "If there isn't, then why pick Alison Pittman to be the project lead. Why kill the last one and dismiss the team?"

Panko reached for his tablet. "Making a note to find out who dismissed the team."

"While you're at it, who picked Alison?" Zoya asked.

Panko nodded.

"Downs has been on the payroll for a very long time. He's been involved in a fairly large number of projects that put him in a position to skim—directly or indirectly—and acquire a significant number of credits," Zoya said.

He squinted at her before looking at Natalya. "Being put in the position doesn't necessarily mean he did."

"We've got evidence that Downs hired some relative to provide the couches," Natalya said.

"As I recall, Alison knew about it," Zoya said. "She chalked it up to small enough that it didn't matter."

Natalya nodded. "At the time, she also thought she had it under control."

"What happened?" Panko asked.

"She did an inventory with somebody who knew inventory management," Zoya said. "She found out how many of those couches got received but were never returned after Downs said he'd done it. It was a large number."

They sat in silence for a couple of ticks.

"I think you're right," Panko said, looking at Zoya. "Unless Tony Downs got really greedy and really stupid, he's not trying to take over the project."

Zoya nodded. "That's the thing that's bothered me about it. Downs doesn't have any motivation to be anything other than a highly respected project lead to maintain his ability to steal from the company. We've scotched that—at least for now—so he might have some animosity toward us, but this has been going on longer than we've been here."

"He's getting rich," Natalya said. "That couch deal alone was worth hundreds of thousands. I'd be willing to bet every one of those expansion projects he worked on gave him a lot more than that."

"Which brings us back to the idea that somebody wants this project to fail," Panko said.

"Not fail, per se," Zoya said. "Just suffer a catastrophic failure of management so they can take over."

"Occam still applies," Panko said. "Why not simply fail? Be shown to be untenable?"

Zoya crossed her arms and frowned. "I agree that the simpler rationale has a better argument but if that's the case, why are so many different things going south?"

"Go on," he said. "Talk it through."

"It would have been pretty easy to scotch it from the beginning," Zoya said. "Just give the design team conflicting task requirements that couldn't be delivered."

"Like what?" he asked.

Zoya glanced at Natalya. "Long legs?" she asked.

"That's a good one," Natalya said. "This ship—if we fixed the flaws with the drive and power—could jump a long way. Could be a record for the commercial vehicle with the longest jump. It's certainly much longer than any ship I've known about could jump."

Panko nodded and his eyes tightened. "Why is that a problem?"

"First, it's unnecessary," Natalya said. "Legs that long don't really help with the kind of mission the ship is designed for."

"Second, it's unheard of," Zoya said. "Whoever set it up might have thought it wasn't possible to do without more mass, more power."

"Clearly, the original design team solved it," Natalya said. "But the redesign looks like it was done by a monkey with a marker."

Panko snorted. "Because of the drive and capacitor?"

"Yeah," Natalya said. "Anybody with a bit of knowledge about how a ship really works would have spotted that in a heartbeat."

"That's another reason why Pittman was a bad choice," Zoya said. "I'm sure she's a terrific administrator but she lacks expertise in two required knowledge domains—how ships work and manufacturing process."

"The only overlap is the administration skills," Natalya said.

"And effective administration of a flawed process doesn't really help you," Panko said. "I get it." He looked at them. "Then who's trying to kill you? Downs, because he wants you out of the way? Or the person who wants control of the project?"

Natalya frowned. "I don't know."

"Maybe nobody," Zoya said. "There were plenty of chances for us to get out of the ship when it started going bad. Nothing actually threatened our safety directly as long as we were taking the proper precautions."

"Decompressing the ship?" Panko asked.

"Any competent test pilot would have worn a softsuit," Zoya said. "And been strapped in."

"Jumping into an unknown spot in the Dark?" he asked.

"Just because it's not on our charts doesn't mean it's unknown," Natalya said. "Only that *we* didn't know it."

He slumped on his chair. "Why would anybody want to get control of a failing project?"

"If they knew why it was failing, they could be the cavalry to the rescue, gaining a huge reputation with High Tortuga," Zoya said. "That ship could have worked as designed until they dropped the second drive and capacitor."

"The couch," Natalya said.

"Yeah, well, the couch was Downs and company getting stupid with their skimming," Zoya said.

"If we can figure out why, that will probably tell us who," Natalya said.

Zoya nodded and looked at Panko. "You know anything about the structure of High Tortuga's management?"

He frowned. "A little. Not much."

"Who wins if the project fails outright?"

"Nobody. At the current rate of service degradation the system will likely blow up from too much success. The company is built on trust. Once that goes, the whole thing goes."

"That would be bad?" Zoya asked.

"If nobody trusts High Tortuga's banking, that's going to play hell with trade which may have an impact on every person in the Western Annex. High Line and Toe-Hold alike," Panko said.

"Follow the money," Zoya said.

"Your granny again?" Natalya asked.

"Older. Confucius, I think."

"Alison Pittman is the loose end," Panko said. "If we can find out who put her into the job, we'll have a pointer back to the person who wants it to fail."

"Wouldn't they use a cut-out?" Natalya asked.

"Probably, but everybody works for somebody," he said. "With a few exceptions."

"Everybody works for themselves," Zoya said. "The only difference is who pays them." She looked at Natalya. "Yeah. My grandmother."

"I think I'd like to meet your grandmother," he said.

"When this is over, maybe I'll introduce you." Zoya grinned at him. "If you can get away long enough to fly over to Margary."

Panko grinned back. "Yeah. That'll be the problem." He rubbed a hand over his scalp and shook his head. "Right now the problem is getting this project out of the lock and into space."

"So, who asks Alison?" Natalya asked.

"You two are going to be ghosts," he said.

"Only for a few stans," Natalya said. "We aren't going to be able to hide very long before somebody spots us." She looked around the ship with an exaggerated roll of her head. "We can't stay in here very long. We're going to need to get back to the *Peregrine* for fresh clothes, if nothing else."

"What part does Call-me-Charlie play in this game?" Zoya asked.

Panko frowned. "Call-me-Charlie?"

"One of the techs. It's like his catch phrase. Says it to everybody, apparently. Even Alison knows him by that name," Natalya said.

"He fixed the lock on *Echo One*. There was a flawed interlock that wouldn't let both doors open at the same time when the ship was in atmosphere," Zoya said.

"What makes you think he's connected?" he asked.

"We spotted him coming out of the bay one evening. When he saw us, he turned and went in the other direction," Natalya said. "It looked hinky as hell. We went aboard and found that the lock access logs had been erased."

"How do you do that?"

"The right commands? It's not hard. Much easier than modifying them," Zoya said. "We've got no way of knowing how many times they've been erased. Alison's supposedly got a team checking for discrepancies but we never found out if they saw anything."

Panko frowned. "So, we have extra players on the field?"

"Are we making this too complicated?" Natalya asked. "We have somebody maneuvering to take over the program and somebody— Downs—running a major skim and scam. You think Charlie is a third player?"

Panko frowned, chewing his lower lip. "Not necessarily, but the level of conspiracy here is getting a bit out of hand."

"A few players in key areas could do it," Zoya said.

He nodded. "I could get behind that idea."

"Well, we can't answer any questions out here," Natalya said.

"We can answer one," he said, standing up and heading for the lock. "You have a deck puller over there, or should I take one with me?"

Zoya and Natalya shared a glance before following him.

"There's one there," Natalya said. "I'll show you where it is." She swallowed her fear and started climbing back into her softsuit.

"Zoya? Would you mind staying here?" Panko asked. "Just in case?"

"In case what?" Zoya asked.

He spared a glance at Natalya. "In case she's right and there's another trap waiting for us."

Zoya's eyes widened a bit but she nodded. "Fair enough. I'm not sure I can fly this ship, so you better come back."

"Can you fly the *Peregrine*?" Panko asked, pulling his helmet up.

"Sure."

"Same ship. Upgraded consoles but it's basically the *Peregrine* with tow grapples."

"That Scout you saw must have really made an impression," Natalya said, her grin more nerves than humor.

"I've been a fan for a very long time," Panko said and latched his helmet down.

Natalya led the way into the lock where they cross-checked each other's suits before closing the inner door.

"Can you read us, Zee?"

"Got you fine." Zoya's voice sounded a little tinny in the suit's headset.

Panko nodded, his face barely visible inside his helmet. He keyed the lock cycle and the outer door opened in a few moments. The safety line still stretched down over the hull toward the smaller ship cradled below. He clipped a D-ring to the line and pulled himself out of the ship hand over hand.

Natalya swallowed hard and followed. Extravehicular activity was never one of her favorite things, even when—rationally—the activity wasn't any more dangerous than jumping across the Deep Dark in the flimsy shells they called ships.

When they got to the *Echo One*, she got the outer door open for Panko and they squeezed into the ship's lock.

Nathan Lowell

Natalya keyed the lock cycle and waited. The lock filled with atmosphere, sounds becoming more distinct as the air carried the vibrations from the hull and the small sounds of their boots moving on the deck, her suit brushing the bulkheads and fixtures.

The green light went on but the inner door didn't open.

"Something's wrong," Panko said.

"Something's right," Natalya said. "I took the actuator off the inner door so it can only be opened manually." She grabbed the dogging lever, pulled it aside, and pushed to swing the door open into the darkened ship. "We don't have enough gases to refill the ship again, so we made it so the computer couldn't trigger both doors open at the same time."

"Clever," Panko said.

Natalya felt a warm flush at his praise as she led the way aft into the engineering space. She grabbed the deck puller from its slot and consulted her tablet. It only took a moment to find the plate she needed and kneel to press the tool against it. With a deft tug on the handle she lifted the plate and tilted it up.

Panko leaned over and aimed a light into the cavity underneath.

The light glinted off the electrical fixtures, pipes, and ductwork all the way down to the top of the tank that ran along the bottom of the ship.

Natalya heard Panko's sigh over the radio. "That's disappointing," he said.

"Don't do this to me," Zoya said.

"It's empty, Zee."

"Damn," she said.

"Well, at least there's room in the deck plan for more capacitor," Panko said, his light playing over the internals, picking out the various points of connection.

Natalya nodded and leaned in. "Looks like enough for a hell of a lot more capacitor. Odd that they'd leave this empty."

"Smuggler's hold," he said. "We should compare the plans a little more closely to see if there are any others."

"How much could you smuggle in—what is that? Not quite a cubic meter?" she asked.

"My plans show it as closer to two," he said. "Anything that's low mass, low volume but highly taxed? That could be a lot of credits."

Natalya pulled the deck plate back into place, latched it down, and removed the tool. "Like counterfeit credit chips?"

"Yeah. You could put a lot of them in a hole that big." Panko led the way out of engineering and forward to the cockpit. "A nice cache of drugs if you're going to one of the interdicted systems. A

265

big pile of gemstones free from CPJCT oversight. There are a lot of things you could put in there."

"Voice of experience?" Zoya asked over the radio.

Panko snorted. "Not exactly." He aimed his light at the couch. "I thought they were going to replace that."

"Replace what?" Zoya asked.

"The couch," Natalya said. "They changed out the actual couch but they were having trouble re-engineering a base for it. Something about the deck fitting and material strength."

He turned to her. "You believe it?"

She laughed. "Not for a hot tick. They were blowing smoke up my pants. With your ships coming off the ways soon, it didn't seem worth fighting over."

Panko grunted. "We'll have to see about making sure we're not getting charged for that thing. It doesn't even swivel, does it?"

"Nope," Natalya said. "But then, neither does the one in the *Peregrine*."

He crossed to the couch and started examining it.

"What are you looking for?" she asked.

"I'm not sure. It just looks—I don't know. Wrong. This base doesn't look like it's meant for this couch at all."

Zoya's laugh came over the radio. "It's not. That's the original base from the monstrosity. They just tacked the new surface to it."

Panko straightened up and stepped back, playing the light around the base.

"What?" Natalya asked, looking back and forth between Panko and the couch.

"This was the original base?" he asked.

"Yeah. Should be. We weren't here when they changed the couch off, but it looks like the same box," she said. "Why?"

"That's a lot of wasted space. No drawers? No cubbyholes to store loose gear in?"

"Well, it's just a prototype," Zoya said.

Natalya watched Panko's light as he walked around the couch to look at it from all angles. He even got down on his knees and looked up under the foot rest.

"How big do you think this is?" he asked, almost as if he were talking to himself.

Natalya measured it with her eyes. "At least a cubic meter. Maybe a little more."

"That's my take as well," he said. He reached in under the footrest and pushed on the base.

"What are you looking for?" she asked.

Panko looked back at her, his face a ghostly pale inside his helmet from the reflected light of his torch. "This is an anomaly. It's been on the ship since it rolled off the ways. It should have been easier and quicker to just uproot it and replace it, but somebody went to a fair amount of trouble to keep this aboard. That strike you as odd?"

Natalya shrugged before she realized Panko probably couldn't see the movement inside her suit in the dark. "Maybe," she said.

He turned his light and attention back to the base. After a few moments of examination he reached in under the footrest and pressed the upper edge of the base where it connected to the couch itself.

Natalya heard a faint click. "What was that?"

"What was what?" Zoya asked.

"I thought I heard a click."

Panko sat back on his heels. "I did, too. I don't see anything that might have made a click."

Natalya walked around the base to get a look from the other side. A small crevice along the top of the back edge caught her eye. "Here's something."

He levered himself to his feet and walked back to shine his light where Natalya pointed.

"What is it?" Zoya asked.

"There's a crack that shouldn't be there," Natalya said.

His light picked out the gap in the casing but no view inside. "That's pretty clever."

"What is?" Zoya asked.

"The latch is under the foot rest, but the door is along this aft surface," Panko said. "Must cut down on pilferage." He reached down and slipped a finger into the crack, making it wider and pulling to reveal a wide drawer sliding open on concealed runners.

His light gleamed off a plastic wrapped bundle that nearly filled the hidden compartment. As the drawer opened and more of the bundle was revealed, Natalya saw what must have been thousands of credit chips through the transparent wrap.

His low whistle shook Natalya out of her shock.

"What is it?" Zoya said.

"Tell you when we get back," Natalya said.

Panko knelt beside the open drawer and examined the bundle closely. After a few moments, he pushed the drawer back in until it latched with an audible snap. "Time to go."

Natalya followed him to the lock, securing the inner door behind her before pressing the lock cycle button. In a matter of a few ticks they were back aboard *Serendipity* with Zoya staring at them.

"Well?" Zoya asked. "You going to spill it?"

"The base of the couch is hollow," Natalya said, stripping out of her suit. "It's filled with credit chips. All stacked neatly and bound with shrink wrap."

"Keeps them together and not rattling," Panko said.

"That's a big base. How many are we talking?" Zoya asked.

Natalya looked at Panko. "What do you think? Ten thousand?"

"Chips?" he asked, his eyes focusing somewhere in the middle distance. A hundred rows with at least seventy-five stacked around fifty deep?"

Zoya's eyes grew round. "Three hundred something thousand."

"Closer to four hundred," he said. "Maybe as many as half a million and we have no idea what may be on them. Even if they're blank, the street value of a blank credit chip is around a hundred credits."

"I bet they're not blank," Natalya said.

"Why do you say that?" Zoya asked.

"Because that's gotta be how Downs has been hiding the profits on his various operations. It's been going on for decades," Natalya said. "We've heard of at least three or four big projects. How many more haven't we heard of?"

Zoya looked at Panko, who shrugged. "Makes sense. More sense than counterfeit chips," he said.

"Why so many, though?" Zoya asked.

"Easier to break a hundred-credit chip than a million-credit chip," Panko said. "A big deposit like that would raise flags."

"Even in Toe-Hold space?" Zoya asked.

"When you've stolen the money from High Tortuga?" Panko asked.

Zoya's eyebrows rose. "I see your point."

"But do they even know they've been robbed?" Natalya asked.

Panko chewed his lower lip for a moment. "That part I'm not so sure of."

He hung his softsuit in the locker and headed for the cockpit.

"Well, we figured it was something on the ship instead of the ship itself," Zoya said. "I wonder how far behind us they are?"

Natalya grinned and gave Zoya a friendly poke in the arm. "They've been ahead of us the whole time. We just need to watch to see who comes to claim the ship."

"Claim the ship?" Zoya asked.

"Bet you a steak dinner that somebody sends out a tug to take the ship off our hands before we get back to the yards."

Zoya pursed her lips and narrowed her eyes. "No bet." She started down the passageway. "We should let Ernst know."

They stepped into the cockpit just as the comms came online with an incoming message. "*Serendipity, Pulaski Towing.* Over."

Ernst gave them a cheesy grin and held up one finger. "*Pulaski Towing, Serendipity.* Go ahead."

"*Serendipity, Pulaski Towing.* I've got orders to haul that ship back to the yards. Over."

"Roger that, *Pulaski Towing.* I can probably have it back in the dock before we can achieve a pass over. We'll be docked in just over eighteen stans. Over."

"Understood, *Serendipity.*"

A brief pause gave Panko time to mutter, "Just following orders."

"Just following orders. I have your track on short-range. We can be alongside in four stans. Free you up. Over."

Panko grinned again and looked at the overhead, obviously waiting.

"Did you copy, *Serendipity?*"

"*Pulaski Towing, Serendipity.* I copy. One tick. Stand by." He keyed the mic off and turned in his seat. "Would you two get back into your softsuits? We've got a little chore that needs to be taken care of before we hand the ship over."

They looked at each other with mirroring shrugs. "Sure thing," Natalya said. "What have you got in mind?"

CHAPTER FORTY-ONE
RAVAINE: 2366, MAY 31

WHEN THE TUG HAD *Echo One* in tow, Panko adjusted his course and kicked in a short burn to change his vector. "It's safe. You can come out now," he said.

Natalya and Zoya came out of his office and settled around the galley table.

"I still don't understand why all the sleight of hand," Zoya said.

"Give it a few ticks," Panko said.

"Do you know?" Zoya asked Natalya.

"I think so." She shrugged. "Somebody's in for a hell of a surprise and they're not going to be happy about it."

"Yeah," Zoya said. "That part I get, but what about—"

"*Serendipity*, Tortuga Control. Over."

Panko's eyebrows rose. "That was fast." He keyed the mic. "Tortuga Control, *Serendipity*. Over."

"*Serendipity*, Tortuga Control. You are directed to dock soonest at High Tortuga. Over."

His eyebrows seemed to climb higher on his forehead. "Tortuga Control, *Serendipity*. That's not exactly on my way home. Can I ask what this is about? Over."

"*Serendipity*, Tortuga Control. Your presence is requested as a witness in the inquiry into the aborted space trial of the ship designated *Echo One*. Over."

Panko's eyebrows finally came down as he frowned. "Tortuga Control, *Serendipity*. Shouldn't the inquiry be held on Pulaski? Over."

When the reply came, Natalya could almost hear the suppressed sigh on the other end. "*Serendipity*, Tortuga Control. You'll need to take that up with the directors. I'm just the messenger. Over."

Panko scratched his cheek, the sound of his nails on the scruff of beard clearly audible in the nearly silent cockpit. He shrugged. "Roger that, Tortuga Control. Soonest is probably thirty-something stans. Over."

The pause ran long enough for the three of them to share puzzled shrugs before the answer came back.

"*Serendipity*, Tortuga Control. We're sending an updated vector. It'll put you here in just over twelve stans. Over."

Panko's console pinged as the message registered with the ship. He scowled at the screen and sighed. "Somebody high up the food chain has a rock up his nozzle." He keyed the mic. "Roger, Tortuga Control. You're paying for the fuel for this burn. Over."

"*Serendipity*, Tortuga Control. I'm just the messenger. Contact Tortuga Local when you reach the outer markers. Control, out."

"*Serendipity*, out."

Natalya raised an eyebrow. "What's that all about?"

"That's going to be somebody who wants his chips back," he said. "I thought they'd come for them at the yard."

"If Downs is on Tortuga, it makes a certain amount of sense," Zoya said.

"It does," he said. "But Tony Downs doesn't have the kind of leverage to get us rerouted on such short notice."

"Who does?" Zoya asked.

Panko's eyes focused somewhere else. "One of the vice directors might have that kind of pull."

"Control said you'd have to take it up with the directors," Natalya said.

"It's a loose collection. Everybody from assistant through vice to full director gets lumped under the title." He grinned. "Unless you're in the room with a full director, and then things get real."

"How many are there?" Zoya asked.

"Seventeen full directors, including the chairman of the board," Panko said. "There are seven or eight divisions and each has a vice-director at the top."

"Depends on the division. Alison is—technically—a vice-director and has full control as CEO. The yard is pretty small as divisions go. Brian Dorion is CEO of the Communications Division with a vice-director over him. I don't know which one, offhand."

"And assistant directors?" Zoya asked.

"Go-fers." Panko shrugged. "I think they're just jumped-up errand runners. They're like directors-in-training, I think. Just along for the experience with the hope that someday they too will carry the title of director."

"Now what do we do?" Zoya asked.

Panko didn't look up from his console. "Now we try to get some sleep, get cleaned up, and eat. You two will have to take turns on the bunk. I can nap in the couch. Won't be the first time."

"Makes sense," Natalya said. "Too bad I didn't bring a change of shipsuit."

"We can pick up a couple when we dock. I'll order ahead and have them delivered."

"Won't somebody ask why you need two women's shipsuits?" asked Zoya.

"That cat is going to be out of the bag as soon as we open the lock," Panko said.

"How do you figure?" Zoya asked.

He glanced at her over his shoulder. "Station security will be waiting to escort me to the inquiry. Your presence will—undoubtedly—be discovered when they sweep the ship for evidence. You may as well come to the inquiry with me." His mouth twisted in a sideways grin. "Nothing like having the 'lost crew' there to cut through the hash they're going to sling at us." He turned back to the console and hit a couple more keys. The stars outside the armorglass appeared to corkscrew around as the ship adjusted attitude before the heavy thrusters in the stern began a deep rumble.

"What aren't you saying, Ernst?" Natalya asked.

He swiveled his couch around to face them. "The inquiry is just an excuse to separate me and—by extension, you—from the ship. They'll need to have access to the whole ship without witnesses so they can find the missing chips."

Zoya's head tilted sideways and she frowned. "But the chips—" She stopped in mid-sentence and her eyes widened.

Panko grinned at her. "Now you know. I didn't expect we'd be called to the principal's office. I thought they'd do this on Pulaski." He shrugged. "Either way, they won't find anything here."

Natalya looked at Zoya. "How far behind us do you think that ship might be?"

"The one that should have picked us up back there in the Dark?" Natalya nodded.

"Hard to say. They couldn't have expected us to jump out," Zoya said. "And they probably expected us to jump back to Ravaine, given our vector."

"Too bad they spotted you. Not finding you would have delayed them more than that," Panko said. "They couldn't be sure you weren't in the system and just couldn't find you."

"Absence of evidence is not evidence of absence," Natalya said.

Panko laughed. "Rudenski still hammering that at the academy?"

"It was a few stanyers ago but she didn't look like she was planning to retire," Zoya said.

Panko shook his head. "She seemed ancient when I was there." He looked back and forth between them. "You don't seem surprised."

"What? That you were at the academy? Or that you remembered the lessons?" Natalya asked with a grin.

"The academy."

"Your class ring," Zoya said. "I noticed it when you gave us the tour with Alison."

Panko frowned and held out his hand to look at the ring. "It's so nondescript. What gave it away?"

"I wanted that model for myself," Zoya said. "Class of '49 was the last year the company made them with gold. After that they used a silver inlay."

He barked a short laugh. "I had no idea."

"It's the little things," Zoya said.

"Thanks for the tip," he said. "Now one of you should probably sack out. The next eleven and something stans are going to get used up fast." He turned back to his console. "Clean bedding in the middle drawer under the bunk. Help yourselves."

Zoya led the way back to Panko's stateroom and Natalya helped her change the bed.

"Think this is overkill?" Natalya asked, shaking out the top sheet with a snap of her wrists.

"What, changing the sheets?"

"Yeah."

Zoya shrugged. "Just being polite. Honestly, I probably wouldn't have noticed. I'm about ready to drop."

Panko's voice echoed down the passageway, barely audible over the roar of the kickers. "Feel free to use the clothes 'fresher while you're sleeping."

Natalya spotted it tucked into a corner by the door to the head. "I'll toss these sheets in. Wanna give me your shipsuit?"

Zoya finished tucking in the blanket and shrugged. She pulled everything out of the pockets and stripped down completely, tossing her clothes to Natalya before slipping between the sheets. "May as well do all the laundry," she said.

Natalya grinned, fed the clothing and sheets into the cleaning unit and clicked off the lights on her way out. "Sleep well. See you in six."

CHAPTER FORTY-TWO
RAVAINE: 2366, JUNE 1

ZOYA STARED AT THE station as they closed on High Tortuga. Fat towers projected above and below a plane. The immense scale of it made understanding the perspective difficult. As they made their final approach to the docking gallery, she asked, "How big is that thing?"

"The basic structure is a three-story sandwich with engineering and life support in the middle," Panko said. "The towers hold the work spaces for administration, data, and finance."

"They're not really gold, are they?" Zoya asked.

Panko chuckled. "No. It's an alloy mostly made of copper, iron, and steel. They mined it all out of the Viceroy systems. It was plentiful and cheap."

"How many people live there?"

"Don't know," Panko said. "I'm sure the administration there knows, but nobody else does."

"Estimate?" Zoya asked.

"Something over a hundred million," Panko said. "Not sure how much over but I've seen speculation that it's closer to a billion." He snorted. "Dark-channel conspiracy stuff."

"*Serendipity*, High Tortuga Local. Divert to dock four-seven-three. Hold at ten meters."

"Roger, Local. Four-seven-three. Hold at ten meters."

"What's that about?" Zoya asked.

"It's just two doors down," Natalya said. "Maybe they over-loaded four-seven-five."

"Probably somebody botched a landing or takeoff," Panko said. "With that much traffic, they have at least one docking emergency a day."

"That's comforting," Zoya said.

"It's seldom anything serious," Panko said. "Landing too close to the doors. Trying to take off before the bay is ready. Just enough to screw up schedules." Panko adjusted their course to line up with the new dock and eased it in, coming to zero delta-v at precisely ten meters. Keying the mic, he said, "High Tortuga Local, *Serendipity* on station. Over."

"Roger, *Serendipity*. Proceed on green. High Tortuga Local, out."

"Not exactly chatty," Zoya said.

"Look at short-range," Panko said, nodding at the window on his console. "With that many contacts, there's not a lot of time to be chatty."

Zoya's eyes practically bulged from her face. "They're not all on our channel, I take it."

Panko laughed. "Hardly. Nobody would be able to hear anything. I have no idea how many operators work in Local, but it's more than a dozen per watch around the clock."

The flashing red light above the lock turned green as the doors opened. Panko gave the thrusters a little goose to get them moving and the ship slid into the lock. In a matter of a few ticks, the cycle completed. The docking bay held a dozen or more landing pads, three or four of them empty—one had flashing green arrows. Panko scooted the small ship over the pad and followed the guide signal down. As soon as he secured the engines, a short squad of armed and uniformed personnel entered the bay and lined up beside the ship.

"Welcoming committee?" Natalya asked.

"Not exactly," Panko said. "Are you ready to do some derailing?"

"Derailing?" Zoya asked.

"You two are missing, presumed dead. Having you show up at the inquiry should derail whatever plans they have for me."

A light cargo hauler scooted into the bay, stopping behind the line of security guards. The operator jumped down and started an animated conversation with a frowning man who didn't appear to be interested in whatever he was selling.

After a few moments of the operator's pointing to the ship being answered by head shakes, Panko said, "We should go bail him out." He climbed out of the couch and headed aft toward the lock.

Natalya and Zoya followed along and waited out of sight in the passageway until the lock doors opened, flooding the interior with station air that smelled of hot metal and hydraulic fluid.

The squad leader met him at the lock. "Mr. Panko?"

"Yeah. Reporting as ordered."

"We'll escort you to your destination. If you'd follow me?"

"Of course, but could you allow that guy through your line? He's got some things we need."

"Everything you need will be provided," the man said.

"I'm sure, but my passengers need fresh clothing."

"Passengers?"

Natalya followed Zoya out to the boarding ramp and stood behind Panko.

The squad leader stared at them with raised eyebrows and a smirking leer. "We weren't told you had any passengers."

"I'm not surprised," Panko said.

The squad leader waved the delivery guy in. "What's in the package?" he asked.

"Shipsuits. Skivvies," the guy said.

"You have any objection if I look?"

The guy shrugged and handed it over. "No skin off my back."

"What do you think?" Panko asked. "We're having booze delivered or something?"

"Can't be too careful," the squad leader said, weighing the compact bundle in his hands before giving it to him.

"I need a thumb," the guy said. He held up a tablet and Panko pressed his thumb to it. The guy nodded. "Thanks and—uh—good luck." He looked around at the gathered security detail. He opened his mouth as if to say something else but apparently thought better of it and scooted back down the ramp and onto his carry-all.

"I assume you'll want them to come along?" Panko asked with a nod toward Natalya and Zoya.

"Do they know anything about the ship and the pilot who died?"

Panko looked at Zoya. "She looks pretty lively to me."

The man looked at Zoya and back at Panko. "What are you saying? She's the pilot?"

"Well, to be honest," Zoya said. "Natalya and I were both on the ship when things started going wrong."

The squad leader shook his head. "I need to check in."

"Thought you might," Panko said. "Gives them time to put on the fresh clothing before we're hauled into a room full of big shots."

The security officer raised his eyebrows at that but shrugged and turned away, keying his communicator and stepping off the ramp.

Panko waved his passengers back into the ship and followed on their heels. He keyed the inner door closed and grinned. "You can use my stateroom to get changed. Or the head if you'd prefer."

"Think our coming back from the dead is going to make a difference?" Natalya asked.

Panko shrugged. "It's grit in the gears, if nothing else. Whoever set this up is not expecting a counter-narrative. You're firsthand witnesses to what happened to the ship. It's going to be hard to argue with your testimony."

"Testimony?" Natalya asked.

"Inquiry. This will be a formal hearing." Panko paused and ran a hand over his chin. "At least in the beginning and on the surface. I expect it'll last several stans. Maybe extend into tomorrow."

"Why so long?" Zoya asked.

He snorted. "Because they won't find anything when they search our ship. Whoever is driving this won't like it if I go back aboard before they're satisfied the chips aren't here."

Zoya's eyes widened. "Oh," she said.

Panko nodded. "Now you know why we couldn't bring the chips aboard."

"We better get going then," Natalya said. She tore into the package and pulled out fresh shipsuits and skivvies, handing Zoya the smaller sizes before going into the head.

Chapter Forty-three
High Tortuga: 2366, June 1

THE LOCK-CALL BUZZED only a few ticks later. "That didn't take long," Panko said as Natalya and Zoya stepped into the passageway.

"What? Us getting changed or getting clearance?" Natalya asked, running her hand down the sleeve of the new shipsuit and trying to get a feel for the fabric. "What's this made of?"

"Don't like it?" Panko asked.

"I love it," she said.

"It's a wool-cotton blend. That's real cloth. Don't put it in the refresher. It needs to be washed."

"Like in water?" Zoya asked.

Panko laughed. "Yeah. With soap. It's much more comfortable to wear but a pain in the ass to care for once you're used to using the refresher."

The lock-call buzzed again—a little longer this time.

"I think our escort is getting antsy," Natalya said.

"Do them good to wait," Panko said. He held up a finger. "Wait for it."

The lock-call buzzed three short pulses and then a single long call.

Panko keyed the lock before it stopped. "Oh. Are you ready to go?" he asked looking at the squad leader.

The officer's face showed just the tiniest hint of red across this cheeks and over his ears. Natalya saw his jaw muscles clench as he bit back whatever it was he wanted to say. "If you're quite through, Mr. Panko?"

"Lead the way," Panko said.

As they stepped off the ramp, he slapped the lock control and the outer door closed. Natalya saw the sly smile flicker across the officer's face so briefly that she might have missed it if she hadn't been looking at him at the time.

"This way," the guard said, holding an open palm to point the way into the station.

The line of officers parted to form a corridor but two of them took point, while the rest fell into step surrounding them with the squad leader bringing up the rear with two more guards.

Natalya glanced at Zoya who simply pursed her lips and gave a little shrug.

The detail marched in step and, once out of the docking bay, the corridor echoed with the cadence of their footfalls. Natalya found herself marching in step with them. Old habits die very hard.

The walk took almost ten full ticks, ending at an airtight door with two more armed guards waiting. The new guards wore body armor and carried automatic weapons. Natalya eyed the guns and hoped they were loaded with glass instead of something armor-piercing that could rupture the hull.

The guard on the right rapped three times on the door. It opened immediately, pushing out into the passageway, momentarily blocking the guard on the left before he managed to step out of the way.

The guard on the inside, an older woman with graying hair and weary eyes, scanned the assembly. "Thank you for coming," she said. "I'm Captain Adams. If you'll follow me?" She stepped back from the door and the squad leader waved them forward.

Panko led the way into the compartment. He nodded to the squad leader on the way by. The small smile playing over his lips seemed to puzzle the man. A frown wrinkled his brow. It was over in an instant as they stepped over the sill. The door thunked shut behind them.

Captain Adams kept a smart pace down the corridor. It looked like any office complex Natalya had ever been in, down to the buffed flooring and the smell of brass polish. Each door sported a small plaque with a letter-number designation but no other identifying marks.

The captain turned her head to one side to speak over her shoulder as she strode along. "We're still waiting on one more participant. It shouldn't be very much longer." She stopped at a set of double doors, pulled one open, and ushered them into a nondescript room.

A half dozen couches, easy chairs, and small tables with chairs huddled in various corners. The industrial beige color scheme from the corridor carried over to the furnishings. A neat coffee mess held pride of place just inside the door, alongside a glassed-in case.

"Help yourselves to coffee, snacks. You'll find pastries and sandwiches in the case. There's hot water in the far urn and teas in the chest beside it. I can have a meal brought if you'd like something more substantial."

"Any idea how long this will take?" Panko asked.

"Unfortunately, no. Generally these things take as long as they take." Adams offered a crooked smile. "The more directors involved, the longer it takes. You're in luck. There are only five today. Get comfy. Relax. I'll be back for you shortly."

"Thank you," Panko said as he started for the coffee mess.

The captain stepped back out of the doorway and it closed with a click.

"Aren't they afraid we'll steal the silver?" Natalya asked, eyeing the door.

Panko shook his head and kept his gaze focused on his coffee. "The room is wired for sound and light and the door is locked." He moved to the case, selected a pastry, and held it up for them to see. "Try these cinnamon rolls. Nice spice without all the sugar slathered on the top."

Zoya followed him down the line while Natalya stood considering the door. "You eat here often?"

Panko laughed. "Not lately. No."

"But you recognize the cinnamon roll?"

"I spent some time here between yard gigs." He shrugged. "What can I say? I'm a sucker for a good cinnamon roll."

"I'm surprised you didn't get Sandra to make some of these for Rudy's," Natalya said, giving up on the door and joining them at the coffee mess.

"I did," he said. "You've probably tried the result. Hers are good but her idea of a cinnamon roll and mine didn't quite mesh. She's the owner. I'm the dishwasher. *Was* the dishwasher."

"Wonder who they're waiting for," Zoya said, snagging a roll from the case. "Somebody from Pulaski?"

Panko rolled his shoulders in a shrug and settled into one of the couch groupings, placing his coffee on the chrome and glass table in the middle. "Maybe a director who's coming from the far side of the station. Might be somebody from the yard. Not sure who they'd call from there unless it's Alison."

The door opened and Brian Dorion walked in with Joe Allen on his heels.

Natalya and Zoya both stood while Panko sat back with his coffee cup in both hands.

"Ms. Regyri. Ms. Usoko." Dorion frowned at them. "The rumors of your deaths seem to be somewhat unfounded." He looked at Panko, the frown turning to a scowl. "Mr. Panko? Care to explain?"

"Hello, Brian. Long time, no see."

Dorion's scowl deepened. "We heard that these women were dead."

"Not from me, you didn't."

"Bullshit. You're the one who told Pittman."

"What I told Alison—on a secured channel, by the way—was that there was nobody on the ship."

"Then where did they come from?" Dorion loomed over Panko.

Panko didn't seem overly concerned. "They came from the ship. They happened to be on my bridge when the call went through. So, when Alison asked, I told her there was no one on the ship, because they weren't. They were on mine." He sipped his coffee and looked up at Dorion for a moment before looking at Allen. "Hey, Joe."

"Ernst," Allen said with a little head nod in greeting.

Panko looked back at Dorion. "Now the interesting question to me is who told you they were dead?"

Dorion settled back on his heels, the frown shifting to a look of puzzlement, his eyes blinking rapidly and his gaze focused elsewhere. "My office got a message from the yards. The space trials for the ship went belly up, the ship jumped out but nobody came back with it."

"Yeah. I gathered that," Panko said. "But the only people who know what happened are in this room. The only message we sent was to Alison. Unless Alison has suddenly gotten loose with her comms, somebody else got some bad data." He nodded at the coffee mess. "Good coffee, Joe."

"Thanks. I have a team who handles it. You'd be amazed how entitled directors can be." Allen grinned and looked at Natalya. "How are you doing, Ms. Regyri?"

"We're fine. The ride was a bit wonky but we managed to bring it back. With a little help." She nodded at Panko. "Zoya's the star. She got the plots and piloting. I was just along for the ride."

Allen turned his gaze on Zoya. "Nice bit of work. Having the ship to tear down should answer a lot of questions."

"I'm sure, but I was mostly concerned with getting myself back, sir." She smiled at him.

"Call me Joe," Allen said. "At least here. We'll be getting the inquest underway in a few moments."

Zoya nodded.

The door opened again and closed behind a distraught-looking Alison Pittman. She crossed the room in a few strides and gave the two women a hug. "Zoya? Natalya? What's going on?"

"Well, we brought your ship back," Natalya said.

"It's a little banged up but luckily we wore our long underwear," Zoya said, hugging Pittman back.

Pittman rounded on Panko and gave him a kick in the leg.

"Hey! What's that for?" he asked, holding his cup out to keep from spilling it. "I got them back, didn't I?"

"You told me they were dead!" she said, practically shouting into his face.

"No, I told you the ship was empty. It was."

"Why would you do such a thing? I've been beside myself. Blaming myself for their deaths by letting them take that jump-capable coffin out."

Allen shifted his feet and stuck his hands in his trouser pockets. "Jump-capable coffin?"

Pittman seemed to notice Dorion and Allen for the first time. "Sorry, Mr. Allen. It's what the first test pilot called it."

"We'll try not to say that where the directors can hear, won't we?" Allen's face softened into a smile. "Although it has a certain ring to it."

The door opened and Captain Adams held it wide. "They're ready for you."

Panko stuck the last of the cinnamon roll into his mouth and washed it down with the last swig of coffee before getting up. "Pity. I bet the chairs won't be as comfortable."

Allen snorted and Zoya chuckled. Dorion just glowered at him.

Natalya stepped between the two men and looked into Dorion's face. "He's not the bad guy here, Brian."

Dorion's jaw clenched as he shot one last venomous glare at Panko before heading for the door.

"What's his problem?" Zoya asked.

"He thought you were dead and that Ernst lied," Allen said. "Which you did, Ernst, if only through omission. Why?"

"Because there are people who are trying to kill them," Panko said. "The fewer people who know they're alive, the safer they are."

Allen's eyes tightened just the tiniest amount. Then he pursed his lips and glanced at Zoya and Natalya. "Fair enough. Shall we go?"

Panko led the parade out of the lounge and into the conference room across the hall.

Across one end of the room ran a long table with five people sitting behind it. If Natalya hadn't known before she got there, their appearances would have screamed money. Hair coiffed just so. Clothing that looked like it came from a fashion newsie. A couple of the younger men sported what she thought of as 'the fashionable scruff' on their faces—as if to prove they were old enough to grow it and high enough on the food chain to flaunt it. The two women looked like they wore no makeup at all, except nobody looked that perfect without it. She wondered if they employed personal makeup artists and how long it took each day to make themselves look like that.

Joe Allen took the only empty place behind the table while Captain Adams escorted Panko, Natalya, and Zoya to the front of the room where they sat in chairs facing the panel. Pittman and Dorion took seats a couple of rows back from the front.

Allen nodded to Captain Adams, who closed the door with a thump.

"Right, then," Allen said. "Recording is active. I hereby convene the inquest into the circumstances of the ship designated *Echo One* on : 2366, May 30 and 31. I am CEO Joseph Allen, presiding." He turned to his right and leaned forward to look at the man on the end.

"My name is Anthony Frobisher. I am a director at large." He settled back and looked to his right.

The woman sitting there said, "My name is Theresa May Caldicott. I am the vice-director of the Data Services Division."

The next man in line said, "My name is Malachai Vagrant. I am the vice-director for Communications Systems."

Allen turned to the man immediately to his left.

"I'm Clarence Wallace, director of Space Operations for Ravaine."

The next man said, "William Bixby. Assistant director at large."

The woman at the end of the row said, "Magda Orlofski. Vice-director for Financial Planning."

Allen nodded. "Thank you." He looked at the three sitting in front. "Would each of you state your names and positions for the record? Mr. Panko?"

"My name is Ernst Panko. I am the captain of the courier *Serendipity* and currently serving as lead designer for Pulaski Yards' new ship production."

The directors behind the table seemed surprised at that. Orlofski and Bixby put their heads almost together and began some kind of whispering conversation. Vagrant simply stared at Panko, a slight crease on his forehead.

"Ms. Usoko?" Allen said.

"I'm Zoya Usoko. I was the pilot for this test run." Zoya glanced at Natalya.

"I'm Natalya Regyri. I'm captain of the Scout *Peregrine* and served as engineering officer for the test run."

Allen nodded again. "Thank you. Mr. Panko, what was your role in this situation?"

"I flew chase for the new ship."

As Caldicott leaned forward, a small silvery lapel pin on her tastefully tailored jacket blinked in the lights in the overhead. "Can you explain what that role entails, Mr. Panko."

"I followed the ship in case something went wrong and the crew needed to be taken off," Panko said.

"That didn't work out very well for you, did it, Panko?" Vagrant said, his eyes hard but not quite a glare.

"No, sir. Not exactly. On the upside, we got the ship back along with the crew. On the downside, we don't know who's behind the sabotage—or why."

Allen looked left and right. All the directors leaned back in their chairs. "Ms. Usoko, to the best of your recollection and ability, please describe the situation starting from the outer markers at Pulaski Yards."

Zoya's head bobbed in a gesture that might have been an acknowledgment. "Without the logs for reference, I may have some of the actual time-stamps wrong. We got underway at approximately 0900. The logs should show the exact time. We cleared the outer marker and began our speed run." Zoya's recitation took only a few ticks. The panel sat in silence, their expressions giving away nothing. "When we met up with *Serendipity*, we powered the ship down to reduce the chance that something else would put the ship at risk again. *Serendipity* took us in tow and jumped us back to Ravaine." She nodded at Allen.

"Thank you, Ms. Usoko. Mr. Panko, how is it your ship has the power harness to jump the courier?"

"It's built on a jump-capable tug's frame. It was easier to strip down the old ship and build what I wanted on top of the spaceframe. Never know when you need to drag somebody out of a hole."

"You didn't build your ship from scratch, then?" Allen asked.

"No, sir. The keel, grapples, and the deck frame all come from a derelict tug I got at The Junkyard. I cut it back, melted the surplus metals, and added a few things of my own."

"Like a power train?" Allen asked.

"A power train, an office, my stateroom, and a cockpit modeled after the old Explorer Scouts. I also added an extra-large head. Since I live aboard, I wanted to make it comfortable."

Allen looked up and down the table. "Anybody have a question?"

"I do," Vagrant said.

"Go ahead."

"Why aren't you dead?" He leaned forward staring at Natalya, laying his palms on the table.

"Why would we be?" Natalya asked.

"According to your story—and I take it you and Ms. Usoko are in agreement about this preposterous tale—but according to her, you lost control of your ship, vented all the atmosphere, jumped into the Deep Dark somewhere, and then jumped back into a holding location instead of coming all the way back to Ravaine." Vagrant's face had turned just the tiniest bit red during his tirade. He glared at Natalya.

After a few heartbeats, Natalya said, "Well, mostly. Except for the 'lost control' part. The ship's computer hijacked us. Is there a question?"

His nostrils flared and he pulled in a deep breath before Allen held up a hand to get Vagrant's attention.

"I didn't hear a question either, Malachai. What is it you want to know?"

Vagrant sat back in his chair and folded his arms. "I want to know what really happened."

Allen raised an eyebrow in Vagrant's direction. "You're calling them liars?"

"I'm just saying none of it makes sense."

Panko raised a hand. "If I may...?"

Allen nodded. "Go ahead."

"The evidence is in the logs. You can easily verify their story," he said.

"Why isn't the ship here?" Bixby asked.

"It was taken off our hands by a tug from Pulaski Towing," Panko said. "They intercepted us a few stans after we jumped back in."

"And you just gave them the ship?" Bixby asked.

Panko shrugged. "I told them they didn't need to do that, but maybe they knew something we didn't."

"Like what?" Bixby asked, his head titled slightly to one side.

"Like we were about to be summoned here."

Bixby snorted. "Point taken." He sat back in his seat and nodded to Allen.

"That does raise another question," Allen said. "Why didn't they bring the ship here for the inquiry?" He looked at Pittman. "Did you order it?"

"No, sir," Pittman said. "I was content to wait for *Serendipity* to return with the prototype."

"Where is the ship now?" Allen asked. "Who's safeguarding the evidence?"

"Evidence?" Vagrant asked.

Allen frowned at Vagrant. "Of course. If nothing else, those computer cores may show who tampered with the programming and when. Who's running Pulaski Towing?" He looked at Pittman again.

"Winfield Tweedie," she said. "He goes by Win."

Allen looked at Captain Adams. "Please, flash a message to Tweedie. Find out what's going on with that ship."

"Yes, sir." Adams slipped out of the conference room.

"You have any other questions, Mr. Vagrant?" Allen asked.

Vagrant crossed his arms and glowered. "Yes. My understanding is that this ship isn't actually the one that's going into production."

"That's correct," Pittman said.

Vagrant looked up at her with a scowl. "Perhaps you'd like to join them here in the front?"

Allen held up a hand. "Ease up. You didn't ask a question and you addressed your comment to the room at large. Ms. Pittman— as director of Pulaski Yards—is the one person with the most direct knowledge." He paused and looked at Vagrant out of the corner of his eye. "Now, do you have a question?"

Vagrant leaned forward, his elbows on the table. "Why did you change the design?"

"Who would you like to answer, Malachai?" Allen prompted before anybody else could speak.

"Panko purports to be the design genius," Vagrant said.

Allen nodded to Panko. "Can you answer that question?"

"I can, sir, yes. But Ms. Pittman brought me aboard to make the change after she made the decision. You might be better served to ask her."

"I'm asking you," Vagrant said.

Panko looked to Allen, who shrugged.

"Well, several things are wrong with that design. First, construction costs are too high. The ovoid hull shape with all the curved parts is expensive—both in materials and time. It's purely aesthetic, serving no functional purpose. Worse, the ship's performance suffers because all those curves cut out useful volume inside the hull.

"Second, it has a single Burleson drive. Nobody runs a single drive. Smaller ships generally use a paired drive design—two drives in one case—to cut down on volume in close quarters. My understanding is that the original plan called for two drives but the decision to remove the second drive happened before I came on the scene—"

"That's rather speculative, isn't it, Mr. Panko?" Vagrant asked, interrupting Panko.

"Which part?"

"That there was a prior plan? One that had both drives?"

Panko frowned and gave a little shrug. "I'd think more hearsay than speculation, sir."

"How so?"

"Well, that's what I was told. I had no reason to doubt that information but it had no bearing on me redesigning the ship."

Dorion raised his hand. "If I may...?"

Allen acknowledged him with a nod. "Mr. Dorion."

"I was shown a design some months back that showed a second drive. I still have the design document in my office. Logically, somebody had to make a decision to change the ship in order for the prototype to be so different from the approved design."

Allen looked at Vagrant. "Satisfied with that point?"

Vagrant chewed his lower lip and glowered. "I suppose. Go on, Mr. Panko. You were saying?"

"Third, its specs are all out of whack. It claims to have very long legs. It's supposed to be able to jump eighteen or twenty Burleson Units, but that's a ridiculous jump. The random jump error is still only five percent but that's a whole BU and may well put the ship in danger. It doesn't really matter, because whoever spec'd out the power system shorted the capacitors. It only has enough power to jump five or six BUs."

Allen scowled. "Who the hell approved that?"

"Before my time, sir," Panko said.

"Alison?" Allen asked, looking up at her.

"When I took over, that was the plan on the ways. We built the first prototype and had ten more on the ways when Ms. Regyri and Ms. Usoko started finding problems."

"Yes, but who approved the last plans?"

"I'd have to go back to the yard and look, sir. Tony Downs might know, if you can find him here and if he'll tell you after I booted him off-station," Pittman said.

Vagrant leaned forward and slapped a hand on the table. "You what?"

Allen turned his whole body toward Vagrant, his jaw clenched. "Mr. Vagrant, director or no, if you cannot control yourself, I'll have security remove you. Is that clear?" He bit the words off through clenched teeth.

Vagrant didn't back down. "She had no right—"

"Think real hard before you say another word, Vagrant."

"Or what?" Vagrant all but sneered. "You're just the CEO of this outfit. I'm a member of the board of directors and you work for me."

"I work for the board," Allen said. "Right now, my board-authorized duties require me to find out what the hell went wrong with that ship."

"But they're not even building that ship anymore," Vagrant said, lowering his voice to something approaching a civil tone. "That doesn't negate the fact that she fired one of the key people managing that project."

Allen didn't look away from Vagrant. "Ms. Pittman, please state your job title."

"I'm vice-director of Pulaski Yards."

"Does your job involve hiring and firing personnel for the yards?" Allen asked.

"Yes, sir."

"Did you fire Anthony Downs?"

"Yes, sir. I had cause."

"What cause?" Allen asked, still pinning Vagrant to his seat with his gaze.

"Profiteering."

Allen blinked at that and he looked at Pittman. "Profiteering?"

"He was skimming off the project budget by giving contracts to his friends and relatives for overpriced goods, then taking a kickback under the table."

Allen cocked his head to one side. "That's a pretty strong accusation. Can you prove it?"

"Yes." She sighed. "What I can't prove is how much he's actually stolen from the company."

Vagrant drew a breath but clamped his jaw shut when Allen glared at him.

"We'll talk about this after," Allen said.

"Yes, sir. I filed a report through HR at the time. It was copied to your office."

"Thank you, Ms. Pittman," Allen said. "Ms. Usoko, why did you make a short jump instead of coming all the way back to Ravaine?"

"We jumped as soon as we had enough forward momentum to get through the hole. We had barely sufficient capacitor to fire the drive and we wanted to get out of that location ASAP."

"Why?" Allen asked. "How much longer would you have had to wait?"

"Probably another couple of stans. We were pushing the power system pretty hard," Zoya said.

"So why jump?" Allen asked again.

Natalya glanced at Zoya and gave her a little nod.

Zoya shrugged. "Well, sir, the ship was sabotaged by somebody who knew the limitations of the design. We thought that—since they knew where they'd jumped us—they'd be waiting to scoop us up. When we spotted an unidentified ship braking hard in our direction, we took the short jump rather than risk being taken."

Vagrant's jaw clenched so tight, Natalya could almost hear his molars grinding. "And how do you come to that conclusion, Ms. Usoko?"

"Which one, sir?" Zoya asked. "That the ship was sabotaged? Clearly the case, since the computer system refused console commands. It didn't simply malfunction. Just before the air locks vented, it displayed a taunt. That's not random malfunction."

"No, Ms. Usoko. That the saboteur knew the limitations of the ship."

"Somebody went to a lot of trouble to remove the ship from Ravaine," she said. "If they believed the ship could jump as far as it says, they could have gotten a lot farther away. There are dozens of open holes out there at ten BUs. Far enough that even *Serendipity* couldn't follow. They programmed a four-BU jump after boosting the ship along a specific axis at high enough speed that it cleared the local threshold. That's almost as far as the ship could go with its limited power supply. We might have gotten another BU out of it, but the capacitor would have been redlined."

"Yes, yes," Vagrant said. "What of it?"

"If they'd programmed it for—say—six BUs, the drive would have shut down before firing. It's a safety feature. It can't jump if it doesn't have enough power to bend space. The program would have run. The jump would have failed. We'd have been sitting out there in Ravaine and only needed to turn the ship around to bring it back."

Vagrant frowned. "Assuming it was sabotage. Assuming the perpetrators knew how far the ship could jump." He shook his head. "You have no proof."

"We have the ship," Panko said. "Or we should have the ship, assuming it didn't get misplaced somewhere between the hand-off and the yard."

"Enough, Malachai," Allen said. "We're here to gather what information we can. Nobody here has done anything wrong. It was an experimental ship. Whatever else may have happened we'll leave to security, right?"

Vagrant turned a fulminating glare on Allen. "This whole program is a mess. You've let this get completely out of control and you're wasting company assets."

"There it is," Natalya said, leaning over to Panko. "Didn't expect to be here to see it."

Allen ignored Vagrant, looking at Natalya with a slight frown. "Ms. Regyri?"

"Yes, sir?"

"You have a comment for the board?"

"No, sir."

He stared at her for several long moments while Vagrant seethed, not quite silently, beside him. The other members of the panel kept casting sidelong glances at Vagrant. Bixby seemed quite distressed, while Caldicott wore a bland expression of boredom. Wallace kept peeking around Allen as if to see whether Vagrant was still there and still fuming.

Finally, Allen sat back in his chair and looked left and right to the panelists. "Does anybody else have something they'd like to ask?"

Caldicott lifted her chin. "How soon will we have transcripts?"

"A couple of stans," Allen said. "Anybody else?"

The door at the back of the room opened and Captain Adams slipped through, closing it behind her. She strode to the front of the room and handed Allen a tablet. As he read it, his eyebrows started scaling his forehead. After several very long moments, he lowered the tablet and looked around the room. "Well, it seems that the idea that somebody wanted the ship badly enough to hijack it wasn't so far off as it might have seemed. Tweedie didn't send a tug out to haul the ship back."

"Who did?" Vagrant asked.

"Good question," Allen said. He looked to Panko. "What do you know about the tug?"

Panko grinned. "PY-1412. Skipper was Dick McDaniels. Yes, I recognized him—and the tug—from the yards."

"Then what the hell is going on?" Allen asked.

"I've an idea," Panko said. "Let's ask the people who are searching my ship right now."

"Searching your ship?" Allen asked.

"Well, I assume they're searching. They breached my lock about three ticks after we came through the security perimeter." He checked his tablet. "Nobody's left yet so I assume they're still there."

Vagrant sat back in his chair and crossed his arms. His scowl evaporated and his expression smoothed out. "What makes you think they're searching for something?"

"Well, there's nothing to steal. The ship's unique, so it's almost impossible to sell even if they can get it underway." He shrugged. "They could be trashing the place. Probably are, because by now they've got to be really frustrated that they can't find what they're looking for."

Vagrant blinked a couple of times, his face going slack for a moment before his mask came back up. "You know what they want?"

"Not precisely, no."

Allen broke in. "Captain Adams, would you secure the docking bay? Keep whoever's in there bottled up."

"Of course, sir." She held out her hand and Allen handed her the tablet. She started typing before she even turned around and strode from the room.

Vagrant's lips tightened but he leaned forward placing his elbows on the table, his forearms flat on the surface. "You know what they want," he said, staring at Panko. "Stop playing around."

"Apparently, so do you," Panko said. A small smile played around his lips.

Allen waved a hand in the air, raising his eyebrows at Panko. "Perhaps you might fill us all in? Some of us haven't any idea what you're talking about."

"Roughly half a million credit chips," Panko said. "I don't know the denominations but I'm guessing something small. Innocuous. Probably under a hundred credits on each."

"Ten million credits?" Allen asked.

"I don't know precisely. And I could be off on the count."

"You're insane," Vagrant said.

"Quite likely," Panko said. "What's your point?"

"Stop, Malachai. That's my second warning. One more word and I'm booting you."

"You don't have the right," Vagrant said.

"He does, actually," Wallace said. "We're here as witnesses, not judges, and serving at the will of the CEO according to the by-laws. He can run the inquiry any way he likes. This is a fact-finding inquiry only." Wallace shrugged as if to say 'sorry' but his expression said he really wasn't.

Vagrant stood, shoving his chair back out of the way, and stormed for the door. "I don't need to sit here and be insulted by a jumped-up bureaucrat." He didn't stop at the door but burst through it as if being chased by a horde of demons.

Caldicott's expression shifted ever so slightly. "Gauche," she said.

Natalya frowned.

"Something, Ms. Regyri?" Allen asked.

"Does he have a ship handy?"

Allen looked perplexed by the question. "Probably. If not a private one, one of his company ships is almost certainly docked. Why?"

"He's running."

"Running from what?" Allen asked.

"My guess is that he's cutting his losses and bolting while he can," Natalya said.

"That would be my guess as well," Zoya said.

Allen shook his head. "What has he to do with any of this?"

"I can't prove anything," Natalya said. "I'd hate to make any accusations. I'm just guessing."

Allen's eyes narrowed. "What does this have to do with the space trials of that ship?"

"I've got a question of my own. Who stands to gain if the project fails?" Natalya asked.

"Why would it fail?" Allen said.

Natalya started ticking the points off on her fingers. "One, the design—which looked pretty good when I saw the original—was gutted to the point where it can't do the job it was designed for. Two, that change didn't happen until the original project lead took a short walk through an open lock without a suit. Three, all the original project architects got scattered to the winds just before the ways started gearing up to build the first prototypes. Four, the new administrator has no experience in ship design or construction." She looked over her shoulder. "No offense, Ms. Pittman."

"None taken," Pittman said. "I'm filling in my gaps as fast as I can, but I'm only now beginning to realize how much I don't know about ships."

Natalya looked at Allen with a slight shrug. "She's a great administrator, but she's over her head. Somebody knew that when they recommended her for the position."

Allen frowned at that. "I recommended her."

"Who suggested her?" Zoya asked.

Bixby cleared his throat. "She's a great department head. As poorly as the project was going, we thought she'd be a good, solid hand on the helm. As it were." His voice tailed off as everybody looked at him.

"Thank you, Mr. Bixby," Pittman said. "I should never have accepted the post. I'm HR, not ship design."

Allen looked back and forth between Bixby and Pittman for a few moments. "Why did you, Alison?"

Pittman shrugged and stared at her hands clasped together in her lap. "I felt like I was at a dead end in HR. There's nowhere to move up from there. When Mr. Vagrant approached me about the post, he convinced me that it could be life-changing." She gave a short, brittle laugh. "He was certainly right about that."

"Vagrant?" Allen asked. "How did he get involved?"

"I did some recruiting for him," Alison said. "Well, the department did. His requirements were difficult to fill but we eventually found him the people he needed."

"How did he get involved with the replacement director?" Allen asked.

Wallace said, "Routine. When we lost Jeffrey, I checked with all the directors for their recommendations. We always do that for high-level posts."

"Vagrant suggested Ms. Pittman," Allen said, his voice dropping at the end as if he couldn't believe it.

"Yes," Wallace said. "He made quite a good case for her."

"He made the same case to me," Bixby said. "With Finance and SpaceOps behind her, he said she'd be a shoo-in and could get the project under control."

"She's an excellent administrator," Wallace said with a smile at Pittman. "Besides, she had one of the most senior structural engineers in the sector as her technical liaison. He should have been able to deal with any issues arising from design and construction. It's what he's been doing here for decades."

Natalya raised her hand.

"Yes?" Allen said.

"How much would Mr. Vagrant lose if the project went through to a successful completion?"

"Why would he lose?" Allen asked. "He's director of communications."

Caldicott cleared her throat and raised one perfectly sculpted eyebrow in Allen's direction.

"Ms. Caldicott? You have some light to shed?"

"One-third of the current couriers are Vagrant's ships. Owned and operated either directly by M. Vagrant Outfitters or indirectly through companies he owns majority stakes in."

Allen's jaw all but dropped to the table. "How was he able to do that?"

"It's not against the rules. His holdings on this were hardly secret." She cleared her throat again. "I might have been doing a little prospecting in the data. He has a lot of companies—both here in the Toe-Holds and in CPJCT space."

"So, if the new ships come online?" Allen asked.

"His contracts would all eventually expire," Caldicott said.

Wallace said, "Well, they wouldn't all expire at once. Some would have to be renewed to give us time to ramp up the fleet."

"You wouldn't need as many ships if you restructured the architecture," Zoya said.

Caldicott's icy expression thawed as she looked at Zoya. "Thank you," she said.

"Explain," Allen said.

"Spoke and hub," Caldicott said. She nodded at Zoya. "You tell him. I've tried talking sense to them until I'm blue in the face."

"If you divide up Toe-Hold space into service regions based on loading, you put a hub somewhere in the Deep Dark where the ships can jump out of. They make a lot of short, fast runs, and dump the data back to the hub. They don't lose days in transit from here to there and back again. Use a few dedicated ships to shuttle crews and data back and forth to the various hubs. The service-time paths get shortened, the service becomes more reliable, and it scales up without major problems as the demand curve grows."

Allen looked at Dorion. "This is your bailiwick. Talk to me."

"They broached the topic with me a little while ago. It makes a certain sense, but it still depends on getting these little hummers out there, which takes us back to the yards, back to the design. It'll still take a goodly number of ships, but maybe not the fleet we originally planned for."

Allen looked at Caldicott. "Why is this the first time I'm hearing this?"

"I haven't been able to get it out of board committee to do a feasibility study," she said.

"Board committee?" Allen said.

"Communications committee."

Allen's eyes widened. "Which Vagrant chairs."

"You see the road block."

Allen scowled and pulled out his tablet, pressing a few keys. One of the battledressed officers from the entry stuck his head in. "Sir?"

"Find Malachai Vagrant. Stop him. Don't let him get on one of his ships. I want to talk with him."

"Is he under arrest, sir?" the guard asked.

Allen paused and looked at Caldicott.

"He's not broken any of the by-laws that we know of," she said.

"Murder? Attempted murder? Theft of company resources?" Natalya asked.

Allen rounded on her, his eyes wide. "What?"

"Somebody killed the first project manager. Somebody tried to kill us. Somebody has absconded with an experimental ship that belongs to the company. Somebody has been skimming off company projects for decades. That last one's probably Downs and not Vagrant, but still." Natalya shrugged.

"You got all that?" Allen barked at the guard.

"Sir!" He ducked out and slammed the door as he left.

They all sat there in the silence for a few moments.

A monster yawn overtook Natalya and her stomach growled. "Sorry," she said. "I got a nap earlier but it's been a rough few days."

"Anybody else have anything to add?" Allen said.

"Not at this time, but I'd like to reconvene if we discover new information," Wallace said.

"Sounds like a plan. I declare this inquest closed pending further development." Allen stood and stretched. "Ms. Regyri, Ms. Usoko. We'll find you some housing and get you fed. Ernst? You might want to get down to the docking bay and check out your ship."

"Yes, sir. I would kinda like to see how much damage they did."

"With any luck they've got assets we can leverage if it comes to compensation for any losses."

"Much obliged."

The group drifted toward the door where they met Captain Adams coming in. "They got out before we could close the door," she said. "Security is tracking cam footage now. We'll find them."

"Thank you, Captain," Allen said. "Please see that these people get unlimited visas and get Mr. Panko back aboard his ship as soon as possible."

"Of course, sir."

"Oh, and put a departure hold on all Vagrant's ships."

"Won't work," Caldicott said so quietly Natalya could barely hear her.

Allen heard. "Why not?"

"It's a shell game. Something like half of the shipping docked at the moment is connected to Vagrant somehow. That's not counting his various yachts under assumed names."

Allen stopped in his tracks and narrowed his eyes at Caldicott. "A *little* prospecting?"

Caldicott shrugged.

Allen sighed and looked at the deck while he rubbed the back of his neck with both hands. "All right. Zoya and Natalya need food and lodging. Ernst needs to get back to his ship. I need to get back to my office. Somebody needs to find the missing ship. And that's just what I can think of off the top of my head."

"Good news on the ship, sir. The tug will have it docked in its berth at the yard by this time tomorrow," Adams said. "Tweedie messaged to let me know. Just a skipper trying to help out. Nothing nefarious."

Allen frowned. "Thanks. I'm not sure I'm buying it, but we've got other fish on the grill."

"I'll escort Mr. Panko to the docks and get his visa." Adams said.

Frobisher spoke up. "I can show Ms. Usoko and Ms. Regyri to the transient housing."

Caldicott gave him a small frown. "If you don't mind? I'd like to pick their brains about this spoke-and-hub idea. I can show them to the Ravaine. They'll have hot and cold running everything there." She smiled at the two women. "My dime. Consulting fee."

"Right," Allen said. "Go. Do. Get back to me."

Bixby, Frobisher, and Wallace said their good-byes and got out of the way. Adams was about to leave when Allen said, "Ernst? Sorry. A word before you go?"

"What d'ya need, Joe?"

"Where are they?" Allen asked.

"The chips?"

Allen nodded.

"Not on my ship," Panko said.

"I gathered that. Where are they?"

"I'll let you know as soon as I can check to see if they're where we left them." He winked at Natalya.

"You won't tell me now?"

Panko shook his head. "Sorry."

Allen's eyes narrowed, giving Panko a thin-lipped, hard look for a moment. "Can't say as I blame ya," he said. "But if that's really contraband, I want our money back."

Panko grinned. "Can't say as I blame ya," he said. He headed for the door, which Adams held open for him.

Chapter Forty-four
High Tortuga: 2366, June 1

AS SOON AS CALDICOTT got them out of the hearing room and walked a few dozen yards down the corridor, she frowned. "Those things always give me agita," she said.

"Inquiries?" Natalya asked.

"Any of the mixed group meetings. Vagrant's bad enough in divisional director meetings. Put him in a group of mere hirelings and he becomes insufferable."

"You mean like Joe Allen?" Zoya asked.

Caldicott bobbed her head a little bit side to side. "Joe was the only one who wasn't a director. It sticks in Vagrant's craw that—technically—the CEO of the mothership outranks all the divisional directors."

"Can't tell the players without a program," Zoya said.

"Even with a program," Caldicott said. "I wasn't kidding about Vagrant's holdings."

Natalya cast a side-eyed look at the older woman. "Pardon my saying so, but none of you are exactly scratching out a living."

Caldicott laughed. "That's true enough, but Malachai's got fingers where most people don't even know there are pies." She winked at Natalya. "I'm not hurting. Nice thing about being Data Division is that I get access to some of the juicy bits."

"Is that ethical?" Zoya asked.

Caldicott glanced at Zoya with a small frown. "Probably not."

"Would you get into trouble with the company if it were known?" Zoya asked.

Caldicott smiled. "I was careful with my contract. I'm actually required to personally investigate data irregularities. I have a team of data miners who work directly for me. Sometimes scraps fall off the table and we're able to pick them up." She shrugged. "A million here, a million there. It adds up for us but in the grand scheme of things? Doesn't amount to pocket change. Not even rounding error. It's dust on the back of a comet. Total GDP for the Western Annex is measured in trillions of credits a day. Wallace can tell you exactly, but it's huge and it's growing."

"That's why Vagrant wants control," Zoya said.

"Control?" Caldicott asked.

"The new ships."

"Ah, well, yes. He's heavily invested in the current network. Losing that investment would hurt."

"It's not just that, though, is it?" Zoya said. "Not just handling the courier duties."

Caldicott grinned at her. "Shrewd one, aren't ya."

Natalya looked back and forth between them. "He's using his couriers to move goods, too."

"And he moves a lot of goods," Caldicott said. "Not as much as his books want us to believe, but still a lot. If he loses that pipeline, he loses a lot."

"What? He's laundering the credits?" Zoya asked.

Caldicott chuckled. "I never said anything about laundering. Or smuggling."

"Why tell us?" Natalya asked.

Caldicott paused and looked Natalya in the eye. She squinted a bit as if trying to see inside Natalya's skull. "I don't know. Call it a hunch. Call it keeping my ear to the figurative ground here and knowing that Joe Allen and Brian Dorion hired you two out of Dark Knight without anybody here catching a whiff. You're both out in the cold as far as data is concerned."

"Out in the cold?" Natalya asked.

"You've got no believable background. Your academy records aren't public although you both graduated the same day. The public records are complete fiction. They're consistent, but that's about all I can say about them. That can't happen by accident. You're working for somebody. You want to tell me who?"

"We work for Brian Dorion," Natalya said.

Caldicott snorted. "You keep getting paid from Port Newmar. A pittance but regular as clockwork every month. A body could live on that if she was careful."

"We don't know who's doing it," Zoya said. "We left Port Newmar under some peculiar circumstances."

Caldicott considered that for a moment. "You wanna share?"

"There might have been a murder involved," Natalya said.

"You didn't kill him," Zoya said.

"I said 'might.'"

"So, TIC," Caldicott said. "That has the smell of a TIC operation. Why did they send two green kids out of school?"

"I don't even know who sent us," Zoya said. "I was supposed to start training as a TIC agent after graduation. Things got a bit out of hand."

"You're actually *that* Zoya Usoko, right? Konstantin Usoko's granddaughter?"

Zoya stiffened for a moment. "Yes. Why?"

"I thought so. It's an unusual name. The other five Zoya Usokos in the Western Annex are all in their eighties. Your records say you're from Margary but don't link to a certification of live birth."

"Is that unusual?" Natalya asked.

"It's not unusual for Toe-Hold space, but it's extremely rare for the High Line. Those people record every time somebody farts." She grinned. "That's good for people like me."

"How did you make the connection?" Zoya asked.

"Financial news. When one of the richest people in the Annex has a kid, it's news. When your father was born, it made a splash. When he walked away from the business, it was bigger news. When his daughter took over as skipper on a mining barge at the tender age of twelve? Yeah. That was roundly reported as both crazy and abusive. It didn't make the public streams, of course, but the smart money tapped you as the heir apparent. Until you went to the academy and dropped off the grid."

"You got all that from the data?" Natalya asked.

"Oh, yeah. Financial records got shifted around, shuffled through some shell companies, but we run the payroll for everybody."

"Not all of it," Natalya said.

Caldicott bit the inside of her lip again. "Yeah. That's true. Chips are a blind spot, even for us."

"Why don't you close it?" Zoya asked.

"We make too much profit from it. We don't know who's using them or what they're doing with them, but they generate a lot of revenue for us. We're not about to cook that golden goose."

"Why are you telling us this?" Natalya asked again.

"Well," Caldicott said, with a shrug. "You asked. I don't know who you're working for—and you won't or can't tell me—but I trust you. Since you've been here, that project has begun to feel more solid than it has since Jeffrey died."

"He was killed," Natalya said.

"I've often thought so," Caldicott said. "But I can't prove it on the basis of the data. Nobody wants to believe it's possible to open both doors on the airlock."

"Of course it's possible," Natalya said.

"Even against the pressure?" Caldicott asked.

"Open the inner door first," Natalya said. "Simple. I haven't got any special knowledge in the case but who said anything about having both doors open at the same time?"

Caldicott stopped and stared openly. "That's the report we got."

"Maybe so, but that kind of malfunction wasn't necessary. Most ships dispose of refuse by stacking it in the lock, closing the door, and popping the override on the outer door. Whoosh. Everything in the lock goes out with the air," Natalya said.

"Jeffrey could have done it himself if the outer door showed green," Zoya said. "That's a software issue. Anybody with access to the station's systems could have done it, left it long enough to do the job, and then pulled the patch out. No fingerprints. No smoking gun."

"That's ... unsettling," Caldicott said.

"Yes, ma'am. It is," Zoya said.

Caldicott's brow furrowed and her eyes focused in the distance. "Wanna bet?" she asked.

Natalya glanced at Zoya. "Bet? On what?"

"That there are no fingerprints?"

Zoya's eyebrows lifted and her mouth opened wide enough for a small "oh" to escape.

"Exactly," Caldicott said. "Just because nobody's found them, doesn't mean they don't exist."

"It might just mean nobody's looked in the right place," Zoya said.

"This long after the fact?" Natalya asked. "You'd need a team—" She saw Caldicott's grin and closed her mouth with a snap.

Caldicott nodded once and struck off down the corridor again. "Come on. While you're getting settled, I've got some business to attend to. Plan on dinner at 1800. I'll pick you up at the hotel."

"Hotel?" Natalya asked.

"What? You thought I was kidding?" She led them around a corner and into an atrium that rose six stories above them and looked big enough to land a freighter in. "Main concourse for Alpha," she said.

"Alpha?" Natalya asked.

"The station's so huge they gave each section of it a name. Like a neighborhood. Alpha is ... well ... alpha."

"The first?" Zoya asked.

"The leader," Natalya said. "The boss."

Caldicott touched the tip of one finger to her own nose. "Now, let's get you checked in. The Hotel Ravaine is right around the corner."

CHAPTER FORTY-FIVE
HIGH TORTUGA: 2366, JUNE 1

CALDICOTT'S PRESENCE brought a dapper manager to the front desk. "Director Caldicott." His smile would have looked cheesy—even obsequious—on a lesser man. "How may we assist you today?"

"Etienne, *mon cher*, these two ladies are stranded here on our lovely station and are in dire need of shelter. Can you find a small space to fit them in for—say—three nights?"

"*Mais, bien sûr.*" Etienne gave Natalya and Zoya each a warm smile. "Do you ladies have any preference?"

"Is my suite available, Etienne?" Caldicott asked.

"Of course, Director. Will you be staying with us as well?"

"Not this trip. Let them have it for as long as they need it, if you would?" She reached across the desk and took his hand. "And put it on my tab. I owe them a great deal."

"Of course, Director."

Natalya and Zoya shared a glance.

"Do you have any luggage?" Etienne asked, looking up at Natalya.

"We do, but it's still at the yard," Natalya said.

"I've notified Veronica. She'll be bringing some more suitable outfits," Caldicott said.

"Of course, Director." He pulled a pair of key cards from a slot on the desk and handed them to Natalya and Zoya with a little flourish. "I can have an attendant show you the way."

"Nonsense," Caldicott said. "I'll show them. No need to bother the staff." She paused and gave him a warm smile. "Thank you so much, Etienne."

"My pleasure, as always, Director."

She nodded at Natalya and Zoya before sailing off across the lobby. "We've got a lot to do and not much time to do it in." She passed the bank of elevators and pressed her palm to a panel mounted on the wall. A door opened and she led the way in. "We'll set your access from the suite." They stepped into the car and the door whispered closed.

"If you don't mind my asking, why?" Natalya asked.

Caldicott gave her a crooked smile. "Vagrant."

Natalya glanced at Zoya who shrugged in return.

"It's simple really," Caldicott said. "I want him out of here. If you two have even a chance of leverage, I want it."

"I don't know how much leverage we have," Natalya said.

"You've probably got more than you think. I've got the team digging now, just based on what you said at the inquest. They'll find something."

"If there's anything to find," Natalya said.

Caldicott snorted. "There is. I know that much already. With these new tidbits, we'll at least break his hold on the Communications Division." The door whispered open to a plush foyer. Caldicott took them to the left. "Use your key. See if it works."

Natalya swiped her keycard on the lock and the paired doors swung inward.

"Good," Caldicott said. "Come on. Elevator first, then what? Food? Drink? Sleep?"

"I could use a snack," Zoya said. "Some water would be welcome."

Caldicott waved them into the entry and pointed to a darkened panel. "Swipe your card, then put your palm on that."

"Slick," Natalya said and did as she was told.

"You'll be able to call the elevator now. If I hadn't been here, one of the hotel staff would have brought you up."

"Isn't this overkill?" Zoya asked.

Caldicott shook her head, elegant coif bobbing at the movement. "When things get ragged, having a secure bolt-hole makes all the difference."

"Where's Vagrant's?" Natalya asked.

"His bolt-hole?" Caldicott asked. "He leaves the station. He's never far from a docked ship with hot thrusters."

"Afraid of getting locked up?" Zoya asked, finishing with the scanner.

"Afraid of getting killed," Caldicott said. "Too many people see a knife in the back as a viable answer to a dispute."

"I thought High Tortuga arbitrated those kinds of discussions," Zoya said.

Caldicott made a see-saw gesture with one hand. "When both parties are rational. It generally works pretty well." She shrugged. "There's always a small percentage who don't like the outcomes."

"And Malachai Vagrant wins a lot of them?" Natalya said.

"Too many," Caldicott said. "As Comms Director, he has a significant advantage that he's not supposed to have. Open access without the moral compass to stay on this side of ethical practice as far as I'm concerned. Not that I have a lot myself." She led them farther into the suite and pointed to an arched entry just around the corner from the entry. "Kitchen. Fridge should be stocked. Fruits. Cheeses. Bottled anything. Wine cellar in the cabinet beside it. Help yourself and we'll get started." She continued on and settled on a couch upholstered in what looked like burgundy leather. "If one of you would grab me a bottle of water?"

Natalya followed her nose into the tidy kitchenette. A half-height stainless steel cooler was tucked under a polished stone counter. She found a couple of bottles of water and eyed the selection of soft drinks. She passed on the food and stepped aside so Zoya could choose what she wanted. Cracking the top on one of the bottles, she wandered back to where Caldicott waited, examining her tablet while perched on the edge of her seat. "You want a glass?" she asked, holding out the unopened bottle.

Caldicott took it, returning a smile and a nod. "Thank you, no. I may be a director now but I wasn't always." She twisted the top off the bottle and took a delicate sip. "Ah. I was drier than I thought." She gestured to the sofa across from her. "Sit. Sit. Get comfy. Then tell me everything you didn't tell the inquest."

Natalya lounged on the sofa, taking advantage of the comfy seating. "This is one thing I really miss. A comfy couch."

Zoya sat on the other end and grinned. "What? The *Peregrine's* couch isn't comfy?"

Natalya took a slug from her water before answering. "It is, but it's not the same." She looked at Caldicott. "What makes you think we didn't tell the inquest everything?"

"For one thing, you didn't say where you stashed the chips." She took another sip from her bottle. "For another, you didn't really say how you survived."

Natalya pursed her lips and considered the questions. "No, we didn't and the location's off the table until Ernst says something."

"Why?" Caldicott asked, her eyes crinkling with curiosity. "Don't you know?"

"Ernst's instincts have been pretty good so far," Natalya said. "I'm good with following his lead on it."

Caldicott gave a short nod. Her frown said she wasn't happy with the answer, but Natalya felt pretty sure the subject would come up again. "How did you keep from getting sucked out the lock?"

"Seat belts," Natalya said. "And we wore softsuits. When the lock popped, everything not strapped down exited the ship. I just made it back to the jump seat before the outer door opened, but the suits kept us breathing and communicating. The only difficulty was making sure we had enough air to get back."

"Obviously you did," Caldicott said.

"The lock doors both cycled closed just before the programmed jump took us out of the system," Zoya said. "We had almost enough reserves and were able to get a little more oxygen from the environmental system. It was enough to pressurize the ship, but only just."

Caldicott tapped the mouth of her bottle against her lower lip and stared into the middle distance. "That tell you anything?" she asked after a few moments.

"It's a tossup," Natalya said. "Either they didn't expect the test pilots to wear suits inside the ship or they had a plan to deal with us in the Deep Dark."

"Or both," Zoya said. "Backup plans for the backup plans."

Natalya nodded. "That's possible, too."

"You said something about them knowing that the ship wasn't up to the stated spec," Caldicott said.

"That's conjecture," Natalya said. "I think it's a pretty good bet but it might just as easily be that they didn't think it was necessary to go any farther than four BUs away."

Zoya stiffened and sat forward.

"Something?" Natalya asked.

"Maybe," Zoya said. "Two things. Maybe three. One, that's about the range of most jump-capable tugs."

"So they were going to catch it and bring it back to Ravaine?" Caldicott asked.

"Maybe," Zoya said. "Maybe they were going to catch it and jump it someplace else. I didn't look to see who else has a station out there."

"It might not be in the database," Natalya said.

"So, the possibility is that they jumped it there because it was halfway to somewhere else they wanted to go," Zoya said.

"That doesn't rule out the notion that they were aware the ship was underpowered," Caldicott said. "Why a tug? Wouldn't they have just removed the pilot and jumped it?"

Zoya frowned. "Maybe it was supposed to have been damaged more. If it weren't for Nats, we'd have had no main engine fuel. It would take a tug to get it under control after the jump."

"We didn't have a lot left over after killing the vector," Natalya said. "We ate a lot of fuel doing it. It was enough, but just barely."

"That why you let Ernst jump it back?" Caldicott asked.

"Partly," Natalya said, then took a short drink of water. "Partly because we wanted to shut down the ship as much as possible. Mostly because we were running out of air."

"We secured as many systems as possible without hampering life support or shutting off the power to the lights, the heat, and the locks," Zoya said. "It couldn't fire thrusters or jump without somebody manually enabling the systems."

"Clever," Caldicott said.

Natalya shrugged and tipped back her bottle, draining the water. "We'll see if it's clever enough." A knock sounded on the door—three short raps, then silence.

Caldicott placed her bottle on the coffee table and stood. "That's probably Veronica. We'll get you some civilian clothes to wear and then go see what kind of trouble we can get into."

"You know, we *can* go to a shop," Zoya said.

"Yes, but I can't," Caldicott said, crossing to the door. "You're not getting out of my sight until you get on a shuttle back to Pulaski." She winked. "Maybe not even then. Data has a significant interest in this project. Maybe I'll just give Alison a bit of moral support. In person." She swung the door open for a pixie hauling a garment rack that looked bigger than the *Peregrine*. "Roni, thank you for coming on such short notice."

Veronica snorted and gave Caldicott a rude gesture with the hand not hauling the rack. "Since when did you ever call in advance, Treese?" She grinned and winked at Natalya. "She's always bossy. Don't let her get to you. She may be a director but she's not *my* boss."

"But you came," Caldicott said.

"Hey, you give good business. Now? You might have given me a bit of a clue instead of having Etienne tut-tut me on the vid." She paused and perused Zoya up and down. "Hello, Fleet. What brings you to the dark side?"

"A small ship," Zoya said. She nodded at Natalya. "Her ship, actually."

Veronica's eyebrows shot up. "Gonna be one of those days, eh? No matter. What kind of clothes you need?"

"Civilian clothes," Caldicott said, before anybody else could speak. "Just a couple of changes. They left their luggage back at Pulaski."

It didn't really seem possible but Veronica's brows climbed even higher up her forehead. "Pulaski?" Her eyes narrowed as she gave both Natalya and Zoya the once over again. "You're them," she said after a few moments.

"Them?" Natalya asked.

"The test pilots for the new birds." She looked at Caldicott. "They're the ones, right?"

Caldicott shrugged. "Maybe."

"Rumor is you're dead," Veronica said, looking back at them.

"Not just yet," Natalya said. "It was closer than I'd have liked."

"All right, then. Clothes for coming back from the nearly dead." She glanced at Caldicott as she began pulling the covers off the mobile rack. "How long? What will you be doing with them? Newsies? Interviews? What?"

"Nothing with that kind of exposure," Caldicott said. "Dinner with friends. Rest and recuperation. We've got a couple of days before Joe Allen will be done with them and I can't stomach the notion that they'll be wearing those ... coveralls ... the whole time." She didn't quite sneer.

"It's a shipsuit," Zoya said. "Very practical for shipboard life."

"I'm sure," Caldicott said. "But tell me you wouldn't welcome a hot bath and a fresh change of clothes."

Natalya gave herself a quick sniff and shrugged. "I could use a shower, I suppose. I'm partial to jeans and pullovers, if you've got anything. And a change of unders wouldn't be amiss."

Veronica nodded, pulling bundles from the bottom of the rack. "Which one's Usoko?"

Zoya raised her hand in a little wave. "That's me."

"Catch," Veronica said and tossed one of the bundles to her. "Three changes of unders and bras. Some athletic socks and stockings." She tossed another one to Natalya. "Then you're Regyri. Same deal. Sizes should be right."

"How—?" Natalya started to ask but looked at Caldicott. "Data."

Caldicott gave a little shrug. "I may have had the office flash a copy of your measurements to Veronica while we were checking in."

"They're probably a little out of date. We haven't exactly been clothes-shopping lately," Zoya said.

"If they're too far off, I can scan you now and get the replacements before dinner," Veronica said. "It's what I do." She pulled a pair of denim slacks from the rack and checked the tag. "You want denims, Usoko?" she asked holding up the pants.

"How much?" Zoya asked.

"Not your worry," Caldicott said. "Board business. Veronica's on my tab."

Veronica beamed. "Makes me glad I brought the good stuff, then."

Caldicott laughed. "You always bring the good stuff, Roni. Just get them dressed so I can take them out without attracting too much of the wrong kind of attention."

"You're so charming, Treese. Makes me wonder why I like you," Veronica said, pulling another pair of denim slacks off the rack.

"You like my credits," Caldicott said.

"Well, that and your charming disposition," Veronica said. She waved Natalya and Zoya over. "You two. Pick stuff. There's two of everything, one in each of your alleged sizes. Grab what you want and give me the hangers so I can charge Miss Bossypants over there. And try some of that stuff on before I get out of here so I know if I have to fix it. Right? Right."

Natalya found some slacks and a couple of pullover tops in her colors and size in a matter of moments. "This will do."

"A dress," Caldicott said. "Cocktail length."

Natalya frowned. "Excuse me?"

"You'll need a cocktail dress. We're not going to stay cooped up in here for the next two days. I've got a couple of places we need to be seen in and you'll need a dress."

Zoya snorted. "I haven't seen you in a dress since ... ever."

"I'm an engineer," Natalya said. "Engineers don't wear dresses."

"Don't tell my Aunt Demi that," Zoya said.

"She an engineer?" Natalya asked.

"A damn fine one, but she leaves the engine room behind when she's done for the day."

"And she wears dresses?" Natalya asked.

Caldicott clapped her hands twice. "Ladies. Focus. Grab some clothing. Try it on. Make sure it fits. Then we can let Veronica get on with her busy day and we can get back to work ourselves, yes?"

Veronica tsk-tsked. "See? Bossy. Bossy, bossy, bossy. She's always like that when she's excited and she's always excited." She turned to Caldicott. "I can leave the rack if you want. There's enough clothes there to satisfy an army."

Natalya held up a dress, black with narrow white piping. "Shoes?"

Veronica pulled a shoebox from the base of the rack and held it out. "Your size, matches the dress. You'll look terrif in it. Go try it on."

By the time Veronica left, dragging her garment rack with her, Natalya and Zoya both had three new outfits with shoes to match.

Eyeing the clothing, Zoya shook her head. "How long did you say we're going to be here?"

"You'll be heading back to Pulaski day after tomorrow, if I'm any judge of how Joe and the gang will go with this." She pursed her lips. "That doesn't give me a lot of time, but I'll take what I can get."

"Well, now you've bribed us," Natalya said. "What do you want in return?"

"You've got it backwards. I already have what I want. Vagrant gone. He can't come back and that leaves a hole in Comms."

"You've got a candidate lined up?" Zoya asked.

"I don't think anybody saw this one coming," Caldicott said. "Maybe Joe Allen, but he plays his cards close to the vest. There'll be somebody bright and clever who'll step up."

"How will you know it's not somebody working for Vagrant?" Natalya asked. "Swapping the devil you know for one you don't?"

"I've got the data." She shrugged. "I'll know if and how they're being paid. Chips are good if you don't need to spend a lot of them or deposit them. As soon as the balances go back into the system, they're where I can see them." She shrugged again. "I won't know where they came from but I can see that they arrived."

"Circumstantial," Zoya said.

Caldicott placed one beautifully manicured fingertip to her own nose. "Right, but I'm not worried about the rules of evidence. I just need to know who I have to be careful standing in front of. If what Panko said about the number of chips is right, that's real leverage." She paused and offered a sly smile. "You don't happen to know where they are?"

Natalya just grinned.

"Can't blame a girl for trying," Caldicott said. Her tablet bipped. Her face clouded over when she read the message. "I've got to go for now. I'll be back. Dinner at 1800. Dressy place. You'll be noticed."

"Thank you for the clothes," Zoya said.

Caldicott didn't look up from her screen but waved a hand in the air in dismissal. "Think nothing of it. Rounding error in petty cash and worth it." She crossed the room in a few strides but stopped at the door. "Unless it's really somebody you know, I wouldn't open this door again."

"Why?" Zoya asked.

Caldicott frowned. "Vagrant may have left the station, but he has a vindictive streak a mile wide. I'd bet he didn't take all of his crew with him when he scarpered off to whatever hidey-hole he's gone to."

"Thanks for the warning," Zoya said.

"Later," Caldicott said and slipped out the door, pulling it closed behind her with a click.

Natalya looked at the clothing draped on the furniture and then at Zoya. "Something's not exactly right."

"Ya think?" Zoya asked. "She's either crazy as a rock miner or playing a game we're supposed to be pawns in."

"Those two things aren't mutually exclusive."

Zoya nodded. "That's what I'm afraid of. Flip you for the shower?"

"Take it. I need to get some sleep on a bed that's not vibrating under me."

"I'll keep the splashing down."

Natalya snorted. "In this place? I'd bet the bathroom is sound-proofed."

Chapter Forty-six
High Tortuga: 2366, June 1

NATALYA AND ZOYA EXITED the elevator dressed in their new finery. Natalya caught a glimpse of herself in the polished doors and shook her head. "Dresses. Really?"

Zoya snickered. "Hush, you. We're hobnobbing with the glitterati. We're going to attract enough attention as it is without looking like rock-knockers in the big city."

Natalya snorted but made no more comments.

Caldicott waited for them near the front desk along with Brian Dorion and Joe Allen. A swarm of hotel staff buzzed around them.

"Oh, good," Caldicott said. "We've reservations at Malloy's for 1830."

"Ernst's not coming?" Natalya asked, looking around.

"Mr. Panko is on his way to Pulaski," Allen said.

"Without us?" Natalya asked.

Dorion shook his head. "We'll get you on a shuttle tomorrow after the inquiry. Ernst's testimony yesterday was sufficient since you two were actually there."

"And didn't die," Caldicott said. "Come along. We've got food to eat and matters to discuss." She linked an arm in Zoya's and pulled her along. "So, talk to me about your notion of hub and spoke. Any idea of the placements?"

Zoya cast a glance over her shoulder at Natalya. "Not at the moment. You probably have people with more insight into the loading distribution than I do."

Caldicott's grin seemed just a bit "I told you so" when she flashed it back at Dorion. "Of course, of course," she said.

Dorion waved Natalya ahead and she fell into line behind Caldicott and Zoya as they sailed out of the lobby, leaving the swarm of staff at the entrance.

"You're probably anxious to get back to your ship," Dorion said.

Natalya shrugged. "A bit. It's not every day one gets to dine with the CEO of High Tortuga."

"Not the first time for you," Allen said behind her.

"How did you find us and why?" Natalya asked, looking back and forth between the two men.

"Small ship expertise is relatively rare," Dorion said. "There are very few courier pilots in Toe-Hold space. CPJCT has them tied up in the High Line. Out here, it's all fast packets like the Unwin Eights."

"We stopped looking for pilots and started looking at couriers," Allen said, leaning in. "*Peregrine* showed up as an unaffiliated courier. When your backgrounds set off alarms, we looked into you both a little deeper." He shrugged. "Seemed like worth a trip over to Dark Knight."

"Alarms?"

Dorion nodded. "Your backgrounds have been scrubbed."

"You can tell?"

Allen coughed into his fist. "According to the data-sigs, we did the scrubbing. That takes some serious doing."

"Caldicott said she pieced together Zoya's background from her sources," Natalya said.

Allen laughed, a low rumble like thunder in the distance.

"That's funny?" Natalya asked.

Allen shrugged. "She probably did the scrubbing. Or can find out who did."

Caldicott, her arm still caught in Zoya's, looked back at them. "You're talking about me again."

Allen laughed again. "You do a lot of remarkable things, Therese. Should be no surprise when people remark on them."

Caldicott laughed and waved a hand in the air. "As long as it's nothing important," she said, tugging Zoya into an open doorway. "Meanwhile, I'm hungry."

Malloy's turned out to be nothing like Natalya thought it would be. Far from being the severe, pastel pavilion of wealth and consumption she'd mentally prepared herself for, the interior felt warm and inviting with what looked like actual wallpaper on the bulkheads and carpet under foot. Tasteful lighting around the overhead and on the tables kept the place from being a dim cave even as partitions broke the space up into cozy rooms of three to five tables. The low murmur of conversations—none loud enough to be overheard—

provided a background for the tinkle of cutlery and glassware and the occasional bell of laughter. She felt the tension at the back of her skull unwinding as they followed a tuxedoed maÃ®tre d'hÃ´tel to a private room just off the main dining area.

"Thank you, Paul," Caldicott said as he seated them around an impeccably dressed table with a single red rose in a cut glass vase in the center.

"Honored to have you with us again, Director," the tuxedo said. "Mr. Allen. Mr. Dorion. Ladies." He nodded to Natalya and Zoya by way of acknowledgment. "Louisa will be your server this evening. Please enjoy your evening." With one last sketch of a bow he left them, gliding smoothly away as if on rollers instead of two feet.

Caldicott leaned toward Zoya. "You were saying? You think you can cut a day off our cycle times?"

Zoya looked around the table, an amused expression lifting the corners of her eyes and the edges of her mouth. "I believe I said I think a properly distributed network could cut at least a day, but that's assuming each hub gets served once every twenty-four standard hours and that no spoke from the hub is longer than a day."

Allen blinked and shook his head. "Care to explain that for the slow and slightly ignorant management at the table?" He grinned and leaned forward on his elbows.

"Right now, when you pick up data, it's up to three days from the time you siphon off the first beacon until that data is transmitted back to the communications core," Zoya said. "Right?"

Allen looked at Dorion who nodded. "About that."

"So, if you have a ship that visits, say, three systems in a day before returning to the hub?" Zoya asked, her eyebrows rising.

"I'm with you so far," Allen said. Before Zoya could continue, his eyes widened. "And if the hub gets serviced every day, then that data gets back to the core in only two days instead of three."

"Exactly," Zoya said.

"That's what I've been trying to get through the Communications Subcommittee," Caldicott said, sitting back in her chair with a broad smile. "With Vagrant out of the way, perhaps we can make some progress now."

"You sound like you don't think he's coming back," Dorion said.

A young woman wearing a white shirt, black pants, and a satiny cummerbund entered the room with a tray of water glasses, which she distributed as she spoke. "Good evening," she said. "Please pardon the interruption and welcome to Malloy's. I'm Louisa. I'll be your server this evening. Can I get you some drinks while you decide what to have?"

"Good evening, Louisa. Is Fernando in the kitchen this evening?" Caldicott asked.

Louisa smiled. "He is, Director."

Caldicott looked at Natalya and Zoya. "Do either of you have any dietary requirements? Something you want in particular or couldn't eat if delivered?"

Zoya shook her head. "I'll eat pretty much anything."

"I'm not fussy," Natalya said. "I'll try anything once. Twice if I'm not sure."

Caldicott fairly beamed and turned the smile on Louisa. "If you'd tell Fernando how many hungry people await and ask him to delight us?"

Louisa's expression slipped for just a moment as she processed the order. She looked around the table and nodded after taking her inventory. "Of course, Director."

"You can tell him Therese is being whimsical. He knows me."

Louisa gave a small nod over her empty tray. "Of course, Director. Drink orders?"

Caldicott waved a hand. "I'll leave that to you and Fernando."

"Could I have a cup of coffee?" Natalya asked.

Louisa nodded. "Of course. Now? With dinner? Or after?"

"Yes," said Natalya. "That would be lovely."

Caldicott rolled her lips between her teeth as if biting back a grin.

Louisa blinked several times, clearly trying to parse the answer. "Of course." She looked around the table. "Anyone else?" After a brief flurry of head shakes, Louisa nodded. "I'll be right back."

Allen watched her leave before turning to Caldicott. "Fernando?"

"A dear boy. Magic in his fingers," Caldicott said, her gaze unfocused into the middle distance. "Simply genius with food." She smiled at Allen. "I eat here every chance I get."

Natalya struggled with the sudden image of the tony director and the chef with the magic fingers. She had to bite her bottom lip and pretend to take a sip of water to keep from giggling. She caught the look Dorion gave Allen and took another sip.

"Vagrant?" Dorion asked.

"He's not coming back," Caldicott said. "Not to HTHC. He may set up shop in one of the Toe-Holds, but my bet's on him heading for the High Line where he can leverage what he knows into something more."

"You think he's given up on the couriers?" Dorion asked.

Caldicott cast her gaze toward the white table cloth and pursed her lips. "I think he's going to reposition his assets to take advantage of the service contracts we'll need to support the hubs." She shrugged. "It won't be as much but he can free up some of those ships to just haul cargo. Knowing his connections, I'd buy stock in M. Vagrant—Outfitters if he sold any. Once he stops spending all his time arguing with the other directors and focuses on his business, he'll probably do great."

"He's going to be pissed, if those are his chips," Allen said.

"You think they're his?" Caldicott asked.

Allen shrugged. "They're his or Tony Downs's."

"You going to lean on Downs?" Dorion asked.

Allen shrugged again. "Depends on whether we get them back or not."

"Somebody killed Jeffrey," Zoya said.

"We'll have some closure on that before I'm done," Caldicott said.

Allen and Dorion shared a glance. "You think he was killed?" Allen asked.

"Yes," Zoya said. "I'd bet on it."

Allen looked up. "How much?"

"A year's pay," Zoya said.

"How did they do it?" Allen asked.

"Bypassed the software override on the outer door interlock," Natalya said. "Triggered the outer door even though the sensor showed no pressure on the outside."

Allen stared at her, his eyes tightening. "Just like that?"

Natalya shrugged. "It's a common routine. Stack the trash in the lock. Close the inner door and pop the outer door. No more trash. Carver didn't kill himself. He had help."

"Somebody knows how to jimmy those sensors," Zoya said. "They opened both doors on *Echo One* to purge the atmosphere easily enough."

Louisa returned with the coffee. "Here you go. Is there anything else?"

Natalya took a sip. "Thanks, no. This is great."

Louisa looked to Caldicott. "Fernando says he'll have an appetizer tray ready shortly. He's fetching a couple of bottles from the cellar now."

"Excellent. Thank you."

Louisa nodded and made a discreet exit.

"My bet's on Call-me-Charlie," Natalya said.

Allen choked back a laugh. "Who?"

"There's a tech at the yard. I forget his full name. Everybody knows him as Call-me-Charlie because that's how he introduces himself."

"Why him?" Allen asked.

"Mostly because he has the knowledge and the opportunity to use it," Natalya said.

"He was working on the lock when we first went aboard," Zoya said. "The inner door wouldn't open if the outer wasn't closed."

"Isn't that what you want?" Dorion asked, glancing at Allen with a half grin.

"Only in vacuum," Zoya said. "Docked? It's a pain in the butt to have to cycle the lock every time you want to leave or enter the ship."

"Hence the interlock," Allen said, almost to himself.

Natalya nodded.

"I'm working on it," Caldicott said.

Allen raised an eyebrow in her direction.

"If there are any traces, we'll find them," she said. "I've had the boys and girls working on it ever since the inquiry adjourned."

Allen looked at Zoya who shrugged without responding.

"It was Charlie," Natalya said. "He'll be gone by the time we get back."

"Why?" Dorion asked.

"He's not one of Downs's. I'd bet he's Vagrant's man on the inside."

"Why not Downs?" Allen asked.

"Downs is a low-level scammer. He makes his profit off the project. The longer and slower the project, the more opportunities he has to turn a profit," Natalya said.

"That sounds like he'd have a motive to kill Jeff Carver," Dorion said.

"I don't think so," Natalya said. "His operation doesn't depend on getting rid of Carver. If anything, it jeopardizes it. The extra scrutiny from a death like that couldn't have made things easier for him."

"No, but having Pittman in charge must have," Dorion said.

"Maybe, but he couldn't have known who was coming in unless he worked for Vagrant, too."

"What makes you think he wasn't?" Caldicott asked, leaning forward on the table.

Natalya pursed her lips for a moment before speaking. "Downs has been at it a very long time. His operation had to have been in place for decades. Maybe longer than Vagrant has been alive. How long has Vagrant been operating out here?"

Caldicott's eyebrows shot up and she leaned back in her seat. "Not that long. A few stanyers. Maybe five."

"So what's Downs? A distraction?" Allen asked.

"Either that or a coincidence," Zoya said. "Maybe Vagrant counted him a stalking goat."

"A what?" Dorion asked.

"Bait for the tiger. He's in place, on the station, doing what he does. Somebody looking into irregularities would find him before Vagrant," Zoya said.

"Your granny?" Natalya asked.

"Gemstone thieves ripping off the company. My grandfather didn't act at once. He waited until he could get the head of the ring."

"Why will he be gone?" Dorion asked again, looking at Natalya.

"Because Vagrant can't afford the loose end. He'll have either tipped Charlie to run or killed him."

"Or both," Zoya said.

Dorion's eyes widened. "When did you two get so bloody-minded?"

Natalya shrugged. "You call us bloody-minded. I call us pragmatic."

Allen chuckled. "They're right, you know," he said, looking at Dorion. "If Vagrant had Carver killed so he could put Pittman in place, he's going to need to tidy up. He'll either take this Charlie fellow with him and keep him close, or he'll drop him out an airlock somewhere in the Deep Dark. Maybe both."

"What about that ship that tried to catch us?" Zoya asked.

"That's a puzzler," Allen said. "Downs must have some confederates working with him to chase it down."

"His brother-in-law," Caldicott said, looking up from her tablet. "They started rolling up the operation after Alison Pittman kicked him off the station." She lifted her tablet and gave it a little wave. "Downs never left the yard, by the way."

"What?" Allen's head snapped up and he stared at Caldicott.

"He never left. According to the data, he's been living there using another name. He's probably staying pretty quiet, but he's buying food and drinks." Caldicott looked down at her tablet. "Lots of drinks."

"How do you know it's Downs?" Dorion asked.

Caldicott cast a sour look at him.

Dorion sat back a little and held up his hands in surrender.

A pale, thin man wearing chef's whites and a scarlet toque bustled in rolling a cart and leading a parade of wait staff.

"Fernando!" Caldicott said, standing and crossing to take both his hands in hers and lean in for air-kisses on each cheek.

"Therese, you minx. You didn't let me know you were coming. I've been scrambling to find something suitable." The man's eyes practically danced in his head as he scanned the room. "Mr. Allen. A pleasure to see you here. Mr. Dorion, is it?"

Dorion seemed a bit nonplussed and merely nodded.

"Excellent. I have just the thing." He looked at Natalya and Zoya, giving each his full attention for only a moment—long enough to give each a small bow from his shoulders. "And guests. How wonderful."

"Now, Fernando," Caldicott said. "A quiet business dinner among friends. Yes?"

Fernando focused his charms on Caldicott and placed one long finger against the side of his nose. "Of course. Please enjoy these small appetizers. Dinner will be along shortly. I hope you enjoy." With that, he bustled out taking most of the staff with him.

It took Natalya a moment to notice that they'd delivered more coffee, served wine, and festooned the table with a collection of small foods, each presented on an oval serving plate, before leaving.

Caldicott took her seat and lifted her glass. "To a job well done."

Allen started to raise his glass, but Dorion asked, "Is it done? I had the feeling we were just getting started."

Caldicott tsk-tsked him. "We may be just getting started, but I'm happy to celebrate the doing of a job well. Would you prefer I toast a job half-assed?" She grinned and kept her glass aloft.

Allen's laugh rumbled from his chest and he lifted his glass to ting against Caldicott's.

Dorion gave a bit of a shrug before joining the toast along with Zoya and Natalya. "It may not be done yet," he said. "But I have a feeling that we're a lot closer today than we were yesterday."

"I'll drink to that," Allen said and tinged his glass again.

Chapter Forty-seven
Pulaski Yard: 2366, June 3

NATALYA NEVER LIKED being a passenger, but she had to admit the High Tortuga Holding Company directors traveled in style. The utilitarian interior felt more like a work of art—or perhaps architecture—than the inside of a shuttle. Every surface carried a polish or a texture. The sumptuous seating looked as comfortable as it felt, padded perfectly and upholstered in a creamy fabric Natalya couldn't identify. The whole experience made her consider washing her hands before she touched anything—or perhaps taking off her shoes before taking another step into the craft. Joe Allen and Brian Dorion flew with them, leaving Caldicott to monitor the data feeds and keep an eye out for Vagrant to surface.

Ernst Panko met them with a broad grin when they stepped out of the shuttle. "Nice boat," he said, casting an appreciative glance down the length of the vessel.

"You have no idea," Zoya said, stepping down the short ladder to the deck.

"You're welcome to come aboard for a tour," Allen said. "I hear you have an eye for ships."

"Thanks, Joe. Perhaps before you head back. We've got some business to take care of first."

Allen nodded. "Can we see the new ship designs?"

"Better than that," Panko said. "We've got a tour laid on for the ways. You can see the ship itself."

Natalya perked up at that. "You've got one ready?"

Panko shrugged and made a small grimace. "Well. Not ready-ready. It's not spaceworthy yet, but the spaceframe is complete. We're still installing astronautics and making sure the pipes are all connected, and there's no finish work done on the inside yet."

"But it's a ship?" Zoya asked.

He grinned and nodded. "It's a ship."

Allen cleared his throat. "About those other *little* things?" He raised his eyebrows with the question.

"We've got the entrances and exits covered. Judging from the way they tossed my ship, nobody's found them yet."

"But you know where they are," Allen said.

"I know where they're supposed to be. I haven't wanted to disturb the scene until you got here." Panko winked at Natalya.

Alison Pittman joined them on the shuttle dock, trailed by an armed security detail. "Mr. Allen. Brian. Sorry I'm late."

Allen stuck out a hand. "Call me Joe, Alison. We've got a lot of work to do together and I don't really like standing on ceremony."

She deep breath before grasping his hand. "Thank you. Joe. I'm not sure about how much work we'll be doing together going forward but ... well ... thanks."

Dorion stepped forward and offered a hand, too. "What's that all about?"

Alison took a moment to look around the shuttle bay. "We need to have a talk about the yard. Later." She cast her gaze around again.

Allen nodded. "Message received. So, show me your baby?"

Alison smiled and pointed to Panko. "His baby. I think she's beautiful, but you can make up your own minds."

"Right this way," Panko said. As he started toward the bay doors, he looked at Natalya and Zoya. "You two coming?"

Zoya grinned and fell in line, but Natalya held back. "Nats?" Zoya asked, looking back at her.

"I need to check on my own baby. I haven't seen her for a few days."

Ernst's grin grew wider. "I'll give you a private tour later, if you want. You'll need to see it before you agree to be the test pilot, after all."

"Thanks, Ernst." She held out a hand to Allen. "Thank you, Mr. Allen. I hope we've helped."

Allen shook her hand. "You're not done yet, but thank you. There are still a few loose ends to tie off but you and Zoya have both helped immensely."

Panko led his troop out of the shuttle bay and down the passage toward the main yards, leaving Natalya to shoulder her bundle of new clothing and make her way in the opposite direction.

The shuttle bay wasn't far from where the *Peregrine* waited, but the walk felt longer. She kept thinking about the *Peregrine* and what she should do with her. The thought that she might do anything with her made tendrils of disloyalty curl in her guts even as the reality of trying to keep her flying loomed as large as a gas giant's exosphere. Couriers flourished in the High Line, but fast packets ruled the Toe-Holds. Without credentials to her name, the High Line might as well have been the Core Worlds for all the good it did her.

She made the turn into the *Peregrine*'s docking bay and trudged up to the lock, keying the code without conscious thought and stepping into the tiny airlock. She found the inner door closed. It didn't open before the outer door started to cycle shut. The malfunction made her sigh. "Don't tell me you're coming down with airlock problems, too," she said. "I didn't think that would be contagious."

Well, she'd fixed it before. She could fix it again.

The inner door opened and a ham-sized fist reached through to grab her by the collar of her shipsuit and drag her into the ship, slamming her skull against the far bulkhead.

THE SMELL WOKE HER. Scrubbers. The stink clawed at her nose and she tried to lift a hand to her face but her arm wouldn't move. Neither would her feet. She managed to get her eyes open but everything was blurry. It looked like the *Peregrine*. Her stateroom. Her head screamed at her, feeling split down the middle. Then she sort of remembered. Something had happened.

"So? Awake, are ya, missy?"

It hurt to turn her head so she just slid her eyes to the side to see who spoke. She knew that voice.

"Where are they?"

"Gone to see the new ship," she said.

"Not them, you stupid bint. The chips."

He swam into focus then, just inches from her face. His breath hot on her skin and she couldn't pull back. "Downs."

"So, you remember enough to recognize me. Now just remember where you stashed my chips and everything will be right."

"On the ship."

"Which ship?" Downs asked.

"The new ship. The one you hid them on. *Echo One*."

"We've tossed that ship three times. They're not there." He sat back on his haunches to peer at her. "Not on Pansy-boy's ship either. So where are they?"

"We hid them."

"Where?"

Natalya struggled against the pain in her skull and the blurred vision to try to see him clearly. "I'll have to show you. Can't explain it."

"Handy," he said. "I'm not buying it."

"Under the Burleson drive. You know how to lift it?"

"What do you take me for, girl?" Downs leaned in, his breath stinking in her nose like a bad set of scrubber cartridges.

"Somebody with bad oral hygiene," she said. The longer she kept him talking, the more the fog cleared. She needed to get untied.

"Don't get smart with me. How do you lift it?"

"Bottom edge of the front cowling cover. There are two latches. Unclip them and lift it up. There's a hinge on the back with a counter weight."

Downs sat back again and scowled at her. "Don't lie to me. I designed that engine room. There's nothing like that there."

Natalya sighed and let her head hang forward. Damn, that hurt but closing her eyes helped a bit. "I can't help it if you can't find it. Take me to it and I'll show you. Or go look yourself. I don't care which."

Another voice. "Tony, we're running out of time. If we don't get the chips and get off this station—like right damn now—the boffins will be back from the ways and we'll be up to our asses in security."

Tony glanced up and behind Natalya. He scrubbed a hand across his mouth and scowled. "Right," he said, almost under his breath. "You. No tricks. There's two of us and one of you. Any silliness on your part could be fatal. Understand?"

"Hey, I just want you to get your damn chips and get out of my face. No skin off my back if you rip off the company. They aren't paying me to be a martyr."

He grinned but it wasn't an expression of humor. "Keep seeing the light, missy, and we'll all leave here in one piece." He reached down and pulled a knot loose around her left foot and repeated it on the right before grabbing her arm and hefting her to her feet. For a few heartbeats she wasn't sure her legs would hold her, but they stiffened and she kept them under her. "Hand me that jacket," Downs said.

The other voice—another man, slender with a bald spot at the crown of his head, wearing an overly ripe shipsuit—reached into her view, dragging her jacket off the bunk. He handed it to Downs.

Downs draped it over her shoulders, arranging the folds so it covered her bound hands. "Here's how it's going to go," he said. "We're going out the lock, leaving the bay, and turning to port.

That ship is all by its lonesome three bays down. They're not even
guarding it. There'll be people in the passageway. You say nothing.
You do nothing. You just walk along. You do anything else, your
lovely little bed-buddy will die."

"Zoya?"

"Zoya. The snooty Fleet bitch. We've got her stashed. You
can't get to her before we can kill her, so just be a good little girl
and do what you're told."

"Why didn't you ask her?" Natalya asked.

"She's insurance," Downs said. "You don't deliver, we'll use her
as backup."

Natalya nodded. "All right. Let's get this over with."

The other guy led the way, opening the lock and checking the
bay before stepping out of the ship. They made a tidy little pro-
cession out of the docking bay and into the wide passage beyond.
Natalya couldn't be sure, but the place seemed deserted.

"Everybody's out gawking at the big shots down in the ways,"
the skinny man said, a smirk in his voice.

"Shut up, Vince. Just make sure nobody gets too close." Downs
didn't seem too pleased with Vince, just judging from his tone.

The longer they walked, the more Natalya recovered. Her head
still killed her with every step, but her vision cleared a little. If
the ringing in her ears would let up, the pain would probably be
bearable.

They passed the next docking bay without incident and continued along the passage.

"Not too much farther," Downs said, giving her arm a little
shake. "Just keep going, nice and steady."

Vince was the problem. Natalya knew that Downs would go
down fast once she moved. He gripped her too tightly and his
reflexes wouldn't react in the time he'd have. Vince was too far
away and she couldn't get them both fast enough.

The distraction she prayed for stepped out of the next docking
bay and turned in their direction. Call-me-Charlie, in the flesh.

"Downs?" he said. "What are you doing on-station, man?"

"Vince," Downs said, his voice a growl. "Shut him up."

Vince had a needler in his hand in a split second, but it was
a split second too long. Charlie was no chump and he took Vince
head-on. Natalya lost track of him after that by falling sideways
and pulling Downs with her. Before he could react she kneed him
in the solar plexus to push him away far enough to get one awkward
scissor kick to his jaw. He collapsed like a chunk of dead meat, his
head rebounding once off the skid coat on the decking. She tossed
herself to her feet and bolted, leaving Vince and Charlie scrabbling

on the deck. Neither seemed to have control of the needler and she saw no percentage in waiting until one of them won.

Each step pounded into her head and running with her hands tied behind her made every step precarious. The damned ringing in her ears meant she wouldn't hear the zing of a needler if somebody fired, which helped her keep her focus on getting the hell out of there.

The end of the passage T came up fast and she had to make a decision. Left into the yards? It was a long twenty meters with no cover. Right into the station? Would Charlie or Vince follow? Could she hide? Maybe make it to Rudy's?

The decision got made for her when she lost her balance and slammed to the deck on her side. She did her best to keep her battered skull from hitting the deck again, rolling to absorb some of the shock. She came to rest by rolling into a sturdy pair of legs. She managed to get her eyes under control enough to look up at Joe Allen looking down at her.

"I found Downs," she said.

"Did you, now?" Allen asked.

"He was out cold down by the *Echo One* dock, last I saw him. Charlie's still here."

Allen looked up and Natalya curled into a ball on the deck trying not to puke on his shoes. "Alison?"

"Got it," Pittman answered.

"Zoya?" Natalya asked.

Zoya leaned around Allen and looked at Natalya. "Yeah?"

The deck vibrated from the thud of running feet in heavy boots and Natalya let that vibration carry her down.

Chapter Forty-eight
Pulaski Yard: 2366, June 4

WAKING UP IN THE AUTO-doc is never fun. Still, Natalya preferred it to waking up to bad breath and the headache from hell. Her mood was probably chemically induced but she considered that to be an advantage. She mused on that for a few moments before she heard the two latches release. The lid opened up and a friendly face peered in.

"What are you doing awake?" the face asked.

"I don't know," Natalya said. "I'm not completely sure why I'm in here."

"You remember anything?"

"Yes. Probably concussion from having my head slammed into a bulkhead."

The friendly face smiled wider. "Very good guess. You had a little tussle after that and then went jogging."

Natalya stretched her face, trying to get her eyes to open properly. "Tell me I didn't puke on Joe Allen's shoes."

"You didn't puke on my shoes." A new face peered in behind the med-tech's. "Hi, there."

"Mr. Allen."

"It's Joe to you," he said. He tapped the tech on the shoulder. "Should she be awake and talking?"

The tech who seemed to be full of smiles shook her head without look away from Natalya. "Not really. She came up spontaneously and I wanted to check cognitive function before I sent her back down."

"Wait," Natalya said.

"Nighty night," the tech said.

Natalya heard the first latch but not the second.

NATALYA OPENED HER eyes to the subdued lighting of night watch. The ceiling above her gave few clues but it wasn't the one in her stateroom on the *Peregrine*.

"Welcome back," Zoya said, her voice creaky.

Natalya turned her head toward the voice and saw Zoya struggling up out of an easy chair beside the bed, her hair tousled like she'd just awakened. "Thanks, I think."

"Doc says you're going to be fine," Zoya said.

"Hard head."

Zoya chuckled and nodded.

"How long?" Natalya asked.

"We docked yesterday," Zoya said but paused. "No, that can't be right. Day before that."

"So a couple of days."

"Yeah. They've all kinda blended together."

"Allen get his chips?" Natalya asked.

"Yup. And Downs. And Call-me-Charlie." Zoya's grin looked positively feral. "He's probably going to wish Vagrant got to him before Allen's done."

"He'll spill it."

"Oh, he's already spilling. They've got him for Carver's murder. The only thing keeping him out of the cold is how long he can keep talking about Vagrant and his dealings."

"Downs?"

"They'll find something for him to do for the rest of his life, I suspect." Zoya gave a little shrug. "Stealing fifteen million credits from your employer is one hell of a black mark on your personnel file."

"That how much it was?"

"Fourteen and change. Dorion's making the case that his penance should be telling them how he did it for decades without anybody catching on."

"I bet he won't last the week," Natalya said, letting her head relax back onto the pillow.

"What makes you say that?"

"You don't think he did that by himself, do you?"

Zoya tilted her head to one side. "Meaning somebody higher on the food chain?"

Natalya gave a little shrug. "He didn't make it to his bolt-hole in time. The knives will be out."

"Sleep, Nats."

Natalya let her eyes close, surrendering to the chemicals in her blood. "Get back to the ship, Zee. Make sure she's ready for space."

"You gonna make a run for it?" Zee asked, a smile in her voice.

"Not just yet, but when the time comes ..."

She felt Zoya pat her on the arm before she fell down the hole again.

Chapter Forty-nine
CommSta Bowie: 2368, January 21

NATALYA TOOK ONE LAST pass through the apartment. The empty space echoed with her footsteps. The furniture wasn't theirs but they'd packed up and hauled out everything that was, not that it had amounted to much. Getting the new ships up and the first of the hubs deployed had taken so much of their time, it hadn't left a lot of opportunity for acquiring new goods.

Zoya waited for her at the door, arms crossed and leaning her shoulders against the bulkhead. "We ready?"

"I think so. I can't help but think we've forgotten something."

Zoya straightened up and hefted the last tote off the deck. "We barely lived here for the last six months."

Natalya nodded. "True enough."

The door buzzer rang. Zoya took a step and swung it open. "Good afternoon, Brian."

Dorion grinned. "How did you know it was me?"

"I suppose it could have been the concierge coming to check us out of the apartment," Natalya said, smiling at him.

He stepped into the room and closed the door. "I know I said my good-byes last night but I had to take one more shot. You sure you won't reconsider? We can always use two good pilots."

Zoya looked at Natalya, one eyebrow raised in query.

She stared at the deck, running the events of the last few months through her mind. The first of those sweet new couriers. The month and a half of moving one of the backup communications spindles. The ongoing path-finding efforts to optimize the routing. She smiled at Dorion. "Thanks, but I can't. I guess I've got itchy feet and we've been at this for nearly two stanyers. It's time for me to move on." She looked at Zoya. "You don't have to come along if you don't want to."

Zoya pursed her lips. "As much fun as this has been, I'm ready for something else."

"It's been lucrative," Dorion said. "You've got to admit that."

They laughed.

"I'll admit it," Natalya said. "The finders bonus helped."

Dorion lifted a shoulder in a shrug. "You guys saved HTHC a lot of credits. Just exposing Downs probably saved us even more. We're still rolling up some of his confederates."

"Any word on Vagrant?" Zoya asked.

"He's out in the High Line. We've sent a report to TIC through an intermediary but it's up to them. We can't do much to him there. "

"He's getting away with murder," Natalya said.

"Well, Charlie did the wet work," Dorion said, looking at the deck and running a hand over the back of his head. "But Vagrant covered his tracks too well. Even with Charlie's information we don't have enough to take to TIC."

"Any idea what he's doing out there?" Zoya asked.

"Caldicott thinks he's laying low, running his outfitter business." Dorion sighed. "Not like he's outfitting anybody but thugs and mercenaries for Iron Mountain."

"You could shut them down in a hot tick," Natalya said.

"We could—and Joe Allen would be the first to tell you he wants to."

"But you can't," Zoya said. "Not without jeopardizing the entire Western Annex."

He nodded. "We can't be the cop. Toe-Holds won't abide that and the High Line can't. They need us to keep the credits flowing."

"Why have they never built around you?" Natalya asked. "They've had a long time to implement a replacement."

Dorion's smile stretched one side of his face. "They keep trying. One day they might succeed but most of the early efforts were based on corporate scrip. Credits you could only spend at company stores."

"Stores that set the value of the credits by how much you could buy there?" Zoya asked.

Dorion nodded. "That's never worked well. The other attempts within CPJCT fail because too many of the administration rely on the Toe-Holds for their income. I don't know if you noticed, but there's a lot of profit to be made out here."

"From what I've seen, the boundary isn't as much porous as it is nonexistent," Zoya said.

Dorion shrugged. "Yeah, well. It exists. You need a few fig leaves to move cargo into the High Line but it doesn't take much to get it out. That's not likely to change either."

"Why maintain the fiction?" Natalya asked. "That's always bothered me. My father always said we needed it but I never got it."

"Why are you leaving a secure job with an established, reputable company?" Dorion asked. "It can't be the credits."

Natalya pondered that. Why *was* she leaving?

Zoya said, "I'm going with her."

"I get that," Dorion said. "You're more than welcome to stay. We're getting the new pilot orientation running in a few more weeks. You'd be a hell of an instructor."

Zoya smiled and gave a mock shudder. "Not for me."

Dorion looked back at Natalya. "So? Why are you leaving?"

Natalya shrugged. "I don't really know. My father would have called it itchy feet. I feel like I've been here too long already and I need to go find the next thing. I'm not ready to settle down." She shrugged again. "I don't know. It sounds kinda silly and shallow, but it's just how I feel."

Dorion smiled. "That is why we maintain the fiction."

The answer blew through Natalya's mind but didn't stick. "Because I'm not ready to settle down?"

"No," Dorion said. "Because the High Line provides for one kind of person. Those who feel best when they've got a solid, relatively secure, and predictable future."

Zoya's eyes widened. "You keep calling Toe-Holds the release valve."

"Exactly," Dorion said. "There's always another system to find. Another piece of space to explore. We've been sifting this section of the Deep Dark for centuries. We still haven't tagged more than a quarter of it."

The swirling ideas gelled in Natalya's head. "And the safety net. It's not just the people. We both need each other's goods."

"And services," Dorion said.

Zoya nodded. "Some people need the frontier. Others avoid it."

"Exactly," Dorion said. After a moment, he shrugged. "Well, I had to make one last bid even though I knew better." He held out a hand to Zoya. "Safe voyage."

Zoya shook his hand. "Good luck with the new architecture. Thanks for everything."

He held out a hand to Natalya. "Safe voyage. I hope you never find what you're looking for." He grinned.

Natalya shook and grinned back. "Oh, I'll probably find it someday. I don't expect to be a seeker all my life, but ..." She shrugged and looked up at the ceiling. "There's a lot to see out there and I got itchy feet."

Dorion's smile crinkled the corners of his eyes. "I'll get out of your way. You ever need anything, let me know."

"We will," Natalya said.

The door snicked closed behind him.

Natalya stood there for a moment before glancing at Zoya. "Well?"

Zoya shrugged. "I guess we're done here." She shouldered her duffle. "Shall we?"

Natalya grabbed her bag and nodded. "Let's go."

The changes in the station struck Natalya. They passed other people in the passages on the way to the dock. A few of the new pilots nodded to them in passing. A couple of pilots stopped to wish them luck. They'd had their going-away party in the back room of one of the new restaurants and a last round of drinks at Frosty's with some of the permanent party.

"It's coming alive," Zoya said.

Natalya nodded.

"You did that," Zoya said.

"*We* did that," Natalya said. "And we had a lot of help."

When they got to the *Peregrine*, Michelle Cecil ran up to them. "Good, I caught you."

"How's life as dock master these days?" Zoya asked.

Cecil chuckled and shook her head. "Busy, busy, busy. We're not exactly on the A-list of must-see destinations, but they're talking about expanding the docks and I had to hire a couple of assistants. You're getting ready to leave?"

Zoya held up the strap on her bag. "This is the last of it."

"One more thing," Cecil said, digging in the sleeve pocket of her coverall. "Here." She held out a small data drive. "This may come in handy."

Natalya took the drive, flipping it in the palm of her hand. "Thanks. What is it?"

"Models for the exploration scout. I don't know if it's a hundred percent. I'm not sure you'd want models for all of it."

Natalya looked at the ship and back at the chip. "Thanks seem inadequate," she said.

"Don't be silly," Cecil said. "They didn't cost me anything and nobody here is using them. At least not yet. I just flashed a copy for you. Seemed the least I could do."

Zoya nudged her with her elbow. "Just think if we'd had those before we took the *Melbourne* out."

Natalya nodded. "I was." She held out a hand to Cecil. "Thank you. Really."

"It may be an antique," Cecil said with a cheeky grin. "That's no reason not to keep it flying." Her tablet bipped and she glanced at it. "Gotta go. Fueling problem on bay twelve." She started out but stopped before leaving the bay to shout "Safe voyage."

"That was nice," Zoya said, nodding at the chip.

"All we need now is access to a couple of printers."

"Dark Knight has some," Zoya said. "Public rental. Flat rate, time plus materials."

Natalya keyed the lock open. "How do you know that?"

"I had plenty of time to explore the docks. It's actually part of the chandlery service."

"We could have printed that coupling we needed?" Natalya asked.

"With the models? Probably," Zoya said. "I didn't find out about it until we got back."

Natalya looked at the drive in her hand. "Probably right."

"Natalya!"

They turned to find Ernst Panko striding across the bay. "Brian said I had to be quick."

"You almost missed us," Natalya said. "Shouldn't you be minding the store at the yards?"

"I wanted to talk to you about selling the *Peregrine*," he said.

Natalya looked at the ship and back at Panko. "You know that's not happening."

"Wait. You haven't heard my offer yet." He grinned at her. "What if I replace her?"

"Replace her?" Natalya glanced at Zoya. "What do you mean replace her?"

"What if I design a ship for you? A modern ship. Custom job. Small like the *Peregrine* but with some cargo capacity. An extra stateroom. Whatever you want."

"You going to build it, too?" Natalya asked, a laugh bubbling out of her at the absurdity of the idea.

Panko bit his lip and shrugged. "Well, I *do* run a shipyard these days."

"Alison going to let you do that?" Zoya asked.

"It was her idea."

Zoya raised an eyebrow.

"Well, all right, I talked her into it but she agreed once I told her about it."

"How are you two doing, by the way?" Zoya asked.

Panko looked at the deck and gave it a little scuff with his foot. "You know. We're still feeling things out as we go."

"I bet," Natalya said. "So, what're you proposing? You build us a ship and trade it for the *Peregrine*?"

"I can toss in a some credits to sweeten the deal."

"We'd have to hang around for a couple of months while you build it," Natalya said.

Panko shrugged.

Natalya glanced at Zoya.

"Your ship. Your call," Zoya said.

Natalya looked up at the *Peregrine* again and shook her head. "She's old. She's scarred. She's an antique." She looked at Panko. "But she's a gift from my father and she's home. It's a generous offer, Ernst, but not one I can accept."

A short laugh puffed almost silently from his mouth. "Figured you'd say that, but I had to try. I've got the beginning of a plan. I'll send it to you. If you change your mind, let me know." He stuck out a hand.

"Thanks, Ernst," Natalya said.

They shook all around before Panko left them standing on the ramp.

"Let's get out of here before somebody else tries to talk us out of it," Natalya said, leading the way into the ship.

"You gotta admit it was a generous offer," Zoya said.

Natalya nodded. "I was tempted." She keyed the outer door closed and they headed down the passageway toward the bow.

"But?" Zoya asked.

"But this is home," Natalya said. "I wouldn't feel right selling it."

Zoya stood in the doorway to her stateroom. "You won't always feel that way," she said.

The tone made Natalya pause. "Bitter voice of experience?"

Zoya shook her head. "Home isn't a place. It's what your heart feels."

"Your grandmother?"

Zoya shook her head, a wistful smile focused somewhere else on her lips. "Pop-pop. He was always the romantic."

Natalya looked around the ship, forward to the cockpit and aft down the passageway to engineering. Zoya's words took root and she decided she liked them there. "I'd like to meet your grandparents one day."

"Got any plans for the next month? I'm ready for some down time and we're pretty flush at the moment."

Nathan Lowell

Natalya dropped her bag on the deck in her stateroom. "I'll start the coffee. You plot the course."

Zoya grinned and offered a mock salute. "Aye, aye, Captain."

Suicide Run

The Golden Age of the Solar Clipper

Quarter Share
Half Share
Full Share
Double Share
Captains Share
Owners Share

In Ashes Born
To Fire Called
By Darkness Forged *

Milk Run
Suicide Run
Home Run

South Coast
Cape Grace*

Tanyth Fairport Adventures

Ravenwood
Zypherias Call
The Hermit Of Lammas Wood

* Forthcoming

Awards

2011 Parsec Award Winner for Best Speculative Fiction
(Long Form) for *Owners Share*

2010 Parsec Award Winner for Best Speculative Fiction
(Long Form) for *Captains Share*

2009 Podiobooks Founders Choice Award for Captains Share

2009 Parsec Award Finalist for Best Speculative Fiction
(Long Form) for *Double Share*

2008 Podiobooks Founders Choice Award for *Double Share*

2008 Parsec Award Finalist for Best Speculative Fiction
(Long Form) for *Full Share*

2008 Parsec Award Finalist for Best Speculative Fiction
(Long Form) for *South Coast*

Contact

Website: nathanlowell.com
Twitter: twitter.com/nlowell
Email: nathan.lowell@gmail.com

About The Author

Nathan Lowell first entered the literary world by podcasting his novels. The Golden Age of the Solar Clipper grew from his life-long fascination with space opera and his own experiences shipboard in the United States Coast Guard. Unlike most works which focus on a larger-than-life hero, Nathan centers on the people behind the scenes—ordinary men and women trying to make a living in the depths of interstellar space. In his novels, there are no bug-eyed monsters, or galactic space battles, instead he paints a richly vivid and realistic world where the hero uses hard work and his own innate talents to improve his station and the lives of those of his community.

Dr. Nathan Lowell holds a Ph.D. in Educational Technology with specializations in Distance Education and Instructional Design. He also holds an M.A. in Educational Technology and a BS in Business Administration. He grew up on the south coast of Maine and is strongly rooted in the maritime heritage of the sea-farer. He served in the USCG from 1970 to 1975, seeing duty aboard a cutter on hurricane patrol in the North Atlantic and at a communications station in Kodiak, Alaska. He currently lives on the plains east of the Rocky Mountains with his wife and two daughters.

Made in the USA
Middletown, DE
01 August 2022